Acclaim for James Markert

"*Midnight at the Tuscany Hotel* is a moving novel of artistic inspiration, love, death, and the nature of memory. Markert expertly weaves the many threads of this narrative together and creates characters that soon come to feel like old friends. Filled with magic, myth, and the spirit of the Renaissance, readers will want to check into the Tuscany Hotel for a long stay."

 —Alyssa Palombo, author of *The Most*
  Beautiful Woman in Florence

"Beautifully detailed descriptions of what life was like during the Dust Bowl, the desperation and feelings of helplessness, are contrasted with small tokens of beauty and bonds of friendship and family. Though heavily spiritual, Markert's (*All Things Bright and Strange*, 2018) non-dogmatic approach to the unknown will also appeal to mainstream readers. Historical fiction at its finest that makes the reader want to learn more about the time and the people who lived there, and those who left."

 —*Booklist*, STARRED review, on *What Blooms from Dust*

"In this enchanting allegory, Markert (*All Things Bright and Strange*) crafts an imaginative tale of the Dust Bowl . . . Markert creatively portrays the timeless battle between good and evil, making for a powerful story of hope and redemption."

 —*Publishers Weekly* on *What Blooms from Dust*

"This is an exorcist story on well-written steroids resembling the best of Stephen King without the nihilism. By the end, I expect readers may be emotionally drained yet ultimately uplifted. Recommended."

 —Historical Novel Society on *All Things Bright and Strange*

"This magical novel warns us to be careful what we wish for. We may get it."

—*BookPage* on *All Things Bright and Strange*

"Screenwriter Markert (*The Angels' Share*) conjures an apocalyptic page-turner that blends Frank Peretti–style supernatural elements with the fine detail of historical novels."

—*Publishers Weekly* on *All Things Bright and Strange*

"Markert's latest supernatural novel is captivating from the beginning . . . Readers of Frank Peretti and Ted Dekker will love Markert's newest release."

—*RT Book Reviews*, 4 stars, on *All Things Bright and Strange*

"A haunting tale of love, loss, and redemption."

—*Booklist* on *All Things Bright and Strange*

"Folksy charm, an undercurrent of menace, and an aura of hope permeate this ultimately inspirational tale."

—*Booklist* on *The Angels' Share*

Midnight at the
Tuscany Hotel

Also by James Markert

What Blooms from Dust
All Things Bright and Strange
The Angels' Share
A White Wind Blew

MIDNIGHT AT THE
TUSCANY HOTEL

JAMES MARKERT

THOMAS NELSON
Since 1798

Published in Nashville, Tennessee, by Thomas Nelson. Thomas Nelson is a registered trademark of HarperCollins Christian Publishing, Inc.

Thomas Nelson titles may be purchased in bulk for educational, business, fund-raising, or sales promotional use. For information, please email SpecialMarkets@ThomasNelson.com.

Library of Congress Cataloging-in-Publication Data

Names: Markert, James, 1974- author.
Title: Midnight at the Tuscany Hotel / James Markert.
Description: Nashville, Tennessee : Thomas Nelson, [2019]
Identifiers: LCCN 2018049925| ISBN 9780785219095 (paperback) | ISBN 9780785219088 (epub)
Classification: LCC PS3613.A75379 M53 2019 | DDC 813/.6--dc23 LC record available at https://lccn.loc.gov/2018049925

Printed in the United States of America
19 20 21 22 23 MG 5 4 3 2 1

For
Bobby Hofmann
God of laughter and humor
Loyal first reader
Uncle

For
Mickey Keys
Goddess of music and kindness
Aunt

For
Gary Markert
God of smiles and friendliness
Uncle

For
Private John Robert Markert
God of bravery and courage
Company C, Eighth Armored Division
Paw Paw

*Memory is deceptive because it is
colored by today's events.*
—**Albert Einstein**

Memory is the treasury and guardian of all things.
—**Marcus Tullius Cicero**

Memory is the mother of all wisdom.
—**Aeschylus**

*I've given my life to the principle and the
ideal of memory, and remembrance.*
—**Elie Wiesel**

The Tuscany Hotel

Gandy, California
Established 1887

Dinner Menu

For April 20, 1946
Head Chef: Johnny Two-Times

Antipasto

Bruschetta	$ .27
Caprese Salad	$ .30
Carpaccio	$ .35
Panzanella	$ .35

Lista del Pane

Focaccia	$ .10
Ciabatta	$ .10
Pane di Laterza	$ .10
Pane con le Olive	$ .10

Entrata

Spaghetti alla Carbonara	$1.50
Lasagna alla Bolognese	$1.75
Linguine con le Vongole	$1.75
Cannelloni al Forno	$2.00
Rigatoni alla Papino	$1.90
Pollo alla parmigiana	$1.50

Lista dei Dolci

Gelato	$ .10
Panna Cotta	$ .15
Tiramisu	$ .18
Amaretto Biscotti	$ .18
Ciambella	$ .10

Lista di Zuppe

Pasta Fagioli	$ .25
Minestrone	$ .25
Pappa al Pomodoro	$ .25
Tortellini Toscana	$ .25

Before

1866
FLORENCE, ITALY

*T*he foundling wheel turned inward with a groan, and the young nurse stifled a scream.

She had extinguished the wall sconce seconds before, unsettled as always by the plunge into darkness, her nervousness heightened tonight by a thunder and lightning storm that had relentlessly shaken the walls for nearly two hours. The overhead bell chimed, signaling the new arrival. The echo drifted. Hurried footsteps filled the void.

Candlelight rounded a curved corner of stone, and suddenly in the glow next to her stood the familiar face of her mentor, brown eyes and black hair concealed under a nurse's cap.

"A midnight baby?" asked Nurse Cioni.

The young nurse nodded and glanced toward the wheel, where an infant lay silent and swaddled. *Why isn't it crying?* She'd only been at the Ospedale degli Innocenti for four weeks but had retrieved enough of the unwanted from the wheel to know the answer—the baby was either sleeping or already dead. Most likely the latter, for most of the sleeping babies awakened and cried as the wheel turned inward. No matter how well they greased the cogs and softened the tiny bed with folded blankets, the quick trip from outside to in was apparently a startling one.

Her voice quivered. "Who would leave a baby during this storm? It was as if the heavens were falling."

"Well, the storm is over now, Nurse Pratesi, so calm yourself. Did you see her? Nurse Pratesi, did you see?"

The young nurse glanced toward the hospital's entrance. She'd forgotten. Probably too late now, but she hurried for the wooden door anyway and stepped out into the cool night air, where low stars had begun to show themselves behind a trail of dark, rapidly moving clouds. Wind whistled through the grand loggia and shadows moved inside its arches and columns. She listened for fleeing footsteps, which often trailed across the cobbled piazza as mothers sprinted away in shame. Except for a distant rumble of thunder, she heard nothing. She was too late, this mother too fast, too eager to leave her burden behind.

She returned inside. Nurse Cioni now stood at the wheel, watching curiously.

"Is it alive?"

"Yes, come look. And it's a girl." The older nurse opened a ledger, placed it on a wooden table beside the wheel, and readied her quill. "Any sign of the mother?"

"No. She's gone."

"What time did it arrive?"

"A girl, you said, Nurse Cioni. Not an it." She looked down, fearing she'd just overstepped her bounds with her retort. She swallowed over the lump in her throat, glanced to the clock resting on the table. "*She* arrived at exactly midnight."

The clock now showed a couple of minutes past.

The young nurse looked to the cold, stone floor, folding and unfolding her trembling hands. Why were they shaking? Why couldn't she bring herself to look at it? At *her*! Because the baby wasn't crying. Because she for some reason felt already connected to her. Because the clock . . .

Nurse Pratesi straightened her posture and spoke with confidence. "She arrived only seconds after I blew out the candle. I extinguish the candle at exactly midnight."

The older nurse shook her head, annoyed for some reason, most likely because she'd been awakened at such an hour. But how could anyone have fallen asleep during that wicked display of thunder and lightning?

They were quiet for a few moments, long enough for them both to hear the clicking of the old circular wall clock hanging above the arched entrance. They stared at each other, listened to the tick-tick, trying to make sense of it.

Nurse Cioni said, "When did that clock start working?"

Nurse Pratesi stared at it, at the thin hands as they clicked. The clock, a donation from a Dutch clockmaker, hadn't worked in more than a hundred years, having stopped during an equally violent storm in the spring of 1761. And now here it was suddenly ticking again.

Nurse Cioni held up her candle for a closer look at the wall clock. The hands showed a time of two thirteen.

"It was frozen at midnight, was it not?" asked Nurse Pratesi.

"For over a century," the older nurse mumbled, unblinking. "It must have started again at the beginning of the storm."

Nurse Cioni placed down her candle and scribbled in the ledger.

The baby. A streak of orange caught the young nurse's eye. She stepped closer to the wheel. The baby had hair like fire and eyes green as plump olives. Still no crying. She smiled, and the baby mirrored it. Were babies this young even aware enough to smile? She'd certainly never seen one smile while inside the wheel. She lifted the infant from the blankets and cradled her in her arms. The closeness brought sudden warmth to her heart. There was no time to be melancholy—she'd been warned of that the first day. The babies were much better off here at the Hospital of the Innocents than abandoned on the streets of Florence.

"You're crying." The older nurse again glanced at the clock. "Check the wheel for any marks."

Nurse Pratesi wiped her cheeks and looked inside the wheel. Often the parents—mostly the mothers—would leave a "mark" or token of recognition with the abandoned babies. Like a charm broken in half, with one piece left with the baby and the other kept by the parent. *In hopes that one day they can be reunited.* The other half would offer proof. She searched the tousled blanket but discovered no such item. "I don't see anything, Nurse Cioni."

The older nurse didn't respond; she was busy running her finger down a list of girl names. The finger stopped, tapped the worn list. "We'll call her Magdalena."

"And a surname?"

The two nurses studied each other. "Salvato?" *Saved.* They shook their heads simultaneously, Nurse Pratesi more emphatically. For some reason *she* now felt more saved than this baby. Though she had uttered her misgivings to no one, she had been on the verge of leaving the hospital in search of different work. But now . . .

"Fortuna?" the older nurse offered.

Nurse Pratesi shook her head. *Luck* didn't seem right either. And then she looked up, eyes enlarged as a thought struck. "Rotile." She didn't form it as a question to her superior, but rather more of a statement of fact. "Magdalena Rotile."

The older nurse pondered and then nodded in agreement. *Magdalena of the Wheel.* The younger nurse gathered courage. "You're crying too."

Nurse Cioni looked away, wiped her cheeks. "Hurry on. Find the wet nurse."

One

*P*rivate First Class Vittorio Gandy walked the narrow sidewalk with a standard army duffel in each hand. The weight of the bags kept his hands from shaking.

American flags rippled from porches, bits of color under a low, gray November sky. Miss Cannon's azalea bushes looked to be blooming, but up close the blooms were just dull remnants of confetti recent rains had glued to the branches. The war had ended months ago, the street parties making way for an uneasy postwar normalcy—a big collective breath of *what now?* The waiting of so many wives for husbands to return home. The grief of widows praying some mistake had been made.

Vitto sometimes wished he'd been among the latter. That kind of sleep could prove deep and untouched.

Wind moved the flags again. He focused on the rippled cadence, slowed his pace as his boots grew heavy, like mud still sucked on them. Maybe he should have warned her he was coming home today. Coopus had said to surprise her, but maybe that wasn't a good thing. Even though Coopus was still officially counted among the living, most of Company C said the man had basically died in Merbeck. *So why did I listen to a man who had no life behind his eyes? No fluctuation in his voice?*

The last time Vitto had written Valerie had been almost two weeks ago, from Camp Kilmer in New Jersey, the place where it all had started after his enlistment in July of '44. Back when the mail was censored and all the men were scrambling to get their wills done, when medics were poking them with this syringe and that—mandatory shots like bee stings. He'd been back in the States since September. Just waiting to be officially discharged, he'd told her in every letter, in response to her weekly question: "When are you coming home?"

Realizing he'd come to a complete stop in front of Mr. Campbell's house, he urged his legs onward. Leaves skittered, and he flinched. His grip tightened on the duffel bags. Last night he'd dreamed of this moment, Valerie jumping into his arms right on the sidewalk, asking what was in the bags. In the dream he'd unzipped them and shown her all the dead soldiers inside, and she'd screamed.

"Just clothes," he whispered as he walked. *And K-rations. A shovel. The knife I took from that Nazi I killed at Unna.* A dog barked from the Levenworths' backyard. His eyes flicked to the sound. The beast sounded hungry, rabid. Vitto fingered the handgun hooked to his belt, but then an image flashed of little William taking his first steps across the living room floor. Steps free from those little braces he'd had to wear, the ones the doctor had put on him too early, concerned when his legs didn't look to be growing straight. Steps that Vitto had missed. Steps he'd urgently encouraged the boy to take in the days leading up to his departure so he *wouldn't* miss them. "*Ticktock goes the clock, William.*" The boy had been almost four and barely walking when he'd left—a delay they had worried about. And now, according to Val's letters, he was sharp as a tack and walking fine. Without the braces.

Vitto stopped again on the sidewalk, knelt down, and buried the .45-caliber pistol in one of the bags, under the box of cigarettes.

Unlike most other artists he knew, he hadn't been a smoker before the war. He'd smoked his first cigarette on the deck of the USS *St. Cecelia* as she cut through waves in the Atlantic. He'd coughed and choked on it before the wind took it out into the froth and Coopus laughed. England had been in the midst of a severe cigarette shortage when they arrived, and they'd handed them out to the dockmen at Southampton like they were dispersing gold.

A month later they'd been begging for them themselves.

Now smoking was as regular as breathing. Vitto lit a cigarette, wedged it between his chapped lips, and zipped up the bag. When he stood back up he got light-headed. Shouldn't have bypassed breakfast. But with his nervous stomach at the train station, even the sight of coffee had made him queasy. He regripped the duffel bags and let the cigarette smolder as he walked the final block toward home.

In the left breast pocket of his uniform was a picture of Valerie on their wedding day six years prior. White dress and brunette curls pinned high in a Rita Hayworth updo. Eyes blue as the oceans he used to paint. Sculpted lips as if carved from one of his father's statues. Lips made to fit his own, as he'd told her at thirteen, the final nudge needed to get her permission to plant one on her right there on the hotel's piazza, carefully concealed behind one of the sculptures as dusk cast giant shadows across the travertine.

When he'd kissed her at the train station, he'd promised it wouldn't be their last. After that he'd sometimes kissed his machine gun before battle. One time he'd kissed the tank for good luck. He'd kissed Stevenson's bloody forehead right before he closed his eyes in the town of Rheinberg. He wondered how Valerie would kiss him now. Like the young, vibrant man she remembered or the shell that now returned?

He slowed his pace again, inhaled on the cigarette without touching it. Remembered that first night on the *St. Cecelia*, when the waves had made half the men sick. Vitto had been sitting on his bunk in the dark, using the flashlight to stare at Val's picture—unbent and fresh at that point—when Private Beacher dipped his head of black hair down from the top bunk and blew cigarette smoke in his face.

❋

"She's a doll."

"Yeah." Vitto smiled, looked up into the drifting smoke tendrils.

Beacher's eyes were ornery. "I'll gladly be the one to give her the news, Gandy."

"What news?"

"That her man died in battle." Beacher's cigarette glowed amber. They were only supposed to smoke on the deck. "Don't worry. I'll treat her good. You know, I'll be a good father to your son."

And then his head disappeared. The bunk creaked heavy as Beacher shifted to get comfortable, and a few minutes later the goon was snoring. Vitto was too stunned to retaliate—it was the first of many instances that told him war didn't always exist in the real world—and didn't sleep all night. In hindsight, he should have grabbed his .45 and blown a hole through that top bunk.

Later, Vitto swore to Coopus that Beacher had tried to get him killed in battle. Twice.

"Why would he do that, Gandy?"

"He wants to steal my wife and kid."

Other than shaking his head, Coopus didn't have an answer for that. Beacher was odd, but he never tried to get Vitto killed again, although he did return home with one less arm.

❋

Vitto stopped in front of their driveway, a nubby concrete append-age leading to the small one-story brick house he'd bought after his father's Tuscany Hotel closed at the tail end of the Depression. He and Valerie had tried for years to get his father to come live with them—pointing out that the hotel wasn't going to suddenly come back to life. But Sir Robert Gandy was stubborn and had refused every time they offered, choosing instead to live alone at the once-opulent hotel that now swallowed him. "Someone has to guard the artwork," he'd said. "Someone has to keep the mice out." Even the lure of living with his new grandson, William, hadn't worked. Then suddenly, the week before Vitto left for training at Camp Kilmer, Robert had finally agreed because "It's what Maggie would have wanted."

"Living in squalor," his father had muttered, standing before Vitto's house with his suitcases in hand, his long white hair wild in the wind, his sculpting equipment weighing down the back of Vitto's Ford Model A pickup with the yellow rims and the sleek running board that Robert refused to use.

"It's not as bad as that, Dad."

"Sure it is."

Robert had insisted that he'd gone from his own hotel to a hole in the wall. "Well, it's my hole in the wall," Vitto had answered, grabbing his old man's bags. "But it's still your town." A town, according to Val's letters, that had been there for Val and Robert the entire time Vitto had been overseas, much as it had rallied in support after Magdalena's death. "Not a week goes by that a neighbor doesn't knock on the door asking if we need anything, Vitto."

Robert had bought the land for the town he named Gandy after returning from his trip to Italy in the 1880s, the one where he'd met Vitto's mother, Magdalena. Robert's father, Cotton Gandy, had willed his only son his quarry and oil fortune, and Robert had spent every bit of it over the decades, first starting the town, then building the hotel.

All for a girl.

Vitto inhaled on the cigarette, wondered what his father looked like now. He'd sired Vitto very late in life and had already been walking hunched over before Vitto left for the war. Valerie hadn't mentioned him much in her letters, saying only that he spent most of his days out back carving on stone, turning their meager backyard into a snippet of what his hotel once had been, and complaining about having to live in what they were now calling a subdivision. Even though the houses were spaced out enough to grow whatever was needed, Robert said they might as well be living in tenements.

The house actually looked pretty good. The grass out front was green and trimmed. Window boxes showed colorful blooms. Valerie wasn't one to sit back and wait. She'd organized blood drives, sold war bonds, and kept her own victory garden on the side of the house. Back in February, about the time Vitto was marching through Holland, she'd taken a factory job to help pay the bills.

"Your father's broke, Vitto," she'd written. "His finances aren't what they once were. And they certainly aren't what his ledger claims. Turns out he's forgotten how to do simple math."

Vitto exhaled around the cigarette butt, spat it to the sidewalk, and crushed it under his boot. The front door flew open as if she had sensed him. Or maybe she'd been waiting in the reading chair next to the window—if not for him, for the daily mail. There she stood in a flowery yellow-and-red dress that ended at the knees, hair done up like he remembered, lips painted red, one hand trying to conceal her shock, the other clutching her stomach. She stepped out onto the porch, one hand still holding on to the screen door, as if afraid to test the waters.

"William, come quick," she called over her shoulder. "Get your grandfather. Your father is home!"

She took a step, and another, and then hurried down the front stoop and across the yard. He dropped the bags in time to catch her. He staggered at first, but then her momentum spun him into a swift circle of laughter and tears. He gathered her in his arms, the underside of her thighs settled into his open hands like a final puzzle piece restored, and he spun her again and again until they collapsed, laughing, in the middle of the front yard. Coopus had been right after all. Surprise was the way to go.

On the train he'd wondered if his face was capable of smiling again or if his heart would ever thrum warm, but Valerie brought about both in an instant. Some of her hair came undone, tickling his neck as she kissed him on the lips and face so rapidly he could hardly keep up. He wanted to ask her when she had started smoking, because he could smell it, but her perfume overrode the tobacco smell, enveloped and brought him back.

Neighbors stepped from their homes, pointed, equally happy that Vittorio Gandy had finally come home. Robert was just looking at it all wrong; a Gandy living with the public wasn't a negative thing. The hotel might be closed down, but their name was still held up on that pedestal.

The screen door closed. Valerie stood from the grass, wiped her dress, and beckoned. Vitto swallowed hard, fought back tears. His boy was five years old now, with unruly chestnut hair that now resembled his own.

"William, come on now. Don't be shy." Valerie waved him toward her.

William shook his head, defiant.

Vitto stood beside her. "It's okay. He couldn't walk straight the last time I saw him."

The boy moved slowly down the steps, then ran behind his mother's leg, burying his face in the waves of her dress.

Vitto hunkered down, blinking back tears—couldn't get over the running—now eye level to his son.

Valerie coaxed the boy out until one of his eyes showed. "William, it's your daddy."

"Not my daddy," said William, hiding again.

Vitto's heart skipped. He'd prepared for this, but hearing it weighed heavy. Uncle Sam had stolen time he'd never get back.

"William, don't say that," she said. "This *is* your daddy."

"Not my daddy."

"It's okay, Val. Don't push it."

The screen door opened again. Vitto locked eyes with Robert Gandy on the porch, anticipating the fatherly embrace he'd imagined after every bloody battle across Europe. Same embrace he'd hoped for as a child, when he'd imagine being wrapped up in those strong sculptor's arms, smelling stone dust and pipe smoke on Robert's loose, half-buttoned shirts. Embraces like the ones he'd share with Magdalena and all the regular hotel guests every time they'd return, but rarely with his son.

Certainly the war would change things.

There he was a few dozen steps away, still larger than life, long silver hair flowing. Vitto nodded toward his old man, then took a step in his direction.

Robert didn't return the nod. He looked at Valerie as if confused.

She said, "Vitto, there's something I didn't tell you in the letters."

Vitto looked from his wife—and his son who didn't remember him—to his father, who stared as if he didn't know who he was.

And then Robert confirmed it, his voice agitated and paranoid.

"Who are you? Valerie, who is this man? Should I call the police?"

Two

*D*r. Aimes thinks it's something called Alzheimer's disease."

Vitto chewed the last bite of his ham sandwich and watched out the kitchen window, where his father stood on a quaint backyard patio of stone and mosaic tiles, staring at a tall slab of marble, carving tools in hand. Two minutes ago, he'd gotten up from the table in a rush, as if an idea had struck him. He'd yet to start chipping away at the stone.

"Vitto, did you hear what I said?" Valerie cleared her throat. "Dr. Aimes says it might be what he calls Alzheimer's. I've never heard of it before, but apparently it happens to people. It's not just hardening of the—"

"What's he doing?"

She shifted in her chair. "He does that every day. An idea strikes him. He rushes out to sculpt, and then he forgets."

"Forgets what?"

"The idea." She nodded toward the window. "And then he stands there trying to remember."

"How long has this been going on?"

"In hindsight, he was showing signs before you left. Repeating things he told us five minutes prior. Calling William by your name. Misplacing his tools. Two months ago he cut his mouth up real good. Got confused in the middle of the night, grabbed a razor to brush his teeth. Now I hide the razor, shave him myself. Fights me like the dickens some mornings."

Vitto watched his wife, perhaps for too long because she caught him staring.

"What?"

"Nothing." But it was far from nothing. He'd been staring at her in awe but was afraid to say it—in awe because of her pretty face he wanted to touch but somehow couldn't or shouldn't, in awe because of those blue eyes that still looked as bright as liquid paint, in awe because of who she still was, that comforting soul, even as a child, who had always seemed to be a bandage for things in need of bandaging. *Like Juba,* he thought, *just like Juba,* wondering why it had taken a war and back to realize it.

Nothing was a far cry from what he felt, but in the saying of it, that one simple yet complex word, he realized there *was* something in him the war hadn't been able to touch or, in the way Val now eyed him, change—his inability to verbalize what he felt, his refusal to show his emotions. She claimed it had started when Magdalena died, but he reckoned that flaw might have started way before that.

Vitto scooted his chair back and struck up a cigarette, spotting William watching cautiously from the hallway. "Come here, boy." He patted the seat next to him, his fingernails dirty with soil or blood—the weathered hands of a soldier now instead of a painter.

William moved with caution, then took the seat in between his parents.

Vitto exhaled up toward the ceiling, watched his son, who still seemed afraid to watch him back. "I got something for you." He opened a pouch on his belt and removed a hand grenade. Valerie jumped in her seat, and William's eyes swelled. "It's a dud," he said to his wife, then pointed at the grenade. "It's German. Took it off a Nazi I killed outside of Ossenberg. We were taking this factory—"

"Vittorio!"

He stopped, tapped the grenade—had the full attention of his son now. "Anyway. Kraut's name was Wilhelm. German equivalent of William. I think." Valerie looked away. He said to the boy, "Go on. It's yours."

William grinned. "What's it do?"

Vitto stuck the cigarette in his mouth, put his hands together, and then blew them apart. He smiled because his son finally did. "It blows stuff up."

"Vitto, that's enough."

William took the grenade and hurried down the hall toward his bedroom. Vitto resumed watching his father out the window. "Why doesn't he write stuff down? Like Mamma did."

"He's stubborn. And he's all too aware of the similarities."

"How long does he stand like that?"

"Five, sometimes ten."

"Hours?"

"Minutes." She folded and unfolded her hands. He took the pack of cigarettes from his pocket and slid it across the table, along with the lighter, but she looked away. "I don't smoke," she said before tapping one out and lighting it like it wasn't her first. She slid the pack back across the table, inhaled like an expert. "Just a couple a day. To take the edge off." She exhaled through slightly parted lips, leaving a red lipstick stain on the butt. For some reason he was in awe of that too.

Val said, "Sometimes he forgets where the bathroom is. Your father. I've had to help change him more than once." By the looks of it, she'd been taking care of two toddlers instead of one. Bags under her eyes, lines where there didn't used to be. Under the makeup was wear and tear; if guilt were a knife, he would have felt the cut from it. She pointed at her father-in-law with her cigarette. Robert had once been a king in both of their eyes. "Doctor said Alzheimer's is when something goes wrong with brain cells in older people. Basically your father's brain is dying before the rest of him."

Vitto reached across the table, offered his hand, and she took it. Tears pooled in her eyes. She laughed it away, although nothing seemed funny.

"You didn't get laid off at the factory, did you?"

She shook her head, exhaled. She'd quit to take care of Robert. "He was starting to hurt himself. It'd be safer to leave William home alone."

"What'd you do with William while you worked?"

"Took him with me. First Lady Roosevelt talked her husband into forming government nurseries while the women worked. Lot of the factories had them for the employees."

"But not for adults."

"Not for adults." She inhaled hard, exhaled harder.

He squeezed her hand. "You look good, Val."

That laugh again—the laugh that wasn't a laugh, but more like an anxious hiccup. She put a fist in the air, pumped it facetiously. "Good ol' Rosie the Riveter." Truthfully, there hadn't been too many women riveters, and none named Rosie. "Poster child in makeup," she said of Rosie, the government-engineered propaganda campaign centered on making women look tough yet still feminine. "They were afraid the war at home was going to make us too masculine. Our factory even gave us lessons on how to apply makeup. Keeping our women looking their best was necessary for morale. Or so they told us." She finished her cigarette and smashed the butt into the plate Robert had left before he'd hurried outside. "They would have laid me off anyway. They laid all the women off as soon as the men got back. Of course, they were only paying us half what the men made."

She slithered her hand from his grip; he wondered if he'd been clutching it too tightly. He'd missed what she'd said last. A memory had flashed, him clutching the hand of a soldier named Hankhorner who'd been shot by enemy fire and was clinging to the tank as it tumbled through the snow. *My hand was frozen. I tried to hold on.* Hankhorner had gone down into the white puff, and the tank had pressed him under.

"Vitto? Where'd you just go?"

He chewed his lip, lit another cigarette. Outside, his father slammed the hammer to the ground, unsuccessfully stabbed the tooth chisel into the stone, and then kicked it into the grass. He stormed inside, teary eyed, slamming the door behind him.

Valerie was up in a flash, coaxing him toward the chair William had vacated moments ago. Robert wiped his eyes as she rubbed his back, and then he took a swing at her, not to hit but to brush her arm away. ". . . Off me . . ."

"Hey." Vitto stood.

Valerie cautioned him. "Vitto, stop. It's nothing. He's angry. Sit back down."

Robert stared at Valerie, his apology evident in his weary eyes. He pointed at Vitto. "Who's he? Your boyfriend?"

"That's Vittorio. Your son, Robert. My husband."

"Oh." He looked at his son with something akin to recognition.

"He's just returned from the war," she said. "From Europe."

"My son." Robert, still strong as an ox, put a hand on Vitto's shoulder and patted it twice, just as he had in this very kitchen an hour ago. "You should change out of that uniform. It stinks." Robert pointed out the window. "I'm working on a new sculpture."

"I see that." Vitto looked away; it was too painful to see his father like this.

"It's . . . it's . . ." Robert scratched his head, digging for a thought. His eyes brightened. "We should tell your mother you're home! Maggie!"

Vitto locked eyes with Val. Maggie, Magdalena to everyone else—Robert had built the Tuscany Hotel for her—had been dead now for six years. Valerie put an arm around her father-in-law and sat him back down. "Magdalena's gone, Robert."

"Gone? Where?"

"She's dead. Robert, your wife passed away." He looked shocked. Her death had shaken him to the core; he'd wept over her grave. Truth be told, though he'd sculpted after her passing, he'd produced nothing worthy of what he'd done when she was alive. How could he not remember? And now Valerie spoke so matter-of-factly about it. Like it was an everyday occurrence. "She's buried at the hotel near the poppy field." She rubbed his back again. Robert nodded, tears in his eyes, like it had just begun to sink in. She pointed to his shirt. "Her picture is in your pocket, remember? Right there."

He looked down, smiled, pulled out the color photograph. "Ah, yes," he said. "There you are."

Vitto caught a glimpse of his mother's orange hair, like fire, but then it vanished inside his father's cupped palm. Robert held the picture to his chest and petted it like he used to do to her back when he'd hug *her*.

Vitto clenched his jaw, soaked in his wife's strength and courage. He knew firsthand the difficulty of telling someone a loved one had passed, and here she was doing it daily, over and over again like a timeless loop. And this was not just about a loved one, but the *most* loved one. The visitors at the hotel had often claimed that Robert and Magdalena had *invented* love.

And for him now, she died again every day.

William's bedroom door opened. "Mommy, it rolls!" They turned at the sound of something heavy rattling on hardwood, and then the Nazi grenade stopped in the middle of the hallway next to the kitchen.

Vitto jumped from his chair, screamed, "Take cover," and then threw his body on the grenade, colliding with the wall, knocking from a hook an oil painting of the Tuscany Hotel's olive groves at sunset. It landed on his back, curved like a turtle shell to conceal the grenade.

William laughed at first and then cried, probably sensing the fear on Vitto's face. Vitto looked up, checked the surroundings. A clock ticked in the hallway. "Is anybody hurt?"

Robert said, "Valerie, call the police. We have an intruder!"

Valerie lit another cigarette, exhaled toward the ceiling.

Three

The bed was no longer their own.

Despite Val's attempts to prove otherwise, he was a visitor in his own home, a stranger in that bed. Three days now, and he'd yet to pick up where they'd left off the way she'd said they would at the train station the day he left for Camp Kilmer. The kiss she'd given him just before he boarded was a fingerprint on his mind, along with the aroma of the peach she'd eaten for lunch and the bright red poppy he'd pinned to her dress. The going-away gift she'd given him the night before—"*just something to remember me by, Vitto*"—was now a distant memory, a memory that had carried him through the war, only to find out now it was just that.

A memory.

He was not the same man she'd married, not the same boy with whom she'd fallen in love. She kissed him every night before bed, but he sensed fear in her eyes. He paced, checked out the windows, and the paranoia grew worse at sundown. Every night since his return, he'd woken from a nightmare, screaming loud enough to put both Robert and William into a frenzy of excitement, and it was up to Valerie to calm them all. And one by one she would, leaving her husband for last, rubbing his neck as they sat bedside, feet dangling, until he calmed enough to lie back down.

"Why do you sleep with your boots on, honey?"

"I got to be ready."

He had a line of weapons on his dresser, all within arm's reach of where he twisted and turned all night, refusing to sleep with the pillow he tossed on the floor before pulling the sheets back. There was the pistol, the knife, and, leaning against the wall, his machine gun. The knife had a stain on the blade that looked like rust but wasn't.

"I don't like guns in the house," she told him on night three.

"Okay."

By day five he'd yet to move them.

Valerie claimed he spent half the day in a daze, staring out the window at the street, but he didn't remember.

"You want to talk about it?"

"About what?"

"About what happened over there."

"No. Not much to talk about."

William was on the floor playing with a toy doctor set—stethoscope and all—and he placed the little circular part on top of a toy Model T as if listening for a heartbeat, paying little attention to their conversation. "Thought you said he was sharp," Vitto said to Valerie, who lowered the newspaper she'd been pretending to read. She looked so shocked at what he'd said aloud—he hadn't meant for it to come out—that she said nothing, which was unlike her.

Saying nothing makes the chasm grow wider. Maybe Juba had said that once. Or maybe it was just something Juba *would* have said at that moment, now that saying nothing was slowly becoming the norm. True as it was, Vitto felt helpless to stop it. And there was nothing easier than saying nothing.

William looked up when Vitto struck a match to light his cigarette but looked back down to his little black car before his father let the match flame burn down to his fingertip.

"Vitto!" Valerie knocked the match away before it burned him too badly, stomping it into the hardwood even though it had gone out before it hit the floor. "Maybe you should see someone. Talk to someone. I read that the new VA hospitals are dealing with . . . this."

He smoked, said nothing.

On the coffee table was a scattering of magazines: *Woman's Illustrated, Woman's Own, Everywoman, The Homemaker, Popular Photography,* and *LIFE*. Robert sat in an armchair flipping through an issue of *Cavalcade* with a pinup girl on the cover, and periodically he'd sketch across the ledger on his lap. "Mamma would have made him write down his ideas."

"What ideas?"

"The ones he gets before he storms out the door to sculpt. Maybe he should keep a paper and pencil in his pocket along with that picture of Mom."

Valerie nodded like she agreed but turned it back on him. "Maybe you should start painting again."

"Maybe you should start *playing* again."

She backed away, wiped her eyes. He'd said it with more force than he'd meant to, but the apology that wanted to bubble up just wouldn't. Somehow it couldn't, because she didn't know and didn't understand. And he'd seen her violin in the corner of the bedroom with dust on it. Before, he'd never witnessed a day gone by when she hadn't played it. He was convinced it was her playing and Juba's voice that had kept Magdalena going as long as she did.

Truth was, red had always been his favorite color. He'd never done a painting that didn't involve at least some shade of it. But all the blood he'd seen—blood so red it didn't seem real—had ruined it. Now he feared that if he saw wet red paint it would turn to blood and he'd start thinking of dead soldiers.

A car backfired on the street, a loud pop like gunfire that sent Vitto out of his chair. He clutched Valerie around the waist and hurried her across the room, into the kitchen, and under the table. "Don't move." Next he grabbed William, who yelled because he'd dropped his stethoscope in the hallway. "Stay with your mother. Keep your head down. You hear me?" William nodded, crying along with his mother. Finally he walked Robert into the kitchen and helped him under the table. Once he had all three under cover, he corralled them close—too roughly by the sound of their groans and whimpering—and then lay down on top of all three. "Stay quiet," he urged them. "Keep your heads down."

William was crying, loudly.

"Vitto, you're hurting him."

"Keep him quiet! They're gonna hear him."

"Vitto, there's nobody out there."

Robert bit Vitto's wrist, screamed, "Maggie! Somebody go tell Magdalena!"

❀

In bed that night, Vitto and Valerie lay with their backs to each other.

"Val."

She rolled toward him. "Yes."

"Hold me." She scooted closer, draped her arm lazily across his side, and after a minute—he could tell she was gathering the courage—clutched his hand, stitching her fingers inside his like they used to on walks.

❀

The next morning the four of them had bacon and eggs at the kitchen table. William suggested they hold hands, and he said a quick prayer.

They dug in, eating silently, utensils clicking against plates.

Vitto poured himself a glass of red wine and placed it right next to his orange juice. Valerie and Robert watched him drink it. Neither said a word.

❀

On night seven, Vitto dreamt of the Tuscany Hotel.

He was eleven and Valerie was a week away from it. She was chasing him through the arcaded brick walkways behind the hotel. Wind from the Pacific wreaked havoc on her hair as she ran, wooden tennis racquet in hand. He was faster, but at that time she was taller than him, with longer legs, and had proven months ago that she could catch him on distance—she'd just beaten him in a set of tennis. So he turned the chase into a series of quick sprints, ducking this way and that, in and out of the rows of Italian cypress trees that soared tall and skinny toward the azure sky, centurion like; they often pretended the trees were Roman soldiers and their tennis racquets were swords.

Lately he'd intentionally let her catch him, like he'd done the day before in the middle of the poppy field, when he pretended to trip and she rolled over him, ending up on her knees with a red flower stuck in her hair and both of them giggling. Today he would not be so easy. He took a tight turn at the hotel's back corner, rounding the castle-like south tower that stretched three stories tall and nearly knocking over a guest and his painting easel—*Why is he mixing those two particular colors together?*—before taking a sharp right toward the grassy dip in the land that led to the olive groves. He had a plan to pluck one from the highest of the four terraces. Those were the best olives, in his opinion. Valerie favored the ones from the lower trees, although they were in agreement that the oil produced from either was delicious. The hotel was now famous along the coast for what they bottled daily, and likewise with the wines produced with the grapes from the hotel's vineyards down below. Juba, the bartender and hotel manager, had promised them a plate of the oil for lunch with garlic and a variety of breads, and Magdalena was known to sneak them sips of wine when Robert wasn't looking.

Vitto climbed the crooked stone steps on each terrace and stood defiant against the rippling wind when he reached the top. But as he went in search of the perfect olive—Valerie was at the bottom terrace doing the same—he saw his mother on the edge of the cliffs, the wind blowing her hair like flames. "Mamma? Don't jump!" Rocks glistened below. Waves crashed, reached up for her.

"Vitto, look."

Valerie stood next to him holding two plump, greenish-brown olives in front of her eyes. They laughed together. But good dreams rarely lasted for long. A Nazi ran out from behind the stone building where they pressed the olives into oil. He fired. Another Nazi came out from behind the building where they hung the grapes to dry.

Vitto stood frozen as they took Valerie away.

He looked toward the cliffs. Magdalena was gone too.

He sat up in bed, screaming. "It was only chocolate! I only gave him chocolate!"

"It's okay." Valerie was touching his shoulder, rubbing his back. She shushed him calm. "What chocolate, dear?"

He couldn't say.

But the next morning he wrote that nightmare down, neatly folded the paper, and buried it in the backyard as Valerie watched from the kitchen window.

❈

On day eight they ate lunch together—skillet-fried potatoes and some sausage Valerie put on buttery biscuits. Only the sound of them chewing permeated the increasingly awkward silence that had come upon the house since Vitto's return.

Robert stared out the window as he chewed, and then he watched his fork as if he'd forgotten how to use it. Valerie snapped her fingers to get his attention and then showed him like one would a three-year-old. Robert resumed eating. He swallowed, said to Valerie, "Are there other people out there like me?"

"Yes."

She left it at that and looked to be wrangling with issues of her own. As in, *Are there other soldiers out there like Vitto?*

William finished his food, asked to be excused. He put his plate in the sink and grabbed what looked to be a half-eaten bar of chocolate from the counter. "Can I finish this now?"

"Yes, honey." She managed a smile. "But only if you give me a bite."

Vitto momentarily froze, then jumped from his seat so fast the chair toppled. He knocked the chocolate bar from William's hands and in doing so accidentally caught part of his son's face.

"Vitto!" Valerie was up in a flash, kneeling with William, shielding him even, as Vitto looked from them to the chocolate bar now angled against the baseboard. William cried, buried his face in Valerie's side.

Vitto approached the chocolate bar as if it were a land mine. He picked it up and tossed it in the trash. Without giving an explanation, he sat back down to finish his lunch, but not before he poured himself more wine and his wife and son disappeared down the hallway.

Robert sipped water, looked at Vitto. "Love is a choice. Not just an emotion."

Vitto stared, gulped wine. "What are you talking about?"

"Just something your mother once said."

Is that why it was so hard for you to ever show any affection?

Robert stared at a toothpick like he didn't know what to do with it—his previous words seemingly forgotten. Just as he was about to put the toothpick in his nose, Vitto scooted over and grabbed it from him, showed him how to use it, just like Valerie had done with his fork. He slid the toothpick across the table, but instead of picking it back up, Robert flicked it to the floor and laughed, but the laugh didn't last long. A few seconds later he was staring out the window at the statue he couldn't seem to carve without his muse by his side.

Vitto finished his plate and scooted back in his chair, noticing that his father's shoes were on the wrong feet, although tied fairly well.

An hour later Vitto had passed out on the bed, drunk from wine. Valerie covered him up.

In the middle of the night, William walked into the bedroom and climbed up in between them with wet pajamas. Vitto startled awake, grabbed for his knife.

Valerie slept the rest of the night with William on the couch.

❖

On night nine, at four in the morning, Vitto jumped out of bed and hurried to the window. He put on his helmet—dented from a graze he'd taken in Nennig—ran to Valerie's side of the bed, cradled her in his arms, and ran down the hallway to the kitchen, where he pushed her under the table and lay on top of her.

"I gotcha," he whispered. "Shh. I gotcha." He rubbed her hair, told her the bombing would be over soon.

At that moment, Robert walked in and poured himself a bowl of Cheerios. Vitto wondered when the name had changed—they'd been CheeriOats before the war. Robert sat at the table with his cereal, his bare feet inches from his son's arm, held protectively over his wife.

She whispered, "Sometimes he gets confused. Thinks night is day and day is night."

Robert finished his cereal and started a pot of coffee.

Valerie went back to bed. Vitto watched her walk down the hallway, in awe of how she could do that after what he'd just done, in awe of how she could be so immune to things most would find unnerving, in awe because maybe he finally realized how much of who she was had been thrust upon her at such an early age—left by her parents at the hotel like she was an orphan, like his mother, left to be raised by the hotel like it was some person in and of itself.

Vitto joined his father for a cup.

Robert said, "Sugar?"

Vitto said, "No. Thanks."

Nothing else was said between them as they sipped.

❀

On night fourteen, Vitto had another nightmare.

An enemy plane flew overhead, unseen in the dark, but engine loud. Bullets cleaved mud, stole leaves from branches. Soldiers screamed and smoke cleared and he straddled a young Nazi on the ground—couldn't have been more than eighteen. They sent them out young toward the end.

Vitto sheathed his knife and put his hands around the boy's neck. "Blut und Ehre," the boy hissed. Vitto blinked, and the Hitler youth turned into a major from the Waffen-SS, silver-gray lightning bolts on the collar, gray eyes bulging as he tried to pry Vitto's hands away. Vitto blinked again, held it longer, wished it all gone. He heard violin music, beautiful music from Valerie's hands—he always swore he did his best painting while listening to her play.

He opened his eyes. He was on his knees atop the bed, straddling Valerie's waist. His hands held her throat. Her face red, her arms flailed, weak hands against his strong wrists.

William stood in the doorway, watching. Crying. Screaming, "You're not my daddy."

Vitto cried, too, and then his hands eased when he realized it wasn't a nightmare any longer and the neck in his grip was real. The love of his life. Best friend since childhood.

Valerie gasped for air as he lay beside her, breathing heavy. Breaths palpable, both of them, eyes glued to the ceiling as the moon blinked outside. Vitto gulped, swallowed over the lump in his throat, his heart and soul all bundled together into one big convoluted knot.

From the doorway, William said, "Mommy."

Vitto got out of bed, dressed in his army uniform, from helmet to boots, and then approached Valerie's side and apologized.

She pushed away from him, and William did the same. She didn't stop him when he left the room either.

He walked out the front door, started up the Ford truck, and drove himself to the local veteran's hospital with the windows open to clear his head, dog tags jangling from the rearview mirror like wind chimes.

Four

Vitto wasn't alone.

After the interview by the white-jacketed doctor with the kind smile and thin-framed glasses, he was escorted into a vast room with metal beds lining all four walls and nurses busy in the middle. Electricity hummed above, lights dimmed. Standard white sheets tucked snug around bodies that moved very little—ex-soldiers sleeping and snoring, echoing like in a cavern.

The doctor's questions followed him: "Do you often feel jittery? Feel soreness? Are you having trouble sleeping at night? Do you feel paranoid? Do you have memory loss? Depression? Nightmares? Tremors in the hands and legs?"

Vitto had checked just about every box, and the doctor had scribbled notes, nodded. Battle fatigue was what he called it. Combat exhaustion.

"Not all psychiatrists have accepted it, Mr. Gandy, but this is a very real thing, this war trauma," said the doctor. "It's what we used to call shell shock or hysteria. It's no longer considered cowardice when a soldier refuses to go back into battle."

"Private Paris was a goldbrick," said Vitto.

"I don't know this soldier you speak of, but he was hardly a shirker, Mr. Gandy. The horrors of battle can be indescribable. You're given a gun and sent to kill, while all around you your friends are shot down. Arms and legs blown off." Perhaps he was trying to get a reaction, but Vitto didn't give it. "You're hungry, filthy, leg weary, and exhausted."

"General Patton would slap 'em. Call 'em yellow. Insist there was nothing wrong and order them back out there. Some didn't have the guts."

"Or they did but lost it. Unlike some of the others, it didn't hit you until *after* the war."

"I never had the guts."

"You had the guts to admit yourself here."

"My father thought war might be good for me."

This seemed to stump the doctor. "Says here you were drafted."

"I was, but I was considering enlisting anyway. He said I needed to make my *katabasis*." He could tell the doctor didn't know what it was. "It's Greek. The hero's journey to the land of the dead. The underworld." The doctor raised his eyebrows as if confused and wanting more. Vitto said, "The ancients called it Hades. Odysseus went there. Heracles. Orpheus."

"You're comparing yourself to the Greek gods?"

Vitto chuckled; it felt weird because he hadn't done it in so long. "My father used to think he was a god."

"And now?"

Vitto shrugged. He didn't know what his father thought now that his brain was mush. He wondered if, even with a clear head, Robert would come visit him in the hospital. Come visit the son he'd never wanted. The son he'd always seen as more of a rival.

"I have a photographic memory," said Vitto, his train of thought all over the place.

"So you have a good memory? And it's—"

"Not just good. Memories are like photographs for me. They're frozen in time, and they never go away. Make up some random numbers, Doc."

"Like what?"

"Numbers—like a hundred of them. Tell 'em to me and I'll repeat 'em back to you. In the exact order."

"Because your mind can take a picture of them?"

"More or less."

"Perhaps this is one reason the war still chases you?"

"I bury my nightmares."

"I can't say I agree with—"

"No, I mean literally. I write them down, then bury them in the ground."

"And this works?"

"Did when I was young."

"But not now? Because combat exhaustion is different, Mr. Gandy. It's—"

"I see color too," said Vitto. "Vivid color. That's my other gift. Color to me is alive—always has been."

The doctor was ready to take more notes. "Explain, please."

"It's the way I've always seen it, even when I was little. Anything colored almost seems to move by itself, like it's alive. Or sometimes it's so vibrant it looks wet. Like the world itself is just on the verge of melting. Like a teary eye getting ready to drip."

"Like paint."

"Yes."

"It says here you're a painter."

"Was."

"You don't paint anymore?"

"Too bloody. These experiences I'm reliving . . . It's like I'm seeing them again in living color."

"So you plan to bury them all? In the ground?"

"You sound like my wife."

"She doesn't approve?"

"She always thought it was silly. She's not one to bury anything."

"Figuratively or literally?"

"Either," said Vitto. "Neither."

The doctor scratched notes across his pad and looked up for more. Vitto said, "I used the war as my quest for knowledge."

"And did you find it?"

"I wanted to prove myself."

"Prove yourself to whom?"

Vitto chewed on it, looked away. "I choked my wife." He said it deadpan, and then his jaw trembled. "I saw it. Men break."

"Yes, they do. And it isn't assumed anymore that those men had any prewar neurosis. It was the war that caused it. There's only so much the mind can handle, Mr. Gandy. There are hospitals going up across the country for the veterans. Psychiatrists are coming from the asylums."

"I'm not a lunatic."

"Of course not. And you've nothing to be ashamed of."

"Who said I was ashamed?"

The doctor's pat on the back was unnecessary, but it felt good. And the next thing Vitto knew, he was in one of the beds wearing skivvies and socks, in between two soldiers who were out cold. The sheets were warm, tucked under his armpits.

A nurse with blue eyes stuck a needle in his arm, and he accidentally called her Valerie, which drew a cute chuckle and a correction. "It's Dolores. Is Valerie your wife?"

He nodded. His head was heavy, floaty. He felt drunk all of a sudden, and his words slurred when he told her Val made him laugh. Always had, since they were little.

The nurse patted his hand. "Your shakes are gone."

He nodded, grinned, didn't even recall having had the shakes. Maybe because it had become the norm.

A minute later he was snoring like the rest of the room.

Vitto slept, but his memories did not.

❀

"I'm finished, Mamma."

Eight-year-old Vitto hurries to his mother in the middle of the hotel piazza, where she's just finished posing for an artist from France. "I'm finished," he repeats, gripping her arm. She playfully runs along with him to find his father, who is carving a replica of Giambologna's Hercules and Nessus.

"He's finished, Robert. Robert, Vitto is finished with the turquoise room. Robert!"

Finally Robert pauses in his chiseling to find them watching. "What is it, love?"

She writes something in her journal and slides it back into her pocket. "Vitto. He's finished in the turquoise room."

Robert smiles toward Vitto, although not exactly at him, and then wipes white dust from his hands and his hairy, muscled wrists. Wrists muscled like the rest of him. Muscled like Vitto one day hopes to be. "Let's have a look then."

Vitto pulls Magdalena along. Robert looks annoyed and preoccupied until she takes his arm and pulls him much like Vitto pulled her, at which point Robert laughs. When he's in one of his sculpting modes— the ones where nothing else around him exists—it is sometimes necessary to pull and tug.

They near the room with the vibrantly colored turquoise door, and Vitto opens it—slowly, theatrically, like the actors and actresses who frequent the hotel might do, were they in his little shoes. The distinctive smell of egg tempera and fresh plaster hits them like a wall. Vitto has spent three months on the wall fresco, a perfect copy of the School of Athens, *by the Italian Renaissance artist Raphael. Vitto opens the door wider to let more air and light into the room, and then he points to his version of the masterpiece, a copy of which he stared at for ten minutes weeks ago before storing it in his memory to be duplicated.*

Magdalena covers her mouth with a shaking right hand. "Oh Vitto. It's . . . beautiful. Exactly like the original, except better. Do you know why?"

"Why?"

"*Because you painted it.*" She gets out her journal and scribbles something in it—hastily, but with pride in her smile.

A great shadow covers the floor. Juba has entered, his massive body clogging the doorway and shutting off the sunlight behind it. "*Oh Vitto. Marvelous. It's breathtaking.*" He pants, pretending to be literally out of breath, and then places a heavy hand on Robert's shoulder. Robert is the only one at the hotel who stands as tall and strong as Juba, who is as black as Robert's statues are white.

But Robert stares at the wall with his jaw clenched. He forces a smile, nods at his son as if to say, Well done, *and then ducks out of the room.*

❁

"Every man has his breaking point. No one is immune, Mr. Gandy."

Vitto opened his eyes, rolled his head to the side, slow motion.

The brown eyes of a sandy-haired soldier on the bed beside him stared. "He tell you that?"

"Who?"

"Dr. Cushings," said the soldier. "Every man has his breaking point?"

Vitto nodded, looked up at the ceiling. Didn't feel like making friends. In war, friends were made only to die. Dixon and Deats, two of his friends from before the war, were both dead. Dixon fought for the segregated Ninety-Second in Italy and died in the Apennines. Deats lost his life in Iwo Jima. Their parents had been loyal guests of the hotel—Mr. Dixon was a respected Negro writer and Mr. Deats was a scientist. Vitto used to play hide-and-seek with their boys at the hotel until the sun went down, at which point they'd play with flashlights or candles. If Valerie wasn't busy practicing violin, she'd play, too, and the four of them had made quite a team. He wondered what had become of their bodies.

"I'm John. John Johnson. The men, they used to call me Johnny Two-Times. But one John will do."

Vitto kept his eyes to the ceiling. "Nice to meet you, John."

"Sometimes they'd call me John Squared. Or John to the Second Power. You know, because of—"

"I got it, John."

"Oh, okay." The bed creaked under the man's bulk.

Vitto spied him from the corner of his eye. John looked like one of those farm boys who could lift a tractor over his head. Hands big enough to crack a pencil in half when he wrote. He sighed, rolled his head back to his roommate. "How long you been here, John?"

"Who, me?"

"Yeah, you."

"Six weeks. You know why they put me beside you?"

"No."

"I'm a barrel of sunshine. And I'm at the end of my stay. They thought maybe I could shine some light on you."

Vitto noticed for the first time that John had some patches of hair missing on his head, near the temples and above the ear. Or not really missing, but much thinner than the thicket of hair around them.

John sensed his question. "Shock therapy. Hair ain't growing back for some reason, but at least my nightmares are gone. Most of the memories, too, although Dr. Cushings said they might resurface upon the right stimulant."

"They literally shocked you?"

John made a bee-sting sound and grinned. "Electric stimulation of the brain. Gave me a brain seizure, more or less."

"Did it hurt?"

"Nah—well, not much. Still got a little jaw pain and some head-aches, but it's getting better." John rotated to his side, faced him like they were two girls at a slumber party. He and Valerie would face each other and talk like that after their picnics in the poppy field. "Your wife sure is a pretty."

Vitto flinched. "How do you know my wife?"

"Met her yesterday."

"Where?"

"Here."

"I wasn't here yesterday."

"You were sleeping. She stopped by with your son and your dad. But your dad had some kind of panic attack, and she took him home."

Vitto let it soak in. "How long have I been here?"

"Three days."

Three days? Vitto faced the ceiling again, felt sleepy. His right arm showed the nicks of more than one needle, and he now vaguely remembered taking some pills by mouth.

"They call it narcosis therapy," said John. "They'll keep you mostly asleep for weeks. Deep sleep too—like twenty hours a day. In between they'll run some personality tests."

"What'd they give me?"

"Barbiturates. Sodium Pentothal. Sodium bromide. You still scream out at night."

Vitto clenched his jaw, couldn't remember.

"You're Gandy, right?"

"Yes? Do we know each other?"

"No. Says right there on your chart. Vittorio Gandy, I like that. You Italian or something?"

"No."

"Huh. Figured you might be."

"Well, sort of. My mother was from Florence, then Pienza. In Tuscany." He was silent for a moment, didn't feel like talking anymore. Didn't feel like explaining his mother.

John said, "You one of *the* Gandys? Like from the hotel?"

After a beat, Vitto confirmed, sleepy. "You been there?"

"No. Always wanted to, though. Heard it was the place to be, especially in the twenties." He paused. "Hey, Gandy, is it true that that reporter jumped from the cliffs way back when? Or was he pushed?"

Vitto rolled the other way, ignored the question, hoping it wouldn't be followed by one about the woman who might or might not have jumped twenty years later.

❀

"Where do we go when we die?"

Father Embry smiles without showing his teeth, the same expression he always shows when Vitto asks him that question. "Well, to heaven, of course." Then he ruffles Vitto's hair and continues conversing with the guests scattered across the piazza, some singing, some playing their instruments, others painting and acting and tinkering with various inventions.

On this day Vitto follows in Father Embry's wake, which is more of a slow shuffle. As long as he can remember, the priest has been old, with white hair and face wrinkles that look like mud after it has baked and cracked under the sun. Except Father Embry's face is always friendly, and when Vitto asks his mother why he's always around, she tells him that it's just a short bicycle ride from the rectory and that the hotel's charm is infectious. She drives the hotel's big Buick or rides her own bicycle daily to Father Embry's church in town for confession, and sometimes Vitto goes with her. He waits in the front pew, staring upward, until his mother is finished confessing, and then he tells Father Embry that one day he will paint the church's low-beamed ceiling like the Sistine Chapel. Father Embry usually laughs and tells him to talk to the monks at the monastery because their church has a better ceiling for painting.

"Father Embry, is there a heaven for pigeons?"

That smile again, along with the pause. "Yes, with millions of birds flying about."

He only asks because every once in a while he'll find a dead pigeon in the grass around the olive mill. The last one he kept in a wooden box once used to carry wine until the little corpse stank up the mill and his father yelled at him. "I told you to bury that! Not keep it as a pet, Vittorio!"

Vitto didn't bury the bird, though. Not because he forgot—he only buried the memories that frightened him—but because he often conjures the nerve to do the exact opposite of what his father asks. He tells himself it's because Robert never seems impressed by his colorful paintings, his copies of the Renaissance masters. But Vitto knows his real reasons to be much simpler. He learned early on that to get the good, it is sometimes necessary to bring about the bad. If he provokes his father's temper, then Robert, who does have a soul beneath his hardened exterior, will most likely come in at bedtime to ruffle Vitto's hair like Father Embry does and to whisper "Good night, son" as Vitto pretends to sleep.

And Vitto will smile into his pillow as Robert leaves the room.

❁

"Father Embry says hello."

Vitto's head was heavy like a brick as he moved it on the pillow toward John. "What?"

"And he said to tell you, 'To heaven, of course.' What's that mean anyway?"

"Father Embry. The local priest in my hometown." He closed his eyes, didn't feel like explaining, then became alert again. "He was here?"

"Stopped by an hour ago." John smiled. "Looked as old as Moses might if he was still alive. Said every day you used to ask him where we go when we die."

Vitto stared at the ceiling, wondered how many days he'd slept away.

"Valerie says hello too. Your wife."

"I know who my wife is, John."

"Anyway, she says hello."

"You on a first-name basis now?"

"She said to call her Valerie. Says you call her Val. Didn't mean nothing by it." After a beat he said, "Your dad looks like a statue. Chiseled, like he just walked down from the pedestal. Except he's old. How old is he?"

Vitto grunted. He didn't know for certain, but he suspected his father was pushing eighty and might be older. He and Vitto's mother had been unable to conceive for decades until, as Magdalena told it, they stopped trying, and "then there came you, Vitto."

He looked at John. "How many days have I been here?"

"Eight."

"My back hurts."

"They rotate you around when you sleep, like a hog on a spit. Keeps the bedsores away. Said it would take four people to shift me around. Like moving a dead bear—that's what Dr. Cushings said."

"How many times has my wife come in?"

"Every day." He chuckled, pointed to a spot next to the foot of the bed. "She doesn't come any closer than there either. You must have scared her something awful. Almost like she *tries* to come when you're asleep, so she won't have to talk to you."

Vitto turned away from John and closed his eyes.

❄

"Finish the story, Mother. Please. Epimetheus and Prometheus."

Magdalena smiles, sits back down on the bed. "Just a little longer. Ticktock goes the clock, Vittorio, and it's getting late."

He settles his head back into the pillow and wonders if his father will come ruffle his hair tonight. He can hear him carving out on the piazza now; the echoing of that chisel and hammer is the music that lulls Vitto to sleep most nights whether his father visits or not. But today he ventured too close to the cliffs after Robert warned him not to, and Robert's tanned face got all red when he yelled.

Magdalena shushes him softly, as if she somehow knows he has loud thoughts running through his head. "Zeus now reigned over all the earth. He tasked Epimetheus to create animals, and his brother, Prometheus, to create man. Epimetheus was very enthusiastic and created all the animals before Prometheus had even decided what mankind should be like. By then Epimetheus had already used all the gifts on the animals. This angered Prometheus so much that he stole fire from Zeus and gave it to man. Zeus didn't like this, so he chained Prometheus to a mountain. Then he had a beautiful woman created and gave her to Epimetheus as his bride. She was the very first woman."

"What happened to Adam and Eve?"

"Well, this is just a different story."

"Like the ones everybody tells at last call?"

"Yes. Sure. Anyway, when Pandora came to Epimetheus she brought a box the gods had given her." *She pauses, sighs, pulls her journal from her pocket, and reads to herself for a few minutes while Vitto waits. This he is used to. Sometimes his mother forgets her own stories, and it seems to be happening more of late. But now she resumes with gusto.* "In that box, Zeus had put a little of each of the gods' powers, and he told her not to open it. But Pandora couldn't help herself; she was curious. So she opened the box. And you know what came out?"

"Powers?"

"All the evils in the world," *she says, referring to her journal again.* "Like pride and envy. Greed and suffering. Bad things like that. Pandora slammed the lid on the box before everything could get out. She kept it closed until a day when Pandora heard whispering coming from the box. And do you know what was whispering?"

"More bad stuff?"

"No. It was hope. And it wanted out."

"So did they let it out?"

"Yes, and hope was released into the world." She stands, tucks him
in tight, makes sure she has her journal. *He asks for one more story, but
she kisses his forehead and whispers, "Ticktock goes the clock, Vitto."*

She leaves the room, and he closes his eyes.

Hope. He hopes his father will come in.

But Robert Gandy chisels all night long.

❀

Dr. Cushings knelt on the floor, touched the corner of his mouth. His
fingers came back bloody.

Vitto flexed his right hand, settled his head into the pillow. His
heart raced; he couldn't believe he'd done it. But he'd told himself, *If
that doctor mentions chemical hypnosis again, I'm gonna paste him.* And
so he had, one good shot across the jaw, and now he lay completely
drained.

"Oh dear," said Nurse Dolores, helping the doctor from the floor.
John was out of his bed, too, standing Dr. Cushings upright. Nurse
Dolores gave Vitto the angry eye and said to the doctor, "Let's get you
a chair."

But the doctor had mentioned hope. As in "our last."

Dr. Cushings politely waved her away. "I'm fine, Dolores." Vitto felt
the doctor's hand on his ankle, patting it. "You rest now, Mr. Gandy."

Vitto suddenly sat up and screamed loud enough to wake half
the room—words about chocolate bars and black smoke and naked
bodies stacked liked cordwood.

Dolores was bedside in an instant with ether on a cloth, and she
quickly placed it over his mouth.

He eased back on the pillow, eyelids fluttered.

As he nodded off, he could have sworn he heard Johnny Two-Times crying.

❁

Even in the waning light of the loft, her eyes are so blue he doubts he could mix a color true enough to duplicate them. To even hint at their warmth, the same warmth now covering his chest like a blanket.

"Tell me a story, Vitto."

And so he does.

❁

"They didn't do the hypnosis with me."

John sat on the side of his bed in civilian clothes—dusty work boots, slacks, and a red-and-black checkered shirt, sleeves rolled to the elbows, arms all bulky strength and farm fat.

Vitto was groggy. "They letting you out?"

John laughed. "Ain't a prison, Gandy. Free to go whenever. But yes, they released me yesterday. I told you that."

He closed his eyes, squeezed hard, tried to remember.

"Valerie says hello."

"I bet she does."

"Your dad seems out of sorts. My grandma is like that—can't remember anything. Maybe we should introduce them—although they'd probably forget five minutes after."

John laughed. Vitto didn't. "Why are you still here?"

"'Cause you are, Gandy." He smirked. "We don't leave soldiers behind." He shifted his weight on the bed, and the frame groaned. "I don't think you're getting much better though. You should try that hypnosis. You see Givens over there?" The dark-haired man was playing solitaire on a board propped across his lap. "He did it, said it helped to bring those memories out. The ones you've buried. Kind of like bloodletting in the olden days. Letting out the humors. They'll get you in what Dr. Cushings calls a twilight state. He talks you through real nice."

"He put you up to this?"

John wouldn't be derailed. "You're completely relaxed, half in and half out. Then they try and get you to relive—"

"I don't want to relive. I don't want to remember."

John chewed his lip. "Opposite of me. I couldn't stop remembering." He pointed to the thin patch of hair at his temple. "That's why they did this." John folded his arms, looked around the room, shook his head. "I had the blues something awful, Gandy. Couldn't stop the crying and the whimpering for nothing. CO called me a sad sack. I vomited on his shoes, and he tossed me in the clink. Let me out a couple days later for a shave and a wash, but as soon as he sent me back out the crying started again."

Vitto felt John staring at him, hands like sandpaper on wood when he rubbed them together. Nervous. John wasn't as cured as he pretended to be. "How about that GI Bill, Gandy? You sign up for the unemployment benefits?" Vitto shook his head. "Twenty dollars a week for us veterans. You should look into it, until you get back on your feet. What'd you do before the war?"

"I was a painter."

"Like houses?"

"No."

"Oh. Like pictures, huh? You can make money doing that?"

Vitto ignored him. The back of his head felt flat as a board, and his hair hurt. Nurse Dolores wheeled a bed into the back corner of the room and parked it against the wall. The man atop it had half his head shaved, and he was drooling. "What's his defect?"'

John looked over his shoulder. "Oh, that's Cheevers. When it gets too bad, that's what they do."

"Do what?"

"Lobotomy. It's when—"

"I know what a lobotomy is, John."

John sat straight, smiled proud.

"What? You just break wind?"

"You just called me by name, Gandy." He nodded toward Cheevers.

"Maybe that won't be you after all."

✳

Vitto grips the table with both hands when the piazza starts shaking, a tremble that lasts three seconds and rattles his plate of tortelloni with porcini before settling.

"What was that, Mamma?"

Magdalena looks around the piazza, where dozens are getting up from the kneeling positions they took when the earth started rumbling. Robert, next to his latest statue, looks up at the sky. Juba, a few feet away, looks down at the travertine.

"That was an earthquake, Vitto. You've felt them before." Magdalena looks up and down and all around but otherwise shows little concern. "Sometimes the earth moves. Or quakes. Especially here in California. But this was little more than a rumble."

"Like thunder?"

"Yes. Like thunder under the ground." She wrote in her journal and closed it.

Vitto says, "So when it thunders and lightning flashes, Zeus is up there moving around?"

Magdalena nods. "Or perhaps some of the other gods."

He points to the stones. "What about just now?"

She smiles to reassure him. "Oh, that was just Hades."

✳

"You feel that, Gandy?"

John bit into an apple nearly the size of his fist, and juice squirted onto Vitto's cheek. He wiped it off. "Feel what?"

"That earthquake." John licked juice from his finger. Instead of the bed, he sat in a wooden folding chair. The man had hooked onto Vitto like a tumor. "More like a tremor, though, instead of a full-on earthquake. Bit of earthly indigestion."

"I didn't feel anything."

"Woke you up, didn't it? Must have felt something."

Vitto grunted, watched the sunlight shift out the window. Suddenly, he craved it on his face, the back of his neck.

"Only lasted a few seconds. Just long enough for Dolores to panic and spill her coffee on Littlefield's sheets over there." Another loud bite of the apple. He offered it to Vitto, who declined. "You know some say the big one is gonna come. Big honker of an earthquake, bigger than the big San Francisco quake back in '06. It'll make California an island, some say."

"You ever get tired of talking?"

"You need to eat," said John. "Bet you've lost twenty pounds in here. I can see your cheekbones. They've got a system for fattening you up *after* you've convalesced." John leaned in, juice from the apple clinging to his lips, his face stubbled with flecks of light-brown hair. "You believe in the power of the mind, Gandy?" Vitto didn't answer, so John went on. "Barrel of sunshine or a barrel of stones. You already know which one I picked. The one that don't sink."

"You still cry at night, John. No such thing as cured. Not with what we got."

"You can lay in that bed as long as you want to, Gandy. Or you can drown in it all the same."

The next morning Vitto got out of bed and with John's help took two slow, aching laps around the room. He ate vegetable soup for lunch and wondered if Val would come by. Dr. Cushings said they were pulling back on how much they'd let him sleep now. Day by day his strength would return. He still screamed out at night but wasn't as restless. The doctor had mentioned insulin shock therapy and again brought up chemical hypnosis.

Vitto refused, even when Dr. Cushings said that nothing stays buried forever.

"Sure it does," Vitto told him, "when you bury it down deep enough. What's the saying—time heals all wounds?"

"Time can be a tenuous dancing partner, Mr. Gandy. And memory the devil. Sometimes the wounds we can't see leave the worst scars, unless they're tended to."

"Well, unless you can give me a Band-Aid I can swallow, we'll just have to wait and see."

Dr. Cushings patted his shoulder. "You speak like you're contemplating leaving, Mr. Gandy."

"I see sunlight out that window, Doctor. I'll fill my barrel with it and see what happens. And I miss my wife."

"You'll give us a couple more days to fatten you up?"

"A couple." He nodded across the room at Cheevers, who was drooling. "I'm not going to end up like him."

Dr. Cushings grinned, condescending. "Very well, Mr. Gandy. Just know that a patient is never—"

A door clicked open, and they all turned.

Valerie hurried in with William in her arms. "Vitto, your father is missing. He took his suitcase and left during the night."

Five

*J*ohn drove his Model A sedan; it had room for two in the back, while Vitto's truck didn't.

The top of John's head nearly hit the car's ceiling and his big hands made the steering wheel look like a black Cheerio. After a minute of contemplation in the hospital's parking lot, Valerie had gotten in with them, making sure she and William were alone in the back. Despite her urgency, when it came to her husband, she'd kept her distance.

In the passenger seat, Vitto looked over his shoulder, caught William staring. He said to Valerie, "Don't worry. John is good people." And then he remembered that she probably knew John better than he did.

She hugged William on her lap like the wind might blow him away. "You mind rolling the windows up? It's cold."

John said, "Sure thing, Valerie."

Vitto watched John, unsure about him using his wife's first name, but let it go. Anyway, he was cold too; he still wore his hospital gown and skivvies. Fortunately, John had grabbed both of their suitcases during their hasty retreat from the hospital, Dr. Cushings following on their heels and warning it wasn't a good idea to leave.

"Mr. Gandy, you're far from convalesced."

Vitto changed in the car—a pair of beige pants and a white button-up he didn't remember packing, along with a pair of brown-and-white oxfords he didn't remember buying.

"They were on sale," said Valerie. "Got them for only three twenty-five." She stared out the window, jaw clenched. Maybe she was used to being in control, and now things seemed completely out of it. Or maybe she'd planned on driving herself and now here she was in an unfamiliar car, at the mercy of two soldiers with what Dr. Cushings called severe combat exhaustion.

In the parking lot, after they'd decided Robert had more than likely run away to the abandoned hotel, the panic level had gone down, but only somewhat. The man was still far from capable of taking care of himself, regardless of his familiarity with the place. There were numerous ways he could get hurt there all alone, especially in the dark where electricity no longer hummed. Not to mention the cliffs and the rocks and ocean below.

No, he wouldn't! Vitto glanced back at Valerie's face and knew she'd had the same thought. Robert wouldn't be the first to jump—or fall—from those cliffs.

Valerie said she'd never seen Robert as agitated as he'd been after last night's tremor—the newspapers were now calling it a minor earthquake—pacing through the darkness of their home like a moth trapped in lamplight.

Vitto decided he could listen to Valerie talk all day. Her voice had always seemed like music incarnate—like sound from the angels, he'd once told her when they were both thirteen. He glanced back, then faced forward again; remnants of purple bruising still showed around her neck from where his hands had clutched it. That memory he'd have to bury, deep in the ground.

He closed his eyes, wished it gone. He'd once promised his mother he'd never put his hands on a woman for any reason. That was when he was seven, after he had watched a drunken guest at the hotel hit his wife across the face. The memory of the smack and then her scream as she collided with the wall had been etched so vividly that Vitto had been unable to sleep, both the violence and the rage from that man wreaking havoc with his mind. So Magdalena had sat him down on the edge of the fountain, lovingly taken his hands in her own, and told him to bury it.

"Bury what?"

"The memory. That's what I do with all of mine, Vitto."

"All of your what, Mamma?"

"The bad ones. I bury them deep down so they never come up."

She'd said it like she'd never been more serious about anything, and then a few seconds later she'd appeared confused, like she didn't remember why she was sitting on the fountain with her son. She'd gotten out her journal and scribbled a few lines before closing it, smiling at him again, pretending all was right with her world.

"And promise me, Vitto. You'll never strike or harm a woman."

And so he'd promised.

The man who hit his wife had been kicked out of the hotel, forcefully removed by Robert's own hand and warned to never come back. And Vitto had taken his mother's advice quite literally, writing the memory down on a piece of paper, placing it inside a small tin can that still smelled of tomato sauce, and burying it the field next to the vineyards, where he'd gone on to bury every bad memory, every argument he'd ever had with Valerie, all the way up until the war.

When Vitto opened his eyes they were already halfway to the hotel, and he wondered if he'd dozed off. He still felt hinky from the drugs they'd been feeding him the past two weeks. With the windows up, the whipping wind got sucked into the noise of a rumbling engine in need of a tune-up and tires that felt uneven. John pushed the car as fast as it would go—through dips and turns on the highway and then through the trees and houses of Gandy, which rested as a small, nose-shaped outcropping of the coastline just north of San Diego. The once-famous hotel Robert had built with Cotton Gandy's fortune perched right on the tip of the nose. A narrow, curving river severed the hotel's property from the rest of Gandy, and butterflies swirled in Vitto's empty stomach as they neared the one-lane wooden bridge that connected it all.

Valerie could have made the trip on her own, he knew, but Vitto understood that her stealing him from the hospital had been a cry for help. Strength can only bend so far before it breaks, and hers was waning. She'd been going it alone for too long now, starting back as far as her childhood, when her parents had brought her for an extended stay at the hotel and then left her behind, with a note for Juba to continue her lessons and look after her. He'd done just that without hesitation, treating her as if she were his own, but the abandonment had still taken its toll.

I'm home now, Vitto thought, willing her to somehow get the message. *Your husband is home, and it's time I started fulfilling again my end of the bargain—war damaged or not.*

Six years ago they'd insisted on getting married in the place they'd first met as kids, right there on the recently closed hotel's piazza with the tall, sculptured fountain trickling in the background and the sun setting over the crenellated stone walls. They'd made promises to each other. The "for better, for worse" one stuck like a splinter in his mind now because things couldn't get much worse. So as they neared the hotel, he bottled those swirling butterflies, leaned over to finish tying his oxfords, and steeled himself like he would just before battle.

John removed his right hand from the steering wheel to wipe tears from his cheeks.

"Why are you crying?"

"I miss your father already."

"You don't even know him."

"I've known him half a dozen times."

Valerie mumbled from the backseat, "At least he gets you talking."

"Talking," said William.

Vitto felt like John had already wedged himself in as part of the family. "Don't you have a family of your own?" he snapped, then wished he could take back the words.

John started crying harder now, clenched that steering wheel like his life depended on it.

Vitto pointed. "Turn here." Then he said, "Sorry."

"It's okay, Gandy."

Vitto glanced over his shoulder again, found his wife and son staring at him like he was some kind of monster, and then turned his face back into the sunlight just as the car's tires roll-thumped over the boards of the rickety one-lane bridge, plunging him into the present and the past in one confused heartbeat. The river they were crossing was really a glorified creek, a wide stream that trickled instead of flowed, with barely enough force to move a stick during the dry months or float one of Mr. Carney's wooden toy ships during the wet ones. Today the water was halfway up the bank, moving just swiftly enough for them to hear the gurgle now that Valerie had rolled her window down, poking her face into the wind like she used to do when they were little.

By now both he and John had tears running down their cheeks, and Vitto did his best to hide them from his family in the backseat.

John whispered, "What's wrong, Gandy?"

Vitto wiped his cheeks dry, the tears gone as readily as they'd arrived.

On the other side of the bridge—fifteen paces across, according to Mr. Carney, the architect who'd built it decades ago, even before the first stone was placed—was a tall sign that read, "Welcome to the Tuscany Hotel." And below it: "Since 1887. Where you put your worries and past behind so your creativity can thrive."

Robert always spoke those words to guests upon their arrival, no matter how many times they'd been there. Ninety percent of those guests had been creators of some sort—musicians, singers, magicians, scientists, architects, novelists, playwrights, screenwriters, famous actors from Tinseltown, and visual artists working every different medium. The rest of them had just wanted to experience the magic of it all. Now only ghosts remained—and the lone security man Robert had insisted on paying. Robert Gandy had stayed until the hotel closed—for a few years even after the staff had up and gone, strolling the courtyards and piazza alone as if waiting for a final rush of people to come trundling over that bridge for one more last call.

On the opposite side of the bridge was a life-sized marble sculpture of two beautiful women, their legs intertwined as if battling for supremacy on a single pedestal. One of them faced in the direction of those arriving; the other looked the other way. They had been carved by Robert at the hotel's conception more than five decades earlier. Now weeds and vines coiled around their legs and waists, climbing upward and branching toward marble arms frozen in motion.

At the end of the bridge, John slowed to take in the statue—transfixed by it as so many had been. Vitto and Valerie had seen it so much as children that they'd wondered if the statue held true powers instead of mythical ones.

William now beside her on the seat, Valerie leaned forward behind John. "The woman facing this way is Lethe, the Greek goddess of forgetfulness. Robert's idea for the hotel was that the guests would leave all painful memories behind while they were here, leave behind the worries of the day so they could relax and create. Which is why the hotel was always full of artists and the like. Vitto's mother—"

"Val."

She stopped cold, leaned back.

Vitto added, "That stream we just rode over—my father named it the River Lethe for the same reason. In Greek mythology, the waters of the River Lethe caused forgetfulness."

"Is he from Greece?" asked John. "Your father?"

"He's from Alabama. Turn right."

Eyes and mood again perked to the surroundings, Valerie continued her explanation. "When the guests left the hotel they'd see the other woman in the statue. Mnemosyne is the Greek goddess of memory." Vitto felt her stare, so he didn't face her while she added, "She's often portrayed with red hair like fire. Seeing her upon departure was believed to restore your memory so that you could return to the outside world."

John steered the Ford down through a valley and then up a hill. Tall Italian cypress trees lined both sides of the serpentine road leading to the hotel, the fields waving with golden winter grass. In the spring and summer, they would be dotted with wildflowers—sunflowers and orange California poppies mixed with the red corn poppies Robert had imported from Italy. When Vitto was a child, the red ones had been limited to a single field near the hotel, but by now they had spread and mixed with the native flowers. Dollops of gold and scarlet now dotted the hotel grounds and beyond—sneaking beside walkways, randomly sprouting between the grapevines and olive trees, playing peekaboo through the cracks of the hotel's limestone façade, springing up along the foundations of Robert's *Leopoldini*—square, stone, mortarless imitations of Tuscany's old countryside farmhouses. One of these housed the olive mill, and the other was used for drying grapes and making wine.

The angled, slate roof of each structure was topped off by a central turret-like home for the property's pigeons and doves. He and Valerie used to feed the birds fresh bread from the hotel *cucina* as the shadows of so many flapping wings flashed monstrous across the lawn, the movement alone conjuring smells of rich olive oil and recently harvested grapes drying in bundles inside the stone houses, each facing the other as if in competition, with the harmonious combination of both always winning out.

"You do know where the pigeon dishes for *pranzo* come from, Vitto?" Val had said one day as they both peered skyward toward the birds.

Until then, he hadn't known. He'd never been as astute as Valerie. John's voice now broke his silent reverie. "Did it really happen?"

"Did what happen?"

"The guests' memory," he said. "Did it leave when they arrived and return when they departed?"

Valerie took a breath to respond but Vitto spoke first. "Of course not. It was just another fun addition to the hotel's lore. Keep following the road." As they climbed the curved road, now potholed in places, sunlight showed glimpses of Renaissance-inspired statues spaced randomly across the grounds and between the trees, their bases covered by weeds and vines, the heads and shoulders and splayed arms pocked by bird dung. No more employees left to clean them off.

John was crying again. Vitto didn't ask why. Valerie patted John's shoulder and the tears came harder, so John clenched his jaw to keep things from getting messy. "Barrel of sunshine or a barrel of stones. Right, Gandy?"

A question of himself to himself, Vitto assumed, John's motto, his crutch to fall upon now that it was clear both he and John had been released—or escaped, in Vitto's case—from the hospital too early.

The road opened. The hotel loomed like a castle in front of a sunlit backdrop. The land dipped and rose in carved undulations, a pedestal of its own, the building a work of art soaring above the cliffs and water below. The scent of ocean breeze and wildflowers entered the car along with ghostly remnants of the region's finest olive oil.

In front of the hotel was an oval loop where guests had unloaded luggage and valets had parked their cars. The grass in the middle was overgrown by weeds but still highlighted by another of Robert's statues, this one named simply *Psyche and Cupid*. Robert had modeled it after Antonio Canova's masterpiece, *Psyche Revived by Cupid's Kiss*.

John slammed his foot on the brake, eyeing the statue. Vitto braced himself against the dashboard to keep from hitting the glass. In the backseat Valerie grabbed on to William. But the boy thought the abrupt stop funny and was even more amused by the way John left the driver's door open and walked trance-like inside the weedy loop toward the two nude figures dominating the statue, Psyche's backside in partial view as she lay in Cupid's arms, awakening from the kiss that freed her from the deep sleep Venus had cast upon her.

John stopped a few paces away, then slowly began to walk around the statue, taking it in from every angle, just as Vitto—for many reasons—had as a young boy, the foremost stemming from what Magdalena had told him one afternoon when she'd caught him staring at the front of the statue, specifically at Psyche's nude form and her bare legs lazily crossed at the ankles. He'd started to run when he saw her watching, but she'd lovingly grabbed his wrist to keep him put. "No reason to be ashamed of beauty, Vitto. Look closely. Cupid has your eyes, does he not?"

But how was that possible? How could Robert have carved the likeness of Vitto's eyes when Vitto had yet to be born? Some said he had his father's eyes, so perhaps Robert had simply carved his own. Regardless, he'd taken it as truth, and later in the day he'd imagined that Psyche's eyes resembled Valerie's. Years later, in front of this very statue, he'd asked for her hand in marriage, to which she'd responded, "Of course, Vittorio, I've known we would since the day we met."

Now they could hardly stand to look at each other.

She and William were now out of the car. William pointed. "Naked butts." Valerie chuckled and pushed gently to lower his arm, her ears tuned in now, as were Vitto's, to the sound of chisel against stone echoing across the piazza.

Robert was here somewhere, alive and apparently safe.

❀

"Love endures against all odds," his mother whispers in his ear, explaining the story behind the hotel's welcoming statue. What he pulls from it is that Psyche, the youngest of three daughters, had beauty that was unparalleled, and the attention the mortal princess received made the goddess Venus—"Aphrodite, as the Greeks would tell it, Vitto"—rage with jealousy. So the goddess urged her son Cupid—"Eros to the Greeks"—to use one of his arrows to make her fall in love with the

ugliest creature on earth. But when Cupid witnessed the beauty first-hand, he accidentally shot himself with his own arrow and fell in love with her instead.

"To make a long story short, Vitto, there were trials and tribulations, breaks in trust, and Venus eventually put a spell on Psyche, a long-lasting sleep that took a kiss from Cupid to finally awaken her. She was made immortal by Zeus, at which point Venus eventually accepted her as Cupid's wife."

Magdalena kisses him on the head, then on both cheeks the way Robert does with all the guests, her perfume smelling of lavender, her breath of cool mint. "Why do I tell you this story, you ask?" He didn't ask, but she's correctly inferred it. "Love endures, yes. But even more importantly, Vitto, the grace of a mother-in-law is not so easily earned. And to whoever that challenge falls upon when the time comes, please warn her to be ready." She gently grips his shoulder, leans in toward his ear, and nods toward Psyche. "And yes, I agree, she has her eyes."

❋

Vitto shook that memory away, and the cold chill along with it. It wasn't so much from what she'd said as from *when* she'd said it. He hadn't even met Valerie at that point; she and her parents hadn't arrived until that afternoon. And in all the years they'd known each other, Vitto had never been able to figure out if Valerie had earned her future mother-in-law's grace. If she hadn't, it wasn't for a lack of trying. But Magdalena had always been protective of Vitto to a fault.

Cupid's massive wings cast ominous shadows across the grass. Vitto turned away from the statue and his mother's voice and faced the Tuscany Hotel in all its grandeur, now six years uninhabited, yet still somehow gleaming with life. Despite the sun-scorched old vineyards down the hill to the left—now gnarled scabs of the lively vines that had once borne grapes so purple they looked blue in the right sunlight and greens ones as plump as small apples—the hotel's wide façade still held the welcoming Italian villa aura that had brought so many to its doors in its heyday. Shaped in a perfect square, two-storied except for the turrets standing higher at the four corners, the sturdy exterior concealed a massive travertine piazza and courtyard—the heart of the hotel's charm—where artists and musicians had done their work and all the guests had congregated day and night.

The clinking of stonework grew louder.

Vitto followed it, then froze on the bricked walkway, staring into the shaded darkness of the portico with its three Roman arches that acted as doorways, where air flowed freely and guests never entered and departed unchanged. The terra-cotta roof tiles showed stains from recent rains, where water would have cascaded the overhang and curtained the second-floor windows, which were shaped as smaller Roman arches—once decorated with flowers of every color but now only pockets of dull shadow staring from rough wedges of limestone shipped in from Tuscany itself. Green vines slithered from mortar cracks. Window ledges had begun to crumble, sprinkling rusty dust on the overgrown hedges below. A few of the stones would have to be replaced.

From afar, the hotel glowed orange in the morning, more yellow and cream-colored at dusk, sometimes red at the exact moment of sunrise. But up close, as Robert had asked Vitto to observe as a boy—so close his nose touched the craggy surface and he sneezed out stone dust—each block had a fingerprint of its own, a unique palette of swirls and specks and fibrous tendrils of red and orange and yellow and creams. On that morning he had stepped away convinced that the walls were somehow alive and dripping.

That was back when Robert was the teacher and he the pupil, back before Vitto's yet-unknown talents with the brush had become a threat to the father. Back before jealousy had turned to rivalry and rivalry to a divide that had yet to be bridged.

I think he wanted me to go off and die in the war, Val.

But that thought was surely nonsensical, so he kept it in.

Valerie clutched Vitto's arm, urged him onward toward the first of three arches Robert claimed represented earth, wind, and fire. John hurried from the statue to catch up, his footfalls heavy beneath the arched ceiling as they passed through brief shade to the vast open belly of the hotel's piazza, where the first-floor rooms opened from canopied entryways and the second-story rooms to an open-air gallery that overlooked the piazza. The door to each room had been painted a different color. After years of disuse, the doors still held the vibrancy intended to make each room unique.

The rooms contained in the eastern wing of the enclosed square— the one comprising the hotel façade, all showed shades of blue, from pale sky to serene periwinkle to inky navy. To their left, on the south wing, the doors were scarlet, crimson, brick—all the various shades of red. To the right, the doors on the north wing shone with shades of yellow and gold. And directly ahead, across the piazza was the west wing, with a walkway behind the crenellations that overlooked the cliffs and ocean. Instead of rooms, this section of the hotel featured a bar and kitchen and bakery and a dining area—where the Saturday markets were held—all under canopied protection.

John turned in a circle to take it all in, as did William, who had let go of his mother's hand as soon as they'd entered the piazza.

"The doors," John said, turning in awe and wiping his wet cheeks. "Like a color wheel."

William pointed across the piazza, to the shadows of the far right corner. "Paw Paw."

He started toward him, but Valerie held him back. "Wait, dear. Let him work."

Robert was clearly safe, unharmed, and perhaps more sound of mind than he'd been in months. It was clear he'd gained some burst of inspiration upon entering the hotel, and Vitto, too, was reluctant to disturb it. He'd learned long ago to not interrupt when Robert was in the middle of one of his manic phases, which was what he appeared to be in now, wielding that mallet and pointed chisel like the magician Vitto had always assumed he was.

"Vitto, look." Valerie pointed to the middle of the piazza, toward the massive, cross-shaped fountain. Tiny square tiles in blues and yellows lined the fountain bed and walls, creating a radiant mosaic sun around which the hotel activities had always rotated. Each end of the fountain cross blended into a mosaic walkway that reached out toward the rooms on each wing, cutting the piazza into four equal sections and continuing around the circumference to enclose it all. Tiled in various shades of blue, the walkways represented river water, a constant flow of life to every room.

Vitto slowly approached the fountain and the ten-foot statue that dominated it: his father's masterpiece, *The Rape of Mnemosyne.* Museums across the globe coveted it, as they did all of Robert's pieces, but none more than this. They had offered money enough to resurrect the hotel, but Robert had always refused. The sculptures were already in a museum. The hotel was *his* museum. Artists from around the world had come to stay and to create, willingly leaving their fingerprints behind in the form of paintings and mosaics, reliefs and friezes, ceiling frescoes and wall murals, religious art and stories about the ancients, each room a new experience.

There had never been any rational explanation for the variety of artwork that adorned the hotel. Religious art seamlessly mingled with secular, ancients, Greek, and Roman with Renaissance and Impressionist and Expressionist. A medieval Madonna and child side by side with a replica of Michelangelo's drunken *Bacchus,* a German-style triptych of Christ on the cross within arm's reach of a classical frieze depicting the battle of the centaurs. Angels and archangels lined up with gods and Titans, goddesses next to saints, the apostles and Apollo with the nine Muses. *The Creation of Adam, Cain Killing*

Abel, gods of dusk and dawn, day and night—each had a place, and each was irreplaceable. Which was why Robert—according to his unreliable books—had used every last bit of his money to pay for a security officer to stroll the grounds in his absence.

Where is the guard now?

The fountain statue had been carved in the style of Giambologna's *The Rape of the Sabine Women* and Bernini's *The Rape of Persephone*—the word *rape* used in the ancient sense of kidnapping or abduction—but with Robert's unique vision. Vitto stopped feet from the mosaic fountain bed, surprised to see a few inches of water sparkling yellow and blue above the tiles. The muscular nude figure of Cronus, the king of the Titans and god of time, wrestled the beautiful Mnemosyne, both forms spiraling upward as the goddess of memory reached for the sky in an intensely passionate struggle for freedom. The goddess Lethe cowered below, one arm clinging to the right leg of Cronus as if unable to watch, as if wishing to take back what she had possibly set in motion or to stop the abduction in the final throes.

Time and memory and forgetfulness all frozen in struggle.

At the base of the statue, spilling from the open mouths of four gargoylelike winged chimeras—each facing one side of the hotel and guarded by carvings of archangels in bas-relief—water fell softly, as if from a half-turned faucet, splashing into the cross-shaped pool below and rippling in a way that gave the tiles movement, life.

Vitto lowered his hand into the fountain, dipped his fingers until water lapped his knuckles, cold and fresh and completely unexplainable—the fountain had been bone-dry for years. He removed his hand as if burned, wiped it on his pants, turned to watch his father chisel away at that tall block of stone in the corner of the piazza.

Valerie pointed to a ceramic goblet on the travertine next to the fountain, lying sideways and wet, recently used. "He drank from it, Vitto. Vitto?"

He was slowly approaching his father in the corner of the piazza. *He drank from the fountain. But why?*

Ten paces from his father, Vitto stopped, noting the dozens of sketches strewn about the stone at the base of his father's next statue. Charcoal studies to use as models, as blueprints. An outline of some figure had been painted on the tall block. Around the base lay a jumble of tools and supplies—plumb lines and mallets, brushes and rags, a bucket of water, and an open bottle of one of the hotel's house wines—Palazzo Tuscano, this one a merlot from 1930—apparently brought up from the cellar.

Robert's concentration was intense as he hammered with a pointed chisel, chipping and cleaving the initial chunks and slivers of marble away. In the weeks and months to come he would switch to the toothed chisels for detail and then, to refine, the smooth chisels and files and rasps. In his mouth was a curved pipe that smoldered as he eyed the next hammer blow.

A genius. Clink—the mallet struck chisel. A madman while at work. Clink. A gladiator. Clink. In this place a god, not the man who confused a razor for a toothbrush. Clink. Marble dropped to the travertine and splintered. He focused on the chisel. Clink! Dust showered down on his shoulders, on the fresh stubble of his face, his long, white hair tossed by the ocean breeze that blew in through the portico.

And then he stopped. Looked around the marble slab, noticing he had an audience of four. The pipe dance-clicked across his teeth. He exhaled; buttery Cavendish caught the breeze, floated with hints of cherry and vanilla.

The memory of those smells alone made Vitto's knees tremble. He swallowed heavily, throat thick with nerves, feeling hungry and suddenly light-headed.

Does he still not know who I am?

"Father?"

Robert smiled, broad and strong, the same smile that had once greeted the likes of Greta Garbo, Carole Lombard, and Joan Crawford unfazed; the presence that Clark Gable, Cary Grant, Charlie Chaplin, and Buster Keaton had spoken of for weeks after their departures. He dropped the mallet to the stones. The chisel fell from his slack grip, rattled sharp against the travertine.

"Vittorio," he said, eyes clear and focused. "My son. You've come home. *Buon giorno!*"

Six

*M*agdalena watched her fellow orphans move about the Cortile degli Uomini, the inner courtyard of the Ospedale degli Innocenti.

She'd passed on their invitation to play, choosing to observe rather than to feign amusement. The game—*whatever it's called*—involved a wolf and a fruit and far too many questions. It seemed fun, and she would have joined in if only she could remember the rules, which they explained to her daily, only to have her forget them midgame and then stand in a stupor while they continued on.

It was easier to decline. And watch. And listen.

The other children laughed, so Magdalena laughed along with them. Sun baked the cobbles and warmed her face. A gentle breeze swooped down into the courtyard and slithered back over the roof; she could hear it faintly whistling in and out of the loggia in front. Up above, hanging from the terrace that Nurse Cioni called the *verone,* clean clothes rippled like flags as they dried under the Tuscan sun.

It was because of Magdalena's memory problems that they all had their names stitched onto their shirts. Nurse Pratesi had sewn them herself, starting the very afternoon the idea had come to her—months ago, after Mass. *Even at your age, Magdalena, you read better than any child here. If you can't remember your friends' names, you can simply read them.* Magdalena had asked Nurse Pratesi to sew her name on her shirt as well. She said she wanted to fit in with the others. But the truth was that Magdalena, on some mornings, couldn't remember her *own* name, much less the dozens of others.

Even at age five, she was aware enough to know that being "the girl whose memories simply would not stick," as Nurse Pratesi was known to put it, would not help her prospects of being adopted—nor would it help in finding an eventual husband. The lack of a dowry was one of the reasons girls were more likely to be abandoned than boys in the first place. And adoptions were not common at any rate, although one girl had been adopted the week before by a wealthy leather merchant. The nurses were happy for her, but at the same time sad to let her go.

"The merchant seemed nice enough," Nurse Pratesi had told Magdalena as they swept out dust from the loggia's arches.

"What merchant?"

"The one who came yesterday. To take Lucia?" Nurse Pratesi was never able to mask her concern over Magdalena's memory issues. The nurses dealt with disabled children on a regular basis—some with deformities, others born deaf or blind or dumb, and there was even an isolation ward for the infants with syphilis. But never had they come across a child who appeared normal in every way but simply could not seem to remember.

On the good days when she recollected small bits of her experience, Magdalena liked all the nurses, but Nurse Pratesi was her favorite, and in secret she called her Mamma Pratesi. They were careful not to let the other nurses hear of this, especially Nurse Cioni, who'd grown colder toward Magdalena over the years and who made a habit of looking cockeyed at the wall clock over the foundling wheel every time she passed it. *Ticktock goes the clock.* Apparently it had been broken until the night of her arrival. The night of the great storm.

Even now, Nurse Cioni looked down with suspicion from the *verone*, pretending to rearrange the drying clothes, but instead doing a rather poor job of spying. Magdalena knew adult words like *spying* but could not remember what she'd eaten for lunch hours ago. She did know she'd had a cup of red wine, though; the dry, fruity taste still lingered on her tongue.

"Why aren't you playing?"

Magdalena turned to find Nurse Pratesi standing behind her. "Mamma."

"Shh. Not when others are around, Magdalena."

The little girl nodded skyward toward Nurse Cioni. "She doesn't like me."

"She likes you plenty, Magdalena. She just has a heavy daily burden and waning patience."

"I consume most of it, I assume."

"Most of what?"

"Her patience."

Nurse Pratesi laughed. "You speak well above your years, my little one. But I won't lie to you—yes, you try her patience." And then she added, "Because of your memory."

"What memory?"

They shared a laugh—it was a common joke between them—and together watched the other kids run through patches of shade and sunlight.

"What's bothering you, Magdalena?"

"Nothing."

"Not true."

"Correct. It's not true. But you wouldn't believe me anyway."

"I'd like to try."

Magdalena started to but stopped, clamping her lips together as if refusing a spoonful of medicine. She couldn't tell her that she *did* remember some things, such as the moment Nurse Cioni's mood first changed—the day the clock above the wheel started working again. The day of Magdalena's arrival. Though she had only been recently born at the time, somehow Magdalena had memories of that night.

Being placed gently on the blanket inside that foundling wheel. The brush of lips to her forehead. The noise of the storm and the soft sound of a mother's voice she would never hear again. The smell of rain and wool and wood, the groan the wheel made as it turned inward toward the belly of the hospital. Sometimes still she would startle awake at night to these sounds and sensations.

Magdalena looked up to the *verone*. Nurse Cioni had disappeared. Dinner would come soon. Bread smells wafted from the kitchen, and her stomach growled.

"Why is Nurse Cioni afraid of that clock above the wheel?"

Nurse Pratesi pursed her lips, exhaled. "I don't think she's afraid. Just leery."

"So why does it stay up there?"

A pause. "So that we will always remember the day you arrived here."

"Why should that matter more than any other?"

Nurse Pratesi didn't answer, just gazed down at the little girl. How could she explain to a five-year-old the uncanny effect she had on people by simply *being*. Even the children felt it, offering little Magdalena a kind of deference instead of teasing her about her memory. Many an adult voice had been silenced by the sight of those olive eyes and bright orange hair. And the painters—they simply could not resist her.

Florence had long been known as an artist's city—crammed with those who created beauty and those who patronized it. And from its founding in the early fifteenth century, the Ospedale degli Innocenti had benefited from that connection. Over the years, statues, paintings, and frescos had been commissioned for and donated to both the hospital and church—works by the likes of Giambologna, Botticelli, and Ghirlandaio—and artists often visited the hospital seeking inspiration from the architecture itself. Brunelleschi's design for the complex had been pioneering—harmonious and humanistic and balanced from portico to piazza. But many who visited left inspired instead by the girl with the orange hair and the olive-green eyes.

Over the past few years, Nurse Pratesi had accepted numerous requests from those who wanted to paint Magdalena. But recently she had begun to refuse them, especially the ones from that crotchety painter named Lippi, who had returned the day after the girl's first sitting to pose an even more unusual request. He had wanted the girl to stand next to his easel while he painted something else entirely—a Tuscan olive grove to be exact—claiming he'd never felt more creative and open-minded than he'd felt around the girl. The man's upturned nose and dark, beady eyes—not to mention the scratchy tenor of his voice—had given Nurse Pratesi the shivers. She'd physically turned him by the shoulders and nudged him on his way.

"I remember the day the clock started again," Magdalena said abruptly, surprising herself that she'd let out the words.

Nurse Pratesi chuckled, patted her on the shoulder, and then, after realizing Magdalena was serious, knelt down beside her. "What did you say, dear?"

"I remember the day the clock went ticktock." Magdalena forced herself to look at the only mother she knew. "I remember I was kissed on the forehead. I remember being inside the wheel, the sound it made as it turned. I remember seeing your face."

"Magdalena, infants can't remember such things."

"Why not?"

Nurse Pratesi scratched the hair beneath her cap. "What else do you remember?"

"That's all."

"That's all?"

"Most of my memories don't belong to me."

Nurse Pratesi bit her lower lip, turned it pale, and before she could ask the question churning in her eyes—*To whom do they belong?*—Magdalena started across the courtyard, dodging the playing children. Nurse Pratesi followed, walking so closely behind that her shadow swallowed them both. She stayed on Magdalena's heels through the open door in the building, down a hallway, then out through the big front door and across the loggia to the piazza, where the little girl stopped, facing the front of the building.

Magdalena pointed up toward the spandrels, the small spaces between the loggia's arches, specifically toward the concave roundels set within. Each framed a mounted terra-cotta bas-relief of a baby. The ten original *bambini* had been added to the building's façade in 1487 and had quickly become beloved symbols of innocence, inspiring replicas on buildings all over Florence. The white glaze over the terra-cotta gave them a milky, lifelike appearance, from the details of the hair to the lines on the hands—and toes of the only one not swaddled. More bambini had been added in 1847, but of those original ten, seven were fully wrapped, two had the swaddles loosened, sagging below the waist, and one emerged completely from the clothes—a sequence generally assumed to represent liberation.

Nurse Pratesi followed Magdalena's pointed finger. "What is it? Magdalena, you're frightening me."

"The artist."

"Yes. Della Robbia. Andrea della Robbia."

"His father made the sculpture in the Innocenti church."

"Yes. Luca. Luca della Robbia. The *Madonna and Child*."

The nurses, wet nurses, and female foundlings often prayed before that glazed terra-cotta sculpture. Magdalena had probably done so just this morning. "I remember these *bambini*. I remember him making them."

"Who?"

"The son. Andrea. I have one of his memories. I think, because it seems old."

"Magdalena, that's impossible. That was nearly four hundred years ago. And you can't have other people's memories." But Magdalena remembered it all the same. "You're frightening me. Is that what you meant earlier? When you said that most of your memories don't belong to you?"

Magdalena lowered her arm, walked with her chin upraised, curious eyes still on the spandrels between the arches and columns. "Nurse Pratesi, who is Mozart?"

"Who is . . . ? Magdalena?"

"Mozart. Wolfgang Mozart." She stumbled a little on the German syllables. "Who is he?"

The nurse touched her brow as if confused or dizzy or both. Her voice trembled. "A composer. A famous composer. Why?"

"I think I have some of his memories too. Just bits and pieces. Of when he wrote one of his operas."

"Don Giovanni? The Magic Flute? The Marriage of Figaro?"

"What was the first one you said?"

"Don Giovanni?"

"Yes, that's the one."

Nurse Pratesi buckled at the waist and then steadied herself with hands on her knees, eyes to the cobbles.

"Mamma Pratesi? Are you not well?"

She sucked in a deep breath, shook her head. Some of the other children had stopped their game and followed from the courtyard. She held them at bay with an outstretched hand. "Have you mentioned this to any of the others? The other children?"

The girl shook her head in a way that said she knew not to, that she probably shouldn't, because they wouldn't understand. "I already know I'm different, Mamma Pratesi."

"Different in only the best of ways, Magdalena." The nurse gently gripped the little girl's shoulders. "What other memories do you have?"

"Too many to count. Sometimes I remember him painting."

"Him? Who is him?"

"He was on his back, way high up to this giant ceiling. Sixteen chapels!"

"Michelangelo." Nurse Pratesi dropped to her knees, closed her eyes.

Magdalena put a hand on her shoulder, leaned closer to hear what Nurse Pratesi whispered.

"Sistine, Magdalena. Not Sixteen."

Seven

*V*itto startled awake in a sheetless bed that smelled old with mildew and damp. The screaming sound of the Nazi warplane faded as he sat up. A tiny lizard clung to the mortar in the stone wall across the room. An arched wooden window hung crooked from a rusted hinge, open to sunlight and birdsong and a chilly breeze.

Where am I? You know where you are. Room 268. The door painted peach.

After his father had greeted them all on the piazza yesterday, somehow like the man of old, kissing each of them on both cheeks, even John—*baci, baci, baci*—Vitto had felt weak in the knees, nauseated by the barbiturates still swimming through his system. John had hurried to help him, but Vitto had waved him away. *I'm fine, just tired.* And then, like a sick dog, he'd slunk away while the others conversed, falling asleep in this second-floor room to the sounds of his father chiseling deep into the night.

As a young teenager, his parents had let him move about the hotel, sleeping in whatever vacant rooms he wanted. This one had been a favorite—mostly because, as a young boy, he'd been allowed to watch the creation of its colorful ceiling fresco, a replica of Correggio's *Assumption of the Virgin,* painted under the dome of the Romanesque Cathedral of Parma in the 1520s. The artist, a Venetian copyist named Julia Francesca, had started the room 268 version in the summer of 1925 and completed it in the fall of '26. Though the room had no dome, she had managed to give it a dome-like appearance using foreshortening, tricks of light, and illusions of depth.

Even today, years after its painting, the fresco pulsed with life as he stared up at it. Apostles at the painting's edge shielded their eyes from divine light, while others showed excitement, their clothing tousled by the force pulling the Virgin upward, through concentric rings of sky-blue clouds full of angels and saints, into the bright glow of heaven at the vortex of the "dome."

A pigeon landed on the windowsill, then flew away, flapping wings giving way to a beautiful violin thrum. *Paganini. Caprice No. 24. Valerie?* Vitto sat up in bed, swung his feet to the stone floor, rubbed his eyes, and slid into the oxfords he didn't recall parking so neatly next to the bed. Something Valerie would do, neat and orderly. Bits of him remembered her slipping them off when the room was dark, giving him sips of wine, wishing him good night, closing the door, her footfalls fading along the second-floor gallery. She must have also come up with the musty throw that lay rumpled next to him.

She's scared of me. She couldn't wait to flee from the room.

He smoothed his wrinkled clothes with his hands and approached the window. It creaked when he opened it wider. Fresh air from the sea mixed with the pleasant aroma of baked bread, and for a moment he felt youthful again, unburdened by the war and that mysterious concept called age, the exact number now muddied by his thirteen months overseas. A twenty-three-year-old boy when he'd left. A grizzled twenty-four-year-old man upon his return. And somewhere in between he'd lost his way.

The fresh-bread smell caught him again. Was someone in the kitchen? He stepped outside to the gallery. Across the hotel, beyond the terra-cotta roof of the south wing, the olive grove loomed high on the hillside, the terraces buried under weeds and brambles, one jagged slope now instead of what he used to pretend were steps in the earth for the giants and Cyclopes from his mother's stories. He leaned on the railing. His father carved below on the piazza. On the far side of the fountain, Valerie stood with her violin tucked under her neck, delicately touching bow to string while William kicked a worn soccer ball around a wrought-iron bench.

When Valerie was a child she'd drawn crowds on this very piazza. They'd called her a prodigy. And now her music soared sweetly again, a little rusty in technique, but shimmering and warm. Had she returned home to retrieve her dusty violin while he'd slept?

Vitto gripped the railing and closed his eyes. If this was a dream, he didn't want to wake from it. If it was death, he'd found the right place. But ever since he returned from Europe, his mind had engaged in a tug-of-war between fiction and reality, truth and trust, and the army doc had cautioned him to approach each day as he would his steps—one at a time.

He held the cool metal rail as he descended the spiral staircase, shoes clunking off each step in a weird rhythmic cadence to his father's mallet blows. An artist from New York had traveled by train in the spring of '05 to install the spiral stairwells, one for each corner of the piazza. An elevator hidden in the west wing had taken care of luggage and other mundane business.

Robert looked up from his work, his white shirt unbuttoned to midchest—dust caught in the curled white hairs—sleeves rolled to the elbows, a dotting of white scruff on his cheeks. "Buon giorno, Vitto." After no response he returned to the statue, eyeing Vitto in between mallet blows. "You're staring. Why?"

"Do you smell bread?" Vitto asked, unsure which father would answer back, the mindful one or the one who'd forgotten how to tie his shoes. "Is this even real?"

"Of course it's real."

"I had some weird dreams inside that hospital."

"You died in the war, Vitto. What you see is Elysium," Robert said. Vitto stared. "Or is it Hades?" Still no reaction. "I'm only kidding." He nodded toward the kitchen. "Your friend John fancies himself a chef. He asked if he could clean up the ovens and test them. Must have gotten them working."

"We have no electricity."

"Who says? You try the lamp in your room? Figured not. You're in 268, right? That artist—Julia, was it? Not as stunning as my Magdalena, but definitely a face to be painted." Vitto should know; she'd allowed him to paint her before her return to Venice, before his father had suddenly and without explanation demanded he paint replicas instead of originals. It had been one of his earliest works, oil on canvas, her sitting in a chair with her back to a blue ocean and a scattering of bright-green Italian cypress trees in the background. His father had looked at the painting with a confused grunt, whispering to Magdalena later that Vitto should stick to copying the masters.

"But why, Robert?" Vitto had overheard that night.

"So I can see it, Maggie!"

It had been the only time Vitto ever heard his father raise his voice to his mother. But what struck Vitto now was the casual way Robert had just mentioned Magdalena.

"So you know?"

"Know what?"

"Mamma . . . that she's dead?"

Robert looked at him like he had three eyes. "Of course. She's buried here at the hotel—out past the poppy field. But thank you for poking an old bruise."

"It's just that . . . Valerie, every day she would have to remind you . . ."

Robert's chisel bit off another small chunk. "A lot has happened since your hibernation yesterday. Water. Electric. We have a telephone line working." He wiped the stone, revealing what could have been the initial pocks of a beard, or perhaps the hair of a woman. "The other evening when the earthquake hit."

"It was hardly an earthquake."

"Tremor, whatever it was, I had a brief burst of lucidity directly after. I made some phone calls. Packed my suitcases and a few other things I thought we'd need." He nodded toward Valerie. "Like her violin. And then I sneaked out of the house. That fountain . . . was running when I arrived."

"How?"

Robert shrugged. "Maybe it was Charles. He was my first phone call. You remember Charles; he used to do maintenance. Or maybe it was something else?"

"Like what?" Vitto was incredulous.

"You're not the only one to have telling dreams, son." Robert held up his hand, craned his head toward the south wing. "Ut in omnibus glorificetur Deus." *That in all things God may be glorified.* The pocket watch he pulled from his pants showed a couple of minutes past noon. "Sext, Vitto. Shh. Listen. I heard them singing Lauds in the wee hours of the morning."

The faint baritone sound of the Benedictine monks chanting carried over the hillside olive grove. From the top terrace the monastery was visible down in the valley, a collection of modest stone buildings for modest men. A church with a tall steeple, stained-glass windows, and a colorful ceiling fresco painted by Vitto in his teens marked it with beauty. The smaller buildings looked like brown paint dots from the height of the olive grove.

Valerie had stopped playing her violin. With William by her side, she stood facing the chanting from the valley.

Robert pointed toward the kitchen. "Your friend, he cries a lot, by the way. He asked to try the ovens. I said be my guest." He grinned, gripped his son's arms. "Our first guest, Vitto."

"Our first . . . What are you talking about?"

"Your friend John. He stayed in one of the Caravaggio rooms. The one with the replica of *Judith Beheading Holofernes*. Vitto, I'm opening the hotel again."

"You're what . . . how? And with what money?"

"Ah." He waved it away as if to say Vitto knew nothing and money mattered little.

"Father, this place closed down from lack of funds, plus a lack of guests near the end. Art is beautiful, but it is not currency. It is not food. The Depression hit hard. And just two days ago you were—"

Robert's glare stopped him. "You don't know why we closed down, Vitto, so don't pretend to."

"It was Mamma's death then."

Robert pointed with his chisel. "You do that, you know? Rationalize. You've always needed to hold something to know it exists. To give concrete reason to things, a hardness"—he knuckled the marble beside him—"when those things just might prefer to be air." He pretended to snatch something from the air in front of his face. "Unseen."

"Really? So who is it you're getting ready to sculpt?"

Robert ignored him, focused back on the marble slab.

Vitto wondered if the water Robert had consumed from that fountain yesterday had done more than restore his mind and memory. Perhaps it had rattled some of the remaining *good* screws loose.

"Don't always ask why or how or what, Vitto." Robert chiseled another sliver from the marble. "Not all questions have answers, nor should they. And not all medicine comes in a bottle."

"So that's what this is? This hotel, the water in that fountain—suddenly medicine?"

"Nothing is as sudden as it seems, Vitto. We are made of mostly water, are we not? Water is life. And to me art is food!"

"You've gone mad. This isn't real."

He laughed. "Perhaps you should look in a mirror, son." He lifted an eyebrow, eyed Vitto's wrinkled clothes and unshaven face. "Or perhaps not. But you've been here only one night and you're already more engaged with life than you were those first two horrible weeks after your return."

"How would you know? You didn't even know who I was. Your shoes were on the wrong feet every morning."

"Oh, some part of me was paying attention," said Robert. "Perhaps locked in a cruel cage, but I was in there."

"And you're healed now? Suddenly let free from your cage? The Alzheimer's disease or whatever is magically gone, just like that? Memory restored?"

"More or less. At least for the moment."

"This makes no sense." Vitto pointed. "*You* make no sense."

"I thought you'd be thrilled."

"Of course, I am . . . but . . ."

"Your friend John calls it a miracle."

"John cries all night. He pretends to be a barrel of sunshine, but deep down he's no different from me."

Robert looked across the piazza toward Valerie, who'd begun playing again—probably to mask their argument—a made-up song in accompaniment with the monks' voices. "It's good to hear her play again. She didn't play when you were gone. The passion oozed from her by the day."

Vitto pursed his lips, fought the urge to go to her.

"She's still frightened of you, Vitto. Give it time." He pulled from his pocket a folded paper. "Read. That went out in this morning's newspaper—and not just the *Gazette*. I made some long-distance calls, got it in the *Union* and the *Times* and the *Examiner*. Expensive, but worth it."

It was a notice about the opening of the hotel. Specifically, it invited the elderly and those afflicted with memory loss. Vitto crumbled it, tossed it to the ground. "You cannot promise healing . . . memory restored. You don't know. This is not right. Who drinks from a piazza fountain?"

"What's not right is to keep this to ourselves."

"This? This *what*?"

"Who is Bed-Check Charlie?"

77

"What do you mean?"

"You screamed it out in your sleep last night. Bed-Check Charlie. Your mind is covering things up, Vitto. You've buried too much."

It was true. He had. Robert had never approved of his son burying those silly little tin boxes of nightmares and bad memories in the field, based on advice from the folds of Magdalena's mind. And Robert had never been comfortable discussing his wife's mental quirks—*because how could his muse possibly be flawed?*

"I craved my mind back, Vitto—my memories. But you *fear* yours. And you have to get past that. You can be hurt by what you remember, but you can also be healed. And the healing will not happen until you allow those memories back out, just as the army doctor said. Who is Bed-Check Charlie?"

Vitto turned on him. "In January of '45, the Eighth was ordered to Rheims. Then we raced more than a hundred miles across France through snow and ice to Pont-á-Mousson, to help stop the Nazis' drive for Strasbourg. We were assigned the call sign Tornado. In Rheims, we saw our first enemy plane. I wet myself as it neared. Is that what you want to hear?"

"Yes, go on."

"He didn't open fire. It was only reconnaissance. But he came back. Every evening at dusk, this lone plane flew above us. We named it Bed-Check Charlie! Why are you smiling?"

"How did that feel?"

"What?" But he knew, and it had felt good.

"Letting go," said Robert. "Allowing that memory freedom. It's already working on you too. Yes, Valerie gave you wine last night. But it wasn't only wine."

"No. She didn't."

"John whimpered all night. He drank too."

"You had no right to bring that horror back. John spent weeks burying those memories."

"He drank on his own accord. And Vitto, memories *can't* be buried. Not forever."

Vitto turned, didn't know where to go. Back to the army hospital seemed the safest place. Where they could poke and prod and dig; he could admit that once, during the war, the sights and sounds and colors had been so strikingly real that he'd attempted to bury himself in a ditch, shoveling dirt in upon him like a man buried alive until Coopus had pulled him out.

Robert touched his shoulder. Vitto flinched. "I drank again this morning, Vitto. The water's effect doesn't last. It really is like medicine—we need regular doses. Daily doses."

Vitto shook his head. He'd been tricked into consuming it last night, but never again.

"Vitto, look at me." He turned. Robert now held a wooden model boat in his hands—a Viking ship three feet long from bow to stern, one of Mr. Carney's maritime replicas. Tiny wooden shields lined the sides, a sturdy red-and-cream-striped mast soared above it, and a tall-necked dragon head adorned the bow.

Robert handed the boat to Vitto; its hull looked wet, recently floated. He nodded toward Valerie across the piazza. "She was skeptical, too, until she saw for herself. I believe you know what to do with this."

Eight

*B*y the time he reached the creek, the Viking ship was an anchor in his hands.

He'd lost so much strength over the past two weeks, the three-hundred-yard walk to the front of the property had exhausted him. The hills of his childhood had suddenly become mountains.

Halfway to the creek he'd rested on the base of a tall statue, a replica of Bandinelli's *Hercules and Cacus*. He'd once told Valerie that someday he'd have a full beard like Hercules did in the statue, with the muscles to go along with it. She'd laughed. "Do you expect to get those muscles from wielding a paintbrush?" He'd grinned, only slightly hurt—they often needled each other—but then she'd quickly added, "If the hotel is ever overrun by this Cacus giant—"

"He breathes fire," he told her.

"Okay, this fire-breathing giant Cacus, then I'll know who to call for help."

These were memories he held dear; the ones from the war could rot where they hid. Remnants of her flirtatious giggle fueled him to the next statue, a replica of one in the Medici Chapels. He paused briefly there before moving on toward the creek. The gurgle of moving water gave him strength to plow on, hugging the wooden ship like one might hold an infant.

The water was high for November, flowing swiftly after recent rains, a mere foot or two below the bank. Often after dry summer months their boats used to get caught on exposed rocks and in little eddies, the flow a murmured trickle instead of a proper current. The best time to float Mr. Carney's ships—thirty-seven of them, if he remembered correctly, all stored in two rooms above the hotel's entrance, the Roman bireme being his favorite—was during the first three months of the year, when Gandy experienced the most rainfall. That's when the Lethe River swelled, and the boats floated faster than he could run alongside as they sped down the valley toward the monastery and the small lake behind it.

Vitto dropped to the grass beside the creek, muddying his knees, watching the water flow. He heard footsteps, looked over his shoulder. John emerged up the hillside—first his head of shiny, wheat-colored hair and then the massive rest of him—breathing like a man who'd spent three weeks in a bed. They both needed to gain strength.

"Valerie said I should come with you. That you'd tell me about the river."

"It's not a river. It's a creek."

John plopped beside him, the weight of his knees displacing grass and mud. "I brought bread." He tore a hunk and offered it to Vitto. It was still warm and tasted of honey. Vitto chewed, watched the water.

John handed him another hunk, sat back on his ankles, and pulled a bottle of wine from his pocket. Vitto hesitated. John promised him it was only wine, so they took turns drinking from it and plucking from the bread loaf.

"Do you know any Greek or Roman mythology?"

"No."

"There were five rivers in the underworld. In Hades."

"Hell?"

"Sure. If that helps. One of them was named Lethe. The river of forgetfulness, oblivion. The murmuring sounds would induce drowsiness."

"I *am* feeling tired, Gandy."

"When the souls of the dead moved to the afterlife, they drank from the River Lethe to forget their past, in order to be reincarnated."

"I don't think I believe in that."

Vitto chewed, watched John. "I don't either. It's a story, a myth. My father was enthralled by the ancients. He wanted this hotel to be a place where guests could come and forget their humdrum lives. To work on their talents free from daily burdens. Some said the River Lethe bordered Elysium."

"Never heard of it."

The way John chewed reminded Vitto of a cow with cud. "Elysium. Paradise."

"Heaven."

"Yes. The final resting place of the virtuous, where heroes were sent to live blissful, immortal lives. The ancient Greeks believed that after death, souls crossed over to Hades and were given a choice to drink from the Lethe, whose water caused forgetfulness. A chance to leave behind any painful memories. Then they were returned to earth, reborn, with a chance to do better."

"I don't think I believe in that either."

Vitto ignored him. "Or they could drink from the fountain of Mnemosyne."

John nodded toward the double-sided statue beside the bridge. "The goddess of memory."

"Very good, John."

"Don't patronize me, Gandy." He tore off another hunk of bread. "I'm not an imbecile."

"And those who chose to remember were sent to Elysium, where they could live out their lives in eternal happiness."

"So where's that leave us?"

Vitto drank wine and chewed bread. "Are we dead, John?"

"Don't think so."

"Then a decision is not yet needed, is it?"

John shrugged, dipped his fingers into the creek water, and then wiped them dry on his pants. Vitto was enjoying a moment of silence, listening to the water, when John said, "What were the other four?"

"What other four?"

"You said there were five rivers in Hades. What were the other four?"

"Do you ever stop talking?"

"That's why my parents said I was still single. My daddy said it was hard enough for a woman to overlook this nose I got, so why did I always have to open my mouth."

"He said that?" John nodded, teary eyed. "Where are your parents, John?"

"They're dead, Gandy. Tuberculosis got 'em both before I went overseas."

"I'm sorry." He raised the wine bottle. "To your parents, then."

John drank next, wiped his mouth. "Daddy said I was a sissy 'cause I always preferred to be in the kitchen with my mom instead of throwing a baseball around the yard." He wiped his wet cheeks. "Said I cried too much too. So I went off to war to show I was tough enough."

"And?"

"I wasn't." He drank from the bottle, a long gulp, swallowed like a snake would. "Robert said I could be the new hotel chef. He tried my bread and liked it. I'm writing out a full menu."

"There's not going to be a hotel, John."

"That's 'cause you still think like a barrel of stones, Gandy."

Vitto chewed the bread. "Styx was the river of hatred. Acheron was the river of sorrow and pain. Cocytus, the river of lamentation. And Phlegathon was the river of fire."

John nodded, let out a brief chuckle that made Vitto ask what was funny. "Just that me and you must have had a good dose of all five rivers then. Hades must just be another name for war."

Vitto couldn't deny it. "They're all here at the hotel, those rivers."

He nodded toward the creek at their feet. "This one's the Lethe. The other four rivers I just mentioned are represented by those blue mosaic walkways leading out from the fountain. Don't ask me why."

"Why?"

Vitto swallowed wine, shook his head.

John went from solemn to smiling in a snap. "You know, Gandy— what you just said about the people that drink from the Lethe to forget? They'd have to do it all over when they died again, right? That would get kind of frustrating, that constant cycle." Vitto shrugged, wondered if a point was coming. John gave it. "It's not too different than what Robert was dealing with. That Alzheimer's, you know? Each day like an endless loop." He tipped the wine bottle back and then wiped his mouth on his sleeve. "Barrel of sunshine, Gandy. Or a barrel of stones."

Vitto looked across the creek, ears peeled to the sound of an approaching automobile. The rumble grew louder, and then a black Chrysler New Yorker pulled up over the ridge and stopped in front of the bridge. The vehicle idled and coughed, hesitating like it had a mind of its own and didn't want to cross over.

"Who's that?" asked John.

Vitto stood, wiped the back of his britches. "How should I know?"

Whoever sat in the driver's seat must have gained some sudden courage, because he or she gunned it over the bridge and continued on toward the Tuscany Hotel like there *was* no turning back. In the passenger's seat sat an elderly woman who stared at them as they passed, and then she raised her right hand, the middle finger extended.

"You see that, Gandy?" Vitto nodded in disbelief. John laughed. "What did that gesture mean back in ancient times?"

"You don't want to know."

The car rumbled down the hill, briefly out of view, and then showed itself again in the distance, scooting along the serpentine, tree-lined road toward the hotel.

All was silent for a moment as the new arrival disappeared over the horizon. "The quiet hurts, Gandy," said John. "It ushers bad memories up. You asked why I talk all the time. Well, that's it. The quiet hurts." He nodded toward the Viking ship resting in the grass. "You gonna float that thing or not?"

For Vitto it wasn't about the silence or lack thereof; it was about what his mind couldn't stop seeing, so he thought it important to keep occupied. He knelt back down beside the creek, wondering now if his delay in floating the ship didn't have something to do with how the water sounded different. It wasn't just that the water was higher than normal. There was something not quite right about how the water was flowing.

"Go on," John urged. "Robert said it was the earthquake that did it."

"Did what?"

But part of him already knew, already could tell. He lowered the wooden Viking ship into the water and let go. Instead of sailing off to the right, toward the monastery and the kidney-bean-shaped lake behind it like it was supposed to, it took off quickly to the left, toward the bend at the poppy field, and Vitto didn't have the legs to chase it.

Nine

Vitto hustled back to the hotel with John beside him, huffing to keep up.

"My mother told me a story when I was a boy," said Vitto. "There's a river called the Limia that starts in Spain and then flows through Portugal. Legend was that crossing it brought about memory loss. They thought it could be the real River Lethe. Then, about a hundred years BC, a Roman centurion led his troops up to the river. He wasn't about to let this myth interrupt his battle plans, so he crossed the river and then ordered his soldiers to cross over one by one, calling each of them by name." He felt the need to explain to John, who looked puzzled and out of breath. "In calling their names, he proved crossing the river did nothing to his memory."

John tripped over a dip in the ground. Vitto helped him up, and then the two of them walked side by side, panting up the winding road to where the newly arrived car had parked in front of the portico. A woman in a green dress pulled a heavy suitcase from the backseat and then helped the elderly woman into the hotel.

"But what about that creek back there, Gandy?"

"It couldn't have suddenly changed directions."

"But it did. You saw for yourself. It was the earthquake. Sir Robert said so. Where'd the *Sir* come from anyway?"

Vitto shook his head, his mind nearly as weary as his legs. "A number of British royalty visited the hotel in the late twenties. Then King George—the old King George, not the one that's king now—invited him to London and knighted him." Before John could ask why—Vitto didn't exactly know why—he took the lead as they entered the arches beneath the front portico and entered the open-aired piazza. In the twenties and thirties, Sir Robert Gandy had been as popular in California as any movie star and the envy of some, and it hadn't been at all uncommon for foreign dignitaries to come for long stays. The walls were adorned with crests and busts and paintings from too many countries to count.

The new arrivals stood before the central fountain. The brown-haired younger woman was chatting with Robert and Valerie while William and the elderly woman stared at each other. She had her hands on her knees, lowered closer to William's level, as if making a game of it. And then the old woman yelled, "Ouch! He pinched me!"

"I did not," said William, red-faced.

"Did too, the little plague rat."

The younger woman stepped between them and ushered what must have been either her mother or grandmother away from the boy, who was crying now. Vitto made a move to comfort him, but that only caused his son to cry harder. Valerie picked the boy up and turned him away from Vitto, as if saving him from a rabid dog.

"He pinched me," the old woman said again, her thin white hair fluttering. "Yes, he did. He pinched me." She made pinching motions with her hands. "Like a crab."

"He didn't pinch you, Grandma," said the younger woman, doing her best to calm her down, but obviously flustered herself.

John, dazed and smitten the instant he saw the younger woman, held out his hand to her, as if introducing himself at this exact moment would help calm things. "Hi, I'm John. John Johnson. My friends call me Johnny Two-Times. But one John will . . ." But his voice was swallowed by the commotion.

"The little crab rat pinched me! Right on the rear end. Got no decency."

Trying hard to regain control of her grandmother, the young woman turned away from John's outstretched hand. She clearly hadn't seen the gesture, but John must have assumed she was ignoring him, which was why his eyes glossed wet with tears. He lowered his chin to his barrel chest and stepped back from the action.

Robert raised his hands—he still held his sculpting hammer in the left one—and encouraged everyone to calm down. A laugh bubbled up from Vitto's throat, but he checked it before it left his mouth, let it settle as a grin. Just a couple of days ago, Robert had been acting like a four-year-old, too, and now he was the voice of reason. But it worked. William calmed, and the old bat stopped her accusations of being pinched, content to just glare at the little boy.

The younger woman unfolded a newspaper, showing the advertisement Robert had paid to run in it the day before. "Have I come to the wrong place?"

Robert kept his eyes on the old woman, who was whispering to herself, as he answered. "You're clearly in the right place, my dear. You're the first to respond."

Her shoulders sagged in relief, like this burden was no longer just her own. "I'm Beverly Spencer." She gestured to her right. "And this is my—" Her eyes widened when she saw her grandmother giving little William the finger. "Grandma!" The old woman put her finger away, playing it off like she was straightening a crease in her long-sleeved blouse. Beverly closed her eyes, took in a deep breath. She opened them and forced a smile. "This is my grandmother, Louise. And she has what the advertisement said you can cure. I still don't believe I'm standing here. My mother, bless her soul, always said I was gullible. But I'm at my wit's end, Mr. . . ."

"Gandy." Despite the stone dust on his hand, Robert reached out to shake hers.

"Pleased to meet you, Mr. Gandy." She stared up at him as if in awe. Those who didn't know Robert Gandy most likely knew *of* him and his hotel. She looked around the piazza, taking in all the colorful doors, each marking its room with artistic distinction. "Newspaper called it a hotel for lost memory."

Robert smiled, toothy and wide. "Senile dementia. Yes. What some doctors are calling Alzheimer's."

Vitto bit his lip to keep his skepticism from ruining things. Besides, Valerie had just given him a look that could have killed a weaker man like John, who was standing on the periphery gnawing a fingernail.

Nonsense or not, unexplainable or not, Beverly was clearly willing to give this place a chance. She folded her arms. "Well, I never heard of any Alzheimer's. But dementia—she's definitely got that."

"I have eighty-seven years under my belt," said Louise, in a moment of lucidity. "That's what I have, you . . . you critter."

Vitto laughed, didn't know what else to do. That old biddy had just called her own granddaughter a critter. Or maybe she'd been talking to Robert.

Robert stepped toward Louise, offered his hand. Louise looked at it, sniffled, and then leaned down and wiped her nose on his sleeve, leaving a trail there like a slug would on a sidewalk.

Mortified, Beverly yelled, "Grandma!"

"It's okay." Robert laughed, approached the fountain, and dipped a cup into it. He offered it to Louise. "Here, take a drink."

She grabbed the cup with gnarled, arthritic fingers that seemed to loosen upon touching the handle. She raised it to her mouth but then stopped to eye what was inside. "What's in it?"

"Water," said Robert. "Just water. Drink. You'll feel better."

Beverly added, "Think of it as medicine, Grandma."

That did it. Louise sent the contents splashing in Robert Gandy's face and then handed the empty cup to Vitto, who'd sidled closer without remembering doing so. Like part of him had wanted a close-up view of the old woman swallowing just to see if this was really happening and not some weird dream stockpiled from the war.

Robert wiped his face as Beverly apologized again. *A professional apologizer by now.* Valerie shot her an understanding look as Louise put her hands on her hips and surveyed the perimeter of rooms that bordered the piazza. "This place is silly, Beverly. The doors look like candy."

Robert, a bead of water clinging to his right eyebrow, motioned toward the rooms all around. "You've got your pick, Mrs. Spencer."

"Call me Louise, and quit getting fresh. Joe will be here any minute."

Beverly whispered over her shoulder toward everyone except her grandma, "Grandpa Joe's been dead for fifteen years."

They all nodded as one collective; they understood perfectly.

Louise pointed toward the wing of rooms with doors in shades of red. Beyond the rooftop were the high-set olive terraces. "I'll take that one."

"Which one, Grandma?"

"The one I'm pointing at, Beverly. The one that looks like a plum." She waddled in that direction; with her hunched turtle-shell back she was a good five inches shorter than her granddaughter. She looked back over her shoulder and said to Robert, "Once I get settled in, sonny, you can bring me up a cup of that medicine—with some Old Sam if you've got it. Or some red wine. On a tray." As they walked, Beverly put a hand on her grandmother's shoulder, and Louise immediately knocked it away. "Where's my bag?"

Robert looked around for the suitcase, then spotted it next to the fountain.

Vitto cleared his throat loud enough to get John's attention and spoke from the side of his mouth. "Get the suitcase. John! The suitcase."

John got the message, hurried to the suitcase before Robert could grab it. "I'll get it, boss."

Vitto said, "Introduce yourself again," then added when John looked confused, "to Beverly."

John nodded, hurried along. Beverly waited, thanked the towering John Johnson, and said, "Nice to meet you, John," when he introduced himself again, insisting that he'd carry the luggage for her. Vitto moved past the fountain to eavesdrop, staying just enough behind them to hear but not seem obvious. Through the corner of his eye he saw that Valerie did the same.

Beverly said, "What do you do here, John?"

"I'm the chef," said John, nervous, and then added, "Lunch will be ready soon."

"And what's on the menu?"

"Bread."

Beverly waited for more, but that's all Johnny Two-Times said. Then, as if his nickname had taken root and suddenly grown to fruition, he said it a second time. "Just bread."

So you're a bundle of words until the ladies come around.

Vitto looked over his shoulder and caught Valerie watching him. Saw a hint of something that once was—the curl of a smile on the right side of her mouth—but then she turned away as if to hide it.

Ten

*T*he sun bled orange across the horizon.

Gradually it shrank to a red sliver, smashed flat by the approaching dark, and then ocean waves rippled it gone. Now a silver sliver of moon shimmered over the same water, begged to be painted.

Instead of grabbing the satchel of paints and brushes Valerie had left outside his door hours ago, next to the easel and canvas Robert had pulled from the basement, Vitto sat stubbornly by the window of room 206 and smoked stale cigarettes. Smashed butts cluttered the windowsill; he only had one left from the packs he'd brought back from the war, and he savored it as his fingers shook. Across the piazza, his wife and son must have gone to bed. Their second-floor light had turned off an hour ago, thirty minutes after she'd stopped playing the violin.

Something was definitely off-kilter. He and Val had nothing but good memories from the hotel, especially with having been married down there on the piazza, but their current relationship was tainting things in a hurry. Maybe he should up and leave. Or maybe he should have opened the door when she knocked earlier.

"I know you're in there, Vitto."

Of course I am. Where else would I be?

If she hadn't turned away from him earlier in the day when he caught her smiling, perhaps he would have opened it. But now he was back to room hopping.

The back wall of room 206 featured a fresco of *The Last Supper*, painted by a Leonardo da Vinci copyist from Berlin back in the summer of 1903. Aside from the beauty of the painting and the coffered ceiling—each square mural told a story from the Old Testament—he'd always enjoyed the view from this room. To the right he could see the road leading to the hotel. To the left and over the rooftop he caught glimpses of the ocean his father used to swim in daily, almost religiously, after Magdalena's death. And the cliff top, where every evening Robert would stand, gazing out upon the open water as if waiting for a lost ship to come back home.

There were mouse droppings under the bed, and the naked mattress looked like it had been through a bomb blast—covered with dust and bits of plaster that had fallen from a ceiling that now leaked. If his father was really going to go through with this, he had months of work ahead of him, months of cleaning out and ordering and restocking. And the cost? Was it even safe to have guests here again—elderly ones at that?

Vitto looked away from the bed. He didn't plan on sleeping on it anyway. The chair would suit him fine, and he had transferred the thin blanket from 268. He hadn't seen which room John had gone into earlier—he assumed it was one of the Caravaggio rooms again—but he could hear the big man snoring like a bear in hibernation. At night the ocean breeze picked up sound as if it had hands and threw it into the open windows.

The newest arrivals had picked a room on the first floor, underneath where Valerie and William slept. The old woman had been true to her word and taken her "medicine," which was why, an hour later, her granddaughter Beverly had run out to the piazza crying. She'd flung her arms around Robert, thanking him profusely as he took a break from chipping away at that stone.

The fountain water must have worked on the old woman too. Which was why Vitto couldn't stop smoking. Or drinking. He'd snatched a bottle of red from the cellar below the kitchen and had about finished it off. The idea had been to keep himself busy at the window, smoking to stay awake and drinking to keep his mind off things, but that plan was proving futile. Sleep tugged on his eyelids, and he couldn't keep his mind off of the fountain down below. The constant, recycled flow of water, the slow splatter into the rippling cross-shaped pool, had hypnotized him.

Hypnos, the god of sleep. He lived in a cave in the underworld where no light from the sun or moon could reach. Hypnos was the son of Night and the brother of Death. In front of the cave grew poppies and other plants that induced sleep.

Just as he was about to doze off he heard the choked throttle of an approaching car. He leaned out the window. At the front of the property, blurry cones of light flashed in and out of the cypress trees, disappeared into a dip of hillside, and then reappeared a few seconds later, climbing the serpentine road toward the hotel.

Vitto finished the bottle of wine, took a long drag to knock off the cigarette, and stepped out onto the gallery. Over the roof, the turnabout at the front of the hotel was visible. The car puttered to a stop. The headlights blinked out. A car door opened and closed, and then another. He waited, heard voices. Head muddled from the wine, he held tightly to the railing on the way down the spiral staircase to the piazza, where an elderly man and woman appeared in the shadows on the far side of the hotel, luggage in hand.

"Hello." The man's voice echoed under starlight.

Vitto approached, stopped beside the fountain, and beckoned them closer.

"Is this the memory hotel?" the man asked.

Vitto nodded despite his misgivings.

"We've come from upstate." The old man moved closer, tugging gently on the woman's hand, coaxing her along. She shuffled like a shy child. "Drove all day. My wife, she's sick. We saw the advertisement in the newspaper and left right away."

"How long have you been married?"

"Sixty-five years." He'd squeezed his wife's hand as he said it, and she buried her head into his shoulder. "Sixty-five years," he said again, this time with a catch in his voice. He was bald except for some white above the ears.

His wife pulled a folded paper from her coat and read from it: "Amy, Norman, Charlie, Belinda, and Peter. Amy, Norman, Charlie, Belinda, and Peter. Amy, Norman . . ."

"The names of our five kids," said the man. "It calms her down."

"How long has she been sick?"

"Two years." He glanced at his silver-haired wife.

She spoke softly, like what she needed to say was between them only. "Where are we?"

"The hotel I told you about, Mary." He patted her hand, both of them arthritic and liver-spotted. "The one we've been driving to all day. Remember?" His voice was calm on the surface but hardened beneath his clenched jaws. Worn out but unable to give up. "The one from the newspaper."

"We need to go to the hospital, Henry. Not the hotel. I've got to get to the hospital. I'm to deliver any minute."

He looked back to Vitto. "She has it in her mind that she's expecting our firstborn."

"Amy?"

Mary read from the list again. "Amy, Norman, Charlie, Belinda, and Peter."

Vitto grabbed a mug from the lip of the fountain and dipped it into the water. He reached it toward them, in a hurry to pass it off because he was already tempted to drink from it as well. "Here, take it."

"I'm not thirsty," said Henry. "But thank you."

"It's for her," said Vitto, looking away. "It's the medicine."

"Oh." Henry's eyes grew large, and he handed his wife the cup.

She sniffed it. "I don't want any. Smells like metal. Like guns. Where are we? We need to get to the hospital." She turned to Vitto.

"My youngest once came to me, tugging on my dress, and he says, Mommy, was I an accident? I said, Peter, what do you mean? Amy said I was an accident, he says, and I laughed. I told him, Peter, you were *all* accidents." Vitto laughed. But then the old woman seemed confused again, anxious. "Henry, the hospital?"

Henry calmed her down, and slowly brought the cup to her lips. "Drink."

Don't drink it, Vitto wanted to say, unsure why. Because every day has its night. Because what goes up must come down. Because memories can cut as much as they cure. And because he'd learned through the war that life too often was fool's gold. Rays of a beautiful sunrise led to rivers of blood. Under lush canopies of evergreen forest, combat stained the silent snow cherry red. Craters and limbs pocked fields and countryside. Last words traveled on breezes choked with smoke and death.

Mary sipped from the cup. She closed her eyes, swallowed, then took a deep breath. Her shoulders sagged, relaxed. She sipped again, eyes still closed, while her husband waited, watching her as if she were a coma patient starting to regain life. And then she opened her eyes, turning toward her husband.

"Henry."

She'd said his name before, but this was different. This mention brought moisture to his eyes. He put his hands on her shoulders as if testing her, making sure she was real. *Because how real are we if we can't remember?* Vitto thought of his mother. *Or if we bury our memories and refuse to remember?* He thought of Valerie as he watched Henry lean toward his wife with an intimacy he now craved. "Mary? Do you know where we are?"

"We're at the Tuscany Hotel, dear." She smiled, wide-eyed and seemingly clearheaded as she took in the entirety of the piazza and the fountain and the colorful doors that circled it all. Her husband nodded, unclenched his jaw, and then wrapped his arms around her slight shoulders.

Vitto stared at the two of them, both slumped with age yet somehow now renewed with life.

Water is life. Water is death.

He shook the thought away and reached down for the cup that Mary had unknowingly dropped to the stones. He approached the fountain, lowered the mug over the edge.

Then the screaming began.

Vitto placed the empty cup on the fountain ledge and hurried toward the spiral staircase, taking two and three steps at a time. John was no longer an annoying sidecar with an overactive mouth, but a fellow soldier in need of help. He followed the screams to room 246 and found John sitting up in bed, wedged into the corner, fighting something unseen, screaming, "I can't feel my toes."

Vitto grabbed at his flailing hands, secured them both, and talked John down, telling him repeatedly that "It's not real . . . It's not real." Knowing darn well that it *was* real, or at least it had been. And the memories were real—memories that didn't need to come up. Memories the shock therapy had kept at bay until the fountain water had set them free again.

John sweated, panting on Vitto's shoulder, so close Vitto could feel his big heart pounding. Vitto rubbed his back, and big John started talking as the Caravaggio replica stared—as if listening too—from across the room.

"The Nazis came out of nowhere, Gandy. We were in the Ardennes Forest. Tired. They broke through our front, surrounded us at Bastogne. We didn't know what was going on. There were Nazi paratroopers falling from the sky, Nazis speaking English, disguising themselves as Americans."

A shadowed silhouette appeared in the doorway, and Valerie called Vitto's name. He raised his hand, held her at bay at the threshold, and encouraged John to continue.

"They were dropping like flies all around me, Gandy. Snow so deep I could hardly lift my legs. They spread rumors to scare us—massacres at Malmedy, Stavelot, soldiers and civilians. Turned out they weren't just rumors, and that was worse. My pals called me yellow every day just to needle me, Gandy, but they were still my pals, you know?" Vitto nodded, knew all too well. "They kept dropping all around me. Beaty got shot in the head, and then a tank ran over him."

He grabbed Vitto by the shoulders, pulled him down so their faces were inches apart. "I wasn't gonna die like the rest of 'em. I wasn't. So I dropped down in the snow, facedown, until I was nearly frozen solid.

"The Nazis were all around. Foreign voices in the air. Boots crunching. I played dead, Gandy. One of 'em nudged me with his boot."

John's breathing had slowed. His arms relaxed. He chuckled, dry-swallowed a memory. "I fooled 'em, Gandy." He wiped his face, smiled. "They moved on. That was brave, wasn't it?"

Vitto nodded. "It was brave, John."

Beverly had joined Valerie at the doorway. Upon sight of her, John sat straighter on the bed. For John's sake and Beverly's ears, Vitto emphasized his next point by prodding a finger into John's thick chest. "You held the lines, John. You did your part to slow them down until Patton arrived."

John nodded as if reassuring himself. He dry-swallowed again and wiped his cheeks as relief washed over him. Vitto stood from where he'd been kneeling on the bed, but John clutched his arm hard before he could step away. "I feel better now, Gandy."

"Good," said Vitto.

John's eyes locked on his. "I mean I feel *better* now. Like a poison's been drained away."

Vitto pulled his arm away at the same time John released him—message given and received. He still wasn't going to drink from that fountain. William stood in front of Valerie, her hands on his shoulders. Vitto hadn't noticed him in the shadows earlier and couldn't bring himself to look at him now. He felt claustrophobic, chest tight, heart racing. He moved past his wife and son and Beverly out onto the gallery overlooking the piazza, where two more elderly couples had joined Mary and Henry and now Robert at the fountain.

"Mommy, look." William pointed over the roof and front portico.

In the distance, headlights from another car bounced over the hotel's bridge, two blurs in a field of darkness, growing large. Up ahead, rounding a curve of cypress trees, another car approached. Vitto hurried down the stairs, light-headed, running on fumes. When had he last eaten? Or slept? He nearly tripped on the tiles as he stepped down to the piazza. The wine he'd consumed caught up to him in a rush. He staggered toward the fountain, where Robert was in the middle of a deep embrace with an elderly man Vitto knew all too well.

Juba's skin was the color of coffee grounds, his halo of hair as white as the fountain's statue, his back still broad and straight. His velvety basso voice had carried easily down to the monastery below, echoing across the piazza every night for decades.

Robert and Juba patted backs and then took each other in, arms' length apart. Was Juba like the other new arrivals, coming to drink from the fountain to restore memories lost? No, he looked too eager, too aware; he was returning to work. An opera-caliber singer and musician, yes, but even better known at the hotel as the pourer of drinks, the tender of bar, the man whose nightly shout of "last call" stopped guests in their tracks.

Valerie had once referred to him as the embodiment of a hug.

"Vitto," he said, stepping away from Robert, arms open for an embrace.

"Juba!" Valerie shouted. Juba turned from Vitto toward the girl who'd come to call him father after her parents left her. Valerie ran across the piazza to steal the hug Vitto wasn't yet ready to give, mostly because he could no longer see straight, but also because he couldn't believe what he was seeing was real.

Despite Juba's age—he had to be at least eighty—he still appeared strong and vibrant. Valerie jumped into the man's arms, and together they spun in a swift circle. He pretended to squeeze the life from her and then placed her down gently on the travertine stones. Vitto noticed she had her violin and bow in hand. *Has she had them with her all the time?*

"Play," Juba told Valerie, eyeing the instrument. "Go on. What are you waiting for?"

Vitto blinked to steady himself, saw a flash of Valerie as a twelve-year-old, playing for him and Juba inside the stone Leopoldino where the olives were pressed—Juba claimed her playing actually increased the oil yield—as dust motes floated through rays of light penetrating the wood-slatted windows.

Vitto blinked again, and the memory was gone. But Juba was home. And Robert didn't look surprised. As if the two old men had been in cahoots.

Mary and Henry danced hand in hand around the fountain like youngsters as Valerie slid bow across strings, the sound resonating through them all, a swollen hum that blanketed the piazza. Vitto took an unsteady step as an elderly man emerged from the shadows of the portico, escorted by someone who could have been his son or grandson. Behind them two elderly women arrived, each with a suitcase that matched their paisley coats. Outside the piazza, at the front of the hotel, two more car doors closed.

Vitto's knees wobbled, his vision blurred. How many more guests would there be?

Valerie stopped playing. "Go on," she said to Juba. "What are *you* waiting for?"

Juba grinned like he'd never thought he'd be asked, although it was clear, with the two suitcases beside him, that he was here to stay and had been brought back for a reason. He cleared his throat. His chest expanded like a windswept sail, and then out came the deep, rumbling voice from the hotel's vibrant past, the one that had echoed every night at midnight from behind the bar, beneath the ticking wall clock Magdalena had taken from the Hospital of the Innocents in Florence decades ago. Everyone on the piazza turned to listen.

"Last call," he said once, pausing briefly as the words reverberated out like a shock wave. He continued: "Last call at the Tuscany Hotel."

And then Vitto blacked out.

Eleven

*D*ecember at the Tuscany Hotel often brought warm sunshine. And now, nearly two weeks after Juba returned to his familiar post behind the piazza's bar, it had ushered in yet more guests. The count had reached ninety-seven, and most of those were out mingling on the cool stones surrounding the fountain that had suddenly given them back their lives.

The past two days, they'd averaged twenty new arrivals, and John, who was adding delicious ideas daily to his menu, had the kitchen running to near capacity. Robert had hired men to clean out the rooms and refurbish them with new bed linens. When Vitto cornered his father on the cost, insisting he know how it was all being paid for, Robert let him in on a secret known only by himself and Juba.

Robert had indeed swept through what he'd inherited from his father's oil fields and quarries, especially in the last few years after Magdalena's death, when the Depression had run its course, the guests had dwindled to a trickle, and his mind had begun to fragment. But apparently Magdalena had possessed a healthy stash that Robert had never touched—money that had made money while Robert spent all of Cotton's, money he'd refused to spend until he could think of a way it could honor her memory, money he'd truthfully forgotten about until the earthquake and the moment of lucidity that led him back to the hotel in a fit of inspiration. This, he told Vitto, was what Magdalena would have wanted. The hotel had closed down after her tragic death, but her death was giving it life again.

Vitto still had questions. "Where did Mamma get the money?"

"She brought it with her from Italy, Vitto. From Pienza."

"And how did she make all this money there as a teen? As an orphan?"

"An orphan who was adopted by a painter who had become quite rich by the time she left."

The time she left—another story altogether that had never fully been explained. Which had brought him back to Juba, another source of mystery.

"Where has Juba been all these years? How did he know to come back?"

"He's been traveling the world, Vitto. And never so far that he couldn't feel the hotel's heart start beating again. Now, enough with the questions. Enjoy the day. Enjoy the excitement."

Excitement, perhaps, but not the kind Vitto used to know. These days the growing crowd made him claustrophobic and confused. Day by day, guest by guest, he witnessed the change in them after drinking from the fountain. With some it was instant. Others took longer, hours in some cases.

And one gentleman, a former cattle rancher named Cane whose son had driven him from Dallas, Texas, had waited half a day for the water to take effect. The son had been hustling him back to the car, crying fraud, when Mr. Cane stopped suddenly in front of the Cupid statue and started crying. Tears streaking his lined face, he confessed that he wanted to go fishing like the two of them used to. He called his son by name—Garrett—when apparently he hadn't done so in over a year. In what must have been a poke at an inside joke, he even snickered and offered to bait the hook. Then, while Garrett stood speechless, he thanked his son for his months of painstaking care, which he vowed would no longer be necessary. He urged his son to go on back to the wife and kids, insisting that he'd found his new home. The two tough men embraced right there in front of the statue.

The son stayed for two more days, just to make sure, and then returned to Texas, promising to write often and bring the family back for a visit. Mr. Cane waved as his son pulled away from the hotel, even stood there watching until the car was a blip bounding over the bridge in the distance. But truth be told, as he would reveal later to Valerie, he couldn't wait to get back into the hotel and the game of bocce he'd promised Ms. Thomerson, the widow he'd met the day before on the arcaded walkway overlooking the ocean, the one with the silver hair and brown eyes and faint birthmark on the left side of her neck that looked like a key. The one whose room had a door the color of the pineapples his own mother used to put on her upside-down cakes.

A lot of the residents were playing bocce these days. Juba had cut a small court into the grass between the two pools on the south side of the hotel. Around the pools, which were in the process of being cleaned, a dozen men and women could be found at any given time—lounging, playing cards, and talking of better days, days they'd never thought to see again.

Vitto's heart should have been warmed by it all, but there was something about all this newfound happiness that cut him like a wound. When he watched Valerie and Juba carry a tray from door to door every morning and pass out little cups of everyone's "medicine," he felt the wound gape. He didn't trust what was happening around him—didn't trust the smiles. And when he tried to smile along with them, especially whenever his wife and kid were brave enough to be around him, it physically pained him to do so. Pained him even to talk, and looking people in the eye became harder by the day. His happiness had been buried beneath too much blood and mud and blown body parts. His happiness had flown the instant he made his first kill and Coopus cheered it.

He couldn't deny, however, that the hotel was full of life again, albeit a different kind of life than that generated by the artists, musicians, and scientists who once graced the piazza. It should have fixed him. Should have made him whole again. Like his father, he had loved the congregating, loved the atmosphere of laughter and gaiety and drinks clinking. The feeling he'd get from it all was something he'd never been able to put a finger on, other than calling it happiness.

But everything felt different now. The more people arrived, the more Vitto wanted to run from them. Which was why each of the past two mornings, after struggling to grasp even an hour of uninterrupted sleep from the nightmares, he'd taken the ax and cutters from the maintenance shed and climbed the terraces to clean out the weeds and brambles and saplings from the olive groves. Hard labor under the sun helped take his mind off of things, and having something to do kept him from drinking wine all day. He did occasionally take a sip from the kitchen sink, which dispensed normal water, but he refused to drink the water from the fountain.

He knew it was winter, with daytime temperatures in the sixties, but the constant sun made it seem almost like summer. His face was sunburned, as was the back of his neck, and it felt good. Every so often, as he worked, he'd glance toward the cliffs overlooking the Pacific. How long would it take to hit the rocks below if he were to jump? How long had it taken the reporter to hit those rocks back in the spring of '21?

"The tragedy at the Tuscany Hotel," the headlines had called it. What was the reporter's name—Melvin something, started with a *T*? No one knew for sure whether he jumped or was pushed—or what Magdalena's role in the tragedy had been, if any. It had only been a rumor that she was out there with him when he went over—a cruel rumor never really put to rest until she, too, went off the cliff almost twenty years later.

From his vantage point on the terraces, Vitto could see the monastery down below. A few of the monks looked like brown inkblots as they tended to their grapevines. Vitto planned on cleaning out the hotel's vineyard next—if he hadn't jumped into the ocean by then. He sat on a patch he'd cleared and wiped sweat from his brow, feeling childish for the nightmare he'd literally buried early in the morning before the sun rose, the mound of dirt visible in the distance from where he now sat. What would Valerie think of him still clinging to that juvenile habit, even now as a grown adult? But it comforted him like a blanket would. Like he was a child sucking his thumb or Johnny Two-Times gnawing on his fingernails.

Vitto was parched, dehydrated, and too thin. Everyone claimed to love John's cooking, and pleasant food smells now constantly wafted from the kitchen—bubbling meats and roasting vegetables and simmering pasta sauce—but to Vitto it smelled like mud. Like bloodstained snow and mud. Once that death smell got into your nose, no amount of sneezing or blowing could get it out. Yesterday morning Valerie had attempted conversation as he'd crossed the piazza toward the maintenance shed for his cutters. *"Bread smells good, doesn't it, Vitto?"* What had he told her? *"Smells like mud, Val."* And then he'd walked on. The wine he'd had for breakfast had made his mouth dry, and the sun, as good as it felt on his shoulders, had given him a headache.

He figured four seconds—five, tops—to hit the rocks below. High tide would take him out into the ocean. Low tide would leave him with the shells and rocks and washed-up litter and dead fish. Main thing keeping him from it was William, not wanting his son to have the same confused feelings he'd had when Magdalena went over. As in, did he have anything to do with why she did it? Was there anything, in hindsight, he could have done to stop it?

John still cried out every night but insisted on drinking his daily dose of fountain water anyway. Claimed he felt better after every episode.

"You should try it, Gandy. It's therapeutic."

"How long you gonna drink that water, John?"

"Until it all comes up. Until it all empties out. We aren't like all these old people, Gandy. I think time can heal what we got. But you got to start letting it out."

Vitto shook his head, smirked. It helped that the woman, Beverly, the one John was sweet on, had started running up to his room every night to comfort him and settle him down after his nightmares. Maybe if Vitto hadn't unknowingly choked his wife, Val would be doing the same for him.

On the opposite side of the hotel, the tennis courts were occupied by four of the guests. From his perch, he couldn't tell if they were men or women, but somehow the thunk of each hit carried. He could see the bocce court better, where Mr. Cane—now called Cowboy Cane by the other guests—played with Ms. Thomerson and another couple. There were five people with mallets on the recently installed croquet court.

Vitto got back to work, hacking at the weeds, pulling and clearing, until he glanced under his arm and spotted his son, William, watching from behind a tree at the bottom of the terraces. Although it was the first time he'd spotted him today, it wasn't the first time he'd caught him spying. All week the boy had been watching from afar—hiding behind a statue, the corner of a wall, the shadow of an arch. One time Vitto had waved and the boy had taken off running.

William now had that grenade attached to a belt loop on his trousers. Maybe Vitto shouldn't have given the boy a grenade. Things might be better now with Val if he'd given the boy a toy of some sort instead of a dud Nazi war weapon. But that grenade clearly meant something to William.

A smile almost bubbled at the boy's clumsy hiding, but Vitto clamped it down and went back to work, cleaving through a thicket of weeds, pretending he didn't see his son watching. Maybe after he finished with the olive grove and the grapevines, he'd get to work clearing out the weeds from around the hotel foundation. Hunched over and dripping sweat, Vitto sneaked another look under his arm. William had climbed the steps of the first terrace and was now hunkered down behind one of the olive trees.

Vitto pulled more weeds. Next thing he knew, William had climbed to the second terrace, and he had something in his hand. Without turning around, Vitto said, "I see you." The boy didn't answer. He didn't run either. Vitto turned, sat on the ground he'd just cleared, and locked eyes with the boy. "Run, and I'll chase you."

He'd meant it to be playful, but the boy now looked scared. Seeing his father choke his mother would be a memory not readily forgotten. Maybe Vitto needed to take William to the field with a shovel and they could bury that memory together.

"You know, I changed your diapers," Vitto said. "Even the nasty ones. I used to rock you to sleep in those first couple of years before I left."

William stared. The boy had big eyes, big olive-green Magdalena eyes, more noticeable now in the sunlight. "You got your grandmother's eyes. You know that?" Vitto patted the earth beside him. "Come up here. I won't hurt you."

William climbed the next set of stairs, paused on the landing, and then climbed up the final one to the top of the grove. He had a cup in his hand. He held it out, persistent. Vitto sighed. "Your mother put you up to this?"

William shook his head no. A toy stethoscope dangled around his neck and shoulders. "You thirsty?" he asked.

"No. But thanks."

William stubbornly held out the cup, and his rigid stance suggested he wasn't going to move until his father took the offering and drank from it. "Doctor says drink."

Vitto said, "Did you drink from that fountain?"

William shook his head. "Mommy won't let me."

"And does she drink from it?"

William shook his head again.

"Why not?"

He shrugged, stepped closer with the cup.

Vitto leaned forward, sniffed it, and cocked an eyebrow. "Smells good." Even though it smelled like nothing. The boy smiled, dimples popped, and before he knew it Vitto had grabbed that cup. "If I drink this, will you help me clear these weeds?"

William nodded, smiled again, watching closely.

Vitto tilted the cup back and took the water in, half a cup's worth. For show, he wiped his mouth on his rolled-up sleeve and smacked his lips. "Best water I've ever had." The boy seemed pleased. Vitto started to pat his son's shoulder, but William stepped back as if afraid he was about to get hit.

Vitto handed William the cutters. "You know how to use these?"

William shook his head but then allowed Vitto to show him. A minute later he was attacking the vines like a seasoned worker. Every so often he stopped to watch his father, as if waiting for that water to kick in like poison would. Or maybe it *was* medicine.

The boy smiled.

Vitto smiled back.

Twelve

*V*itto watched the goings-on in the piazza from the railing outside his second-floor room.

He'd always believed the elderly turned in early. But here they all were, ten minutes before midnight, mingling around the fountain, around the stone fire pits, around where Valerie periodically played her violin with Juba singing beside her.

They'd gained another musician today, an eighty-one-year-old woman named Elenore Eaves. Once a concert pianist, she had struggled with memory loss for four years, according to the daughter who'd brought her, and had not played for longer than that as she increasingly struggled to remember how. She'd taken a dose of medicine soon after lunch, and by dinner the daughter had noticed a difference in her mind, a clarity in her eyes and thoughts. She'd even begun reciting memories thought long forgotten.

Robert had then insisted that Juba roll the hotel piano out onto the piazza next to where Valerie had been playing her violin.

Juba did as requested but was dubious. "It hasn't been maintained in years."

"I had a tuner out last week," Robert admitted with a wink. "The thing sounded awful. And I assumed you'd be here to play it eventually."

Juba smiled as if he couldn't wait to play it again but would gladly now wait his turn.

Mrs. Eaves hesitated but finally sat down and touched the keys. A few tentative notes. A scale. A few familiar lines. Valerie lifted her bow. And soon the two musicians were flowing harmoniously into pieces by Mendelssohn, Schubert, and Brahms, luring Vitto from his cleaning at the olive terraces to follow the sound, the music, the memory of what the hotel used to sound like for large portions of the day, when talented musicians would come to write and practice and perform. Too many concerts had been held on the piazza to count.

Now, as he watched from above, the piano bench stood empty. Mrs. Eaves stood among a cluster of women near the brightly lit bar, drinking wine and no doubt being apprised of what was about to occur on the piazza at midnight. Juba, as was his custom after sundown, wore his tuxedo as he stood behind the bar wiping wineglasses. Robert had found the brightest corner of the piazza, near the bar, and was feverishly chiseling away on his statue. Beside him, a table of old men played cards, laughing and gnawing on cigars, engulfed in a cloud of smoke that even the ocean breeze couldn't penetrate.

Valerie was down there, too, mingling with the crowd. Periodically she'd look his way, the awkwardness between them still lingering like a splinter. He was resisting the urge to write down their argument and bury it in the ground the way he'd done after the handful of times they'd argued in the past—yes, she'd thought that silly, too, but in a cute way. But he honestly wouldn't have known what to write. He couldn't quite pinpoint exactly what this argument was about, or even if this roadblock was an argument at all. It was like a wall had come up between them, and walls weren't easily buried.

At least today she'd spoken to him, even though it was out of frustration—unwarranted frustration, in Vitto's opinion.

Earlier, while taking a break from cleaning the terraces, he'd shown William different ways to properly throw the grenade he'd given him. Ultimately the boy had decided he liked the kneeling position best and had used that position to lob the dud weapon onto the tennis court, where two old guys were hitting a ball around.

"No harm done," Vitto had tried to tell her, even though one of the men had fallen into the net when the metal object bounced onto the court and clanked to a stop around the service line. The two men had then gotten into an argument over whether or not to replay the point and had not even seen William hurry onto the court to retrieve his Nazi plaything.

"It could have given them a heart attack, Vitto," Valerie had argued.

"But it didn't," he'd said, laughing. Then both of them had realized simultaneously that he *was* laughing, which had prompted Valerie to bring up the fact that he'd consumed some of the fountain water earlier in the day. She'd thanked him for at least trying to get better, to which he'd answered, "It was only water, Valerie. I don't feel any different than before." She'd huffed, turned on her heel, leaving him standing alone in the grass.

That was hours ago. Since then he'd shaved and washed up for the first time in days. And now, as he overlooked the buzz of excitement down on the piazza, he could no longer deny the nerves coursing through his bloodstream, the same jittery feeling he'd gotten before the first time he kissed her, before he asked for her hand in marriage. The nervous feeling he'd get *for* her before every one of her hotel performances, when famous actors and directors or well-known musicians would sometimes show.

When Valerie caught him laughing over the grenade incident, she'd assumed it came from drinking the water. But the laughter and warmth had actually started hours before that. As soon as he swallowed the water, he'd felt warmth coating his heart, like melted caramel over an apple, and it had stayed with him the entire time he worked side by side with a son who still didn't believe he was his father. But progress had been made, if not measured. The warmth had followed him from the olive groves the instant he heard Valerie playing alongside Mrs. Eaves in the afternoon. He had come running from the terraces, spying on them from the shadows much like William had been doing earlier, suddenly filled with emotion and anxiety.

"Let it out, Gandy."

John's voice.

But let what out? The tears? They were there, certainly, because ever since he'd swallowed that water he'd been on the verge of breaking down, like what went in as water would come out as salty tears. Was that how it worked? Despite the feel of it, he refused to believe it. That water was a placebo, nothing more.

Then why was he upstairs watching while everyone else was congregating down in the piazza? Because he didn't want them to see him cry. Didn't want them to see him become a bumbling mess.

Even now, as he looked down at his father chipping away at that stone, he wanted to know why, after all these years, the man was still so consumed by his work? On the surface Robert Gandy was the father of all fathers, loving and flamboyant, but Vitto knew the connection between them had always been tentative, teetering on a slippery surface. Robert had never really let him in, never loved him the way he loved Magdalena. The way he loved his work, his sculptures, the art inside his hotel, and the idea of being the Renaissance man, as numerous magazines had called him in the twenties. Vitto had never had that easygoing, conversational connection with him that he'd had, for the most part, with his mother, and even more so with Juba.

It had been the same with Valerie and many of the other kids who stayed for long periods at the hotel. While the parents were working, creating, and mingling, Juba had done the dirty work. The behind-the-scenes bandaging of knees and administration of discipline, the tucking in at bedtime and reading of stories. Juba's had been the shoulder Vitto and Valerie leaned on while Robert chiseled deep into the night.

Vitto watched his father now, hammering and smoothing while life went on around him. "Who are you?" he whispered aloud. "Who am I?"

An artist. That's what I am. Or that's what I used to be.

Vitto's talent had always been undeniable. Born with the unique ability to look at the world and recreate what he saw and remembered—and surrounded by adults who made sure he had the resources he needed—he'd been creating beautiful works of art when most children his age were learning to correctly lace their shoes. The same had been true for Valerie and her violin, her training begun by her parents and teachers and continued by Juba.

Two prodigies, people had called them. Destined for each other, like two pieces of a puzzle finally rejoined. And, especially, just like Robert and Magdalena. People loved to talk about that—how Robert hadn't been so much drawn to Tuscany for the art and sculpture as he had been drawn there for her. But Magdalena was just a memory now. And Vitto had not touched a paintbrush in years.

So who am I now?

Tears streaked cold toward the corners of his lips. Vitto wiped his cheeks. Down below, Juba had just cleared his throat, and the piazza had hushed in anticipation. Even Robert put his hammer down and faced his old friend behind the bar.

"And ticktock goes the clock," Vitto said to himself, sniffling like a baby. He moved on instinct, migrating now toward the action, his shoes clinking step by step down the spiral staircase as the rest of the hotel awaited Juba's next words.

On previous nights Vitto had holed himself up in his room during last call, distancing himself from all the stories and laughter. Tonight he stopped on the travertine, facing the canopied bar and the clock from Florence on the wall that used to be stuck at midnight. Vitto had always assumed that was why they started last call at exactly that hour.

Juba used to glance up at the clock just before the ritual. "Last call," he'd shout in more of a singsong than mere spoken words. Then, after a pause, he would finish: "Last call at the Tuscany Hotel!" Then the people in the piazza would gather round for drinks and stories, just as they were gathered now.

They'd resumed the tradition after Juba's return, and the guests had taken to it like ducks to water. Juba would pronounce last call. And immediately the chatter would begin anew as the guests—older than those during the hotel's heyday, but no less exuberant—moved toward the bar. Juba would already be pouring wine, red and white, into rows of glasses, which they snatched one by one. They would be the last glasses of wine served at the hotel for the night, but the goal was to make them last as long as possible while the stories were spun. And the new guests had plenty of stories to tell. They had lived long lives, many of them fruitful, and now that they could remember, they were eager to share.

The stories usually came out through a social game called truth or lies, which Magdalena had started in the summer of 1903. One full-moon night when she happened to be engaged in the camaraderie and not strolling the grounds alone, she'd clapped her hands to draw everyone together and proposed the game. The idea was for the players to swap brief stories with one another—quick bursts from either memory or imagination—and for the listeners to guess which stories were real and which were made up. Guess wrong, and the listener had to drink. Guess correctly, and the teller had to drink. Players who ran out of wine were out of the game and had to watch from the sidelines, though Juba would often sneak more wine to those watching the final rounds. Eventually the game would dwindle to two. Back when the hotel was booming, the writers and actors had been tough to beat.

Vitto found himself joining the crowd as Juba's familiar greeting rang out. He even picked up a glass of red wine as the stories began flying around him. *Maybe I'll even play.* The thought surprised him, but he found himself warming to the idea. As teenagers, he and Valerie had been allowed to join in the game, and he'd gotten quite good at sifting through the malarkey.

Apparently the old cowboy from Texas had won last night. "Quite the storyteller," Louise Spencer had whispered to her daughter, Beverly, nudging her with an elbow as if smitten. Cowboy Cane now walked high-and-mighty across the travertine, his Stetson tilted against the moon glow. Vitto decided to confront him first.

"Why are you crying?" asked Cane when Vitto stepped up beside him.

"I'm not." Vitto wiped his eyes, found them wet. "It's the wind."

"What wind?" And then Cane got right to it, didn't even shake hands for a proper introduction. "When I was your age, I got hit by a train. A steer got lost and took a nap right on the railroad track. The train was coming. I waved like this." He showed Vitto, somehow without spilling a drop of his red wine. "I eventually got that steer up and moving. Must have been having a good dream. The train started braking, a real loud screech that hurt my ears, and I kept on pushing that steer. But it was groggy and slow, and I wasn't about to let it get hit—mostly because I didn't want to clean up the mess. So I just didn't get out of the way quick enough. It was a glancing blow, but the train knocked me clear off my feet. I landed about twenty yards away in the dust."

Vitto didn't even hesitate. "You're lying."

"You're wrong, pal. Drink up." And then he rolled up his sleeve to show a scar that looked more like an old shark bite than evidence of a train collision. "Almost lost my arm. Couldn't use it for months after. Steer got away without a scratch, though."

Vitto sipped his drink, still not believing it. *Easy to win the game if you cheat.*

Cane started to walk away, but stopped. "You know why I have to win this game?"

"Why?"

"I don't like wine." Cane winked. "Real men drink whiskey." He moved on, started in on the next person with the exact same train story.

John approached next, smiling large. Behind him, Beverly was smiling too. Clearly, she wasn't only hanging around to watch over her grandmother. She and John had been hit by Cupid's arrow, and they couldn't stop glancing at each other. Vitto's first notion was to punch John in the stomach because the obvious exchange of affection was making him nauseated. Instead he just faced John head-on, without a specific story to tell.

John spoke first. "What are you crying for, Gandy?"

"I'm not." He wiped his eyes again. The top of his hand came back wet. "It's the wind."

John looked around as if to find it, but then looked back a little flummoxed.

Okay, so it's the water. It made all the old people able to remember, and it made Vitto an emotional mess. At this point he didn't know what he would prefer, memory of everything or memory of nothing.

They stared at each other for a few beats, like neither one of them had a story to tell, when Vitto knew darn well that they both did. Plenty of stories, probably, and none of them the good kind.

"All right, Gandy, since your tongue seems to be stuck in the mud, here we go. Every night I still cry out because of my war nightmares."

Vitto chuckled because it was so easy. So simple, too, just like John. "Truth, John. Drink up. That was a dumb story."

John laughed, pointed with his glass. "You drink up, Gandy. Because I made it up."

"You didn't make that up. We hear you crying out every night. The entire hotel does."

John lowered his face toward Vitto as if to plant one on him and then lowered his voice. "My nightmares are gone, Gandy. That water brought 'em back up, but then it cleared 'em out."

"What are you talking about?"

"Barrel of sunshine, Gandy. My nightmares are gone." He looked over his shoulder toward Beverly, who now stood listening to a story from an animated Robert, and added, "I'm just *pretending* to have them now."

"Why would you do that?" asked Vitto, and then it dawned on him. Lately, Beverly had been the first one to come running when the screaming started. She'd taken to holding John's hand and rubbing his back and smoothing down his sweaty head of wheat-colored hair.

"So you're a liar?"

"But for a good cause, Gandy. I'll wind it down eventually, but I've never been this close to having a woman interested in me, and I want to make sure things stick, you know?"

"Not really, no."

John wouldn't be derailed. He smiled again and winked. "Drink up, Gandy."

Vitto drank, wiped his mouth, cursed the moisture still puddled in his eyes. He watched John move on to the next victim, hopefully with a better story than what he'd just had to endure. And he reached quickly to wipe his eyes again. If one more person asked him if he was crying, he decided, he'd just chug the rest of his drink and head up early. Shouldn't have come down in the first place. The water was messing with his mind, and not in a good way.

Next he was confronted by a man in his fifties, who said his memories had started going early, right about age forty-nine, and the doctors had been completely confused by his early senility. Said he felt like he'd been dealt a brand-new hand at life now that he was at the hotel. Vitto listened but was also trying to focus on a story to tell. He finally went with a story he'd used often during last call, about the day he and Valerie met when they were kids. Most people thought it sounded too much like a fairy tale and assumed he'd made it up. But this guy immediately said, "You're telling the truth."

He'd guessed right—except it didn't sound like a guess, more like he already knew. Then he confirmed it, pointing across the piazza toward Valerie, who was telling a story to an old woman with poorly dyed black hair and a movie-star dress that didn't quite fit anymore. "That your wife?"

Vitto followed his finger, nodded.

The man patted him on the shoulder. "She told me the same story last night."

Vitto took his mandatory sip, and after five more minutes of bouncing from guest to guest, his glass was empty. Probably for the best; his head hadn't been in the game. Whatever edge he'd once had, he'd apparently lost. He blinked, and a tear dripped down his cheek. As the cluster of active players dwindled, Vitto found himself sitting on the lip of the mosaic fountain, listening to the water trickle. The moon cast a shadow of Robert's fountain statue across the travertine. The god of time stretched across the stones as old people unknowingly stepped on him. In his shadow arms was the goddess of memory. At his feet, the goddess of forgetfulness.

Vitto was thirsty for more wine now that he'd started. But instead of crossing to the bar, he dipped his empty glass into the fountain water and drank it while he watched the game play out. He counted fifteen people left, and Cowboy Cane was still going strong with his train story, probably adding to the lies with every person he told it to. He had Valerie in his grasp now, and she was trying not to laugh— Vitto could tell from how her chin quivered and the left corner of her mouth twitched. She looked good in her purple dress, her feet bare against the stone. She was carefree like that.

Vitto had unknowingly finished off his water and gone into the fountain for a second scoop. Tears flowed now, big wet ones like raindrops, but silent—just enough for him to let it all go but not be noticed. Cold tears, too, unlike any he'd ever experienced. Cold like the memory of ice and snow at Pont-á-Mousson. Cold like frostbitten toes and the pale skin of the frozen dead. He downed the second glass and cried so much his eyes were blurry.

Valerie was out of the game now. She'd fallen for the cowboy's scam and was across the way talking to Elenore Eaves. The game was down to ten now, and John was one of them. So was his woman, Beverly, and they were exchanging glances like a pair of lovestruck teenagers. But Vitto found that he didn't mind the flirting. For some reason he felt unconcerned, even peaceful, like he'd been given some morphine from the war or ether from the military hospital.

John nodded toward him. Vitto finished off a third glass of water and nodded back. And then John did a double take because he must have just noticed the tears dripping down into a puddle between Vitto's Oxfords.

Vitto was feeling it now, the fountain water churning through him like a storm front. He dipped the wineglass into the fountain a fourth time and chugged it so fast that some dripped down his neck and wet his collar. "I've got a story to tell," he said aloud.

They didn't hear him at first. *Did I slur? Is it possible to get drunk off this water?* So he said it again, louder this time, interrupting the game. "Excuse me! I've got a story to tell. Several stories, actually."

John stepped closer, spoke under his breath. "You okay, Gandy?"

"Never been better, John." Vitto wiped his face. Probably should have felt like a fool, but instead he felt oddly right with the world. "There was this time," he said, all eyes on him. "There was this time." *Why am I smiling? Crying and smiling at the same time.* "During the attack on Berg. I was selected to crawl behind enemy lines. There was a Nazi pillbox holding up our platoon's advance. We wiggled like snakes. One minute Private Nelson—we called him Dandelion—he was crawling next to me. One minute he had a face. The next minute he didn't. Happened too fast. I kept going, though. Like a good soldier."

John stepped toward him. "Gandy, let's get you up to bed."

Vitto held him back, shook his head as more tears dripped. "I knocked the pillbox clear out with my bazooka and captured ten Nazis by myself. Marched them like little schoolchildren." He'd migrated away from the fountain, where those left in the game had backed away to give him space. This wasn't how last call was supposed to go, and they all looked confused. "In the town of Roermond," said Vitto, "I accidentally shot a woman."

Robert said, "Vittorio, that's enough."

"Not yet, it isn't. Can't ever be enough. Isn't this why you wanted me to drink the water?" He tilted the empty glass back; finding nothing, he tossed it to the ground, smashing it into dozens of pieces. "She fired from a window of an abandoned house, and I fired back. Innocent civilian from Holland. A Hollander. The Netherlands. Dutch—is that right?"

No one answered. They stared, like they didn't know if they should answer or ignore.

Valerie's soft voice broke the silence. "Vitto, that's enough for tonight."

He shook his head, wiped tears that kept flowing, gesturing to everyone listening. "I don't know if you know this, but I strangled my wife a few weeks ago. Nearly killed her. In my nightmare it was a Nazi."

"Vittorio." It was Robert speaking. He'd never stopped Vitto from acting up before—the discipline had always been Magdalena's or Juba's job—so his use of Vitto's full name as a warning now held little weight.

Juba arrived from behind the bar and gently took Vitto's elbow. Vitto walked with him willingly, but he stepped away again as they passed Robert, buying himself more time because the water wasn't finished. "At Buchenwald . . . I learned what burnt Jews smelled like." He nodded, took in all the horrified stares. Valerie was crying. "You know, a burnt Jew doesn't smell any different than a burnt Gentile. Or a burnt Christian. Or a burnt atheist. Black smoke still comes up from the chimney, and it's all the same. It's this horrible smell that gets in your lungs. Makes you choke. That's what wakes me up every night—the smell of bodies burning."

He walked back toward the fountain, and no one made a move to stop him. On the way he grabbed Cowboy Cane's wineglass, which was still mostly full—the man was on his way to winning truth or lies again with his fabricated train story—and downed the wine. He then dipped the empty glass into the fountain water and drank that, too, his chin wet with water and drips of red, his eyes blurry and tear-filled.

He faced the crowd, spotted his son hiding behind his mother's leg, and plowed on anyway. "We didn't know what we found at first. Like a hidden village in the woods. Tanks drove right over the electric barbed wire so fast the fence shorted out. We expected to see some Germans, but they were gone. We stood watching all that black smoke billow. Biggest chimney I've ever seen. Then all of a sudden these people started coming out. Ragged, real skinny, most of 'em in these prison uniforms that looked like pajamas. Vertical stripes. Dull gray. Dark blue."

Vitto wiped his eyes, set the glass down, and then sat beside it on the edge of the fountain, no longer shouting because he didn't need to. He had everyone's attention. "They crept out from in between the buildings. Out of holes and crevices, showing their hands. Skeletons with skin. Eyes sunken in like walking dead. *'Don't shoot.'* One spoke English, asked if we were American. Yes, we said. Joy touched their faces. We pointed our weapons to the ground, followed them inside the camp."

He stood from the fountain, started pacing. "That's not accurate. The higher-ups went in first while we waited, stood guard. Left to wondering about that smell, that smoke. And then they came out. I'll never forget the look in their eyes. Thought they'd seen every horror a war could stir up, but they hadn't. They told us we were about to see what was called a concentration camp. About to see things we were in no way prepared for. They warned us to look just as long as our stomachs lasted.

"On the main gate, German words were fashioned in iron: *Jedem das Seine*. 'Everyone Gets What He Deserves.'" Vitto grinned, scratched a chin that quivered like his voice. "Nice design—kind of art deco. I heard it was made by somebody famous." Juba's big, muscular hand was on his elbow again, not in an attempt to lure him away anymore, but to comfort.

"Go on." It was John's voice. "Let it out, Gandy."

"Barrel of sunshine," said Vitto.

"Barrel of sunshine," repeated John, with little emotion. Beverly was hugging one of his arms, her head resting against his big shoulder.

"Once inside, we followed our sergeant to the right, and there they were." Vitto locked eyes with his wife. "Cover the boy's ears, Val." She did, but then Mrs. Eaves offered her hand, and William took it. She walked him back toward the kitchen and promised him a piece of chocolate. The gesture made Vitto tear up again.

"Piles of naked bodies stacked like wood." He showed them with his hands. "Bottom layer positioned north-south. Next layer east-west. Alternating up five feet high. Aisles of human bodies down the hill. Any arm that dangled free, Coopus—that was my CO—would tuck back in. Eyes that were open, Coopus would close. Stacks of humans all set to be thrown into the biggest set of ovens anyone could imagine."

He wiped his eyes again, exhaled as the stench of memory enveloped him. "The crematorium had a roar to it. We could feel the heat from out the doors. At least thirty trays fed into that furnace, three bodies to a tray. And they still couldn't keep up. I ran out, got sick in the woods. Same woods where they'd tie prisoners' wrists together behind their backs and then hang them a few inches off the ground until their arms dislocated. Called it the singing forest because of their cries."

Vitto paused, lowered his chin to his chest, stared at the stones. Silence permeated the piazza. "The funny thing is, I wasn't even supposed to be there. My division was a hundred miles away. But there was this photographer woman with a double-barrel name. Margaret Bourke-White. She was famous, worked for *LIFE* magazine, and she'd traveled with my division for a while. I'd kind of been her assistant when she was with us. So when she went over to the Sixth Division and they were closing in on Weimar—that's the town right outside Buchenwald—she asked for me. Said I had the best eye for setting up shots she'd ever seen—apart from her, of course. So they got it approved for me to go over to the other division. Lucky, huh?"

He directed the question to the stone floor, not expecting an answer, and he didn't get one. He made a point of not looking up—didn't want to see the faces of those around him—and he went on with his story.

"Patton assigned us there for four days. He was so mad, he went to Weimar, grabbed the mayor, and told him to have every citizen in town ready by morning. And that next morning he marched them all up to Buchenwald and made them walk through the camp to see what we'd seen. He wouldn't let us start burying those bodies until they saw.

"We found other camps too—subcamps, hundreds of 'em. We got out our K rations, I was about to dig in, but there was a prisoner holding his hands out to me, starving. I opened up my waxed paper, gave him my chocolate bar. He devoured it. So I opened my twist key and was fixing to give him some canned pork and maybe some cheese, but by then he'd gone pale. He died in my arms—so starved that the chocolate bar was too rich for his system."

He paused to let that sink in. "I wasn't the only one to kill a prisoner by giving him food. Even chicken broth was too rich for their stomachs. We were ordered not to give them any food as they sat there and begged us for it." Vitto shook his head, stared blankly. "My toughest kill of the war."

He stood there for a minute, listened to the weeping of those around him. He couldn't produce any more of his own tears; he'd finally been drained dry. He turned toward his father. "When I was little, you used to talk about the hero's journey—a quest for knowledge. Remember? Well, I went to hell and back—there's your Greek tragedy. Consider this our catharsis." Purged of every emotion possible, he stared at the crowd. "Sorry for interrupting the game."

Vitto was a dried-out cornhusk, but somehow better for now. Lighter. Cleansed. He walked over to the spiral staircase and headed up, each step like a hammer blow on the metal. Finally he was in his room—his bed, the covers, the soft pillow. He turned toward the wall, tucked his knees into his chest, and buried his hands between his thighs because he was suddenly freezing. He listened to the sounds from the piazza below. Feet moving. Whispers of "good night" and "see you in the morning." Old-people whispers, which meant half of them were practically yelling.

Doors opened and closed.

Ten minutes later his father was chiseling on his statue. They all had their ways of dealing with things, and Robert's always involved a hammer.

Vitto was on the verge of sleep when the door opened and light footsteps whisked across the floor. The mattress sagged under the weight of a lone knee. One by one his shoes were removed and placed neatly on the floor. Then Valerie nestled up behind him. She pulled his hands out from beneath his thighs and held them, fingers intertwined.

She kissed his neck. "Your father just called you the boatman."

"I bet he did."

"Said you helped that prisoner cross over by holding him in your arms."

"I saw lamp shades made out of human skin, Val." She kissed his shoulder, squeezed his hand. "Photo album covers made of skin too. The first camp commander's wife sought out inmates with tattoos because she wanted their skin. They called her the Witch of Buchenwald."

She shushed him, held him so tight he could feel her heart thumping against his back. They stayed that way until he could no longer take the silence.

"I don't want any more of that water, Val."

"Okay."

"Val?"

"Yes, Vitto."

"Tell me a story."

After a beat she squeezed his hand, exhaled into his neck. If it was possible to feel a smile, he suspected he just did. Her voice was the best medicine. Always had been. "In the summer of 1929," she said, "my parents brought me to this grand place called the Tuscany Hotel . . ."

Thirteen

LATE SUMMER, 1929
THE TUSCANY HOTEL

*V*alerie didn't want to leave her friends in San Francisco. Especially not for, as her father had put it, possibly weeks at a time.

"Months," her mother had enthusiastically corrected, carefully stowing Valerie's violin case in the car with Mother's flute and Dad's cello and the rest of their luggage. Her parents couldn't wait to get to the Tuscany Hotel. They'd been talking about it all year.

But Valerie didn't get it. *Who stays at a hotel for months?* "And what about school—will I be back in time? And my lessons with Signor Vitale . . . ?"

"We'll take care of all that when the time comes. Besides, experiences like these will teach you so much. They're an education in itself."

Valerie had known from experience that she just couldn't win when her parents embarked on some new enthusiasm, so she'd just given in and packed. Mother had pushed her to take just about everything she owned; by the time they left, her room back home looked barely occupied. And now, as their car hurtled south down the coastline, Valerie brooded with her arms folded and jaw clenched, refusing to answer out loud when her parents looked over their shoulders to the backseat to ask her questions.

"Did you pack your toothbrush?"

Head nod.

"Did you bring the bag of games?"

Head nod.

"Your music?"

I don't need it, she wanted to say, but settled for another nod, at which point they left her alone for the next hundred miles—a precursor, in hindsight, for eventually leaving her alone for the rest of her life.

"You'll love it here, Valerie," her father had said. "You can play your violin all day out in the open air. Your mother and I . . . it'll be like a retreat. Rumor is, at the Tuscany, you forget all your worries, so your creativity can thrive."

Her mother smiled over her shoulder. "There will be plenty of other children there. Plenty of artists and musicians like us. And actors—even engineers."

Valerie rolled her eyes and straightened a crease in her red dress, pretending to be unimpressed. But, truthfully, the more they talked about the place and the closer they got to the coast, where the air was salty and fresh and white birds soared, the more her bones hummed with excitement.

Magical was the word that came to mind when she heard the descriptions—like some of the shows she'd seen on the big screen. One of her most memorable, a silent film called *Sunrise*, told the story of a farmer who became bored with his wife and fell under the spell of a city-girl flirt, who talked him into drowning his wife so that they could be together. The wife became suspicious, ran off to the city to hide. And the husband pursued her, only to end up slowly regaining her trust and rekindling their love for one another.

Some might say the content was too old for Valerie. But her parents were different. They had exposed her to a lot in her young life, claiming it was all for the sake of art and culture and you could never get too much of it too early. *"You might as well dive into life sooner than later, Valerie,"* her mother had said, convinced that Janet Gaynor was a lock to win the Academy Award for best actress.

Turns out Valerie's parents were right on all accounts. Janet Gaynor had indeed won best actress back in May. And as soon as her father steered their Model T over that one-lane bridge, drumming his thumbs on the steering wheel and craning his neck to get a good look at the welcoming statue of the two nude women—and getting a playful slap on the arm from Mother—it seemed that Valerie instantly forgot all of her fears and misgivings.

A field near the building was splashed with bursts of red flowers that matched her dress. The land—marked with skinny, cone-shaped green trees and scattered statues—rolled and tilted, curving in and out of sight. To the left and down the hill was a vineyard where green and purple grapes hung, looking like dollops of paint. And on the hillside above the hotel—it was so magnificent from the corner of her eye, she was trying not to look at it yet—was what her mother pointed out as the olive groves. Four steep terraces of olives waiting to be turned into oil or cut up and tossed into pasta.

The hotel itself was like a castle, with crenellations along the top and turrets at all four corners. And the central piazza was full of people—artists drawing and painting, sculptors carving, musicians singing and playing instruments, actors working on lines, writers sitting on benches, eyes fixed on the blue sky as they pondered. Scientists tinkered with their latest experiments. One man sat at a wooden table carving a fancy wooden ship, a glass of red wine to one side and a plate of olive oil and bread to the other. The air smelled of fresh bread and fruit and sizzling meats, the aromas so rich her stomach growled.

In the middle of the piazza, a giant fountain churned water that rippled clear above blue-and-yellow mosaic tiles. And the kids—her parents had not been lying. Dozens of them ran about, seemingly unattended to, which seemed normal to Valerie. Bandaging her own bumps and bruises had been custom for as long as she could remember, since her parents were so often busy or out or home but never quite in.

Valerie stood by the fountain and surveyed the piazza. Rooms surrounded it on three sides, two floors high, with doors of every color imaginable.

Runaway poppies spied through cracks in the stones. A man in the corner, next to the bar, sold meats. Another sold bread. Another, vegetables. The man behind the bar had skin so dark you almost couldn't see him in the shadows, but you could hear him; his heavy bass carried easily over all the other noise. Nearby stood a man in a hat who could have been one of those gangsters she'd read about in the newspapers—the new organized types of crime brought about by Prohibition. He leaned in close to speak with another man who might have been a gangster as well, both with clipped Italian voices and pinstriped suits. They seemed nice enough, though, both of them smiling and sidling up next to two women with bobbed hair and fancy dresses as bright as the hotel doors. Valerie wondered if those men were responsible for the drinks the bartender was openly purveying.

"Isn't alcohol illegal, Mother?"

Instead of answering, her mother pointed out a cluster of actors across the way, chatting and laughing. "There's Buster Keaton, darling. And Douglas Fairbanks Jr. He was just in the movie with—oh my, there she is, Valerie—look. There's Greta Garbo."

Starstruck, Valerie began to think—though she would never admit it—that the months-long stay her parents had described might not be long enough. The hotel was so beautiful and exciting, and there was even a touch of tragedy to add mystery to the place—something about a reporter who had disappeared over the cliffs. That had been a long time ago, when Valerie was just a baby, but her parents had already warned her to stay away from the cliffs.

The hotel owner welcomed them with open arms—muscled arms specked with white dust—and introduced himself as Robert Gandy. Valerie eyed the man curiously. He gripped a hammer in one hand

and a glass of red wine in the other. His skin was tanned to near leather, his wild hair a dirty blond streaked with white, his eyes blue as the California sky. He was tall, taller than any man she'd ever seen, and his persona seemed larger than life as well, larger even than the movie stars and gangsters around him.

He introduced his wife, Magdalena, whose hair was beginning to fade at the temples but still showed evidence of the vivid, bright orange it had once been. Her demeanor immediately relaxed them, her smile a deep breath, her gait showing a grace no Tinseltown set could ever muster. She showed them to their room on the second floor, the only vacant one at the time, which was why her parents had been in such a hurry to get there.

"Stay as long as you like," Magdalena told them in a lilting accent, eyeing Valerie as they approached their room, whose door was painted a rich burnt sienna. "My son is around here somewhere. He's about your age."

"Eight?"

"Then he *is* your age. I'll introduce you—if I can find him. That boy, if he's not painting, likes to hide."

She unlocked the door, pushed it open, and the three of them gasped as they entered. The entire ceiling of the room was covered in fresco paintings, replicas of both the *Creation of Adam* and the *Creation of Eve* from Michelangelo's Sistine Chapel.

"Who painted this?" Father asked as they stood there in awe, necks craned and faces tilted upward.

"My son, Vittorio," Magdalena said proudly. "He just finished it. You're the first to stay in this room since the completion."

"Your son?" asked Valerie's father. "The one who is eight?"

She nodded but offered no more.

An hour later Valerie had claimed a spot on the piazza and was playing with two other violinists, both grown adults who apparently needed to follow sheet music, so she pretended to do likewise just to fit in. She played for an hour on the travertine stone, bathed in sunlight. Never had she felt so loose and free and flowing in her movements—and how beautifully the sound carried!

Magdalena was out and about, buzzing like a bee from one artist to another, every so often pulling out a journal to jot down thoughts. Periodically Valerie spotted a child or two running across the piazza, chasing one another and laughing. Outside the hotel and in the distance, she heard the thwack of a tennis ball being struck and splashing from the two swimming pools her parents had promised she'd be able to use after she'd practiced.

After a dinner of pasta with meatballs and mushrooms, as the sun began to cast shadows across the piazza, many of the kids—two dozen at least—congregated around the fountain. She wondered which one was Vittorio, the child painter. Magdalena came over and encouraged her to join the other kids for a game of hide-and-seek. A black boy named Turner Dixon introduced himself with a handshake and a kind smile. His father was a writer. Another boy named Charlie Deats did the same and told her to just call them Dixon and Deats—everyone did. He was the son of a scientist and an actress—"They're around here somewhere." He also claimed that their games of hide-and-seek at the hotel were legendary.

"And you can hide anywhere on the grounds?" asked Valerie.

Deats nodded. "Well, there's a security guy at the bridge, so no one leaves the grounds."

"And another at the cliffs so no one goes over," Dixon said.

"Otherwise," said Deats, "we're free to go anywhere—which means he could be hiding anywhere on the property."

She rubbed her hands eagerly, glad to get away from her violin and feel the fresh breeze in her hair. "But who are you talking about?"

"Vitto. He's always it."

She looked around the clustered group of kids. "Which one is Vitto?"

Dixon laughed. "He lives here. He's already hiding. We have to find him."

"How long has he been hiding?"

"Apparently since lunch," said Deats. "He does that. And sometimes we don't find him; he just shows back up. But just in case." He grinned, gently tapped her arm. "We'll say you're it as well."

"Me? I don't know my way around yet."

"Then you should be easy to find," said Dixon.

"And what better way to learn the grounds," said Deats.

They closed their eyes, hunkered down, and started counting, as did the rest of the children.

"How long do I have to hide?"

"A minute," said Deats, his voice muffled as he crouched. "Less than that now."

She turned in a circle, took in the surrounding rooms, imagined she was in a grand Roman arena. The group had already counted to thirteen by the time she got moving, walking briskly at first. But with each step taken her anxiety waned, and by the time she reached the arches beneath the portico, she was sprinting, carefree, eager to find the best place to hide on the hotel grounds so that she could prove them wrong.

In between the tall cypress trees, sunflowers dotted the hills. Statues stood like gods frozen in time. To her left, the poppy field called to her, with its thousand blobs of red moving in the breeze. But it wasn't a good hiding spot; the grass was too short. She turned right and headed down toward the vineyards, where the branches twisted arthritically under the weight of so many grapes—plump orbs of green and purple, so purple they shone blue in the dusk. The vines were too narrow and crabby to hide behind, although she did take the time to pluck a grape from a vine on her way back up the hillside. Sweet juice exploded in her mouth as she surveyed the grounds— walkways running here and there, jutting off in angles and tangents, corners concealed by trees, the rough stone of the hotel itself, more statues. She eyed the olive groves at the top of the hill, four tall terraces linked by steps big enough for giants, but the trunks were also too narrow to hide behind, and now she heard the other kids scattering and laughing. They were on their way, and here she stood, still in view of the hotel wall.

Voices chanted in the distance, somewhere behind the olive groves. She followed the sound, not to find where it came from but to get herself out of the trance she'd found herself in—the place *was* magical, just as her parents had said. And then she nearly ran into the two structures in between the olive groves and vineyards. She'd noticed them when she arrived, but only now did she really *see* them. Built of stone the same color as the hotel, the two buildings—more like little houses—faced each other with a narrow sidewalk running between them. Each was two levels tall, not counting the square appendages atop each one that seemed to house pigeons. Two symmetrically placed windows on each wall opened like eyes into the dim interiors. The front doors of both were open and gave the impression of never being closed.

She stepped into the stone house farthest from the hotel. Her footsteps clacked off the wood floor. Wooden racks holding thousands of grape clusters, bundles of purple and blue and green and red, soared up toward the ceiling, where dust motes floated and the aroma of fermentation pinched at her nose. Large vats lined the wall, and some kind of a machine loomed on a counter. A few grapes lay smashed into the floorboards, but she saw no other sign of human presence. Even the workers must take time to socialize at the hotel.

Sunlight glistened through the doorway. Valerie grabbed a cluster of purple grapes and stepped back outside, paused when she heard approaching voices, and ducked into the neighboring building, where the air smelled pungently of olives. Dark bottles and big glass jars lined up on shelves nearby, along with a collection of bins and barrels.

An unfamiliar contraption occupied the center of the room; she guessed it had something to do with olives. As she rounded one of them, she bumped into a ladder, looked upward toward a loft, and decided it was the place to go.

She clamped the stem from the grapes in her mouth and climbed the tall ladder slowly, feeling it might tilt with her if she leaned back too far. Tension broke out as sweat across her brow. Her heart raced, more so with every rung, until finally she reached the floor of the loft and clambered over the edge. It was warmer up here by the rafters, which were supported by thick, wooden beams. The loft's floorboards were littered with pigeon droppings and hard, shriveled olives someone must have thrown up there for fun.

"You can't hide here."

Startled, Valerie looked up toward the voice. In the corner shadows hunkered a boy about her age. She flinched and accidentally knocked the ladder with her foot. Before she could grab it, it teetered and then fell in the opposite direction. They both cringed, fearing the crash would give their hiding spot away, but the ladder snagged in a thicket of netting someone had piled up and gave no more sound than a hand puffing a pillow. Dust scattered but had settled by the time Dixon and Deats—those two seemed to be connected at the hip—entered the stone house for a quick look around. The boy in the loft clamped his hand around Valerie's mouth to keep her quiet. His fingers smelled like a mixture of olives, garlic, and paint.

As soon as Dixon and Deats left, Valerie lightly bit the boy's finger, and he yanked it away, shaking it.

"What'd you do that for?"

"I was hungry."

He pointed toward the cluster of grapes resting near the edge of the loft, a few of them dangling over. "If you're hungry, then grab the grapes you stole. Lucky those two didn't notice."

She retrieved the grapes and popped one in her mouth.

He leaned over the edge, which was a good fifteen to twenty feet down. "How are we gonna get down now?"

"We could call for help."

"And then we'd lose." He watched her, his brown eyes suspicious. "Why are you hiding, anyway?"

"Because they said I was it."

He pointed to his chest. "I'm it."

"Well, I guess we're both it, and now we're both stuck. Do you want a grape?" He plucked one from the stem but didn't say thanks. "How long have you been up here, anyway?" she asked.

"Since lunch."

She scoffed, looked away, spied out the window as another kid darted past and disappeared. Atop the roof, on the opposite side of the ceiling, pigeons roosted, tiptoed, and cooed. She glanced up nervously.

He said, "They won't poop on you under here." She pointed to the hardened spots on the floor, and he explained, "From the other birds. Sometimes they find their way in and can't find their way out. Juba catches them with towels and sets them free."

"Who's Juba?"

He didn't answer. He was too busy spying out of the circular dormer window behind him. "I think we're in the clear." Finally, his eyes settled on her and then stalled, as if he was fond of what he'd just found. If not for the loft's shadows, she could have sworn he was blushing.

"Why are you laughing?"

"I'm not laughing."

"You're grinning, then."

"Little odd, is all. Hiding hours before the game even starts."

He looked away, bashful for the first time since her arrival. "I suppose this loft is big enough for two."

"If not, were you thinking of tossing me to the floor?"

He scooted closer, held out a jar of giant green olives pickled in brine. "Tell me your name, and I'll give you one."

"Valerie's my name."

He did as he'd promised, and she took an olive, savoring its salty fruitiness. For a few seconds the silence was awkward, and then she held her grapes out toward him.

He took one. "Aren't you going to ask my name?"

"No."

He paused midchew. "Why not?"

"I already know who you are. You're the boy they call Vittorio. Your mother and father own the hotel. Magdalena and Robert Gandy. That makes you Vittorio Gandy." She pointed to the spots of paint on his fingers and wrists. "And I've seen that you're quite the painter."

He covered them as if ashamed. "My friends call me Vitto."

"Is that what I am? A friend?"

"Right now you're the girl who stole my hiding spot."

She huffed and folded her arms for effect, but truthfully she enjoyed the give-and-take more than even playing the violin. Until now she hadn't had much use for boys, but Vittorio Gandy was different. He seemed wise beyond his years, and judging by the work she'd seen on the ceiling of their hotel room, he had a talent with a brush that even the most gifted of adult painters would covet.

She didn't really know him, but she understood him immediately.

He asked her what her parents did and said it like he knew they did *something* with the arts. So when she told him her father played the cello and her mother played the flute and both of them were also composers, he nodded. "They'll fit in really good then."

"Well."

"Well, what?"

"They'll fit in really well."

He didn't answer, just shrugged. After another awkward silence, he checked out the dormer again. Night was almost upon them, and the temperature was dropping. She said, "And what do your parents do?"

He looked at her as if she should already know but said, "My father is a sculptor." *That explains the dust and the hammer.* "He built this place. He considers himself a Renaissance man. Not only *a* Renaissance man but *the* Renaissance man. Oh, and I think deep down he believes he's a god."

Valerie laughed, but then covered her mouth. "And what if he is?"

"He isn't. Although he carves statues like one."

"You sound like you disapprove of him."

"Of my father?"

"Isn't that who we're talking about?"

"He doesn't like me."

"I doubt that."

"How would you know?"

"Because it's obvious you idolize him. And who wouldn't like that?"

"He's jealous of my talents."

"I doubt that too. He's your father. And you're still a . . ."

"A what?"

"A boy."

He grumbled. "Maybe not so much my talent, but the attention it steals from him. Once I even did subpar work on purpose, but he saw right through it and accused me of being arrogant."

"If not arrogant, then silly."

"Whose side are you on, anyway?"

"Since we're both stuck up here, I suppose I'm on yours."

Vitto folded his arms. "That's good to know, I guess." But he didn't look convinced.

"So what about your mother?" Valerie asked. "What does she do?"

He bit his lip, pondering, and then smiled. "She makes people do this."

"Get stuck in lofts?"

"No. Smile. She makes people smile."

Valerie laughed. "And that's her talent?"

He sat rigid, as if offended. "What better talent is there?"

Cold now, she folded her arms and noticed the breath crystallizing before her when she breathed. "Should we call for help?"

"And lose the game? Trust me, they're still out there looking."

"And our parents?"

"They won't even know we're gone. That's just what it's like out here. The place does something to people." He was leaning with his back against the wall, the top of his hair skimming a wooden beam. He patted the floorboards beside him. "I won't bite." He laughed. "Unlike you."

She recalled biting his finger earlier and apologized as she scooted next to him. She pressed down her dress so her knees weren't showing. His legs were longer than hers, his shoes muddy and worn. His clothes smelled of paint and turpentine, of olives and oil. They sat silent for a minute as the ocean breeze hugged the stones and moved the rickety branches in the vineyard outside. Laughter carried from the belly of the hotel.

He said, "I don't usually like girls."

She nearly choked on the olive she'd just tossed in her mouth. But the bluntness of his statement somehow opened them up, and within minutes they were talking like old friends, like she was a repeat guest come home to roost instead of a new arrival. They spoke of his painting and her violin playing, of her life in San Francisco and his at the hotel. She told him how left out she felt at times, with her parents so focused on their careers—or lack thereof—and how she was practically raising herself. He answered that, by the looks of it, she'd done a swell job so far, and she smiled.

And then he told her that he'd been an accident, which made her laugh. Said his parents had tried for years—no, decades even—to have a child, with no luck, until suddenly—here he opened his arms theatrically—"Here comes Vittorio Gandy." Her laughter seemed to fuel him, because he continued on, and she was glad for it, because she liked to listen to him talk and it felt good to laugh. He explained how, in autumn, the olives would be harvested and pressed or brined—"We do it all right here"—how the wine was made—"That happens next door, in the other house"—how the hotel had been decorated by visiting guests for nearly three decades.

They paused in their conversation to listen to the singing from afar—he said it was the monks chanting their nightly prayers—then continued on about the hotel food, the Tuscan recipes and flavors, and the many hotel customs. And then, come midnight, Juba made his call. She nearly hit her head on the beam when his voice first reverberated. She'd been on the verge of falling asleep on Vittorio's shoulder.

"He does it every night," he said. "At midnight. Last call at the bar."

He told her about the nightly game at last call, truth or lies, and after he explained how it was played, she rested her head back on his shoulder and said, "Tell me one."

"One what?"

"A story. Tell me a story. We'll pretend we're playing too."

"Okay." He sounded hesitant, as if thrown off guard. She could somehow feel his nervous heartbeat humming through his shoulder, his voice an echo in her ear. He said, "There once was a woman named Psyche. She was a mortal princess."

"Psyche? What kind of a name is that?"

"The name she was given," he said. "Now, let me finish. She was the youngest of three daughters. And she was the most beautiful woman ever. But the goddess Aphrodite—the Romans called her Venus—she became jealous. So she urged her son Cupid to use one of his arrows to make Psyche fall in love with the ugliest creature on earth. But when Cupid witnessed Psyche's beauty firsthand, he accidentally shot himself with his own arrow and fell in love with her instead."

"Not true," said Valerie, half-asleep.

"How do you know?"

"Because those people aren't real. Does that mean I win the game? Vittorio?"

He didn't answer. But then he rested his head on hers and said, "My friends call me Vitto."

"Mine call me Val."

And soon they both fell asleep.

Fourteen

*V*itto's eyes had grown heavy during Valerie's story, recalling her arrival much as she told it.

"True," he whispered. It was deep into the night by now, and his father was still out on the piazza chiseling stone.

"Of course it's true," Valerie said into the back of his neck, both of them remembering that night they'd spent in the loft overlooking the olive press.

"But you never let me finish my story that night."

"No, I didn't."

"There were trials and tribulations," he said. "Breaks in trust."

"I know the story of Psyche and Cupid now, Vitto. I've seen the statue."

He continued anyway. "Venus puts a spell on her, a long-lasting sleep that takes a kiss from Cupid to finally awaken her." Valerie's heart raced against his back. "My mother once caught me staring at that statue outside the hotel," he said. "It was the morning you first arrived here. She told me that story. So I told it to you."

"And I said not true."

"Because those people weren't real." He tilted his head back toward her. "What would you say now? Truth or lies?"

"I'll tell you if you tell me how you really got down from the loft the next morning. It wasn't Juba who helped you reposition the ladder, was it? Because I never saw or heard him."

"No. I climbed down on my own and then reset the ladder for you."

"You climbed down on your own?"

"I'd never used the ladder to get up in the first place. The stone wall has niches and grooves, perfect for climbing." He smiled, and the emotion cracked through the rest of the rust that the fountain water hadn't gotten to earlier. "I'd been up and down that wall to that loft so many times I could have scaled it blindfolded."

The bed creaked. She'd slapped his arm, leaned up on an elbow to see if he was kidding her. She playfully slapped him again. Rolled him on his back and straddled his waist.

"You didn't answer my question," he said, looking up at her.

"What question?"

"Would you call that story I first told you a truth or lie?"

Her answer was a kiss on the lips, the one she'd promised him from the train station the day he was carted off to war, and for the first time in months he felt human again. She stared down at him intently, as if trying to wish back time, but the best she could do was act in the now. "I missed you." She didn't give him time to respond. She just kissed him again, passionately, and when he said, "Are you sure?" she said, "Of course I'm sure." But she stopped abruptly a few seconds later, giggling.

"What?"

She grinned and pulled him from the bed. Told him to come on and follow her and he did, out onto the landing and around to the opposite spiral staircase so that Robert wouldn't see them come down. She squeezed his hand like she'd never let go again. They tiptoed down the stairs like two sneaky children and spied on Robert across the piazza, who never looked up from his work as they slipped into the shadows of the main portico, still holding hands, and exited the hotel.

"Where's William?" he whispered.

"Asleep," she answered. "Remember, kids police themselves at the Tuscany."

"But . . ."

"I asked Beverly to listen for him. Now, quiet."

She didn't tell him where they were going, but he had an idea, and as they approached the stone house where the olives had once been pressed into the finest oils in the region, his heart was ready to jump from his chest. Inside, he expected mold and mildew, cobwebs and stale air, but instead found the wood floors newly cleaned and glimmering in the moonlight that shone through the windows. The smell of fresh cedar oil permeated the air, along with ghost remnants of freshly pressed olive oil and baked bread.

He asked who had done this. She said the house had been the first thing she cleaned upon their arrival.

He took her in his arms, and she gently backed him against the window, their shadows dancing across the floorboards. His shirt untucked. Dark strands of her hair came loose from her pinned-up curls and hung across her eyes. He brushed them away, kissed her forehead, kissed her nose, kissed her mouth, only to be halted again as she led him toward the ladder, which she'd apparently angled perfectly against the loft floor. He asked if the ladder was still sturdy, and she said yes. He asked if she'd cleaned up there, too, and she said yes and then told him to stop talking. He did that when he was nervous.

She went up first, and he couldn't help watching as she navigated each rung. Once atop, she helped him up, and they rolled as one away from the drop-off, eyes locked and breathing heavily.

"That day we met," he said, voice quivering like the youth he now felt like, "I accused you of stealing our grapes. That wasn't the only thing you stole that day, Valerie."

Her weight settled on him, her breath on his neck. "Vitto, shut up."

And so he did.

Fifteen

SEPTEMBER 1883
PIENZA, ITALY, SOUTHERN TUSCANY

*M*agdalena didn't remember why, but out of habit or even instinct she waited for the clopping of the horse hooves to fade across the cobbles outside before getting out of bed.

The sound that meant he was gone.

And *he*, she would remind herself upon opening the leather-bound journal on the bedside table, was Francesco Lippi, the famous painter who, seven years prior, had adopted her from the Hospital of Innocents in the weeks before it closed. All this was written on the first page of the journal, right under the sketch he'd done of himself. The portrait showed a handsome man with a thin nose and a kind smile hinting at an easy disposition. Something in Magdalena knew the truth was different, although she couldn't remember exactly *why* she knew it.

Beside the journal lay a note he'd left with her instructions for the day; without it, she wouldn't remember what to do or even where she was. She'd gotten to the point where, with practice and notes and habit, she could remember enough to get through the day, but then it was as if her memory reset every night. Every morning was a blank canvas. But she'd looked at the journal and the instructions often enough now over the years that it had become a habit, as regular as combing her hair at night and brushing her teeth in the morning.

And flinching every time he came near. She shook that residue of memory away and focused again on the note. She was to clean the kitchen, sweep all the floors, and launder the clothes. He was off to Florence to sell his two latest paintings and would expect dinner by the time he arrived home. He wanted chicken with mushrooms and pecorino, a bowl of olives, and a bottle of their finest wine. He was expecting his paintings to sell for quite a sum and thought they should celebrate. And then they had work to do in the evening— another masterpiece to create.

As usual, at the end of the note, he reminded her of the dangers that lurked outside and that only fools give in to the temptation to venture out. He'd hammered it into her head daily that they had moved from Florence for that reason. But Magdalena knew somehow that this was a lie as well, that there were other reasons. If only she could remember them.

You're mine now. Another bit of memory residue she shook away. She dropped the note on the journal and stepped away from the bed, toward the middle of the room, where her reflection watched from the large mirror above the dresser. Hair like a Botticelli angel, fire-orange and cascading now to her lower back. She winced upon the next step as pain shot across her hips, sore as if they'd been beaten. She removed her nightgown and washed her face with water from the basin. She cleaned under her arms and noticed fresh bruises on her wrists, bruises from what looked to be strong hands. She stepped closer to the mirror and noticed another bruise fading along her right collarbone.

She swallowed over the lump in her throat and fought back the tears of frustration that struck her every morning. *Why can't I remember like everyone else? There must be some purpose. What is my purpose?* she silently asked the mirror, but to no avail. So she dressed in a plain blue dress and combed out her hair until curls bounced.

The chores could wait. In the main room, sunlight bled through curtains Lippi insisted they keep closed. But the Pienza street noise beckoned. She peeked through the divide and saw vendors and carriages and merchants, heard hammering and music and singing and laughter. Her heart raced in anticipation, but of what? Had she been out there before? Had she dared go against his word and venture out?

She smoothed her hands down the sides of her dress and felt something in the pocket on the right side. A note. She pulled it out and read, "Look under your bed, Magdalena." She smiled, folded the note, and did as it said. This all seemed familiar to her now. Back in her bedroom, she dropped to her knees with a grunt and felt beneath the framing. Out she pulled another journal, the worn journal Lippi knew nothing about, the journal where she kept the truths and not the lies. She sat on the floor and opened it to years of notes, years of pages, years of words that took the place of her memories.

Ever since her adoption, she'd made it a habit to write in it every night before falling asleep, quickly jotting down what she remembered during each day. Writing only what was necessary and penciling it smaller and smaller because the pages were nearly running out. Perhaps God had been cruel to grant her a life without memory, but at least he had granted her the ability to read and write, two talents she'd mastered much earlier than the other orphans. By following her own words, she could fight her helplessness.

Now, reading from the beginning, Magdalena was reminded that they had moved to Pienza because Lippi had wanted to get away from the swarms of artists wanting to carve and paint her or simply to have her by their side as they worked. And he'd been especially eager to get away from the "pestering" Nurse Pratesi, who for months after the adoption had visited his humble stone house overlooking the Arno River daily to make sure Magdalena was being cared for properly.

"Like a gnat," Lippi had said of her old caretaker, the only woman she'd ever called Mamma. The nurse who'd wept the day Magdalena was taken away, literally pulled from her arms while Nurse Cioni watched down her angled nose, arms folded, with a smirk on her face, secretly pleased that the orphan who couldn't remember was finally being adopted and the lines of artists appearing daily to see her would soon end.

Nurse Pratesi had then walked across the stones and slapped the smirk from Nurse Cioni's face. The first must not have satisfied, so she'd slapped her again and again in quick succession, flat blows that had echoed across the loggia and somehow etched themselves into Magdalena's memory that wasn't. She had recorded all this in the journal Lippi knew nothing about, adding that the older nurse had terminated Mamma Pratesi's employment right then and there.

The journal didn't say what had happened to the nurse, but it did remind Magdalena that Lippi had frightened her from day one. Sometimes his breath smelled of garlic and his clothes of sweat and his pores of stale wine. He yelled when he was drunk, and he drank every night—drank until he passed out. He broke wind more than he laughed, and when he laughed his teeth showed yellow. And there were other things, too, things that made sense of the bruises and the suffocating feelings that descended on her when he walked in the door. On more than one occasion she'd contemplated cutting his throat with the knife they used to cut apples or pouring the smelly liquid he used to clean his brushes into the wine until his eyes bulged and he choked on it.

"I'll never call him father. No matter how many times he begs me, I will never call him father." She'd written that more times than she could count, hard enough to indent the pages.

She flipped through more pages, catching herself up on her own history, wondering how much of it would stick past noon. When she'd gotten her first monthly blood at twelve, he'd told her it was a sign, a warning of what would happen daily if she ventured out while he was gone. She'd bleed until there was no more coursing through her veins. "Not true," she'd scribbled in the margin. "More lies, Magdalena."

She turned more pages, familiarizing herself with herself. One page held an account of a time in front of the Duomo in Florence, when she'd accompanied Lippi to the great cathedral on business. She'd wandered into the crowd while he was engaged in conversation, bumping into men and women gazing up toward Brunelleschi's famous dome and wondering over the millions of bricks used to construct it. She somehow remembered seeing the plans before the work on it began in 1420. She'd never been inside the cathedral, yet she remembered the frescoed interior of the dome as if she'd painted it herself.

She'd bumped through the crowd, having lost track of Lippi, and upon tilting her head up to take in the scaffolding masking the new façade that soared white, ornate, and heavenly toward the blue sky, her hood had fallen from her head and her orange hair had unfurled for all those to see. Then, suddenly, arms were reaching toward her hair. Voices murmured. An artist, as if on instinct, turned her way, lured along by the rest of the bodies as they pressed close, too close, until it became hard to breathe.

Then, somehow, she was able to breathe again. That was the first time she'd seen the black boy, roughly her age, with skin dark as night, leaning against the green-and-white marble of the neighboring baptistery, singing. His voice was angelic, "from the heavens," she would write that night in her journal. And the sound of his prepubescent soprano had lured enough of the crowd away from her to allow Lippi in to grab her, "roughly about the elbow," she'd write, and pull her away. Never again would he take her to Florence.

You're mine now, Magdalena.

She turned more pages, faster, fingers racing nearly as rapidly as her heart toward the end of the journal. "He's a brute. He's a beast. His hair is greasy and his nose upturned. My back hurts from the standing while he sits and paints and looks upon me. And then he does those things to me, knowing that I won't remember come morning." She didn't know why she had refrained from writing down exactly what

Lippi did to her, but part of her was glad. Perhaps some experiences in life were better not remembered. Perhaps it could be a blessing to forget, especially when she had no means of changing her fate.

But now she flipped to the end of the journal, where the final pages—soon she would have to write in the margins—brought about a smile even though she'd yet to read what was written. She moved from the bedroom for the second time that morning and slipped on her brown shoes, the soles—unnoticed by Lippi thus far—more worn by the day. She ignored the threatening note Lippi had left on the front door, warning her about the streets. She wrapped the light cloak around her shoulders, hid her bundled hair beneath the hood, and stepped out into the warm September air of the hilly Val d'Orcia. Into the air and sunlight that apparently, according to her notes, she had braved for fifteen days in a row now.

For a boy.

"A boy already built like a man," her journal had told her, "with unruly blond hair that brushes his shoulders as he chisels away at his stones. He wields the hammer like a god, like a Titan."

Her palms began sweating as she walked down the cobbled alley, the confusing soreness from the morning waning with every step toward the town square, which still looked as it had during the Renaissance, harmoniously laid out and strategically placed overlooking undulating hills.

A small town in the province of Siena, between Montepulciano and Montalcino, Pienza had been birthed from a dream, the ancient village of Corsignano transformed into a new utopian city combining the principles of classical times with those of the Italian Renaissance. Her journal had told her this too. It was the creation of one Enea Silvio Piccolomini, a wealthy humanist who would later become Pope Pius II and spend his summers as pontiff in the Palazzo Piccolomini with his Flemish tapestries and rooftop gardens. Magdalena imagined his court of cardinals meeting like flocks of red birds and getting fat off breads and wines and cheese, so plump they would have to walk instead of fly.

Wind swept over the hill and down the valley. As she navigated the perfectly proportioned streets, narrowed by tall walls of brick and bright travertine stone, Magdalena held her hood with one hand while gripping the open journal with the other, following a crude map she'd drawn at some point in the past few days to get her to the right destination. Chatter picked up as she neared the central Piazza Pio II, stepping in and out of sunlight and shadow, triangles of bright and shade, warm and cool against her face.

The piazza teemed with excitement, some kind of festival not mentioned in her journal. Shops and vendors hawked wine and home-made pasta, spices and perfumes, wheels of pecorino cheese. Kids played games, darting through the crowd, behind the town hall and around the well she had labeled in her notes as the well of the dogs. A circle of men took turns rolling the rounds of cheese around a wooden spindle, and Magdalena couldn't help but laugh at the spectacle. She kept her chin pointed down, the hood around her ears, but spied from the top of her eyes.

A black boy stood across the piazza, chatting in a cluster of men and women, and periodically he'd glance at her. She looked to her notes, going back through the days, and noticed that she'd recorded the same experience each day she had come out. His skin was shiny black, his smile kind. More of a well-muscled man than a boy.

"Could he be the same one who saved me from the Florence crowd outside the Duomo with his singing years ago?" She'd written that question on each of the last seven days. "Does he watch me, or is he watching over me? And who is he?"

And then, as if on cue, he started singing. According to her notes he'd done the same on several of the days. If this was the same boy, his voice had changed. It was now deep, cavernous, echoing across the piazza. Her heart grew warm at the sound of it.

She listened until he finished, and after the applause faded, she stepped deeper into the piazza. The front of the Pienza cathedral stretched upward like a mountain on the other side of it.

Sometimes Lippi would usher her inside the cathedral to pray for his continued success—*their* continued success, for she was at least aware enough to know she was an integral part. "He is nothing without me," she'd written in the journal he didn't know about. And sometimes, instead of praying for their continued success, she'd startled herself by praying for his death—a violent death. Other times she'd simply pray to God for her memory to be restored. With memory she could escape. With memory she would be normal. So she'd secretly petition God to be rescued from this place—this beautiful place where she lived with a horrible man.

She heard the hammering before she saw him. Then there he was, outside the Palazzo Piccolomini's loggia, standing in the shadow of a block of white marble carted down from the quarried hills, the stone looming two feet taller than his six-foot-plus frame. Her heart jumped into her throat, so she swallowed to get it back down.

A crowd of at least two dozen had gathered around him, watching him chisel into the stone. She flipped through her notes. In the past days she'd written down things the crowds had whispered about him.

"A talent to rival the greats. The equal to Michelangelo and Bernini and Donatello. A man born centuries too late.

"He astonished crowds in Florence before coming to Pienza. Lured to Pienza, they say, for a mysterious girl.

"He's creating his own David.

"He's come from the United States. On a steamship to Sicily. On a boat to Naples and up the coast to Pisa. Then Florence. Then Pienza."

She stepped closer. He looked up as if he'd sensed her. Their eyes locked.

He stepped away from his statue, recognizing her, just as the notes said he would. But she was seeing him for the first time. Again.

"Your confusion—he finds this adorable," her book had said. "He calls you his muse. He claims he's crossed oceans to find you. He claims to have dreamt of you. Every artist needs his muse."

She moved slowly, reading and learning as she walked, so she wouldn't make a complete fool of herself. He told the crowd around him to stay put, that he had quick business to attend to. They listened, none of them moving—as if afraid to lose their spot—as he stepped around the palazzo and ushered Magdalena into the shadows where they could talk undisturbed.

Except he didn't talk at first. His intimate embrace took her by surprise. His arms powerful, the hairs coated with dust. He kissed her on the lips and she melted, just as her notes said she would. She closed her eyes and imagined escaping with him to another place. He looked down upon her and smiled. "Magdalena."

She'd practiced this on her way through town. Memorizing his name. "Robert."

He hugged her, let go, stared into her eyes—his blue and hypnotic, hers swimming. "Magdalena, why is it that every time I kiss you it's as if it's our first?"

She smiled.

Her notes said he'd ask that too.

Sixteen

1946

The *Gandy Gazette* called it the Memory Hotel.

Newspaper and magazine articles were now being written about the "fountain of youth" in the middle of the piazza. Reporters from across the country, one from as far as Maine, came daily to witness the goings-on inside the Tuscany Hotel, which was as full as it had ever been in its heyday, only now with the elderly instead of the artistic. Not all were elderly, though. They had learned with the arrival of a dozen men and women over the winter months that senility—or Alzheimer's disease, or whatever it was—sometimes struck those in their fifties. One guest was as young as forty-nine. Even for them, the water from the fountain seemed to bring them back to themselves.

The medicine also seemed to help those suffering from war trauma. Nine war veterans, some from each of the world wars, now had rooms inside the hotel. After a few weeks of drinking their daily doses of medicine, they'd shown the same elements of catharsis that John and Vitto had experienced—what John called bloodletting, letting free the humors, bringing out the war memories so that they could be talked about.

From the hundreds of recently arrived elderly guests, two of the men had been psychologists before dementia had derailed their careers, and they were both more than willing to meet daily with the war vets. John, despite being previously cleansed—*it's an ongoing process, Gandy*—joined their daily sessions near the cliffs overlooking the ocean when he wasn't cooking. Sometimes he still left with tears in his eyes. But at least he now had help in the kitchen. So many of the women—and a handful of the men—couldn't wait to cook again, so John had to organize them in shifts.

One day Valerie caught Vitto watching a meeting of the war vets from afar.

She'd sneaked up on him, slithering her arm through his. He could tell she was trying to rekindle the magic they'd shared inside the olive press house weeks before—the laughter and stories they'd shared, her sense that her Vitto was back, finally back. But he was all too aware that his breakthrough that night and the handful of positive days that followed had been fool's gold. The fountain water had churned up dirt that wasn't ready to be flipped. He wasn't really back. Maybe he never would be.

She sensed the slipping—the two steps backward, as she'd called it one afternoon—and was now trying desperately to keep him from reverting to what he now considered his new normal since the war. And that's what they were like now—him distant, her trying to bridge the gap, trying to *be* the bridge for both of them because he was still not emotionally ready to hold his end.

"You should join them, Vitto."

"I told you. I'll never drink from that fountain again."

"Then don't. But drink something. Do something."

She squeezed his arm and walked away, but not before getting in her last two cents, which was not her custom—not something someone trying to save a relationship would do unless she, too, was close to giving up. "You're becoming too much like your mother near the end, Vitto."

Perhaps those words had been meant to soften him, to leak into the cracks of his broken façade, but they only proved to do the opposite. Valerie had always loved Magdalena, but unlike Vitto she had no soft spot for his mother's frailties. To her, Magdalena was not a perfect being. She was a woman who was beautiful in almost every way, who had encouraged Valerie's friendship with her son, only to later resent her for stealing his heart and taking his attention away from her. *There's a dark spot on her heart, Vitto.* Valerie had said this to him when they were teens, and it had led to their first argument, because to him his mother was nothing but good, nothing but kind. That argument had lasted ten minutes, the cold shoulder only a day; after all, he'd written down their disagreement and buried it in the ground within minutes after she stormed from the room, calling him blind when it came to his mother.

Now she was saying he was too much like Magdalena. And maybe that was true, but it didn't really change anything. It didn't make him any more inclined to join the other war vets. He'd let enough out on that night during last call. And it certainly didn't convince him to drink the water. In fact, as he and Valerie and, by proxy, William all seemed to grow more apart by the day, he watched the fountain with greater disdain.

He felt it each time a new arrival walked through the arches and into the piazza, bags in hand, surveying the stone and color and surroundings as if they'd entered some grand stage or made an early entrance to Elysium. They took their so-called medicine, those sips of water Vitto knew now weren't just sips of water. His mother had once told him that if something looked too good to be true, it probably wasn't.

Not totally.

"There's two sides to every coin, Vittorio. Memory can be a double-edged sword. There's always a pull and a tug, and eventually someone has to win."

She'd looked solemn when she said it, and older. The moment was etched in his memory. He had been sixteen, and she'd already been showing the signs of, not dying perhaps, but certainly being on the tail end of something.

So every day he looked for signs when the guests—he tried not to call them patients—drank the water from that fountain. A wince of pain? Signs of choking? Rough going down? But most closed their eyes as if they'd just swallowed peace in liquid form.

I'm not blind, Valerie. In fact, I may be the only one here who sees clearly.

But he wasn't the only one skeptical about the water. Now that the hotel was full of men and women his age, Father Embry, the priest at St. Dymphna's in Gandy, had begun to visit daily, parking his ancient bicycle with its patched tires in the corner of the piazza. He never drank from the fountain, either, although he certainly took note of who did, spying curiously as the guests sipped and swallowed. But, unlike Vitto, who watched in wonderment of what might happen, Father Embry gazed as if waiting for something he knew *would* happen eventually. Like he'd seen it before and was waiting for the other shoe to drop.

Father Embry, who'd celebrated his ninetieth birthday during last call three weeks earlier, had soft hair layered like dove feathers and bushy white eyebrows to match. He was nearly as tall as Robert and Juba but thin as the brooms he used daily to sweep off the steps of his church. Lately he'd not only been spying on the fountain but also partaking in the card games and croquet matches and bocce games out on the lawn. He'd become one of them, in a sense, except for the fact that his mind was still sharp as a tack. Maybe he'd begun to hang around because, despite his mobility and mind, he was at the tail end of his life and priests get lonely too. Or maybe he was spying because he knew more than he and Robert and Juba were telling.

Father Embry had just left the hotel grounds to make his pastoral rounds when the hotshot reporter from San Diego made another scene on the piazza. His name was Landry Tuffant, and to Vitto he looked like someone who'd been perpetually needled on the playground as a kid. Short and thin and sickly, with dark hair pomaded back, he was the type that used his words as a substitute for physical toughness.

And for days now he'd been sniffing around the hotel like a dog in heat—interviewing guests, pestering the staff, and insinuating that the so-called fountain of youth was nothing more than a confidence scheme, a way to steal money from the elderly and desperate. His recent articles had been the only ones to cast the hotel in a negative light, and he took pride in doing it. "Someone has to be the bearer of truth," he'd sniveled to Vitto in passing just yesterday.

"A placebo," Landry Tuffant now yelled across the piazza—Vitto noticed he'd waited until Father Embry was out the door and only a blip on the hilly distance—loudly enough to interrupt more than one conversation. "A placebo . . . or worse."

The second time he yelled it, Mrs. Eaves stopped playing the piano and Valerie lowered her violin bow. Vitto had been on his way to the hotel entrance for another day of avoidance, another day of working on maintenance-type chores in the sun where no one could bother him, but Tuffant's voice slowed his walk.

It wasn't his blabbering about the water being a placebo that angered him—this was the second day in a row the man had pulled this stunt. But as soon as Tuffant mentioned Magdalena, Vitto stopped cold. Valerie took a step forward, and the nearby guests stared. Even Robert looked up from his sculpture, which had, in recent days, begun to take the shape of a woman Vitto suspected was Magdalena. Robert had never sculpted his wife before. He'd always said it was impossible to capture her beauty—*"only a god could do so,"* he'd once said—but it sure looked as if he was trying now.

Vitto strode toward Tuffant. "What about Magdalena?"

Tuffant pushed thin-framed glasses up his blade-like nose and smiled like a chimp that had just been fed a banana in a menagerie. "Why did she jump from that cliff? That's the story, is it not?"

"I'd like you to leave," said Vitto. "Right now."

"Why was there never a story written about her death? Just a meager mention in the obituaries."

Because, at the time, Robert threatened to kill any reporter who tried.
But Vitto said, "Some reporters showed the respect that was due."

"A devout Catholic who selfishly took her own life."

"She slipped," Vitto said, tight-jawed. "It was an accident."

Tuffant let out a quick laugh, a burst like a punch in the air. "Tell yourself that if it makes you feel better. A slip on purpose, I'd say, Mr. Gandy. Who in their right mind would venture so close to the cliffs without having the notion of going over?"

"Get out." It was Valerie who'd said it now, storming across the piazza with bow in hand, gripping it as if preparing to strike. Valerie may have been aware of Magdalena's flaws, but she was also quick to take up for her. "Get out now."

"Or what?"

She got as far as raising her elbow to strike him before catching herself. She lowered the bow but didn't retreat.

The reporter looked back to Vitto. "A future story will, no doubt, cover all these questions, Mr. Gandy. I'll be happy to present your take on them if you will allow me an interview."

Robert had moved away from his statue, shuffling close but not too close to the reporter, still holding his hammer and chisel but showing no sign of using them. He might have threatened reporters years ago, but he was no threat today. Vitto noticed for the first time, in the sunlight spilling over the hotel's crenellations, that his father looked frail and uncertain, no longer equipped to fight his own fight. Even when struggling with Alzheimer's, his physical appearance had never wavered from that of a warrior, of the god he'd always claimed to be. But now he just stood there looking . . . old.

Tuffant paused as if hoping he'd get more of a reaction out of Robert and even seemed disappointed when he didn't. So he again faced Vitto, who looked ready to fight right there in front of everyone. "Your mother was famous, was she not? Artists traveled continents to be around her." He turned in a slow circle, gesturing toward each wing of the hotel. "To be around this. But who was she? Where did she come from? That's what I want to know."

Vitto took a threatening step toward the man, who took one back and pointed at the fountain. "This isn't the only story, Mr. Gandy. Stories start from something. They aren't birthed from midair. Your mother came from Italy. From Florence. A foundling baby left at an orphanage with no marks to identify her. She was adopted by a man named Francesco Lippi, a painter who suddenly found fortune and a bit of fame because of her. His muse."

"Get out." It was Juba this time, walking across the piazza like a man on a mission. The hotel guests watched nervously, backing away as Juba said it again, this time like a rumble of thunder. "Get out before I throw you out."

"Or throw me off the cliff!" spat Tuffant.

Juba froze. The accusation had clearly been meant—and taken— as more than a threat.

Tuffant knew something. And then it hit Vitto; he'd heard the name before. *Tuffant*—that was the name of the slick-haired, sus-pendered reporter who'd gone over the cliffs in the early twenties, his body broken and disfigured on the rocks below. Melvin Tuffant. The hotel's tragedy had obviously been rekindled in the person of Melvin's son, Landry, who was grown now and had grabbed hold of the thread the father had dropped prematurely.

Tuffant pointed at Juba. "I know what you did, and I'll prove it. There was a fire at Lippi's house the night Magdalena fled Pienza. She was ushered away by Robert Gandy and a mysterious man with skin so black some confused him with the shadows. Lippi burned inside that house, but I have suspicions he was already dead."

He backed away from Juba, unknowingly toward the rim of the fountain. "I've sent letters to Pienza. I learn more daily. I'll prove what my father couldn't."

"And do what with it?" asked Valerie. "Magdalena is already gone."

Tuffant held his finger up. "Well then, perhaps she'll burn in hell for multiple sins, suicide being the least of—"

His sentence ended in a squawk as Vitto reached for him, grabbing Tuffant's extended finger and pulling it back until it popped. Valerie covered her mouth and then William's eyes; he'd sidled up against her leg during all the commotion. Vitto pulled Tuffant's arm around to his back and duck-walked him to the fountain, where he kicked his legs out from under him, and forced his head over the rim, Tuffant's chest resting against the wet blue-and-yellow tiles.

Vitto dunked the reporter's face and head into the water, held it down for a couple seconds, and then lifted it back up. "Drink." He did it again and again. "Lap it up like the dog you are." Water streamed from Tuffant's face as Vitto lifted his head again, clutching it by the loose strands of the reporter's greasy hair.

"Stop," Tuffant gurgled, choking.

"Drink!" Vitto hissed, only vaguely aware of the shouts behind him, the sound of William crying. He wished not only memories but also a storm front of nightmares on the man. But part of him couldn't help wondering, *did Mamma have something to do with Melvin Tuffant's death?*

"Vitto, stop." Valerie's arms clutched his. And Juba's. And John's. They pulled him away as the reporter gained his equilibrium on the side of the fountain, positioning broken glasses on his nose. Blood leaked from Tuffant's chin where it must have hit the tiles on one of the plunges. He wiped it with a soaked shirtsleeve.

"I'll be back, Gandy. I'll shut this place down."

❃

Vitto found Juba behind the bar that night after last call, cleaning wineglasses that already looked clean.

The game of truth and lies had been played at midnight as usual.

But after the stress of the day with the reporter, attendance had been sparse, with many guests shuffling off to bed instead of the piazza. Vitto had stayed away, aware that most of the guests had steered clear of him after what he'd done to Tuffant inside that fountain. Some of them during the day had even given their medicine a second look before drinking, as if it was now tainted or, at worst, littered with a strand of Tuffant's hair or remnants from his broken glasses.

Vitto sat on a stool now while Juba poured him a glass of red. He poured himself a glass as well and leaned forward with his elbows on the bar top, ready to take on any questions Vitto might conjure. They drank for a minute, watching each other from their respective sides of the bar. Vitto finally said, "Did you do it?"

"Do what?"

"Push that reporter's father off the cliff? Back in the twenties?"

Juba swallowed wine, said decisively, "No."

Vitto didn't know whether he believed Juba or not, but he'd known him long enough to know he wouldn't get any more out of him. Juba was a vault stuck inside of a vault and he'd swallowed the key long ago. "You would have done anything to protect my mother?"

Juba nodded, wiped his mouth. "Still would."

"Why'd she jump?"

"She slipped."

"No she didn't," said Vitto. "I can handle you and Dad and even Father Embry concealing the truth like you've always done, but what I won't take is a full-out lie. Why'd she jump?"

Juba sighed and flicked a bread crumb off the bar. "She was troubled."

"Not at the beginning."

"She got worse as the years went by."

"Why? What troubled her?"

"Her past. And who she was."

"What past? And who was she, Juba?"

"She was your mother."

Vitto downed his wine and pushed it forward for a refill, which Juba poured, but with hesitation and the kind of glance a father might give to a son when something needed to be monitored.

Vitto pressed. "What happened in Pienza?"

"Just like the man said. Me and your father helped her escape."

"Why did she need to escape?"

"That man Lippi beat on her."

"There's more. Did she set that house on fire? Was Lippi inside? Did she steal his money?"

Juba stared across the piazza to where Robert had paused his chiseling to stare at the moonlit statue. Vitto changed course, nodded toward his father in the distance. "I heard you two arguing earlier."

"Is that not allowed?"

"It was heated. What was it about?"

"Something we disagree on." A pause. "I promised him I wouldn't tell you . . . yet."

"Which means you might."

Juba nodded. "Which means I might. If your father doesn't soon come to his senses."

"About?"

"About all of this."

Vitto finished his second glass in two gulps and made as if to step from the stool and approach his father.

Juba's voice stopped him. "Don't. He won't talk to you about it."

"Why not?"

"He's not ready."

"Look at him, Juba. He's thin. He's pale. He's weak. I've never seen him like this. His mind might be whole again, but his body is taking the brunt. These weeks have somehow taken off years."

"Let him deal with it in his own way, Vitto."

"Deal with what?"

"His mortality."

Vitto laughed, folded his arms. "He once told me he was immortal."

Juba started to say something but stopped. Vitto looked from Juba to his father. "Why could he never love me?"

"He loves you, Vitto."

"Then why did he never show it? He was always consumed with his work. And he never really had any real interest in my paintings. I could tell. He'd just nod and walk away while others stared in amazement."

"But it wasn't like . . . Vitto, it's complicated."

Vitto laughed. "Yes, it is."

"He couldn't—" Juba stopped.

"Couldn't what?"

"Couldn't see it the way others did." Juba gathered himself, lowered his voice but not his intensity. "He's color-blind, Vitto." He paused to let that sink in. "He at one time wanted to be a painter, but from the beginning, he could never see color. Flowers were gray. Grass was gray. The sky was white. Clothing, shoes, anything he set his eyes upon, he saw only white and black and shades of gray at best."

A lump formed in Vitto's throat, and he gave it a moment to settle, although his heart fluttered like a caged bird. "So that's why he turned to carving stone."

"Yes, Vitto. That is why he turned to carving stone. He was brilliant. And then he found your mother and become even more brilliant. They became . . ."

Vitto watched Juba, who looked away, having already said too much—much more than he'd ever leaked before. Perhaps they were all dealing with their mortality. The two of them went silent for a minute, both watching Robert watch his statue. And then Robert surprised them both by placing his hands on the woman's hip— Magdalena's hip—and shoving. The half-finished sculpture rocked, then began to topple.

"What's he doing?" Vitto moved toward his father, but this time Juba grabbed his arm.

"Let him be."

The marble statue he'd been working on for months now lay in chunks around the pedestal. Robert cursed and swore and kicked one of the smaller marble pieces across the travertine. He dropped the chisel and hammer and walked slump-shouldered toward the first-floor room where he'd been staying since their arrival—the same one he and Magdalena had used their entire lives. The one with the door the color of goldenrod.

"I'm surprised it took him this long."

"To do what?"

"To give up on the notion that she could be recreated," said Juba. "I told him not to try. But he had to see for himself."

Seventeen

*Y*ou're not well, Vitto."

What burned him more than the words was the fact that Valerie couldn't look at him as she said them, sitting on the side of the bed, hands folded on her lap, facing the far wall as William slept.

She was right. He was not well. But hearing it from her lips was not the medicine he needed, the medicine he'd hoped for after nearly drowning Landry Tuffant in the fountain. After again instilling fear in his family.

"I'll go," he'd said, hoping she'd respond with, "No, don't. Please." But she hadn't. She'd just nodded silently, and so he'd gone. Not from the hotel—as confused as he was about things, he couldn't bring himself to leave the hotel, and he truly believed Valerie knew that. Otherwise, perhaps she would have stopped him.

He decided to sleep in Mr. Carney's old room on the second floor, one of the two that stored the wooden ships that he and the other kids used to sail on the creek, and brought with him a case of wine. His assault on the reporter had unsettled the majority of the guests and their visiting children, so he thought it best to be holed up for a while. He spent the next few hours cleaning dust from Carney's ships, picking up each one in turn and eyeing it closely as he had when he was little.

William should be floating these ships.

But William was back to hiding, scared of his father yet again. That in itself was a dagger to Vitto's heart, a sign that the father-son bond between him and Robert—the bond that wasn't—had been successfully passed down. The best way to become a Gandy man,

166

apparently, was to not be one. To shirk and avoid and distance yourself until the lack of communication felt comfortable. Which was why, at twenty-five years of age, he had just learned that his father was color-blind.

He spent the rest of that night in that ship-filled room, drinking wine and contemplating the strange injustice of his very existence. That while Vitto had been blessed with eyes that could see and imagine the brightest, most robust of colors, his father saw nothing but black and whites and grays. And while Vitto had been blessed with a memory like a vault, like pictures frozen in his head, his mother often had trouble remembering her own friends' names.

What was denied to each parent had been given to him as gifts.

More like a curse, he thought early the next morning, stepping out onto the gallery overlooking the piazza. Below him the elderly guests were out and about, eating breakfast on wrought-iron tables, playing cards, mingling, reading newspapers and magazines. A silver-haired woman finished off her milk and then slid her teeth back in her mouth. Unlike the guests in the hotel's heyday, the current ones were usually up before the sun rose. And none of them seemed agitated or upset. Maybe they'd forgotten about what had happened with the reporter at the fountain. Or maybe they were just better than he was at moving on.

Robert was down there too. Somehow he'd gotten another block of marble onto the piazza and cleaned up the remnants from the broken statue. Juba had probably helped. They'd once had a pulley-and-crane system for loading the marble from the seemingly endless supply kept in storage—perhaps that still worked. But now that the block was here, nothing was happening with it. Instead of carving the marble, Robert just stared at it, hammer and chisel in hand, as if the Alzheimer's had returned.

Valerie was down there, too, bustling from table to table, taking breakfast plates and stacking them and carrying them back to the kitchen. Every so often she'd glance up. He could tell she had spotted him, and he didn't know what to do about that. He loved her more than ever, but for some reason he felt like he shouldn't. She deserved better than him.

Perhaps he would have been better off with a lobotomy.

"Vitto." He turned toward the voice. Cowboy Cane stood a few paces away, watching with a toothpick in his mouth. "Got a minute, partner?"

"What is it?"

Cowboy Cane had become the leader of the guests. Just last week he'd begun a weekly dance on Wednesday evenings. Now he tipped his hat, looking oddly nervous, which was strange considering how sure of himself Cane usually was. "I was talking with the other folks. Like what we heard with the hotel's olden days, last call has become a special time for us all. We're old, and we've got plenty of stories to tell." He chuckled. "And I've even taken a liking to the wine of late."

To all the widows too, Vitto thought.

Cane paused, long enough for Vitto to prompt him onward. "And?"

"You noticed how early we get up? Well, that midnight time for last call is tough for many of us."

"Last call has always been at midnight."

"I understand that, and believe you me, us old folks don't like change. But if the point of last call is to get everyone engaged in the telling of stories, attendance would be much improved by an earlier time. Not to mention the quality of the stories."

"Did you ask Robert about this?"

"Sure did."

"What did he say?"

"Said to go ask your wife."

"And what did *she* say?"

The old man grinned. "Said to go ask you. Said it'd be good for you."

Of course she did. Vitto mulled on it, figured Cane wasn't going anywhere until he got an answer he liked. "What time do you propose?"

"We took a vote, and most said nine o'clock."

"Fine."

"Really?"

"Yes." *Just go away.*

Cowboy Cane tipped his hat, thanked him.

"But tell me," Vitto said. "Did you really get hit by a train?"

He winked. "Far as you know."

Vitto watched him walk away, and a minute later Cane was down on the piazza spreading the news about the new time for last call. Vitto was about to return to the room when John approached, smelling like bread dough and garlic.

"Hey, Gandy. Got a minute?" He didn't wait for a response. "We're pals, right?"

"Sure."

"Well, you know how me and Beverly have been getting along real good? I was thinking about asking for her hand in marriage."

"Sounds like the logical next step, John."

"You think so, Gandy?"

"You spend every waking minute together, John."

"Good." He rubbed his hands together. "That's good. That's what Valerie said too."

"You asked her first?"

John nodded. "She said to go get your opinion. Said it'd be good for you. How'd you do it?"

"Do what?"

"Ask Valerie."

"I said, will you marry me? She said yes, that she'd always known we would."

"That's good, Gandy. That's good information. You think Beverly will say the same thing?"

"I don't know what Beverly will say, John. You've been lying to her since you met her."

John looked flummoxed. He scratched his head, chewed on his lip. "That I have. So you think I should stop pretending to have those war nightmares at night?"

"I think you hooked her a long time ago, John. You can probably cut off the playacting."

"Okay." He rubbed his hands together. "But I like the attention, Gandy. She gets right up on the bed with me and falls asleep. I smile the rest of the night, even when she snores."

Vitto shook his head, wished he'd sneaked outside the hotel before he'd become the morning's sounding board. John said, "Did you get down on one knee or both?"

"One knee, John. Who would get down on both? Who would do that?"

"I don't know, Gandy. I've never done this before." John stepped away, nodding, seemingly satisfied with how their talk had gone. "Just want to get it right, you know?"

"I think someone's calling you from the kitchen, John."

"Oh, okay." John moved down the gallery, then turned suddenly. "Thanks, Gandy."

"Sure."

"But when are *you* gonna cut out the playacting?"

John clearly meant it as a joke, but when Vitto didn't smile, John's melted away, and he returned to the kitchen.

The February sun felt good, at least, so Vitto walked discreetly down the spiral staircase and out the hotel's entrance while everyone else was busy eating and talking. Last month he'd cleaned out the Leopoldini—the month before that, the vineyard. For the last week he'd been working on the hotel walls, filling in the exterior cracks where mortar had crumbled loose and weeds and vines had taken over.

After an hour in the sun, he admitted to himself that things weren't so bad; he felt peaceful almost. The sky was azure and cloudless, the stones glistening like a ripened peach, the field grasses golden and green. As it had been since he was little, every color was like a dollop or smear of paint, sharp and vivid and wet. The whole earth seemed like a freshly painted canvas yet to dry, and now he knew his father couldn't see it.

Vitto pulled a vine from the cracks beneath the stone wall and dropped it into the basket at his feet. He moved down the wall toward another cluster of vines and began to pull those. He looked over his shoulder at the sound of laughter.

Down the hill to his right, an elderly couple walked hand in hand in between the vineyard rows. He didn't know them; too many had arrived in the past months for him to meet them all. Many were widows and widowers, but a number had arrived as couples, some married for decades, fifty to sixty years even. But only rarely, Vitto had noticed, did both husband *and* wife need to drink the medicine; usually it was one or the other. Maybe that was nature's way of keeping at least one wheel on the track. But Vitto had also noticed that it was usually the spouse unafflicted by the memory disease who showed the most joy at the rebirth. After dark times, sad times—*how awful to have your spouse of fifty years not even know who you are*—it was like they'd been given again the gift of their loved one, and to Hades with the consequences.

The couple stopped as the monks began chanting down over the hillside. Vitto listened, too, like he'd done as a boy, imitating his mother's actions. She had never failed to stop whatever she was doing when the monks prayed. After a moment he left the basket of pulled vines on the sidewalk and followed the sound of their rhythmic voices.

He climbed the olive grove steps and watched from atop the hillside. To his right he could see the cliffs from which his mother had leapt to her death. Below lay the lake, the scattered buildings of the monastery, and the stone monastery church. Beyond that was the Pacific Ocean and the endless horizon.

He sat for a while on the hilltop and listened but then felt called to go closer. He lowered himself over the lip of the terrace, which dropped steeply—what Magdalena had called dangerously—toward the valley below. What made it dangerous was the rocks and the craggy, uneven ground. But instead of using the paved walkway bordering the creek—as Magdalena had done daily when she'd walk to the church for confession—he and Valerie and Dixon and Deats used to navigate straight down the hillside, using the rocks and grassy shelves, made slippery by ocean mist, as steps.

Vitto made his way down the rocky slope and moved across the knee-high field of grass toward the lake below and the stone buildings of the monastery. The church was just inside the gates, to the left. He passed through the open doorway, touched fingers in the font, crossed himself, and genuflected before entering the back pew. It had been years since he'd entered any kind of church—since his mother's death, in fact. She'd been the one to bring him faithfully every Sunday since the day he was born, either here or to Father Embry's little church in town. But the familiar motions came back to him without his having to think.

The air was cool inside the darkened space. Sunlight cast prisms of color through the stained glass. Stone columns soared toward a vaulted ceiling and the fresco Vitto had painted as a teenager. The chanting brought him back, the candles and incense enveloped him like a cocoon, and he sat with his head lowered, chin to his chest, until the midday prayer was over and the monks silently shuffled out. He didn't open his eyes until he felt bony fingers on his shoulder.

"Come for confession, Vitto?" Father Embry said.

He looked up in surprise. "No, Father." He twisted in the pew to look up at the old priest. "But this isn't your church. Why are you here?"

"I like the chanting." The old monk patted Vitto's shoulder and sat in the pew across the central aisle. "And I, too, go to confession here."

At ninety, Father Embry's face was more wrinkled than Vitto remembered, his posture a little more stooped, but his brown, comforting eyes had not changed. His mind and soul seemed untouched by the age that marked the rest of him.

"My mother came to you for confession," said Vitto, fishing. "What would she talk about?"

"Her confessions, Vitto, were exactly that. *Her* confessions."

Vitto nodded; he'd figured as much. *I know she jumped. She didn't slip.* He remembered the priest on the day of his mother's burial, more nervous and emotional than Vitto had ever seen him. Father Embry had choked up halfway through his eulogy, specifically after he'd said that "Magdalena is not inside that coffin"—he'd paused to gather himself—"but has been reunited with the gods." And then he'd cleared his throat to correct himself. "With *God*." Now he was looking up at the frescoed ceiling as if to avoid Vitto's eyes.

"Have you picked up a brush since your return, Vitto?"

"I have not."

"And why is that?"

"Has Valerie been to see you?"

"She has." The priest held up his hands up as if guilty. "I admit it. And she asked me to come talk to you. To get you painting again. She believes that is what will fill the void."

"And what do you think?"

"I don't disagree. But I told her I wouldn't come to you. I'd wait until you came to me."

"That's not why I came down here, though. I didn't even know you'd be here."

"Then why *did* you come down here, Vitto?"

Vitto folded and unfolded his hands, wrangling with his thoughts until he nearly stood and left. "There's a reporter snooping," he finally said.

"There seems to be more than one reporter snooping at the hotel of late."

"But this one dug deeper," said Vitto. "Wanted to know more than just the present." He looked across the aisle and waited for Father Embry to look his way, which he eventually did. "He said Mother is in hell for jumping off that cliff. Was what she did a sin? I know she jumped."

"And how do you know that?"

"Was it a sin? Killing herself like that?"

"Was it a sin nearly drowning that reporter for saying something you should have had the strength to ignore?"

"I suppose. Want me to say a few Hail Marys?"

"It's never a bad idea."

"But is she in hell? Is that how it works?"

Father Embry's jaw quivered, but then he pursed his lips and steadied himself in the pew. "This reporter . . . seems pretty sure of things he knows nothing about."

"At the funeral," said Vitto, treading carefully, "you said she was called home. What did you mean?"

"She was dying, Vitto, on the inside and out. Her time on earth had come to an end."

Vitto stared at him, wanting to prod more but knowing from experience that Father Embry often spoke in riddles. If he were to tug one way, Father Embry would pull the other way. No matter how he peeled that apple, he'd never get to the core. So he just asked, "What do you think of all this?"

"All what, Vitto?"

"That fountain. The water acting like medicine, curing people's Alzheimer's or whatever it is. You believe it?"

"What's there to believe, Vitto, when it's right before our eyes?"

"But how do you explain it?"

"I don't. How do you explain the weather? The changing of the seasons?"

"I'd imagine it has something to do with the world turning."

Father Embry laughed, mouth closed as if to muffle it.

"What's funny?"

"A story your mother once told," he said, "decades ago." He waved his hand dismissively, and after Vitto insisted on hearing it, he told it. "Your mother won last call many more times than she lost. She had so many stories that most guessed as lies but she'd insist were true, and we'd let it go. She'd carry her journals with her and read from them. This particular one—you know of Hades and Zeus and Poseidon?"

"The three brothers," said Vitto. "The Olympians. After they won the great war with the Titans, they drew lots to see who would rule what."

Father Embry nodded. "Zeus got the sky, Poseidon the sea."

"And Hades the underworld."

"That's right," he said. "Well, one night your mother told us a story about Hades, how he became captivated by the beauty of a woman named Persephone. So he kidnapped her. Carried her right down to the underworld to be his wife, and as your mother told it she went kicking and screaming. Once there, she begged and begged to be returned to the world above. And meanwhile, Persephone's mother, Demeter—"

"The goddess of grain and growing things."

"Yes. Demeter grew distraught after her daughter disappeared. She roamed the earth in search of her. And that was a disaster, because nothing would grow while she was searching. There was no wheat, no barley, no fruit. So rather than let the world starve, Zeus ordered his brother Hades to return Persephone. And he agreed, which meant that Demeter would allow the earth to bloom again. But there was a problem. It turned out that while in the underworld, Persephone had already eaten the seeds of a pomegranate."

"So?"

"Vitto, anyone who tasted the food in the land of the dead could not return to the land of the living."

"You speak of this as if you believe it."

"I speak of it as an intriguing story that I'd eventually like to finish."

"I'm sorry. Go on."

"Well, as a compromise, Zeus allowed Persephone to spend a portion of the year with her mother and the other portion of the year in the underworld with Hades. During the months when she returns to her mother, the world grows green and warm and plentiful. That's spring and summer, you see?" Vitto nodded because he got it, but he didn't really see the point. "And in the months when Persephone returns to Hades, the world darkens and cools." He clapped his hands together. "Fall and winter. Her comings and goings explain the changing of the seasons, and the queen of the dead also becomes the goddess of spring."

"So you just explained the changing of the seasons."

"Did I? Or did I just tell you a good story—a Greek myth your mother believed to her dying day."

"My mother was a strict Catholic."

"And so am I."

"Then how did she believe in all these Greek myths? She told me one daily, if not more often."

"Their ideas were not so different from our own, Vitto. Take the afterlife, for instance. The ancients believed that the spirits of the dead were separated into the just and unjust. The good were taken to Elysium, the bad to the torments of Tartarus. So there was reward and punishment, the idea of immortality of the soul. Plato advanced things even further. His rewards and punishments for life lived on earth are quite similar to the Christian notions of judgment after death. And I'd say the church's idea of purgatory, at least as it was imagined in the Middle Ages, conveniently resembles the idea of the underworld's Acheron River. A place of sorrow and pain where souls are purified after death."

"Sounds familiar. So maybe I died in the war after all."

"And this is now your purgatory?"

"It sure isn't my Elysium."

Father Embry smiled.

"What?"

"Nothing." He looked down, eyed Vitto again. "You could make this into your Elysium if you wanted to."

"You been talking to John? This some kind of barrel of sunshine or barrel of stones talk?"

"I don't know what this is, Vitto." Father Embry shook his head and laughed as he stood, using the pew back as a crutch. He grunted straight. "And to answer your earlier question, whether that fountain water is really helping to restore memory—yes, I believe it. And do you know why?"

"Why?"

"Because I believe in miracles, Vitto. I've seen them. And I believe that not everything can be explained the way your mother explained the changes of the seasons. I do *not* believe your mother is in hell, or Hades, or Tartarus, or whatever you want to call it. I believe she had her reasons for what she did. And yes, I believe you should start painting again." He held up an arthritic finger, which in the colorful stained-glass light looked more like a hooked talon. "In fact, I think it's imperative that you start painting again. I'm tired of seeing you walk the hotel grounds in a posture of doom and gloom." He pointed to the ceiling fresco. "You painted this. Do you remember?"

"Of course I do." It had taken him eleven months.

"Create, Vitto. Create."

"I copied, Father Embry. I didn't create; I copied. Everything I've ever painted was a reproduction of a work by some old master.

Some legend of the Renaissance. I had the ability to see something and duplicate it perfectly. And what I did might have brought joy to others, but not to me."

"So why did you do it?"

"You know why I did it."

"To gain the favor of your father."

"Yes, to gain his favor. His approval. To earn a 'job well done' from the great Renaissance man. But I never could, and now I know why. Juba told me. Father Embry, why did no one ever tell me my father could not see color—couldn't truly see my paintings. You knew, didn't you?"

"He had his reasons."

Knowing he'd get no further with that line of questioning, Vitto tried a different tack. "Why are you watching the fountain so closely? You're watching the guests drink that water as if you're waiting for something. What is it? Is the water doing something to these people besides restoring their memory?"

"I don't know, Vitto."

"But why do you suspect it might?" And then it hit him. "Did my mother drink from that fountain? Was she drinking from that fountain before she died?"

Eighteen

"You're slowly killing yourself."

Vitto stormed across the piazza toward where his father leaned back in a wooden chair, eyeing the slab of untouched marble. "Don't deny it."

Robert leaned forward, suddenly too old to stand quickly. "Hush, boy."

"Mamma drank from that fountain."

"Lower your voice." Robert surveyed the piazza, then grabbed Vitto by the elbow and walked him into the shadows nearby. When a cluster of guests emerged from the same spot, he redirected Vitto outside the hotel, where more guests played bocce and croquet. He redirected him again, this time along the wall toward the ocean. The thwack of a tennis ball echoed in the distance. Ocean breeze whipped Robert's hair into a frenzy. And even though he appeared even weaker than he had yesterday, his hands still proved strong as he braced them on Vitto's shoulders and looked deep into his eyes.

"Who told you this? Juba? Father Embry?"

"I guessed it. Father Embry was unable to deny it." Vitto stepped out from under his father's grip. "It was Juba who told me you've never been able to see color. Why did you never tell me?"

"I had my reasons."

"I don't care about your reasons, Dad. I spent my entire childhood trying to impress you with paintings you simply could not appreciate. Now, what is the water in that fountain? And why was Mamma drinking it?"

"I don't know where to begin."

"Try."

"Vitto, it's too hard to explain things I've never fully understood myself."

"What did the earthquake do to that water?"

"Nothing. The water has always been the same. The earthquake did nothing."

"It restarted that fountain."

Robert pounded his chest with a fist. "*I* restarted the fountain, Vitto. With the turning of some knobs. Just as I turned it off the day your mother died."

Vitto pointed out toward the front of the hotel, toward a stream he couldn't see. "And what about that creek? Your River Lethe?"

"Stories, Vitto."

"I know that, but the changing of direction. The water flow. You sent me down there with a boat to see for myself."

"To get you to believe."

"In what?"

"This."

"What is this?"

"It's not the first time a river or creek has changed directions, Vitto. Uncommon, yes, but the earth rumbles, shifts, moves under our feet. The land has been changing for centuries. That creek has changed direction before."

"So that had nothing to do with the water in that fountain?"

"No."

Vitto stepped closer, his voice more stern. "What is coming from that fountain, and why did Mamma drink from it?"

"I didn't know she was drinking from it. We promised each other we'd never drink from it."

"Why?"

"For the same reason God put Adam and Eve in the Garden of Eden and told them not to eat from the tree of the knowledge of good and evil." He raised his arms incredulously, defeated. "I don't know."

"Water is life," Vitto muttered, staring out toward the ocean. "Or is it death?"

"We live, Vittorio!"

"This isn't the Garden of Eden," said Vitto, "or the Elysian Fields. What was it about that water? From the beginning, what made you not want to drink it?"

"The stones that make up that fountain, they were there before we built the hotel. They fell from the sky one night. There was a storm—thunder and lightning so great the heavens rumbled. The locals thought them to be meteorites. We used them to make a fountain, and then we placed more stones around it. We built the fountain first and then built the hotel around it."

"More unbelievable stories."

"Your mother, she had no memory when I met her. And near the end of her life it had gotten so bad again that she could remember very little."

"Again? What do you mean *again*?"

Robert looked away, refocused, and replaced his hands on Vitto's shoulders in a posture of dominance. "Listen to me, son. There was something in her, memories that needed to come out. Horrible memories she'd suppressed since her childhood. She knew the water would bring them out, but she also knew they'd do her in."

"Like what it's doing to you now."

Robert didn't deny it. "I didn't know she was drinking the water until it was too late. She couldn't handle the memories. You remember the months leading to her death?"

"Yes, she spoke little, cried a lot, and wandered about the grounds like a woman who'd lost her mind."

"I didn't realize it until it was too late. I was too preoccupied with my work. I was deep into a depression of my own."

"Why?"

"She kissed me that night like she did every night." Another redirect. Robert choked up, then composed himself. "Instead of saying good night she said good-bye. I was half-asleep and didn't even notice."

"She came to my room too," said Vitto, remembering. "Here I was, a man grown, and she comes in to kiss me on the head in the middle of the night. She told me she'd always loved me and that she was finally free." He took a step back, eyes wide. "She was telling us good-bye. We're fools."

Robert nodded slowly, shoulders sagging, as if he agreed that he'd been a fool. As if he had carried this guilt for years and was only now letting it surface. "Vitto, do you remember the outlandish story she told that night?"

"No, what story?"

"At last call. Her final . . ." And then Robert must have remembered. "You weren't there."

"I skipped last call that night."

"Yes, you were angry. You'd had an argument with Valerie. She was concerned about Magdalena's well-being, concerned that she might . . ."

"We both skipped last call because of that argument." *I buried that argument too.*

"And perhaps that's why Magdalena told it."

"Told what?"

He waved the question away as if it was nothing. "Just another one of her imaginative stories, Vitto. You know, one of those stories she would tell that took over the entire game, the kind that would be bandied about by the guests after she returned to her room and discussed the next morning too. It would have been, too, if not for what she did that night after everyone was in bed. It's just that . . . I should have seen the finality in it."

Vitto watched his father, looking for cracks in the façade. He was holding back as usual. "What was the story she told?"

Robert touched his head, fingers to his wrinkled temples. "I . . . I don't remember it all."

Vitto believed him. Magdalena's stories were not that easy to remember unless you had a memory like Vitto's. They went this way and that, forward and back, twisting upon themselves, and often they left the listeners confused. No doubt Magdalena's last story had been like that.

But as his father continued to speak, Vitto's mind shifted from the fuzziness of the past to the clarity of the here and now. He gazed into his father's eyes, so intensely blue and alive, but framed by the skin and flesh of a rapidly aging man. He felt weak in the knees and suddenly nauseated.

His mother had begun drinking the water in the months before she jumped. And she, too, had appeared increasingly older and frail over the course of those months. Valerie had been the first to point this out, but he'd been too stubborn to listen. He'd assumed she was sick from lack of sleep, lack of eating. But that wasn't it, was it? It was the fountain water. While it was bringing back the horrible memories Robert spoke of, it was also killing her, moving her life forward at an accelerated pace.

He glared at his father. "You're dying."

"We're all dying, Vitto."

"You've led them all in here like lambs to the slaughter." Vitto laughed. "The water, this magical water you've still yet to explain—it's restoring their memory yet shortening their lives. And you've known this!"

Robert didn't deny it. "The earthquake did one thing, Vitto. It made me see the truth—the same water that helped kill your mother could bring pleasure to others. Like me." He gestured toward the hotel, to the gathered guests in the distance. "Like them."

"I can't believe I'm hearing this."

"Look at them, Vitto. Happiness abounds. This is what Maggie would have wanted."

"But you've no right to play God. It must be their choice. You're bringing them here so that they can die."

Robert's voice swelled with passion. "I'm bringing them here so that they can *live!*"

Vitto grew light-headed, mumbled, "For their last call."

Father and son watched each other as Robert whispered, "Yes, for their last call." But in those words Vitto's argument had finally taken root. "You're right, son. They must decide for themselves."

"Yes, they should," came a nasally voice behind them.

They turned simultaneously to find the reporter Landry Tuffant standing in the grass, taking notes on his pad.

Nineteen

$\mathcal{B}$y the time Vitto realized the potential damage Tuffant could bring down on both Robert and the hotel, the reporter was in an all-out sprint toward his car.

Vitto gave chase but slowed after twenty paces. What would he have done with the reporter had he caught him? He couldn't hold him hostage, and he really didn't want to lay hands on the man. He was fortunate no charges had been filed after he'd nearly drowned him. But what was done was done, and now they had to quickly decide how to fix it.

"So this is what you and Juba argued about last night?"

"Yes."

"And this is why Father Embry has been watching things so closely?" Robert nodded, an uncharacteristic worry in his eyes. "We have to tell them."

"No one has died yet," Robert said. "In the eyes of the law, we've done nothing wrong."

"We have to tell them."

"Yes, I know, but—"

"They'll have to take your word for it," said Vitto. "Just as they trusted you that the water would restore their memory. You're the great Robert Gandy. They'll believe you."

"If the police come—"

"When, Dad, not if. You saw him. Landry Tuffant thinks his father was murdered here. He thinks Mamma . . . He wants to bury us."

"Then let him try." Robert inhaled ocean air, and his chest swelled with sudden pride that Vitto couldn't deny he felt too. "Find Juba and the priest. And Valerie."

"Did she know?"

"No. But just a few months ago she was helping me dress and spooning food into my mouth. She, more than anyone, needs to be told before the rest of them."

❃

They met inside Robert's room to discuss the best way to inform the guests that the water that was restoring their memory and giving their lives back was quite possibly also killing them. They needed no more proof than to look at how frail Robert had become over the past few months. He'd been drinking the water longer than anyone, and probably more of it as well.

Valerie admitted that she'd noticed her father-in-law's physical depletion over the past months but had been afraid to verbalize it, probably because of how Vitto had reacted when she suggested the same thing about his mother years ago. And then, as if to steer them away from that past, that pain, Valerie said, "Beverly's mother, Louise. She's still feisty, as we all know, but you can see it on her too. She's aging quickly."

"And Cowboy Cane." Juba glared at Robert; their argument had come to fruition, and he'd proven himself right.

"Don't." Robert held up a hand. "I know, Juba." He faced Vitto and Valerie. Father Embry stood quietly to the side, wide-eyed and every so often crossing himself and mumbling prayer. "But how do we tell them?"

"Individually," said Vitto. "This is too personal to do otherwise."

"We don't have that luxury anymore," said Valerie. "That reporter can come back at any minute, and think of the anger from these guests if we've yet to tell most of them. They can't hear it from a third party. They'll think Robert is a murderer"—she looked at him—"when I truly believe his intent was the exact opposite."

Robert nodded, eyes wet. Vitto wanted to reach out to him but couldn't. And then Valerie did, with an ease that showed why she, like Juba—was this why the two of them had always gotten along so well?—was the glue that held them all together.

"Juba," Valerie said now. "Call everyone together on the piazza. I've been the one bringing them their trays of medicine every morning. So I'll be the one to tell them."

"You?" asked Vitto.

She nodded toward Vitto and Robert. "The two of you have the bedside manner of a two-by-four."

Vitto couldn't disagree. "But how? What exactly will you tell them?"

"That sometimes miracles come with a catch."

There was an old church bell in the corner tower closest to the ocean that Robert used to chime when he needed all of his guests to gather. But since none of the current guests had heard it and probably would not know what it meant, they decided to have Juba call them in. And it worked. Even though it was many hours before last call, they still responded. Everyone trickled in eventually—Cowboy Cane coming from as far as the tennis courts. They gathered on the piazza, clearly curious about the sudden gathering.

Juba had them all squeeze in tighter around the fountain, where Valerie stood atop the rim. As they noticed the serious look on her face, the atmosphere quickly transformed from jovial to solemn. Some guests began whispering and surveying the crowd to make sure no one had passed away. It had always been openly discussed that the water had magically restored their memories and minds but could do nothing for their aging hearts and lungs and other physical ailments they had brought with them.

The whispers quieted, and Valerie got right to it. "We have a serious announcement to make, ladies and gentlemen, and not much time, as you'll no doubt appreciate once you've heard what needs to be said. We've all witnessed firsthand what this fountain water has done to our minds." She paused, and the crowd nodded in unison, sharing glances but apparently eager to have the other shoe fall. "We've accepted this benefit, even though we've had little to no explanation as to why and how it has occurred, because it has spun life in our favor. Now it seems we'll have a similar lack of explanation in regard to the other side of this coin."

"What is it, Valerie?" Mrs. Eaves asked from the front row. "We've lived through hell, all of us, because that's what losing memory was for us . . . so we can handle the truth." She eyed others in the crowd. "Because many of us sense what you're about to tell us, and I for one appreciate the honesty."

Valerie nodded, sighed as if a weight had been lifted from her shoulders. "Robert Gandy had a feeling this fountain water could restore your minds and was eager to help and share the benefits with you all, as outlandish as it had seemed at first. But, well, he also had a hunch that the same water could also cause harm."

"In what way?" a man asked from several rows back.

Cowboy Cane said, "Earl, it's getting us to the finish line faster than we would get there otherwise."

Baldheaded Earl looked shocked by the news, but many to most didn't. They could probably feel it in their bones and notice it in the mirrors every morning when they brushed their teeth and combed their hair and patted on their colognes and perfumes.

Valerie looked out over the crowd; Vitto had never admired her so much for her courage. Her voice calmed them. "It's true. Robert was unsure of the repercussions at first." Vitto didn't know if this was true, but her love for Robert was obvious, and she wasn't going to throw him to the wolves. "But this effect has clutched him deeply enough for him to realize and fear that the same could be happening to all of you."

Whispers permeated the crowd. Someone quietly sobbed.

Cowboy Cane said to everyone, "So basically we have a choice to make, folks—our bodies or our minds. I know which one I'm choosing." He turned away and began to politely burrow his way through the crowd, his wooden tennis racquet held high.

A man with salt-and-pepper hair and a bushy matching mustache said, "Where you going, Cowboy?"

"Back to the tennis courts," said Cane. "Me and Rufus were in the middle of a set."

The rest of the crowd looked at one another as if wondering what to do. Then, in a trickle at first and then a steady flow, the guests began peeling this way and that, most seemingly returning to what they'd been doing before the gathering.

"Well, I'll be . . ." Vitto said under his breath, right about the time the sirens began approaching outside the hotel's entrance. And then it became obvious that, while a good majority of the guests were neither surprised nor disheartened by the announcement and might even be relieved that they could go on with their newly found lives of aging faster, not everyone felt that way. Some were standing in shock, some crying, some clearly angry, and one in particular had already exited his first-floor room with his suitcase in hand. Mr. Franklin—if Vitto remembered the name correctly—shook a few hands and headed toward the entrance just as Landry Tuffant hurried in with four policemen flanking him, clubs pulled as if they'd really need to use them on Robert and his elderly guests.

Their arrival instantly added a level of anxiety to an already tenuous situation. Beverly was one of the ones still standing near the fountain, stunned over the news, while her grandmother Louise seemed unbothered. John stood between as if he was about to do something stupid and untimely, which turned out to be true.

A police whistle blew, shrill enough for most in the piazza to cover their ears.

"There he is," Tuffant shouted, pointing at Robert. "He's a murderer. He's slowly poisoning these poor souls."

The coppers moved in, and Robert stretched out his hands, offering his wrists for cuffing. But if he wasn't going to put up a fight, Vitto would. He stepped in front of the first copper, the chubby one who acted like he was in charge of things but who in reality looked like a teddy bear in way over his head, as antsy as the elderly guests surrounding him.

"What crime do you accuse him of?" Vitto screamed over the throng.

"Euthanasia," shouted Tuffant. "Assisted suicide! He's a regular Nazi!"

Officer Tubby nodded as if to second the accusation and attempted to move around Vitto with his wrist bracelets. "You've no proof of anything," said Vitto. "We've lost no one in the months they've been here, Officer. Not one." He eyed Tuffant. "You're taking a foolish man's word over the truth."

Tuffant yelled, "He tried to drown me in that water yesterday."

Officer Tubby paused, unsure of what to do. Robert, uncharacteristically, stood passive, ready to be taken if that's what was decided. Mrs. Eaves, in an attempt to ease the growing tension, crossed over to the piano and began playing Mozart, but for once the music seemed unequal to the task of soothing the agitated guests. Many seemed angry toward the reporter and the coppers and were speaking on Robert's behalf, while others who'd been on the fence before began to look at him accusingly.

Beverly was one of the latter. And just as she was about to say something seething to Robert, Johnny Two-Times grabbed her hands and knelt before her on the travertine, apparently deciding that now was the ideal time to propose. Or perhaps he'd been so determined to do so that he thought he'd better get it done before the situation slid further downhill—Beverly looked like she was on the verge of grabbing her grandmother and leaving, and he probably sensed that too. So he not only dropped to one knee; he ignored Vitto's earlier advice entirely and went down on both, sweating like an overheated mule as he asked for Beverly's hand in marriage, all while Mrs. Eaves played louder on the piano keys and a trio of liver-spotted men who in the past month had named themselves the Tuscan Tenors started singing along.

Beverly, instead of crying and saying, "Yes, yes, oh, yes," as John had probably envisioned, slid her hands out from his and slapped him across the face quicker than a snakebite, to which her grandmother Louise cried, "Beverly, my lands, girl," and proceeded to give the tubby copper the finger.

It dawned on Vitto that John had probably asked Beverly's grandmother for permission to propose and that this had not been the result Louise expected. Perhaps she blamed the officer for messing up what could be a good situation. At any rate, she seemed distinctly put out when Beverly grabbed her arm and hustled her away.

All got quiet for a few seconds, just in time for everyone to hear young William Gandy's voice shout from somewhere unseen. "Fire in the hole!"

Heads tilted upward, eyes peered toward the blue sky as a German-style hand grenade soared over the fountain and the marble Cronus, bouncing to a stop a few feet from Tuffant and the coppers. By the time it rattled still, Tuffant had dived under a nearby bench and Officer Tubby had pulled his pistol, firing aimlessly. The bullet ricocheted off the church bell in the southwestern corner of the hotel, pinging loud enough to make everyone duck a second time—the first had been when the gun went off—before it whistled back toward the piazza, causing the crowd to duck a third time just as the bullet burrowed into Juba's right arm.

Officer Tubby got to his feet with a grunt and wiped nervous sweat from his reddened forehead. "Everybody okay?"

And then Juba dropped to the piazza's stones with a thud.

Everyone gasped.

Robert was the first to his side. Vitto was second, realizing when he got there that Juba had somehow known the bullet was heading right for Robert and had decided to protect him.

"One last time," Juba whispered, and then closed his eyes.

Twenty

*H*e loves me, and I love him."

Saying the words aloud, even if whispered in the dark confines of her bedroom, proved even more powerful than reading them from the last page of her journal, the one Lippi knew nothing about. As impossible as it seemed to fall in love with someone unremembered each sunrise, Magdalena knew she had managed it. How else to explain the smile every morning upon opening her eyes, when she had no other earthly reason to do so?

Now, as she lay beneath the blanket, her tears flowed, even fresher than the bruises he'd given her an hour ago, spitting on her as he screamed, her crawling back on her elbows, he straddle-walking above, aware of her deceit and dishonesty. The citizens of Pienza had seen her on numerous occasions strolling about town during the day, and someone had reported to Lippi. As much as she tried, she could not hide her hair.

He wept when he first saw it.

"Who is he?" Lippi had demanded.

"Who is who, Francesco?"

"Some say they've seen you speaking with a man." He'd sat on her midsection so she couldn't move, pinning her with his bony knees squeezing against her rib cage. "The one who shows off in the piazza daily, carving his own statue of David. The tall American with the long hair and blue eyes." His nasally voice grew strained as he raised it. "And they're calling you *his* muse!"

She'd had no answer; there was so much she couldn't remember, so much that had melded together until very little made sense.

"Should I keep you chained?"

"No, Francesco."

"Francesco who?"

"Francesco Lippi."

"Francesco Lippi who?"

"Francesco Lippi the Great."

The pressure his knees had been applying eased, but only somewhat. Since he'd adopted her at age nine, his paintings had become well-known throughout Tuscany, and the commissions and sales had increased yearly until he'd become a very wealthy man, a successful painter in a region so full of artists, historical and present, that it was nearly impossible to stand out.

"Whose muse are you, Magdalena?"

"Yours."

"Louder."

"Yours."

"Mine and mine alone," he said, his voice easing along with his insecurities. "You're an orphan of the wheel, Magdalena. Unwanted. Abandoned. Unloved."

"Lies." It had come out before she could stop it.

He slapped her across the face. If a bruise formed there, he would make her stand the opposite way while he painted so that he couldn't see it. "What have you done with this man? This American who dares to compare himself to the masters?"

"Nothing. I don't know who he is."

"Of course you don't." He stood, wavered. He'd already finished a bottle of wine but now shuffled across to the kitchen to open another. Lank hair askew, he drank from it, watched her on the floor with hateful eyes of black. "I'll deal with the American in the morning."

"How?" she whispered.

"Like any man deals with a nuisance. A rat. He kills it."

He wouldn't.

Upon seeing the bruises on her arms earlier in the day, Robert had nearly gone mad, seething, hissing that he'd kill this man Lippi with his bare hands. She had no doubt that he could, and would. He was well-muscled, with hands stronger than the stone he chipped into daily. Magdalena was nowhere near strong enough to stop Robert, though she'd tried to do so with her words.

"No, Robert."

"We'll run away then. Tonight. Under the cloak of darkness."

"I can't."

"Why not, Maggie? You're not his slave. He adopted you—that doesn't mean he owns you."

No, he doesn't, Magdalena thought now as dusk bled to night, trembling under the bedcovers as if cold, clinging hard to the memory of Robert gripping her shoulders in the afternoon, staring into her eyes as if they were portals to her soul.

I'm seventeen years old, a woman grown. Sneaking out had not increased her monthly blood the way Lippi had warned. *More lies.* She reached again to her fading memory of the afternoon—Robert telling her of the news he'd learned the night before. He'd been investigating the disappearance of her old friend at the Hospital of the Innocents, Nurse Pratesi, who for years had pestered Francesco Lippi for his treatment of her Magdalena until the nurse, months before, had disappeared altogether. Lippi had told her she moved away—to Venice, he'd said when she insisted on knowing. He'd stalled in his answer to conjure another lie. According to Robert, the nurse's body had washed up weeks ago on the banks of the Arno.

"He's a thug and a crook, Maggie, and he's surrounded by thugs and thieves. Come with me tonight. I'll be waiting here . . . at exactly midnight."

Magdalena flung the covers from her trembling body and steadied her feet on the floor. *You can do this, Magdalena.* Both Robert's voice and her own. *Do it before you have to start all over again in the morning.* From the bedpost hung a cotton satchel in which Lippi used to carry his paints and brushes when he was unknown; she vaguely remembered grabbing it from a closet earlier in the day with the purpose of storing her belongings when she fled. Now she filled it with clothes, shoes, a brush, her journal and pencil, and finally the round wall clock Nurse Pratesi had given her the day Lippi had taken her from the orphanage. Tears welled; if what Robert had heard was true, the woman she once called Mamma was dead, possibly even murdered by the man now passed out drunk in the neighboring room.

She opened the bedroom door and walked quietly into the hall. A red candle burned in the kitchen, wax dripping like fresh blood onto the lip of the brass holder. Lippi was no longer snoring. A stubby hallway off the kitchen gave access to his studio, and Lippi was visible from where she stood. His eyes were open, watching her.

"Magdalena . . . bring me my wine," he slurred, slouching in his wooden painter's chair, the easel shielding the left side of his face. His hair was a mess, his right eye reddened from too much drink. His shirt was untucked, his belt unlaced.

She closed her eyes, hard, pushing back a sudden memory wanting to come up. She swallowed, opened her eyes, and faced him, each peering at the other down the short hallway, where a bag of onions, peppers, and garlic hung on the wall and a wheel of cheese rested on a small table next to a jar of olive oil.

"Magdalena . . . bring me my wine."

Run. He's too slow and drunk to catch you. Run, Magdalena.

Instead, she discreetly placed her satchel on the counter and grabbed the bottle, clutching the throat as one would a hammer. She shuffled toward the hallway, paused when she saw the bone-handled knife beside the wash basin, the blade curved and sharp but marked with apple remnants yet to be washed clean.

His nasally voice grew louder. "Magdalena . . . bring me my wine."
And so she did.

❄

Magdalena stumbled through the narrow streets and alleyways of
Pienza.

Tears dripped cold down her cheeks as she navigated through
moving shadows and dips in the cobbles. She braced herself on buildings of brick and stone that soared high enough to blot out the moon
when she needed it the most.

As her memory faded, she moved on instinct. Her heart pounded.
Her hands were wet, covered in red. Sticky red. Congealed red. She
smelled smoke, then saw it rising from atop a stone building behind
her, blocks away. *From where I've come?* Black, acrid smoke turned the
night darker. People left their homes, moving toward the source just
as Magdalena ran away from it.

A woman screamed. Once, twice—so shrill. Magdalena moved
now with her hands over her ears, but the screams still penetrated.
She'd made it to the piazza. Moonlight blinked. More people hurried
from doors and migrated toward the smoke and a new sound—the
crackle and roar of a true fire.

"Maggie."

That's what he called me. Robert. Yes, that's his name. Robert.

"I love him, and he loves me," she whispered.

He emerged from the shadows and ushered her away from the
increasing commotion. "Maggie, there's blood on your hands." Even
in the darkness, his eyes shone as blue as the cobalt of his cloak. "And
on your neck. Did he hurt you? Are you hurt?"

She shook her head no but couldn't remember. She didn't feel
hurt, only confused and tired and oddly free—as if something deeply
buried in her had been released. Across the piazza, his statue of David

towered, finished now, left as a gift to the town where he'd finally found his muse after years of searching.

Whistles trilled, echoed down the alleyways. Flames grew, and a pocket of Pienza now glowed orange and bright. Robert protected her, concealed her, made sure the hood covered her hair as they sneaked away together into the dark, through streets she should know but didn't. His words were jumbled in her mind; she'd lost all sense of direction. They were walking downhill now, to where the valleys and hills spread out like a Francesco Lippi landscape painting.

Fragments of memory filtered through—Robert's words, his plan: get to Florence, and then to the Arno River, and on to Pisa, where he had passage to the sea. She watched the ground as they walked, ran, hurried, waited, down the hillside, waiting again. Not simply running away anymore, but fleeing for their lives. *What have I done?* Cobbles and stone turned to grass and mud. She heard moving water and current, lapping against wooden docks, but when she looked around she saw no river. *Memories of sound from another time. Why are we turning around?*

"Keep your head down, Magdalena."

What do you mean we've been spotted? He knew? Lippi—he knew? He'd had Robert watched. *Why is there blood on my hands?*

"There she is," a man called.

A crowd moved toward them from the hillside, a cluster of toughs and roughnecks paid to guard the outskirts of the town. More running, back up the hillside, back into Pienza, more turns and tight streets, down an alleyway so narrow he had to sidestep. Her heart raced as she followed him, confused and lost but aware enough to know she was in good hands. Safe, even.

They left the alley, found themselves in a small open area surrounded by more brick and stone. The mob closed in. Black smoke swallowed the moon. And then from the shadows came a man dressed in a cotton shirt stained by too many hot summers, brown trousers cinched above muscular calves, worn leather sandals twisted around massive feet, his skin dark as molasses, brown eyes alert.

"Follow me."

"Who are you?" asked Robert.

"No time for questions," he said, voice deep.

A memory emerged—she'd written of him in her journal. He sang daily in the piazza, with a basso voice so deep her heart thrummed. She had wondered if this same man, years ago and a boy himself, had saved her from the mob of people in Florence when she'd wandered away from Francesco Lippi.

He led them through more darkened alleys and narrow streets, through a church of candles and incense and marble statues and stained glass, where praying clerics lifted bowed heads and paused in their whispered Latin to follow their escape. Unlike her and Robert's frantic movements before his sudden arrival, his escape was fluid, like water sluicing through channels and viaducts. He knew the terrain like the back of his hand.

They moved out a wooden door and back into the night, the smoke and flames behind them now. They passed through a heavy gate, burst through a cluster of trees, down another slope into a valley, where a carriage and two horses awaited. The man opened the door and ushered them inside. He got in with them, slammed the door, and knocked twice on the roof. The driver clucked to the horses and they pulled away, clip-clopping, the carriage lurching over the uneven terrain.

Magdalena nestled close to Robert, who grabbed both of her hands, kissing her knuckles, the dried blood on them. The dark-skinned man sat across from them, watching as if he'd known them for years instead of minutes.

He finally spoke. "My name is Juba."

"I'm Robert. Robert Gandy. And this is—"

"I know who she is," Juba said with the hint of a grin. "I've been watching over her since before we were all born."

❋

The Tyrrhenian Sea was choppy, but the night had given birth to warm sunshine and a picture of freedom.

The man Juba had proven true to his word. The fishing boat he'd promised had been waiting for them on the shore of the Paglia River, which carried them to the Tiber and on to Rome, where a group of men and women Juba called friends had done exactly as he'd said they would—first hiding them and then, come sunrise, securing them passage on a boat with massive sails. He said it would carry them south past Naples and Pompeii to Sicily, where he promised an even larger ship that would take them far away.

For now, Robert soaked in the sun's rays and clutched Magdalena to his side, the top of her head resting in the crook of his shoulder. Her long hair fluttered against his neck. In Rome, the crusted blood had not been easy to remove from her hands and arms and neck and forehead, so he'd helped her scrub into the basin, trying to be as gentle as he could, until finally she'd insisted on doing it alone, scrubbing furiously until her skin turned pink and then red and tears formed in her eyes as if she were battling the memories of what had happened back in that house. He didn't ask, and truthfully didn't want to know; the searing flames, even though he'd seen and felt them from a distance, were still etched vividly in his mind.

With the bloodstains finally gone—proving, indeed, that none of the blood had been hers—she'd spoken stoically, without looking at Robert, choosing instead to stare at the cold brick wall above the water basin. "I'm free."

What had that man done to her? The beating and the mental abuse were evident, but Robert feared more. Feared the worst, and in her smile as she stared out across the choppy sea, he realized it as truth. If she'd killed the man, he hoped he'd suffered.

The longer Magdalena watched the sea, the more it calmed, as if from some mystic command. The waves settled. The ship no longer rocked. Sunlight shimmered off the low ripples—to Robert, in various shades of gray and white—and a sense of peace overwhelmed him. He couldn't explain it, but he sensed it had everything to do with the water, with the power held inside every wave, every lap and gurgle and spray of mist.

Like the water back home, the water he'd found bubbling from the ground months ago, in California.

Fearing for her mental well-being, for their future, he hugged Magdalena tight. *How can she remember bits of memory from centuries ago, but nothing from the here and now? Who stole your memory, love?* And now he'd taken her from the only land she knew—a land that had surrounded her with beauty even when its residents brought her pain. She might not remember it, but he knew she would miss those hills, those cobbled piazzas, those blowing poppy fields and art-lined streets, with an ache deeper than memory. Though he barely knew her, he knew this with a certainty that surprised him.

"I will bring Tuscany to you, Magdalena," he whispered, kissing the top of her head, kissing that orange hair that was nearly so bright it made him squint. He told her about the land on the southern coast of California, the land he'd first seen in his dreams and had recently found. He told her about the Renaissance hotel he planned to build on it. "It will be unlike anything ever seen."

She nestled deeper into the niche created by his chest and shoulder, seemingly comforted by his words. He couldn't take his eyes from her hair.

Juba had been misted by enough waves to soak his shirt, so he removed it, revealing a broad, muscled chest, the cavern from which that deep voice bellowed. He watched the waves as if they calmed him, too, closing his eyes to the occasional spray. It was as if he were speaking to it, to the water. To the sea.

"We were all birthed from the waters, were we not?"

Robert watched their new friend, confused.

Magdalena tilted her head out toward the vast waters, ears perked as if she'd heard some distant voice calling her name. She smiled, leaned back into his shoulder. "From the waters we shall rise."

She and Juba shared a smile.

Juba told them that he, too, was an orphan—from a tiny Sudanese village called Juba, near the White Nile. Robert said nothing. He didn't tell them that he was also an orphan. That Cotton Gandy had found him on the banks of the Conecuh River in Alabama while fishing and had taken him home. After his pregnant wife miscarried two days later, they'd played it off as if *he* was the newborn—their gift from God—and nobody had ever been the wiser.

He especially didn't tell them—not then, anyway—that ever since he was old enough to read about the ancients, he'd believed he was somehow one of them—that he was a god wielding that hammer and chisel. And that his fourth-grade teacher, after explaining that Leonardo da Vinci was not only a sculptor and painter but also an inventor and mathematician, had asked him during class, "Robert, how do you know so much about the Renaissance?" And he'd answered, standing with his arms outstretched: "Mrs. Peters, I *am* the Renaissance."

But it was Magdalena's hair that had brought about his now-constant smile. He'd seen flickers of orange the day he first set eyes on her, flickers of colored strands every day thereafter, and he'd wept. For what he wouldn't tell them, couldn't even begin to explain, was that except for in his dreams, in seventeen years on earth, the fire-orange of her hair had been the first color, other than black and white and gray, that he'd ever seen.

Even now, as the waves lulled them and the mist sprayed and the water somehow whispered the unspoken, her hair shone so starkly colored in his otherwise gray world that it looked wet, like fresh paint. He couldn't take his eyes from it. And then, upon her stone-colored shoulder, where her dress sleeve and arm and hand and fingers had been a mixture of grays and whites and stone colors since he'd known her, he suddenly saw the smallest hint of what he knew to be yellow— first as a flicker and then as a dollop as the true colors of her clothes and her skin revealed themselves to him.

Twenty-One

1946

*J*uba was adamant that they call no doctor, ultimately convincing them all, even a panicked Valerie, that he was fine and would take care of what he called the metal splinter on his own. So he pulled the bullet from his arm with some tweezers, a leather belt made into a tourniquet, and a few slugs of Old Sam whiskey John had found behind the bar to ease the pain. He was bandaged and standing fully alert by the time the new last call went off at nine.

The bullet had hurt like the dickens, he said, and the blood trickling from it had certainly been real, but the collapse on the piazza had been for show: "Seemed like the perfect time for a diversion." And the diversion had worked. Officer Tubby had been so rattled from accidentally shooting someone—and not just someone, but a Gandy celebrity—that he and his officers seemed to have forgotten why they were there at all. After cautiously approaching to help the felled giant, who halted them with an upraised hand and eyes that said *come no closer*, they had fled the hotel. The reporter, Landry Tuffant, hadn't been far behind. After promising Vitto he'd be back, he'd chased after the coppers, asking why they weren't pressing charges or arresting Robert Gandy for attempted murder and euthanasia.

"Has anyone died?" Officer Tubby had called over his shoulder on his way out of the hotel.

"No . . . not yet, at least," Tuffant had responded.

"Then there's nothing I can do. There's no proof that water does anything but restore people's memory, just as the newspapers have been saying all along."

❈

Dinner that night had been a quiet affair. The day's excitement seemed to have sucked the energy from the piazza, from the hotel itself, and now that night was upon them, many of the guests seemed lost in the contemplations of their next move. To stay or go? To continue drinking the water and take their chances or to stop drinking it and return to the painful life that had brought them here in the first place?

Now, with the sun below the horizon and darkness creeping in, Vitto sat on the lip of the fountain, listening to the water spill and ripple. Most of the guests had gone into their rooms, and even Robert was nowhere to be seen, his slab of marble still untouched. Juba, too, had opted to rest until time for last call.

It had been a frightening thing to see Juba go down. And for Vitto, the worst part hadn't been the blood coming from Juba's arm, as alive and red as it had been, dripping onto the travertine, but the fear he'd seen in Valerie's eyes when Juba fell. Seeing the panic in her eyes had nearly paralyzed Vitto.

The quickness and desperation she'd shown running to his side had reminded him in a flash that Juba was much more to her than a friend. After her parents abandoned her at the hotel, Juba had been her father figure from day one—from minute one—holding her hand the instant she walked from their room, rubbing the sleepers from her eyes and asking where her mother and father were. He'd held her hand as he walked the grounds with her, turning it into a game to find them—"*They're surely around here somewhere, Miss Valerie*"—held her hand when the entire hotel began looking an hour later to no avail, held her hand when they realized the car was no longer in the parking lot and the dressers in the room were empty of the clothes that had been neatly stacked and folded within. And later that evening, when they found the note Valerie's parents had left on Juba's windowsill— hard evidence that they'd deliberately left their daughter, who they'd claimed was better off there without them, better off learning her music and learning life from Juba than from two parents still searching for themselves—Juba had gathered her in his arms and held her close.

It was all this that Vitto saw flash before his wife's eyes when Juba hit the travertine. He now sat on the fountain seeking to breathe fresh air, to clear his head, to avoid holing himself back up with Mr. Carney's wooden ships, but mostly because, like a child scolded and awaiting punishment, he knew his was coming—and well deserved.

If it hadn't been for his temper, his near drowning of Landry Tuffant, perhaps the reporter would not have been so dead set on ruining them. If he hadn't given his young son a hand grenade, William never would have thrown it across the piazza at the most intense of times. If he hadn't thrown the grenade, Officer Tubby would never have panicked and fired his weapon. If he wouldn't have fired his weapon, Juba would have never been shot, and Valerie wouldn't have had the second worst scare of her lifetime.

Valerie's approaching footsteps sounded a few minutes later, signaling the beginning or end of something. She sat beside him on the fountain, but not too close. A good minute went by, and neither of them said a word. If it was possible to have a silent argument, they were doing so now. He'd have a hard time writing this one down to bury it.

Finally, he gathered the courage to speak. "I'm sorry."

"Me too." She glanced up at him but then looked down between her narrow feet.

Her apology put him on edge. She couldn't be sorry for anything she'd done because she hadn't done anything wrong. So the alternative was that she was apologizing for something she was about to do, something she was about to say.

He braced himself for the worst. But still she said nothing, which might have been hardest of all, because the two of them throughout their childhoods and early-adult lives had never been lost for words. And then finally she said, "I don't know how to fix this, Vitto."

"I don't either."

"I thought a few weeks ago we'd done it, but it . . . it didn't hold."

He looked at her. "But at least it was a glimmer."

"A glimmer of what?"

"Of some hope."

She nodded, couldn't deny it, which meant that there was some left. Hope. His posture eased on the fountain. He wanted to reach out and touch her, but he didn't. Wanted to rub her back and shoulder and tuck the loose strands of hair behind her ear in order to see her face more clearly, but he didn't. "We had an argument the night Mamma died. You remember?"

She nodded.

"You were right in worrying about her. We were blind, me and Dad. And after that I was just . . . angry."

She bit her lip. "I have scars, too, Vitto. This hasn't been easy."

He didn't have to ask what. All of it. The war. Dealing with Robert when his mind was gone. Living with an angry, unpredictable husband who frightened their son. But it now made some sense that his anger had all begun with his mother.

"Her death made me angry, Val. The mystery of it. The rumors. I was angry at her. Angry that she wasn't alive to be at our wedding. Angry she wasn't alive for William's birth. Angry because . . . because she wasn't perfect like I thought was. And I was angry at Dad because he didn't do enough to stop her. I just . . . I don't know . . ."

He felt Valerie looking at him, longer than a glance, and they locked eyes. "You're angry at yourself, Vitto."

He didn't disagree; it was easier to admit now that it had been verbalized. He was angry at himself, and he'd taken that off with him to the war, which had made him even angrier.

"Your mother was a wonderful woman," Valerie said. "But she wasn't flawless. And there near the end, she was falling apart."

"I know that now. I think I knew it then."

"Me and Juba," she said. "We would play for her. He sensed it, too, that something wasn't right. The music helped calm her in the last weeks."

"Did you know she was drinking that water?"

"No. But she killed herself because she had stuffed it down, Vitto. She killed herself because she had *buried* it." She stressed the word *bury*—hating the way that, even as a child, Vitto had buried his own unhappy memories. "She never should have told you to do that. As innocent as it was, it was misguided. Here she was, a woman with the inability to remember giving advice to a little boy who couldn't stop remembering."

She stared out across the piazza, toward the bar where Magdalena's round wall clock ticked. *Ticktock goes the clock, Vitto.*

"You can be hurt by your memories, Vitto, but you can also be healed by them." She gestured to all the rooms, all the guests still residing within. "Look around." She nodded toward Robert's room, his closed door in the shadows. "You've always resented your father, but he's the one still alive. There's still time with him."

He scooted closer, inched until their legs touched, and then he draped his arm around her shoulders. She rested her head against his. "Dad said Mamma told a story during last call, hours before she jumped. We'd argued about her, so I didn't attend that night."

"Neither did I," said Valerie. "But I remember an eerie silence across the piazza after she finished. Like the story she had told weighed heavy on people's minds."

"Or it was too confusing to understand."

She nodded, and they shared a smile. "And then it was lost in the sorrow the next morning. I asked Juba about the story she told that night."

"And?"

"He said that maybe sometime he'd try to tell it."

"Of course he did."

"But not yet."

Vitto laughed. "But not yet." He held her, listened to the breeze circle in from the ocean. He tempted fate. "Is this an argument I need to run out and bury with my shovel?"

She elbowed him in the ribs. "It's a conversation, Vitto, one we probably should have had before now. But promise me you'll never bury another."

"I promise."

"Good," she said. And then, "This is a start."

"Yes." He kissed the top of her head, thought about suggesting they sneak up to the loft of the olive mill.

"Are you ready for your penance?"

I'd rather go up to the loft. "I suppose."

She disengaged, gripped his hand. "Practice being a father. William's in the room waiting for you."

"He's still awake?"

"It's been an exciting day," she said. "You're the one who gave him that stupid grenade. You can level the punishment."

Twenty-Two

I promise to not throw the hand grenade where there's people."

"Good," Vitto said, sitting on the bed opposite his son, the two facing each other, one with his feet firmly on the floor, the other dangling.

William adjusted the notepad and pen on his lap. "How many times do I have to copy it?"

"How about a hundred," Vitto said. "Can you count that high?"

"No."

"How high can you count?"

"Ten."

Vitto figured ten times would be too lenient for Valerie's liking. With that look she'd put on him earlier—the one that said *you'd better take this seriously*—he probably needed to come down harder on the boy than he was inclined to do. Vitto was impressed William could write at all, let alone a full sentence, albeit just a copy of one. To him ten times was plenty. But instead he said, "How about you copy that sentence until your hand falls off?"

"Really?"

"Or how about until it gets tired?"

"Okay."

William reached his hand out, and Vitto shook it. "Are you really my dad?"

"I am." Vitto waited through weird silence. "Does that work for you?"

"Does what work for what?"

"Is it okay that I'm your dad?"

William shrugged. "You always been my dad?"

"Yes. But I had to go away for a while."

"Mommy says you're my dad, but you came back different."

"True, but how about I promise to fix that? I'm better now." *At least I know our relationship shouldn't have restarted with the gifting of a Nazi hand grenade.* William stared, nodded. Vitto said, "I'm sure I've done and said some things since my return that have frightened you."

"I asked Mommy if I should bury those memories in the ground like you do."

"You've noticed?"

"Yes. But she said that would be a silly thing to do."

"Yes. Very silly. As childhood habits sometimes are."

William nodded. "I thought Grandpa Robert was my dad."

"That's 'cause you don't remember me from before I went to war."

"Maybe if I drank some of that fountain water I could remember you better."

"No, William. You don't go anywhere close to that fountain water. Do you hear me?"

He nodded. "What's in it?"

"We don't know for sure."

"What's war like?"

Vitto appreciated the change of course, although not the direction. He didn't feel the need to sugarcoat his answer, though. This was already the longest talk he'd ever had with his son by far, and he thought some truth medicine might help bridge the gap between them even faster.

"War is terrible, William. People die. They kill each other. You know what that means?" William shrugged. "That grenade I gave you was something that could kill some people. That's why everyone reacted like they did. They didn't know it's a dud."

William nodded and changed course again. "How's Juba?"

"Juba is just fine."

"Good. I like him."

"We all do. Now, time to get to work."

William focused hard on copying that first sentence, the tip of his tongue protruding from his pale lips. The pencil scratching over the paper and through the quiet room was poignantly palpable. William finished it successfully and moved down to the next line to begin again.

He looked up midsentence. Vitto nodded his approval and walked to the window. Robert was out there now, staring at that marble slab. Otherwise the piazza was empty. Last call had come and gone. Had anyone bothered to attend?

In total, so far, only twenty-seven guests had checked out of the hotel after Valerie's announcement, and nearly all of them had a loved one making the decision for them, as Beverly had done with Louise. He'd heard more than once, "It's not your life to be deciding about." Or variations of those words. And they were right, but that didn't make the situation any less difficult. If the water was killing at the same time it was restoring, he didn't want Robert drinking it either, and he'd told him as much.

He'd gotten the answer he'd assumed he would.

"Not your life, Vitto. I'm not going back to being what I was—a child needing to have my rear end wiped."

A life gone full circle.

A shadow moved near the hotel entrance, and Vitto flinched at the window. A stooped-shouldered man in a fedora walked across the moonlit piazza, went right to the fountain, and dipped a cup into the water. Mr. Franklin, who'd been the first to leave in the afternoon, was apparently the first to return. Did he crave the water like a drug? Or did he just miss the way things had been? The way *he'd* been. Mr. Franklin drank from the cup and stood there for a minute as if content. Then he walked to the room he'd vacated that morning and closed the door behind him.

William said, "My hand's tired."

"How many have you done?"

William counted, looked up. "Six."

"That's good enough."

William put the notepad aside and swung his legs again. "How'd I throw it?"

"Excuse me?"

"The grenade. How'd I do?"

Vitto laughed, and his heart grew warm. Maybe laughter was even better medicine than that water. But William was serious, and Vitto wanted to take him seriously. *How'd I do?* How many times had he asked that question inside his own head when he'd finish one of his paintings or frescoes and Robert came in to gaze upon it, only to grunt and walk away as if annoyed or disappointed.

Vitto sat back on Valerie's bed and faced his son. "You did good, William. The throw must have been executed perfectly with the arc you put on it. Sailed right over that fountain statue. Thought for a minute I saw Cronus's head move to watch it."

"Who's Cronus?"

"God of time, the guy in that fountain statue. But I was kidding. Statue heads don't move."

William grinned. "I did feel like I really let it loose."

"That you did. Perfect throw."

They sat for a minute, looking around the room. William gazed up at the ceiling, pointed. "Mommy said you painted that when you were fourteen. All the girls have Mommy's face."

Vitto eyed the ceiling, already knowing he'd painted all the faces to look like Valerie but feeling the need to look anyway. It's probably why she'd picked this room out of all the others; it had been a big surprise to her that summer to see what Vitto had painted for her.

"What is it?"

"It's a replica," said Vitto. "Of Raphael's fresco, *The Triumph of Galatea*. I was going to paint it on the wall but decided to paint the ceiling instead. That's Galatea in the middle there, in the red robe, eyeing the heavens. She's in a clamshell chariot pulled by dolphins."

"Why not horses?"

"Horses can't swim. And she's a nymph of the sea."

"What's a nymph?"

"Uh, they're minor divinities. Mythological spirits of nature . . . typically beautiful maidens."

William blinked at the big words, clearly not following. But he knew *beautiful*. "That's why you painted Mommy?"

"Yes, that's why I painted your mother."

William looked back up. "What else?"

"Well, there's a Triton—half man, half fish—abducting another sea nymph."

"Like the fountain outside."

"Yes, sort of."

"Why are men always stealing all the mommies?"

Vitto chuckled, said under his breath. "I don't know."

"Why's everybody naked?"

This, too, gave him pause. "They're not all naked. Galatea has the red robe on."

"Those naked babies got wings on. I didn't know naked babies could fly. Why are they shooting her with those bows and arrows?"

"Those are putti. You see them a lot in Italian art. They're toddler boys—often chubby and winged."

"Little fat baby boys with wings."

"Yes, little fat winged baby boys." Vitto pointed again. "In this painting they're firing Cupid's bow and arrows. Cupid is the god of . . ." He hesitated; Magdalena had told him the story of Galatea when he was a few years older than William. ". . . the god of attraction and affection. Galatea was known as the goddess of calm seas. She attracted the attention of the giant Cyclops Polyphemus, who tried to woo her with music from his rustic pipes. But she instead fell for a youth from Sicily named Acis. Polyphemus grew jealous and crushed the boy beneath a big rock. Galatea was stricken with grief, so she transformed the boy Acis into a stream."

Vitto watched William for a reaction but saw only confusion or boredom or a combination of both. "What's depicted on the ceiling is Galatea sailing through the water. She hears the giant's love song and turns her head with a smile."

"Which one are you? The giant? Or one of the little fat baby boys shooting the arrows? Or the guy stealing that woman?"

"None," said Vitto. "It's not real."

"Oh," said William, still staring.

"Let's get you in bed." It was part of Valerie's deal—go in and discipline the boy and then get him tucked in for bed. Apparently he didn't frighten William anymore; otherwise their conversation wouldn't have gone as deep as it had gone.

Vitto ripped the first page from the notepad, folded it, and shoved it in his shirt pocket. William kicked his shoes off and slid under the covers. "How many times you gonna tell Mommy I copied that sentence."

"Enough. You copied it enough. How's that?"

"Good."

Vitto tucked him in, although he was a little unsure exactly how to do so. He had helped with the boy as an infant but hadn't been involved with any bedtime ritual since he returned from the war. The boy smiled, so he must have done something right.

"I forgot to brush my teeth."

"I won't tell if you don't." He ruffled William's hair, shut off the light, and headed for the door.

William's voice caught him at the threshold. "Paint the real."

Vitto turned toward the bed, found his son eyeing the ceiling again. "The real?"

"You said this wasn't real," said William. "So you should paint the real."

Twenty-Three

*V*itto hurried through the loggia outside the hotel's southern wing, wooden easel in one hand and a freshly stretched canvas in the other.

Valerie followed excitedly in his wake. "Vitto, what are you doing?"

I'm painting the real. He looked over his shoulder as he moved through an archway and out onto the piazza. "What does it look like I'm doing, Valerie?" He said it with a smile, not as a wise guy, and her positive reaction spurred him faster. She covered her grin with the same hand he'd kissed—surprising them both—moments ago, right after he'd closed the door to the room, finding Valerie waiting and possibly spying just outside. "I need my paints!"

It wasn't a demand or even a suggestion—he'd planned on retrieving them himself—but she was off in an instant, running for his satchel of tubes and brushes before he could change his mind. He walked past the fountain and set down his easel twenty paces from where Robert sat slumped in a chair, staring at the untouched slab of stone before him.

At first, after the surge of adrenaline he'd had after leaving the room and running into the eavesdropping Valerie, he hadn't been sure what to paint; he'd only known he had to paint something. But then it had quickly dawned on him that the subject was right in front of him, out there on the piazza.

Vitto moved the easel a few steps to the left for a better angle of Robert's position, slouched in his chair with a fist propping his chin up—a clothed, elderly version of Rodin's *The Thinker*. The slight up-and-down movement of his chest signified he was alive. Otherwise, he gave no sign that he saw his son suddenly set up to paint him. Or perhaps he had seen but didn't care.

Valerie returned a minute later with Vitto's satchel and an old jacket—"It will get chilly in an hour or two"—and watched over his shoulder while he centered the canvas on the easel, readied his stained palette, and focused on his father across the way.

"Is he asleep?" Valerie whispered.

"I dunno."

"I'm not asleep." Robert sat up straight as if he'd been toying with them all along. "And you two cake-eaters interrupted my train of thought." He stood from the chair, shuffled slowly into the shadows on the edge of the piazza. A few seconds later, the closing of his door echoed like a gunshot.

Valerie folded her arms in defeat. She patted Vitto's shoulder. "I'm going to bed. Don't lose the inspiration."

Her door closed a minute later, leaving him alone on the piazza. All was silent except the familiar sound of ocean waves pounding the rocks below the cliff. Memories flashed like perfect snapshots: his mother's hair tousled by coastal breeze, Father Embry's choked voice during the eulogy, Robert unable to look at the casket they were about to bury in the ground. Valerie at the violin. William in the olive grove.

Vitto looked toward the chair his father had just vacated and pictured him there exactly as he'd been moments before. He didn't need him to pose; the scene had already engraved itself in his memory, just as all the classic Renaissance paintings he'd copied over the years had done. Except his father was real, and now he would paint the real. Something of his own experience. From his own life.

He needed better light, though. The moon and the lampposts that circled the piazza gave sufficient light for sculpting in white marble, but not for painting in color. Vitto surveyed the piazza, thought a minute, then picked up his supplies and crossed over to the deserted bar, where he switched the lights on. Vitto shoved a few little tables against the far wall and set up his easel in the middle of the floor. And then, for the first time since the weeks before the war, Vitto put brush to canvas. The initial touch of the stiff bristle crunched against the tightly pulled cloth, but soon the paint ran smooth, his strokes more confident, and within an hour he'd captured the vision of his father sitting slumped and thinking in that chair, the untouched slab of marble looming like a mountain of unanswerable questions.

He stood, stepped back to view it from a different perspective, approved of what he saw, and a title popped into his head: *A God, Fallen.* He didn't know if Robert would love it or hate it, kiss it or put a fist through it, but he didn't much care. He'd finished the first painting of his rebirth—he'd painted the real—and now he yearned to do more. In the basement, where earlier he'd dusted off the canvas for what would become *A God, Fallen,* he grabbed five more canvas-stretched frames and brought them out to the piazza.

Alone, except for the waves and the breeze and snoring reverberating from behind colorful closed doors, he squeezed color after color onto his wooden palette and painted through the night, finishing four more paintings before sunrise.

The first one recreated a vivid memory from Buchenwald. It depicted the back of a soldier standing, head lowered in defeat, while the furnace glowed in the background, bodies in stacks all around. Although the face never showed, in his mind the soldier was him.

He named the painting *A Soldier's Lesson.*

The second painting showed the instant Valerie had stepped out onto the porch the day he returned from the war. The joy on her face warmed him—at the time, he had hardly been able to feel a thing. That one he named *A Soldier's Return.*

The next canvas captured a memory from only hours before, of himself and William sitting in profile on two beds facing each other. He named it *A Father's Return.*

The last painting of the night showed a memory from back at

the veteran's hospital, when he'd opened his eyes to find Johnny Two-Times sitting on the side of the neighboring bed, watching over him and smiling. As soon as it was finished, he marched it right to the door of John's Caravaggio room and knocked. He knew he was awake because he could hear him crying. Apparently the loss of the only woman he claimed would ever love a big baby like him had reversed the progress he'd been making—at least temporarily.

"Who is it?" he called now through the door.

"It's Gandy."

"Go away."

Vitto opened the door and closed it behind him. John was sitting up in bed with his back against the headboard, legs drawn up and in, his wrists hanging lazily off his trouser-covered kneecaps, boots still on like he never intended to go to sleep.

"What do you want, Gandy?"

Vitto showed him the painting.

"Why'd you paint me?"

"Felt like painting a big, ugly crybaby."

John nodded, resigned. "It's good."

"I'm calling it *A Soldier's Calling*."

John scoffed. "Ain't no soldier, Gandy. Never was."

"That's not the point," said Vitto. "And yes you are. Look at your face."

John pointed across the room toward the desk. "Bring me that mirror. Although I already know what I look like."

"No, your face in the painting. What are you doing?"

"I'm smiling."

"Yes, John. You're smiling."

"So?"

"So . . . barrel of sunshine or a barrel of stones."

John nodded as a grin formed. "Barrel of sunshine, Gandy."

"Right. Barrel of sunshine. Your outlook on life can save lives."

"You think so?"

"I know so. And Beverly will be back. Trust me."

John smiled like he believed it now himself. "But she slapped me, Gandy."

"She was upset over the news. You asked for her hand in marriage at the worst possible time, John. Why did you do that?"

"Just felt it, Gandy, you know?"

"Did you tell her you'd been faking the nightmares so she'd come up to your room?"

He nodded. "Right after I asked her to marry me. It just came out. Then she slapped me."

"She'll be back, John."

"Do you think so?" He considered the idea. "I hope so."

"But both knees? I warned you, nobody does that."

"I told you, Gandy. I was feeling it."

They shared a laugh, then shook hands. Before Vitto walked out the door, John pointed at the painting propped against the bed. "Gandy, your painting."

Vitto nodded toward it. "I didn't paint that for myself, John. It's yours."

Vitto stood outside his father's room for a good minute before he knocked.

"What?" The voice was weak, almost inaudible.

"It's Vitto. Can I come in?" He waited, but after no answer he tried the knob, found it unlocked, and let himself in. Robert was in bed with his head and shoulders propped up on pillows, the blanket pulled up to a chest that didn't look so strong anymore. In the corner of the room a candle flickered, and in the shadows Robert's eye sockets looked so sunken, his head resembled a skull. "Dad, you okay?"

"What do you want?"

Robert seemed confused; his eyes wandered. On the bedside table was a tray with three medicine cups of water, still full.

"You stopped taking your medicine, Dad." Robert's eyes flashed, but he didn't answer. Vitto repeated, "You stopped taking your medicine."

"So?"

"Why?"

Robert didn't answer; he just looked toward the wall as if he'd given up. Vitto said, "You afraid to die?"

Robert swallowed, licked chapped lips. "I can't work anymore. I haven't carved anything of worth since she died." A smile flickered, then hid back in the shadows. "But what we created together . . . Vittorio, I never was at a loss for inspiration. It was instant, came to me the moment I saw her. She was more than a wife. She was my muse."

He said it like there'd never been a more rock-hard truth ever spoken. And then, softer. "My muse."

"You created brilliant sculptures before you met Mamma," said Vitto. "You can do it again."

Robert's head swiveled toward his son. "Can I? Seems I have two choices. Drink my medicine and remember, only to realize I can no longer create. Or not drink it and let my mind go."

"I can't make that decision for you." And didn't know what he would choose if the decision was his to make. Watching his father die was painful, but seeing him return to what he'd been months before could prove even more so.

"What about what you said earlier? Dad?"

"What did I say earlier?"

"I said that all the guests were coming here to die. You said no, they're coming here so they can live."

"So?"

"Then live." He couldn't believe he'd just said that, and he wondered how much it had come from his own selfishness. Not wanting to deal with his father's affliction, as Valerie had for so many months. Not wanting to help him dress and eat and do every little piece of daily life they all took for granted until it was gone. And it was true. He hated the idea of all that.

But there was something else, too, something deeper. He'd never felt closer to his father than he did right now. After the hours he'd just spent painting on the piazza, he felt like he was finally alive again too. Like he'd already practiced what he was now preaching. He'd lived most of his childhood and all of his adult life with questions about both of his parents and felt he was suddenly on the verge of learning some answers. Like a bridge had begun to construct itself over the chasm.

Robert's eyes settled on the framed canvas Vitto had propped against the bed. "Show me."

Vitto hesitated, suddenly wished he hadn't painted it, hadn't brought it here. Maybe painting the real wasn't what was best for everyone. Truth medicine was often hard to swallow. And what would he do if his father responded the way he always had—that familiar shrug, like nothing Vitto did was ever good enough in his eyes, when in truth, he'd never been able to really see what his son had created.

He steeled his nerves and turned the painting and showed it to his father anyway.

Robert stared, blinked, and clenched his jaw as he viewed himself on canvas—the slumped posture and the blank gaze toward that untouched slab of marble. At least he didn't look away or eye it as if it mattered little. The painting had clearly struck some chord.

Vitto cleared the nerves from his throat. "I didn't use any color on this one." He tapped the canvas. "Just used black and grays. So you could see it as it is."

"Is that supposed to make me feel better?"

"It was an attempt."

Moisture pooled in Robert's eyes. "What's it called?" Vitto didn't answer right away, was even considering changing the name at the last second, when Robert said, "Every masterpiece has a name, Vitto."

Masterpiece? Vitto's eyes lifted, and his heart swelled from the apparent approval. "It's called . . . *A God, Fallen.*"

He waited, waited. The hint of a grin showed on Robert's unshaven jawline, so Vitto allowed his own to emerge.

And then Robert said, "Get out."

With those two words Vitto's heart stopped, then seemed to lurch into his throat. Two words laced with what he construed as hate and venom—whether aimed at himself or his son, Vitto couldn't yet tell.

Vitto opened the door, turned back toward the bed. "What if perfection isn't possible?" Robert looked at the wall.

Vitto said, "You've spent your entire life trying to create perfection, until it consumed you and burned all others in your wake. Why, I'll never know. Maybe that can only be answered by you. But what if you've already created perfection and never realized it?"

Robert eyed his son again. "You think you're perfect, Vitto? How do you think you got that way?"

Vitto pointed out the open door, toward the piazza, toward the hotel itself. "I wasn't talking about me."

Twenty-Four

*V*itto points toward the door.

Robert says, "Turquoise."

They walk to the next room, the next door, the next shade of color to be memorized by Vitto's four-year-old brain. Vitto points. His father says, "Viridian."

And the next. "Cyan."

The colors are so real and alive to Vitto that they all look recently painted, wet and edible, like he could put a finger in whatever it was and taste it. According to Juba, colors don't have taste; he said that after Vitto asked one day what yellow tasted like. Vitto isn't sure he believes it. But he does know his father is losing interest in this fascinating game. With each door viewed and each color learned, Robert's voice loses life and energy, his mind preoccupied with the statue Vitto pulled him from moments ago, begging him to name the colorful doors.

Vitto walks to the next room, points.

Robert hesitates, then says, "Sky." And at the next room, "Cobalt."

The colorful doors grabbed Vitto's attention even before he could walk. When Magdalena or Robert or Juba would carry him from room to room, place to place, across the grounds, his eyes always locked on the doors, and he'd point at the color. His first word—even before Mamma or Da-da or mine—was boo. Blue.

He points at the next door, but Robert has had enough. "Enough for today, Vittorio."

Vitto protests, but Robert leads him down the spiral steps toward the piazza, where other children congregate. He tells him to play with the others and returns to his work. But instead of playing, Vitto recites *the colors over and over in his head until they are in there for good, chiseled into his mind the way his father's statue was chiseled in stone, imprinted like when he'd look at something real hard and the image would stay forever.*

Vitto counts the grownups on the piazza. Not including his mother and father and Juba—who is behind the bar cleaning glasses—eighteen men and women are doing various things like painting and designing and acting and writing and playing music. His mother, Magdalena, walks amongst them, in between and around them like the breeze itself, like a bee skittering from flower to flower, except slower—more like the syrup Juba pours on his hotcakes.

Magdalena stops when she sees Vitto watching her. He waves, and she smiles as her orange hair ruffles in the ocean breeze he can smell and feel but not see.

He memorizes the moment—that smile—somehow knowing it isn't as real as the sadness he saw in the morning when he spied on her from the hallway. She was cutting an apple at the table and paused halfway through to look down at the knife in her hand, like the blade itself meant more than just cutting fruit. That's when the tears came, then the sobs, and he didn't know what to do, so he tiptoed out the door and into the bright sunshine, where he stared until he saw spots.

Juba once said the sunshine here was so bright it was white. Vitto answered that he could see through the bright and that the sun was all kinds of colors. And Juba laughed and patted him on his shoulder and smiled, because that's what Juba does—he smiles when Vitto's parents sometimes will not. Vitto memorizes moments like that too. Juba's smile is as real as the colors of the rainbow, his teeth white like jarred milk, his eyes the color of chestnuts, his skin like the dark melted chocolate he sometimes pours on Vitto's ice cream.

Vitto likes all those things, just like he likes Juba. Once he fell on the piazza and skinned his knee, and Juba covered the scrape with a bandage. Another time a guest dropped a chess piece, a knight, and the horse head came off. Juba used glue and put the head back on. That's what Juba does. He fixes things. Vitto guesses that's why Juba gives such good hugs, his arms powerful enough to show that memory can have a feeling as well as a look, a smell, and a sound.

Even at Vitto's young age, he's observed enough to realize what Juba's role is, not only for the hotel but specifically for his parents. He is the bandage and the glue when things get scraped or broken, the hug when hearts need fixing. And Vitto is well aware that a lot needs fixing around the Tuscany Hotel.

Vitto sometimes hears people talking, the guests whispering when they either don't know he is listening or maybe think he is too young to comprehend what is being said. And he has surmised from what he hears that his parents haven't always been like they are now—often distant and confused, his mother always trying to figure out some unsolvable puzzle, his father painstakingly trying to get back to . . . something.

Magdalena, according to the whispers, seems more and more forgetful by the year. She's taken to writing in her journal more and more often, even carrying it around with her during the day. Of her love Vitto has no doubt. Her hugs are nearly as good as Juba's. But on a couple of occasions she squeezed so hard it felt like she was trying to squash him, and she left tears on his shoulder. Meanwhile, his father grows more agitated and frustrated under the surface, showing it only when people don't see him. In public, Robert is the boisterous and flamboyant man of the hour, the life of every party ever held on the piazza, just as he's always been before.

Before what? Vitto asks himself. But he already knows, already senses it, because if Juba has one flaw it is that he has eyes that cannot lie. So when Vitto asks him one day if his parents were different before he was born, Juba's voice catches, and his eyes flicker just enough for Vitto to know the truth. So when Juba says, "Different how?" Vitto can tell he is being evasive, even though he doesn't yet know the word.

"I mean, what were they like?"

"As they are now, Vittorio."

But Vitto knows that not to be true.

❊

"Vitto, wake up."

He rolled on his back. *Viridian. Cyan. Sky. Cobalt. Where am I?*

Valerie hovered above him, nudged his shoulder. "Wake up. It's your father."

Pulled alert, Vitto leaned up on his elbows. He was in the same room as his family; he'd come here last night after his father sent him away. He'd slid under the covers with Valerie and hugged her as they slept. In the middle of the night William had come from his bed and joined them—all three in one bed, packed in like sardines in a can, but perfectly so.

On the floor and leaning against the far wall were two of the paintings he'd done last night. He nodded toward them.

"They're beautiful, Vitto. Thank you."

He pointed to the first one. *"A Soldier's Return.* That's what it's called." Valerie covered her mouth like she was about to cry. He pointed to the second painting, which depicted him and William sitting on the sides of their beds, facing each other. *"A Father's Return."*

And then he recalled the painting he'd done for his father and remembered why he'd been rustled awake. "Where's Dad?"

"Outside," she said, not panicked but concerned. "Oh Vitto, he's as lost of mind as he was before he arrived here," she said. "I think he's completely stopped taking his medicine. Several of them have."

Vitto laced his shoes, tucked in a fresh shirt, and walked out to the piazza. As usual, the space was full of their elderly guests eating breakfast at scattered café-style tables, apparently unafraid of the water they'd been told would shorten their lives. A life without the medicine is a life not worth living, an eighty-year-old man with a

walker had said the day before. Now he was among the group playing cards. Some read the newspapers. A dozen had formed a walking
club that slowly traversed the blue-tiled outline of the piazza until
tired, twice daily—a couple with canes, three more in wheelchairs.
Mrs. Eaves played the piano.

John emerged from the kitchen with a plate full of fresh bread,
and his sunshine smile was contagious. The guests loved him, not
only because of his cooking but because he'd somehow assumed the
role of son or grandson to them all.

All in all, a typical morning at the Tuscany Hotel. But Valerie
was right that the behavior of a few of the guests seemed off. Or
rather, they'd seemingly slipped back to their previous behavior, the
way they'd been before their arrival to the hotel—lost and confused,
clutched by the cruel hands of senility. They asked for spouses long
dead. They moved with questions in their eyes and hesitation in their
steps and an endless litany of "Where am I?" and "Who are you?"
One frantically insisted that he was late for work and had to catch the
train, although he'd retired fifteen years before. Other guests, who'd
become their friends, fretted over whether to get these lost ones to
drink the water or simply do their best to calm them without it.

So far, Valerie had said, the regressing guests seemed to be in the
minority. Most still took their medicine without wrangling. But some
of their children, after reading Landry Tuffant's latest newspaper
article claiming Robert Gandy was *possibly* performing a form of
euthanasia *right under everyone's noses*, had arrived at the hotel, either
to stop their parent from drinking the water or at least to have the
discussion about what continuing to drink it might mean. Oddly, few
seemed to doubt that the reporter's claims were true. After witnessing
firsthand what the water had done in restoring memory to begin with,
it seemed that most could believe anything.

Vitto turned in a circle on the piazza, taking it all in. Tuffant
was on the second floor with a notepad, observing the piazza from up

high like a vulture. Was he waiting for the first to die? Was he that desperate for copy? That determined to revenge his father's slip from the cliffs decades ago?

Valerie pointed toward the northern wing. Robert paced the tiled walkway in front of the first-floor rooms where, at every door, he'd stop with his nose inches from the painted wood as if waiting for his eyes to adjust and see something other than gray. He moved to the next one, and the next. Juba was with him, following him from door to door like a shadow, waiting to catch him if he should fall. Then Robert moved toward the northern entrance and passed through the archway leading out. Juba stayed with him.

Vitto and Valerie hurried to catch up, finding Robert and Juba around the corner, on the walkway outside the western wing, where the ocean loomed to the right and the wind rippled their clothes. Robert had paused as if confused, staring off toward the cliffs in the distance. Was he picturing Magdalena jumping, as Vitto often did?

"Magdalena," Robert whispered. He turned, confused, and pointed toward the ocean. "She's not in there. Where'd she go?"

Juba tried to corral Robert's arms, but he batted them away and shuffled toward the cliffs.

Valerie ran after him. "Robert," she called out, "let's go back to the piazza." Her father-in-law turned, stared as if he'd never seen her before, and continued on.

Vitto's dream was still vividly imprinted in his mind—Robert naming all the colors of the hotel doors. It wasn't the time, but Vitto felt pressed to say it anyway: "You memorized the colors, didn't you? Since you couldn't see them."

Robert stopped, turned toward his son, then looked at Juba. "Who is he?"

"That's your son, Robert. Vittorio."

"Vittorio?" His eyes surveyed as his mind searched through the muck.

Vitto stepped closer and reached out his hand, but Robert only looked at it.

"Where'd Maggie go?" Robert asked Juba. "She's not in there."

Juba tried to turn Robert back toward the hotel, but he wasn't having it.

"Why aren't you drinking the water anymore?" Vitto asked, following again. "Some of them back there—they're following your lead. Not drinking it because you aren't."

"Drinking what?" Robert asked Juba. "Oh, the water. Don't drink the water. Magdalena drank the water."

"You scared to die?" Vitto blurted in frustration. "Huh? Or are you scared to live?" Realizing right after he said it that his father wasn't the only one. Until last night Vitto had been scared to live, and the same could be said of his mother, Magdalena, before she jumped.

Robert stopped, asked Juba again. "Who is he?"

The question stung.

Juba said, "That's your son, Vittorio. And that's Valerie, your daughter-in-law."

Robert grinned, reached out and kissed Valerie's hand. "How do you do?"

Valerie nodded, "I'm well, Robert. Please come back inside."

Robert shook his head. "I can't. I need to find her. I need to go to her. I need to swim in the ocean." He started again toward the cliffs. Waves crushed against the rocks below them, misting the air. He used to swim in the ocean daily, every morning without fail—sometimes two or three times a day after Magdalena's death.

Vitto raised his voice above the wind. "You haven't always been color-blind, have you?"

Robert turned.

Vitto continued. "There was a time when you could see color."

Robert's jaw quivered. "Magdalena's hair. Orange was the first color I ever saw. Her hair, like flames from a fire." He smiled, but it faded. "You stole it all."

"What?"

"Magdalena?" He'd turned toward Juba again. "She's not in there."

Not in where? Why does he keep saying that?

Robert pointed at Vitto but spoke to Juba. "If he comes any closer, I'll jump. Tell him that."

Juba didn't need to; Vitto had already stopped following. *"You stole it all?"* What does that mean?

Valerie had her arm linked around Vitto's just in case. But Juba gave them both a look that said not to worry, he would escort Robert safely to the cliffs as if they'd done it numerous times before. He'd be careful not to let him get too close—just close enough to see the vastness of it all and hear the power of the waves and surging tide. Juba's presence would be calming for him. It always was.

"You stole it all." Had he? He recalled his mother's issues with her memory. Had he somehow stolen that too? He had no way of knowing his parents before he was born, because—other than in pictures where the two of them were always smiling—that was impossible. But he'd once heard a guest describe them together as being seamless as an eggshell. Two equal parts made whole the instant they met in Italy and later married upon reaching the States, with no seams or stitches to prove they'd ever existed apart. They'd been put on earth for one another.

"A puzzle of two, connected," one guest had said, "the two for whom love was invented."

"The original targets of Cupid's arrow," another had observed.

Seamless as an eggshell.

Until Vitto was born and a crack showed on the shell's pristine surface.

A wound in human form.

Twenty-Five

*J*uba eventually talked Robert away from the cliffs.

He'd been in his room ever since, and Juba had returned to his work around the hotel, although his eyes never ventured far from that door, in case it were to open and Robert wander toward the ocean again.

After what Robert had said—*"You stole it all"*—Vitto had fought the urge to do the same, to hole up inside his room, but when he returned to the piazza to find William talking to Cowboy Cane and the old man laughing, he'd stopped to spy. Around William's neck was his toy doctor's stethoscope. Cowboy Cane squatted low so that William could listen to the man's heart through his shirt. William focused, serious as he listened, and then he nodded some sort of approval. Cowboy Cane patted the boy's shoulder and moved on, as did William to his next patient, an elderly woman in a wheelchair who smiled as if she'd known little William for ages. *How much have I missed?* His son was apparently now the pretend hotel doctor, and his bedside nature seemed second to none.

Across the piazza, Vitto's easel loomed. He surveyed for his next subject, spotted the couple he'd seen walking hand in hand through the vineyard the other day, both of them laughing and lucid then, but now the wife appeared troubled and confused and the husband saddened. Like Robert and many others, she'd apparently stopped drinking the water. The longer Vitto watched, the more he could tell it had not been her choice. The husband wasn't letting her drink. The pain of losing her too real to take the chance. But every so often he glanced at the fountain as if tempted.

Torn.

With one drink he could have her back. *Was it that easy? Was it that hard?*

Vitto brought a handful of canvas frames from the basement and sat down near the fountain to paint. Colors mixed and blended and soon formed a landscape, the hotel's vineyard, the couple he'd seen holding hands taking form on the canvas just as he'd memorized the scene, like a snapshot, days ago. A dozen or more guests gathered to watch him work.

William continued to make his rounds. Valerie had begun playing her violin and several listened to her; the music especially soothing to those again stricken by memory loss. Their confusion detoured by the lovely notes, the fluidity of her movements, the bow effortlessly gliding across the strings.

Vitto put the finishing touches on his painting, stepped back to view it, and, after deciding it was exactly as he'd remembered, he carried it across the piazza toward the elderly couple he'd spied on earlier. He introduced himself to the distraught husband and shook his hand. His name was Phillip Rosenberg. His wife's name was Anne. Vitto showed Phillip the painting; the old man stared for the longest time before looking up, wet-eyed.

"Thank you, young man," said Phillip, eyeing his short, silver-haired wife watching the clouds, temporarily contained, temporarily focused on something, anything. "We've been married fifty-eight years." He stole glances at her as he spoke. "I keep telling myself. It's not the person who's changing, it's the illness. You try to put yourself in their shoes . . . You have to. You keep yourself busy to deal with the loneliness, but . . ."

Anne lowered her gaze from the sky to her husband. "Where am I?"

"The Tuscany Hotel, dear. Remember?"

"How long have we been here?"

He paused, gathered himself for a smile. "All of our lives, dear."

"Oh . . ." She looked around again, as if seeing it for the first time. "It's beautiful."

Phillip squeezed her hand lovingly and laughed. To Vitto, he said, "Humor is the universal language, is it not?"

Vitto nodded in agreement, and then Anne looked at him and pointed to her husband. "Who is this man holding my hand?"

"Your husband, Mrs. Rosenberg. Phillip."

She lowered her voice so only Vitto could hear. "He's handsome."

It was clear Phillip heard her anyway; he smiled and gave her hand another squeeze.

Vitto said, "I think you should marry him, Mrs. Rosenberg."

"Oh, call me Anne." She looked up at her husband. "And I just might."

Phillip took both her hands in his. "Will you marry me, Anne?"

She blushed, looked away. "Well, I don't know. We've only just met."

Phillip forced a smile; her words had stung him, but he tried hard not to show it. He looked into his wife's eyes. "What do you say? I predict we'll have six children. Twenty-three grandchildren. And six great-grandchildren."

"Oh my. We'll have to get busy then," she said.

Phillip laughed and teared up at the same time. He said to Vitto, "You try hard to make humor of the things that upset you, because what else can you do?"

"What else can you do?" Vitto repeated softly to himself.

"Show her the painting," said Phillip. "See if it registers."

Vitto held it in front of his chest while she stared at it, knowingly, he hoped. The silence was awkward, so he felt the need to explain. "You struggle to remember the past, Mrs. Rosenberg. So I painted it for you. In the present." He swallowed, suddenly nervous. "I'm painting the real." She seemed to be ignoring him, her eyes focused on the painting. Vitto felt foolish and said, "That's you and—"

She pointed at the canvas, glanced at her husband as if the memory had suddenly hit her. "That's me and you, dear. In the vineyard."

"Yes," said Phillip, excitedly. "Yes. That's me and you in the vineyard. Good. Good. Would you like to take a walk there now?"

She nodded, slowly, eyes alert for now. "Yes. I think I'd like that."

Vitto painted six other canvases throughout the day, recalling his memories of others from recent weeks and months and showing them to those who'd lost them, all with similar results to what had occurred with the Rosenbergs. By nightfall, two patients who'd stopped drinking the water had given in and gone to the fountain again. They had returned to the state they'd been in before, their memory restored, although they now showed a hint of trepidation and fear as they moved about.

Valerie was out on the piazza with a few stragglers after last call, playing her violin, possibly finding new purpose with her music, just as he had with his art. Vitto walked William to their room and tucked him into bed and pulled up the covers to his chin. Outside, the piano started up in accompaniment to Valerie's violin. Vitto assumed it was Mrs. Eaves, although he'd felt certain she'd retired to bed when the night's stories ended. Out the window he found Juba at the piano, playing as well as any concert pianist. Seeing the two of them play together again was a blessing in itself.

"Can you tell me another story?" William asked from the bed. "Like last night."

Vitto faced the bed, tried to recall what story he'd told, and then remembered after glimpsing the ceiling fresco. "What kind of story?"

William shrugged. "I dunno. Start from the beginning."

The beginning of what? Vitto sat on the side of the bed facing William's and chewed the inside of his mouth while he thought of something to tell. He spotted William's stethoscope on the bedside table. "You going to be a doctor when you grow up?"

"I already am."

Am what? thought Vitto. *Already a doctor or already grown up?*
The way he talked with the elderly guests, Vitto thought both could
be accurate. "You looked good out there today."

William shrugged, still waiting for his story. Vitto thought back
to the stories his mother used to tell him at night and decided to
start there. The thought of duplicating them for his own son made
his heart warm, especially now that he could see the reflections of
their lives in the stories more clearly. "How about we start with the
ancients?"

"The who?"

"The Greek gods and such."

"Are they funny?"

"Well, no, not really, although some of the stories are so fantasti-
cal that they could be a bit humorous."

"Okay. Are there giants?"

"Yes. And those one-eyed beasts called Cyclopes too."

William grinned and nodded for Vitto to go on, so he did. He
thought back to exactly how his mother had started, and all the weird
names came back in a flash. "There was a guy named Hesiod, who
wrote something called the *Theogony*."

"This is boring."

"It gets better. Now, Hesiod claims the first deity was—"

"What's a deity?"

"Like a god. As my mother and Hesiod tell it, the first deity was
named Chaos. And out of Chaos jumped Erebus."

"What's that?"

"The god of darkness. But that's not all. Out came Aether too. That's
the god of light. And Nyx—night . . . and Hemera—day. Tartarus, the
underworld. And Eros."

"Who's that?"

Here he paused. "The god of procreation."

"What's that mean?"

"Another night."

"So Eros is the god of another night?"

"No, forget him. For now. But these primordial gods typically depicted places. Like Gaia. She was the goddess of earth, or Mother Nature."

"What'd she look like?"

"She was beautiful."

"Like Mommy?"

"Yes. Just like Mommy."

William's eyelids grew heavy, and Vitto wondered if Magdalena had told the story better, but he plowed on regardless; he found the remembrance of it all somehow cathartic. "So in other words, Gaia was another daughter of Chaos. Along with Uranus, the god of the heavens, and Pontus, the god of the sea, and several others."

William yawned as if to say something good better happen fast.

"Well," said Vitto. "Uranus and Gaia—"

"Brother and sister?"

Vitto nodded. The kid was half-asleep but still sharp as a needle. "They gave birth to the Titans. The Titans ruled during the Golden Age."

William closed his eyes but said, "Keep talking." So Vitto did, reeling off names of Titans as he remembered them, and before he could exhaust his mental list, William snored softly.

Vitto whispered that he'd continue where they'd left off tomorrow. Tonight he'd only begun setting the stage. The various generations of gods would eventually go to war against each other, but that was a story for another day.

Vitto hovered at the bed for a beat, then bent to kiss William's forehead before leaving the room. As he reached the door, William said, "Good night, Dad."

Vitto's heart grew warm for the second time in ten minutes. "Good night, son."

Twenty-Six

T he next morning Vitto joined Valerie for a quick breakfast at one of the scattered piazza tables. Both of them found enjoyment in watching William make his rounds. He'd added a small leather bag to his doctor ensemble, and from it, after he'd briefly spoken with a "patient," he would pull out a pad to jot down notes. This reminded both Vitto and Valerie of Magdalena, but in a way that brought them smiles instead of sadness.

Mr. Rosenberg patted William's shoulder.

Vitto finished his bacon and wondered what had been said during that conversation, what little William had written down. John had fixed bacon and eggs and toast, all soft enough for the guests to chew without trouble. Cowboy Cane had suggested as much early on in his stay. "Personally," he'd said, "I could still chew through a rare steak with my eyes closed, but some of these people's teeth aren't even real." So John made sure all his food was easily chewable. Vitto wiped his mouth with a cloth napkin and dropped it on his empty plate.

Valerie sipped her hot coffee, reached across the table to give Vitto's hand a quick squeeze, and they shared a smile as William moved to his next patient. Those gestures said more than words could. He got up with a boost to his step, ready to paint the real, ready to help some of these old folks remember the present.

The Rosenbergs stood together, only a few paces from the fountain, and something about the way Anne held Phillip's arm told Vitto that she'd started drinking the water again. He watched some of the others, specifically some of the ones who'd stopped drinking in fear of the possible repercussions, and noticed that a handful of them also looked more together and aware than they'd been yesterday. Then he spotted Juba walking through the piazza with a tray of tiny cups and handing them out as he usually did. The daily doses of medicine. But today the doses looked smaller.

Vitto called Juba over. "What's going on?"

"An experiment," he said.

"What kind of experiment? These people are old, Juba, but they aren't mice."

"Nothing like that." Juba smiled and handed out another cup to an elderly woman who quickly downed it, smacked her pale lips like it was sweet nectar, and placed it back on his tray. "It was William's idea—so simple I can't believe we didn't think of it sooner." He handed another cup to a man who sipped on his way to a table of friends. "We were so distracted by the thought of what could be," said Juba, "that we overlooked the obvious."

"What are you talking about?"

"William, he comes to me this morning . . ." Juba stopped as William himself approached. "Here he is. William, you tell him."

"Tell him what?"

"What you told me this morning."

"About the eggs being good?"

"No, about the . . . chocolate bar."

Vitto knew why Juba had paused, probably realizing too late the significance of what those two words would mean to Vittorio. What the chocolate bar he'd given to that concentration camp victim had ultimately done. But William held no such qualms, or perhaps didn't realize how badly the memory still hurt.

"Oh," he said with a snap, as if just remembering what Juba was talking about. "You know how you gave that chocolate bar to that man at that place? In the war?"

"You heard all that?" He recalled someone walking William away that night so he wouldn't hear it.

William nodded. "You were talking real loud. Anyway, I wondered what would have happened if you didn't give him the entire chocolate bar? Maybe if you gave him just a pinch at first he wouldn't have died." Vitto stared, not because some revelation had just struck him, but because he'd thought the same thing for months. That was the burden he carried.

William bravely went on. "Mommy always tells me too much of anything isn't good, even too much of a good thing. That's why when she gives me candy, she only gives it to me in pieces."

"Smaller doses," Vitto whispered to himself.

"What's a dose?" William didn't wait long for an answer. "Anyway, I asked Juba what if we give 'em smaller pieces of the water to drink? Then they won't die as fast."

Vitto looked over at Valerie and covered his smile. Oblivious, William moved on to the next table.

Juba said, "So I cut back on the doses. I didn't pressure anyone, but some of the guests who'd stopped drinking decided to try it and see what happened. Maybe it won't last as long. Or maybe it won't work as well. Only time will tell." He focused on Vitto. "But if it doesn't work as well, I figured you could help fill whatever void ensues."

"How might I do that?"

"With those paintings. Capture everything you see here. Paint the memories for them, just in case they start forgetting. Then show them the paintings like you did for the Rosenbergs. It helped them, Vitto. And—" He broke off, attention diverted across the piazza. Vitto followed his gaze and saw Robert emerge from his room and step out onto the sunlit piazza, more alert and steady on his feet than he'd been when they followed him to the cliff. Robert shook hands with several of the guests, patted a few others on the back, and then made his way to his untouched sculpture, where he picked up his hammer and chisel and resumed his now signature pose in that chair, waiting for inspiration, for an idea.

Waiting for his muse.

Vitto caught Juba's eye. "I assume he's drinking the water again?"

"I'm afraid so. But to what end I can't say."

❈

"What does *castrate* mean?"

Vitto sat on the edge of the bed, stumped over how to explain the word and mentally kicking himself for letting it slip out during tonight's bedtime story. But the word had been crucial to the story, and if the boy was to become a doctor one day, a real doctor, it was a word he probably should know.

"When the Titans were in power," he had said, "Uranus ruled over all the universe. But he hated his children."

"Hated his children? Why?"

"He just did," he'd told William. "He even locked up some of them, like the Cyclopes and the Hecatonchires"—William had enjoyed learning about them—"in the depths of the earth, the place called Tartarus. That's Hades," Vitto had explained.

"Why'd he send them there?"

"I don't know, but probably because they were big and ugly and looked different. Gaia, their mother, didn't appreciate this too much, so she decided to take revenge on her tyrannical husband, Uranus. She created a giant sickle—that's like a huge knife—and told her children to castrate their father, then overthrow him."

That's what had prompted William's uncomfortable question, which Vitto decided to answer as simply as he could. "They cut off his manhood."

William nodded, serious looking, like he understood but really didn't, but that was good enough for Vitto. "Hyperion was a Titan, one of the sons of Uranus and Gaia. He married his sister Theia."

"His sister?"

"Yes."

"That's weird."

"You bet. But listen to this. They had three children, and their names were Helios, Selene, and Eos."

William chuckled.

"Funny names, I know, but they were gods too."

"Of what?"

"The sun, the moon, and the dawn." William's eyes grew large, and Vitto used the burst of interest as fuel. "Back to Hyperion. He was one of the four pillars holding the heavens and earth apart."

"Why?"

"So the sky wouldn't fall down and squash us flat."

"Like one of Johnny Two-Times's hotcakes?"

"Exactly," said Vitto, reminiscing back to when he was William's age and in bed and Magdalena was telling the same to him, except without all the questions. "Since Hyperion's daughter was goddess of the dawn, he was probably the pillar of the east. The other three pillars were Hyperion's brothers: Coeus in the north, Crius in the south, and Iapetus in the west. These were the four Titans who held their father Uranus in place while Cronus did what he did with that sickle. The blood of Uranus fell down and splattered on the earth, creating three more sets of children."

"How's that even possible?"

"I don't know, but it happened, according to this Hesiod guy."

"And Grandma."

"And Grandma. The blood created the Gigantes, or giants." William's eyes flashed with excitement. "They were mean and ugly. And the Furies, these three goddesses of vengeance, who would punish people for bad things they did. And then there were the Meliae. They were tree nymphs or something. But the blood of Uranus that fell upon the sea created Aphrodite. The goddess of love and beauty. Born of sea foam."

William blinked like he couldn't believe it and didn't want to. Vitto said, "Although Homer claims Aphrodite was the daughter of Zeus."

"Who's Homer?"

"Another ancient storyteller, like Hesiod."

"Okay. So who's Zeus?"

"Oh, I'll get to that."

"What happened to the guy who got it with the sickle?"

"Well, Cronus overthrew him, and *he* became the ruler of the universe instead of his father." Vitto held up a finger. "But not before Uranus made a prophecy." Vitto anticipated William's question: "That's sort of like a prediction. A telling of the future. His prophecy was that Cronus would also be overthrown by *his* sons. So, fearing the same fate, Cronus became a paranoid, tyrant god like his father. He put his brothers in Tartarus."

"In Hades."

"Very good. And so his own children wouldn't turn on him like the prophecy said, Cronus, he, uh . . . he . . ." Vitto bit his lip, contemplating how to explain this one.

"What did he do to them, Dad?"

"He ate them."

William's eyes popped. "Eat 'em in bites like a cookie? Or in one pop like an olive?"

"Probably in one pop. Remember, he was a god. He could do that. But he didn't manage to eat them all, which is where Zeus comes into the story . . . But that's enough for tonight."

At that point Valerie had come in, so he halted the story in fear of her disapproval of the content. "I'll tell you that story tomorrow night."

William was asleep ten minutes later, and Vitto was at the window watching his father watch that slab of marble on the piazza. He wanted to go down there and tell him that it wasn't going to carve itself, that he wasn't getting any younger, and if he was going to carve that last great masterpiece he'd better get started before the water finished him off.

"Vitto, come to bed."

She didn't have to ask him twice. He joined Valerie under the covers, and they shared thoughts on Juba and William's experiment during the day, both agreeing it could work if monitored correctly. They'd have to get paperwork drawn up, though, to avoid future lawsuits. If the water really was doing what Robert said it would, they needed written proof that the guests were well aware of what they were doing. Maybe that would help keep that reporter's nose out of their daily business.

The goal, they both agreed, was to give each guest the minimum amount of medicine possible to get them through the day. Juba apparently agreed, because they'd noticed him taking notes on the doses for each guest so they could track the results. It was already clear that several who'd taken the smaller dose in the morning had begun to lose some of their mental facilities by sundown, and many more became confused after last call. Keeping records would let them adjust the dosages accordingly and try to reach a balance between mental and physical decline.

"And then you fill in the gaps," said Valerie. "With your paintings."

Vitto nodded, thinking about Cowboy Cane and what had happened after dinner that night.

Cowboy Cane had not been enthused with the new lower dosage, pleading instead for his right to live his life how he pleased, to the utmost and, in his exact words, until he "keeled over and bellied up in the sun." He had finally agreed to participate in the experiment and took the smaller amount. But he was one of the ones who began to lose his train of thought and grow agitated as darkness fell.

As soon as Vitto noticed Cowboy Cane getting aggravated and confused, he'd called him over to his easel and had him sit for a portrait. And to the basic picture of Cowboy in the chair, Vitto had added some items the man had used in the past months—a tennis racquet leaning against the chair's arm, a basket of bocce balls on his lap, and a glass of wine in Cowboy's right hand to remind him of the nightly last call. He got the piazza and fountain in the background, with a few of the colorful doors and some of Cowboy's friends mingling. When he finished, he showed the painting to Cowboy, and the old man smiled. Vitto helped him carry that memory painting back with him to his room and set it up on the dresser while the old man crawled into bed. He was already snoring when Vitto turned off the lights. Come morning, hopefully, the wet canvas would be dry and the next dose of water would give him a restart. In the meantime, the painting had indeed helped.

"But I can't fill in the gaps all alone, Val," he said. "There's a reason you're here too."

"And what would that be?"

"Your music. You've noticed how your violin affects the guests. Tonight even, when a few of them started getting confused, your music calmed them down quick. And John's food, his smile, they need that too. Food often conjures good memories."

They lay silent for a minute, staring up at the waves of the ceiling fresco, and he could tell they'd come to the same thought simultaneously as their heads rolled toward one another on their pillows.

He said it out loud: "But Val, what if that fountain water starts to run out? What if at some point the water becomes just . . . water?"

"Then with your paintings and my music and John's food, at least we'll have somewhere to start."

Twenty-Seven

"H ey, wake up," someone said in a hushed whisper. "Vittorio."
Vitto opened his eyes, figured he'd been dreaming his
father's voice, only to find him hovering bedside, wearing a canvas
jacket and a soft hat. Vitto tried to sit up, hit his head on the headboard. Valerie remained asleep.

"What are you doing?" Vitto whispered. "It's the middle of the
night."

"Follow me." Robert sipped from his ceramic chalice as he stepped
out the door.

Vitto slipped his shoes on and followed his father outside into the
crisp night, where Robert waited next to a door that looked purple
under the moon glow but Vitto knew to be closer to blue in the day-
light. Robert stared at the door, sadly almost, as if trying to make it
something other than gray. His face was dotted with fresh stubble, his
skin looser around the neck and arms, where previously muscle had
pushed it taut.

"You were right earlier." He sipped water from the chalice, which
held far more than the doses Juba had given out the previous morning. "There was a time when I could see color." Robert moved slowly
out toward the piazza and Vitto followed, listening. "I was born color-
blind, but with a curse."

"What curse?"

Robert shuffled toward the fountain and grunted as he sat on the
edge. He patted the tiles beside him, inviting Vitto to join him. The
shadow of Cronus stretched across the travertine at their feet. "My
curse was that I knew what color was. I had a deep understanding of

it, like I'd not only seen it before, but had been able to touch it. To *be* it, Vitto, if that makes sense."

To Vitto it did.

"I would have dreams at night." Robert smiled, reminiscing. "Vivid dreams in color, of oil paintings and frescoes and mosaics. Dreams of the Renaissance, Vittorio. At night when I closed my eyes, I'd walk the streets with Michelangelo and Leonardo. Raphael and Botticelli. Titian and Masaccio. And not just artists, but places. I'd walk the streets of Milan and Florence. I'd see the beautiful Tuscan countryside, with green cypress trees and red poppies blowing in the fields. I was there, Vittorio. It was all somehow . . . inside of me."

"And then you would wake up."

"And then I would wake up," he said, his stark blue eyes now distant. "And see only black and white and shades of gray. It was like God was teasing me, showing me nightly what I couldn't have, couldn't be. But still, I was consumed with the art. Italian art. The Italian Renaissance. I read books. I saw pictures. I had my father take me to museums." He laughed, a quick burst. "All black and white and gray. I thought that maybe if I searched long and far enough, I'd find that painting I could see fully, and my color would be returned."

"Returned? But you were born without the ability."

"Seemingly, but then why did my mind see it at night? Somehow I knew those weren't dreams, Vitto. Those were memories."

"Of the Renaissance? That's not possible."

Robert held out his chalice of water. "Is *this* possible?"

"But . . . how could you have memories of a time when you could not have possibly lived?"

"Oh, that's where you're wrong. I think part of me did live out the Renaissance, Vittorio."

Vitto couldn't help laughing, but he stopped when he saw how serious his father's face was, how stoic and unmoving and statuesque he sat.

Robert took another sip and stared across the piazza toward the bar, the clock ticking on the wall behind it. "I was convinced of this even as a young boy. I know it's nonsensical, but that's how I made myself believe. Not only did I study the Renaissance, but also the ancients, the gods, until eventually I began to pretend I was one of them. A god who'd accidentally fallen from the sky, flawed now, his power stripped somehow.

"I tried painting, you know. My parents bought me brushes and paints, but it was hard to get excited about putting shades of gray on canvas. My father, before he struck oil, he owned a quarry. One day—I was eight or nine, I believe—I went with him to work, and I took my paints along. I was determined that that would be the day I'd squeeze the paint tubes and color would emerge. So I sat there and painted while Father and his men pulled stone and rock from the earth. But nothing changed. It was still just . . . nothing.

"I got upset and turned my little table over, scattering the paints. My father watched, as did his men, as I stormed across the quarry and picked up a small hammer. I went to the stone wall and chipped away at it, violently slamming that hammer into the stone with no purpose other than to let out my frustrations. At first Father tried to stop me, but then he just let me go, let me attack that wall wildly."

Robert sat silent for a moment.

"And?" Vitto prodded.

"Well, finally I backed away from what I'd done to the wall. And as I stepped back to look, I saw a face in the stone. Roughly carved, since I had only a hammer, but a clear face nevertheless. The workers were amazed, if not a bit frightened. But my dad was intrigued, and I—for the first time in my life I felt like I had connected to who I really was. Who I was meant to be. The next day Dad located a sculptor's hammer and chisel for me and then took me back to the quarry. He set aside a big chunk of granite for me, and I went to work. I created, Vittorio. Chiseled into a medium that I could see as it was—those stones of white and gray."

"So you were a sculptor after that."

Robert nodded. "I worked at my craft, studied, developed my skill. And for years I assumed that was what I was meant to be—not only a sculptor, Vitto, but a god. A god fallen, just as you titled that painting, and trying to create something so brilliant that the heavens would call me back up. To be immortal."

"So that is why you've always been so consumed with your work? Dad, you're trying to create something that cannot be created. Trying to get somewhere that doesn't exist."

Robert took a heavy gulp of water. "I know that now. I don't have long, Vittorio."

"Then stop accelerating the process." Vitto took the chalice from his father's hands and poured what remained into the fountain. "Now tell me, when did you first see color?"

"Orange was the first color I had ever seen." Robert smiled. "It was your mother's hair. Brilliant and bold, vivid like the color I'd see in my dreams. My memories."

"But *how* did you see it? This makes no sense."

"Because you're too grounded by things you can hold and feel, Vittorio. You always have been."

"I'm grounded by reality."

"What reality?"

Vitto started to respond but didn't, suddenly couldn't, as his own reality swarmed him with memories of color, his ability at such a young age to take pictures in his mind and paint them perfectly, life and art recreated in pigment. His ability to remember numbers and lists and names and statistics. His inability to escape the war memories because they'd been so vividly engraved. *What reality?*

Robert patted Vitto's leg. "My entire childhood, and into my teenage years, I'd always felt something missing. Something beyond my inability to see color and that sense that I was part of something bigger and higher. I had friends growing up, but while they wanted to hunt and fish and throw rocks into the river, all I wanted to do was carve. To create. When they got to the age where girls stole their attention, I waved them on. I'd seen enough girls about town and in the schoolhouse to be aware of their beauty and attraction, but even as many sought my attention, none of them could lure me from my work. For there was only one girl for me, Vittorio. I began to see her in my dreams. In my—"

Don't say it.

"In my memories." He said it anyway. "The orange hair and those olive-green eyes. The most beautiful woman on earth. I didn't know her yet, but somehow I knew her. I attempted to carve the way I saw her in my mind but found it impossible.

"By the time I was sixteen, with too many statues under my belt to count, I was ready to set out on my own. Fortunately, my father understood and granted me this freedom. As my memories of my dream girl intensified, I set out to Europe. To Italy. Started in the south. Sicily. Up the coast to Pompeii and Naples. To Rome. Siena. Then to Florence, where I stayed for months—carving, soaking up the sun and atmosphere, walking streets and passing buildings I felt sure I'd visited before.

"And then one day I heard some men talking, some artists chinning about a beautiful woman they'd seen on the streets. A woman with long, flame-colored hair, so beautiful and striking she was forced to hide it beneath a hood. Artists, when they saw her, felt the urge to paint her. A real muse, the whispers said. Pienza, they said. The daughter of an artist named Francesco Lippi, they said. So I gathered my tools and luggage, and off I went to Pienza."

"And there you first met her?"

"*Found* her, Vittorio. *Found* is the word used for things that have been lost. Separated and then reunited. I've no other way to explain it."

"Seamless as an eggshell," Vitto said. "I once heard a guest refer to you and Mamma that way."

"That's not inaccurate." He pondered it. "I saw her on the piazza one day, following behind that man Lippi. A strand of her hair had fallen loose beneath the hood, and I saw it. I saw the color, Vittorio. A flash of orange in a world of gray, and then it was gone. We made eye contact, stared for a few seconds—an eternity. She'd seen me before, she'd later tell me, but had forgotten.

"You, see, Vittorio, we were both born with something missing. I was stripped of my ability to see color, and she was stripped of her memory. Well, she had memories, but they were not her own. Somehow she could recall things from before she was born—little flashes of memory about the greats—from Raphael to Shakespeare to Mozart. Music. Art. The written word. Memories somehow from the past, from history. But she couldn't remember her own life from day to day, from hour to hour even."

"The journal?"

"Yes. It was her salvation, the only way she could piece together a life for herself. She'd write details to remind herself and read it the next morning, and that's how she was able to sneak out to meet me. Vittorio, do you know how difficult it is to be in love with someone who doesn't remember you from meeting to meeting, who every day when she first sets eyes upon you, it's as if she's seeing you for the first time?"

It wasn't a question meant to be answered, so Vitto didn't. His father had never told him of how he and Magdalena had met. Robert had rarely told *any* stories of his past—and Vitto didn't want the flow to stop. But he sensed where this was going—his mother had been able to remember things at some point, just as Robert at one time could see color. Magdalena had been cursed at birth with some kind of memory loss, and Robert had been her magical water, just as she had somehow been the key to him seeing color.

"We fell in love as if we'd invented it," said Robert. "And she was my muse. Not just my muse, but *the* muse—like all nine of the Greek

Muses molded into one. We had to be together. So we plotted to escape Lippi. Your mother was basically a captive in his house, and he abused her. Thought he could get away with what he did because he knew she wouldn't remember the next day. But she wrote it all in her journal—a secret journal Lippi didn't know about—and she showed me. I threatened to kill him, but she begged me not to. She managed to escape, and we fled."

"But the reporter, he spoke of the house being burned down. And the man Lippi dying?"

"Another night, Vittorio. I can't explain what I never fully understood myself. What I didn't witness." Robert's eyes grew wet. "And your mother, she . . . she never spoke of it, although I fear it haunted her until her final days—at least once she was able to remember."

"How does Juba enter into this?"

"Because of whatever happened inside that house, it seemed the entire town was after us. Lippi had thugs in his employ, unscrupulous men, and they were especially determined to find us. I'd devised a plan of escape but found my route to the Arno blocked, so we hurried back into the city, and there he was. Juba. Like he'd been watching out for us and waiting. He had an alternative plan of escape for us already mapped out—first by carriage and then by river to Rome and on to the western coast, where we boated out to the open sea."

Robert paused, eyes glistening. "I'll never forget that voyage. The sun dappled over the water. Endless water. The three of us floating on the waves. I was watching her, your mother, and in the shimmer I saw her hair—the beautiful flame of her hair. A few strands at first, like I'd seen on the piazza, and then all of it came into my view as if painted by an unseen brush. And she looked at me without seeking her journal, Vittorio. She called me by name, remembering me. Juba was there, just relaxed against the side of the boat with his arms stretched out on either side, smiling as he watched us."

"And from then on you were able to see color?"

"Not right away," he said. "At first it was just her hair, then part of her dress. And then, after we came here, to the spot where we would build the hotel, I saw the green of her eyes. Soon colors began to pop from flowers, from grass, from clothing. Sunsets and sunrises. Ocean waves. Works of art. And as my ability to see color settled and became reliable, so did Maggie's memory, until eventually she no longer needed her diary to remember simple daily things. Oh Vitto, those were heady days. We built this place together, the three of us, out of a single vision. I'd stolen her from Tuscany, so I wanted nothing more than to bring Tuscany back to her. And we always had a sense that somehow we might be able to recreate the Renaissance—or at least bring a taste of it to this little plot of land."

Vitto had so many questions. *How did they come to arrive in California—in this specific part of California? Does Dad know more about the fountain and the water than he's letting on?* But the story was still so far from his reality that he didn't know where to start, and he wanted his father to keep talking.

"The walls came up, and rooms soon filled. Word got out that this was a good place to create, and people came in droves—artists, musicians, actors, and scientists. And as for me and my work—Vitto, it was my golden age. Every month I was turning out new pieces— beautiful pieces—that I refused to sell because I wanted them around me. I always said that the hotel was my museum.

"And now that there wasn't a color I couldn't see, I was determined to fill the hotel with it. I painted the doors one by one, each one slightly different than the next, until I one day stood next to the fountain, turned full circle, and realized I'd created the entire color wheel. That's when we started referring to the rooms by the color of the doors instead of the room numbers. Later, we'd also name the rooms after the art-work inside them—the copies of Renaissance masterpieces that I hired people to do—until you came along to do them.

"This hotel—the way it was—was once the envy of every hotel

built before it and the goal of all that came after. But that was a fool's dream, because this"—he gestured to the rooms and stones and sculptures all around the piazza—"cannot be duplicated. It was my Maggie that made this place tick. She was the one who inspired all of this artwork and inspired me to turn my Renaissance dreams into reality. I soon realized she was not only my muse, Vittorio, but everyone's muse. Painters came to put color on these walls and ceilings, but none . . ."

"None of them what?"

"None of them could do what you could do. Not with the precision and detail and innate understanding of color that you were born with."

"You encouraged me to paint replicas because you'd once seen them in true color."

Robert nodded.

"But you were married for years and years before I was born. Decades. Why did you wait so long?"

Robert let out a chuckle that then settled as a deep, heavy sigh, and looked at Vitto with sad eyes filled with guilt. "You want the truth, Vitto?"

Vitto nodded.

"I never wanted a child."

Vitto waited for more of an explanation to help soften that blow, because the words had punched him hard. Had Magdalena fought Robert about that? Had she wanted a baby and he'd finally given in? Had they been trying for that long only to finally, miraculously, conceive? Was he an accident, unwanted by the both of them?

"We were truly happy, Vitto. I was a god here—at least I felt like one. My dreams were being realized every day. And . . . the idea of a child felt like a threat. That sounds selfish, I know, but you have to understand what things were like back then. The tenuous nature of what your mother and I believed we'd been given—and not just given, but given *back*. Like we'd been given so much, and it could be taken back in a minute. And then there were all those stories your mother used to tell you at bedtime—those outlandish stories about sons overthrowing fathers, castrating them with sickles, the fathers eating their children."

"You feared the son."

"Yes. As foolish as it seems now, yes. But it wasn't that I merely feared the son, Vittorio. I feared altering the life we had. What we thought was perfection."

"Your return to the Renaissance."

He smiled. "Our rebirth."

"So what happened?"

"Well, we never stopped trying, even after your mother reached the age we assumed a child was unlikely."

"I assumed as much."

"Your mother was convinced that her purpose was to bring a child into this world. She prayed for a miracle, and I suppose you were that for her. It made the headlines, you know—everyone was astonished that a woman her age could bear a child. Although she didn't *look* her age or act it. She was still vigorous and beautiful—not a hint of gray in that glorious hair. Maybe those years without memory protected her somehow, slowed her aging. Or"—he shrugged—"maybe it really was one of those miracles Father Embry likes to talk about."

"But my birth changed things for you, right?" Vitto didn't really want to hear it, but somehow he needed to. "I was the crack in that seamless shell, wasn't I?"

Robert's nod was slow, reluctant. "It didn't happen right away, but over time it did. At first we held you with nothing but love and joy. How could we not? You were beautiful in every way. But you're right—your birth changed things. Changed *us*.

"Within months, colors became blurry to me. By the time you were walking, they were fading, as was your mother's memory. She took to carrying her journal around with her again, jotting down things she feared she'd forget. Now that she had a child to take care of, she worried she'd forget to feed you, to do the daily things of comfort any right-minded parent should do. And as for me, by the time you showed me your first painting, I saw only grays and whites again. And I was bitter about that—I admit it. When everyone else looked upon your walls and ceilings and canvas frames with amazement and joy and disbelief, I saw only what I *couldn't* see. What I'd had for a time but lost.

"So I turned back to my work, except not with the joy I'd had during my golden age but with a newfound drive to create something so great that the gift of color would be returned to me, along with your mother's memory. Some kind of offering—or maybe a bribe—to the gods who had wronged us."

He sighed. "It wasn't a conscious thing, of course. At the time, I just felt compelled to work. But I can see it so clearly now, looking back. I spent *your* entire life trying to create that next sculpture, that next masterpiece, until I was consumed by it and suddenly you were off to war."

The words were on the tip of Vitto's tongue, but he couldn't say them, not with the ball of nausea wanting to emerge with them. *I'm sorry.* But it wasn't his fault. He knew that. He'd somehow stolen his gifts from both mother and father; but he'd had no control over what was happening.

Robert braced his arms on the edge of the fountain; they trembled as he pushed himself up to standing. He laid a large, bony hand on Vitto's shoulder. "Don't ever apologize, Vittorio. Don't ever. I've come to realize things now."

"What could you possibly realize from this?"

"That I wasn't wronged by anyone or anything. I was righted, Vittorio; my ship in the water—it was made right. And now I'm thinking that perhaps your mother and I were given those gifts for a short time so we could pass them on to you, perfected. My only regret is that I didn't see that earlier. And for that I'm sorry."

"No, I should—"

"I told you." His voice grew stern. "Don't ever. Parents sacrifice for children. You've been given gifts. Use them." He straightened slowly, and his shadow mingled with the shadow of Cronus. "Do you remember when I'd take you to the creek when you were a boy, and we'd float Mr. Carney's wooden ships?"

"Yes."

"You once asked why boats float."

"I remember. You said it was because they had to in order to get from here to there."

"But then I explained."

"An object will float if it weighs less than the water it displaces."

Robert smiled. "Our friend John is on to something. A barrel of sunshine or a barrel of stones, right? Be the sunlight, Vitto. Move in the water, but try to stay on top of it. Even the tiniest of stones can sink. The most massive of boats can float." His smile simultaneously showed both life and a welcomed death. He turned, walked slowly away.

"Where are you going?"

"Back to bed, Vittorio, as should you."

Vitto watched him walk across the piazza, and just as he'd nearly disappeared into the shadows, he called out, "Dad."

Robert turned. "Yes."

"Good night."

"Good night, son."

Twenty-Eight

The next morning Vitto rustled William awake, and, while Valerie slept, walked his son out into the sunlight. They found a table and shared pieces of sweet bread and glasses of milk.

William wiped his mouth free of crumbs and asked, "What're we gonna do next?"

Smiling at the eagerness in the boy's voice, Vitto leaned in close. "Do you know why boats float?"

His son thought on it. "Because they'd sink if they didn't?"

"Correct." It wasn't the answer he was thinking about, but it made as much sense as any, and he didn't feel the need to go any deeper. That wasn't the point of his morning plan, the idea that had come to him during the night and kept him up until the sun rose. He'd begun to share stories with his son, but other than working together in the olive groves and vineyards, they'd yet to *do* anything that fathers and sons should. "Have I shown you all of Mr. Carney's boats?"

William shook his head no.

"Then I haven't been doing my job." Vitto took William's hand, both of them under the curious gaze of Robert, who had taken his usual spot across the piazza, and led him up the spiral steps to the second floor, where all of Mr. Carney's wooden ships awaited. Vitto, when he was holed up in that room, had taken the time to clean them all, so they now gleamed dust free—ancient ships of Greece and Rome and Vikings and pirates. Ships of exploration and ships of battle. After thirty minutes of perusing the shelves and tables, William selected the ancient Greek trireme, while Vitto grabbed the smaller Korean turtle ship, a boat he claimed had beat Valerie's boat choices on many occasions when they were younger. They hurried with their boats back down the stairs, out the front of the hotel, and through the fields until they reached the creek and the one-lane bridge.

Vitto was a little worried when they first got there. Every boat he'd ever sailed had meandered toward the monastery, so now that the creek had changed course, this outing would be uncharted waters for them both. They knelt in the grass and let loose their boats, and immediately the water swept them away. They gave chase, each cheering on his respective ship. After ten minutes of following the creek bed as it twisted and turned, they grew tired, and for the first time Vitto wondered how far the creek ran. They ducked under branches, stepped over brambles, walked through side streams, slipped in the mud and wet grass, laughing as they continued onward in pursuit of the fleeing ships that rocked, eddied, and nearly capsized on two different occasions before breaking free yet again.

After thirty minutes the boats had sped out of their sight, but they followed the water until, an hour and a half later, they found both boats stuck in a small alcove and jetty that William swore looked like a palm of a hand, a tiny lake of calm as the rest of the creek sluiced by, both of their ships nosing the mud as if expertly docked.

Their boats were not alone, as William was eager to point out. The ship Vitto had sailed upon their arrival months ago rested there, now muddied and torn by the weather, overturned against a muddy rock. Next to it lay the carnage of what could have been wood from boats of decades past. At least that's how they described it to Valerie and Robert when they returned near sundown, muddy and sweaty and grass-stained. Valerie, who'd had no idea where they were and was beginning to worry—her "let kids run free at the hotel" attitude apparently had its limits—opened her mouth to scold them both until she saw the childlike smiles on both their faces. Then she relented with a smile of her own and a laugh-charged demand that they both go inside and clean up before nightfall.

Which they did.

And that night, at William's urging, Vitto continued his story.

"For the sake of the story, if it helps you to picture it, think of Cronus popping his children into his mouth like olives."

"All at once?" asked William.

"No, but as soon as each new child was born, he'd pop them into his mouth to get rid of them. Remember his father's prophecy—that he was destined to be overthrown by his own child."

"He chewed them up?"

"Yes. No. I don't know for sure. But you'll find out in a minute why I think he probably swallowed them whole."

"What were their names?"

"Let's see, there was Demeter, Hestia, Hera, Hades, Poseidon."

"I've heard of him."

"And Zeus."

"I've heard of him too."

"But Cronus didn't eat Zeus."

"Why not? Was he too big for his mouth?"

"No, Cronus's wife Rhea tricked him."

"What was she the goddess of?"

"Fertility."

"What's that?"

"Having babies and stuff. So she was getting sick and tired of her husband eating all of their children right after they were born. So when Zeus was born, she swaddled up a rock instead."

"Rocks don't look much like babies."

"No, they do not. But Cronus fell for it anyway. He swallowed down this rock, thinking he'd just eaten Zeus. That's why I think he ate all his children whole."

"'Cause he would've cracked his teeth on the rock."

"Probably. And so Rhea hid Zeus in a cave on the island of Crete, where he was raised by a goat named Amalthea."

"I don't believe that."

"You believe he ate his kids whole, but you don't believe in goats?"

"Not talking goats."

"Who said it could talk?"

"Figured it would have to if it raised Zeus."

"Well, you're right. Amalthea was a kind of goddess-goat. But she must have done a good job, because Zeus grew up without being found and eaten, and later he even became his father's cup-bearer, and Cronus never even knew it was him. But Zeus knew his father had eaten his brothers and sisters and tried to eat him, and he wanted revenge. There was another Titan goddess named Metis who decided to help Zeus. She gave him a mixture of mustard and wine to put in Cronus's cup."

"Ick."

"I agree. But Cronus drank it. And you know what happened?"

"What happened?"

"Cronus vomited up the children he'd swallowed one by one, setting them all free."

"And they were still alive?"

"They're gods. They can do just about anything."

"Like Grandpa Robert?"

"Sure. Like Grandpa Robert."

"What's wrong, Dad?"

"Nothing. I'm fine."

"So what did Zeus do next?"

"He gathered up all his brothers and sisters and convinced them to start a rebellion against their father, Cronus. This is what started the Titanomachy."

"The what?"

"The great war between the Olympians and the Titans." He ruffled his son's hair. "But we'll save that for another night. Ticktock goes the clock, William."

Twenty-Nine

*R*obert knelt in the grass, held out a hand to keep Magdalena from coming too close.

Odd, how the stones were configured, most of them half-submerged in the mud and scattered haphazardly. Possibly fallen from the sky, as the locals insisted. Certainly not carefully placed. But they were smooth, as if they'd once been part of something now broken.

Wind whipped across the cliff, the outcropping of land overlooking the ocean he'd seen in his dreams. Down below, hammering echoed. A monastery was being built for a cloistered gathering of monks.

Robert ran his hand over one of the stones, wet from the water eerily bubbling up from the surface, the real reason he held Magdalena at bay. He sensed pressure beneath and feared it could erupt suddenly, like a geyser.

Footsteps stole Robert's attention. Juba approached from the east, having gone exploring close to an hour ago.

"There's a creek over the hill, with water that flows to a lake next to that place they're building down that way. A small bridge could easily be constructed over it."

Robert nodded, smelled the air. He'd seen the creek in his dreams too. "This is the place."

"What place?" asked Magdalena, hugging her arms against the cool wind, her eyes on the water coming up from the ground.

"I will build my hotel right here, Maggie. I will bring Tuscany back to you and the Renaissance back to the world."

"What is this place called? It's like the edge of the world."

"California," said Juba, turning slowly to take in fully the rolling hills and vast ocean.

"I'll name it the Tuscany Hotel." Robert wondered if Juba was imagining the building as he now was. The sculptures he would create. The guests who would come.

He focused again on the stones, like perfect teeth half-buried in gums of mud and grass. The bubbling water. He put his fingers in it, brought it to his lips. A memory flashed—of his adopted father, Cotton Gandy, cradling him in his arms seconds after he'd rescued him as an infant from the banks of the river.

Magdalena's orange hair rippled with the wind. Her face to him was still the color of stone, but her eyes now showed olive green. The top of her right hand had begun to show a smooth tan, and her dress held hints of blue along with the yellow he'd seen on the ship.

He dug out one of the stones, wiped the dirt and mud from it, and showed it to Magdalena and Juba. "We'll use these to build a fountain. And around it a piazza . . ."

Thirty

*M*arch rolled in with a wave of late-spring heat, and by the ides, early blooms of gold and scarlet had emerged in the poppy field. The olive trees he had trimmed and tended on the terrace were already showing buds, and in the vineyards, the dried-out vines he'd pruned and watered showed signs of leafing out. Vitto had no idea how long it would take to regain the quality of oil and wine the hotel had once produced, but he was determined to get there again.

In the weeks since he and Robert had sat talking by the fountain in the middle of the night, Robert had aged visibly; his hair thinner, veins and bones starkly visible beneath the pale skin on his arms, and his eyes retreating into deep sockets. While most others in the hotel—even Cowboy Cane—had smoothly transitioned into taking the lighter doses of water, falling into the pattern of lucidity and awareness during the morning and gradually becoming more confused in the evening, Robert had resisted all efforts to slow him down and continued to drink the water at will.

"I don't wish to spend even one more moment alone, Vitto," he insisted.

"You're not alone."

"When the disease takes you, you're never more alone."

He spent his days outside in the sunshine, not carving—he barely even stopped to look at the untouched slab of marble anymore—but shuffling slow and methodically around the piazza, smiling and mingling, telling stories of the hotel's golden age to any guest who would listen. Often they'd find him gazing at various parts of the hotel grounds as if proudly overlooking his vast kingdom.

"It's the hotel's rebirth, Vittorio," he said more than once.

Vitto couldn't deny it. In an ironic twist, the hotel full of dying people had come alive again—alive with laughter and camaraderie, guests and hosts united by the unmentioned bond of battling the same deep, dark monster that was age and memory loss and the end of full lives lived.

The days had fallen into an easy rhythm. John and his helpers served meals across the piazza. William played at being everyone's doctor, visiting every guest daily with his stethoscope and leather bag—he also carried the grenade in there, but had promised not to throw it while on his rounds. Valerie played her violin when she wasn't helping John. Mrs. Eaves was often at the piano, while Juba occasionally took breaks from whatever hotel chore he was doing to sing or to play as well. But Juba never lost track of Robert's whereabouts, and Vitto noticed that he often looked to the wall clock behind the bar, as if waiting for something only he and Robert knew about.

And Vitto painted.

He strolled the hotel grounds daily, spying various scenes of everyday life, and then painted them for the guests, capturing memories they could have in their rooms at night when they grew confused. He painted portraits of singles and couples, of widows and widowers, of husband-and-wife pairs with decades of marriage behind them as well as a few couples who'd only recently become an item and were beaming from the newness of it all.

Most guests now carried a leather journal with them to record whatever they did during the day, and they'd made it a habit to read through their notes at night and again in the morning. Vitto had gotten the idea of giving out the journals on the morning after his fountainside talk with his father, about how Magdalena, after he was born, had been forced to again use a journal to help get her through the day. And Robert reminded him of the little notebooks that used to be inside the bed stands of every room. It had become tradition for every guest at the hotel, at the end of their stay, to write down stories and memories from their time at the hotel. One of the first things a newly arrived guest had done was to read the accounts left by the previous residents of the room—the food they'd eaten, the celebrities and artists and musicians they'd met, and especially the interesting stories they had heard at last call.

"This hotel is full of memories, Vittorio. Memory seeps from every wall, every stone, like fuel. Memories from decades of guests."

So full of memories that it spilled into the water? Vitto hadn't spoken the idea, although it seemed as plausible a theory as any. But the next day he'd contacted a local shop, purchased every journal they owned, and then had the shop order enough for each guest at the hotel to have one. And now, whenever he looked about the piazza, he saw dozens with journal in hand, scribbling down their thoughts. The results were noticeable. They remembered a little more, felt a lot more content and less lost.

Several doctors had come to visit—real doctors, William called them—to observe the goings on, the morning behavior as it transitioned to day and finally night, taking notes of their own as the water's effect ran its course throughout the day. They interviewed some of the guests and even invited a few to their offices for more detailed analysis. So far, all had declined. No one wanted to leave the hotel grounds.

One doctor asked if he could visit regularly, and Vitto told him that the guests—he was careful not to call them patients, as the doctor had—could have any visitor they desired. But then Valerie jumped in and warned that a doctor's appearance implied sickness and that no one here wanted to be reminded of it.

"This is not a hospital," she told him.

"Then what exactly is it, Mrs. Gandy?"

"It's a retreat," she'd said and then added, "from life." And then: "A place that promotes living over dying."

Vitto held up his hand to stop her—though he agreed with what she was saying. Valerie had grown more passionate by the day about what they were doing and had become sensitive to those who questioned it or hinted that they were about to—which the doctor then did.

He leaned in to whisper: "That reporter Landry Tuffant claims the water is killing them."

"And Landry Tuffant scours the grounds like a vulture, daily, as if waiting for just that." Valerie stepped toe-to-toe with the doctor. "Do you see any of them dead?"

Vitto hoped at that point that Robert wouldn't shuffle by. In the wrong light he looked *nearly* dead. The same was true of Mrs. Eaves, who had been ninety when she arrived months ago and now looked closer to the century mark.

The doctor said, "I can't say as I do."

"Are they not happy?" Valerie asked.

"Seemingly."

"And if one of them were to suddenly die, Doctor?"

"Well, then . . . I don't know . . ."

"Old people die," she added, turning on her heel and leaving the doctor standing with his mouth open but no words coming out.

"I fear I've unintentionally made an enemy," said the doctor to Vitto, who patted him on the shoulder and took him on a tour of the grounds, showing him the tennis and bocce courts and the croquet lawn, all full, and the pools lined with elderly guests lounging in the sun and drinking sweet colored beverages on ice brought to them on trays by the crew of young people Vitto had hired from nearby towns to help with daily operations.

The doctor visited daily after that, but not to take notes or observe or study. When Vitto asked why, he admitted, "I don't know exactly. But this place makes me smile."

He was there with Vitto when Johnny Two-Times, carrying a tray of dirty breakfast plates and utensils across the piazza to the kitchen, suddenly stopped, his ears alerted to the sound of a distant car rumbling over the bridge and onto the hotel property. The tray of dishes began shaking, unbalanced now in his extended hand, as if he'd been struck by his own personal earthquake. The doctor and nearby Cowboy Cane took the tray and rested it on one of the piazza's wrought-iron tables, while John moved catatonically toward the sound of the approaching car.

A car door closed outside the hotel entrance, and then another, and by the time Vitto reached the three Roman arches, the two new guests were coming through with suitcases in hand.

"New arrivals?" the doctor asked Vitto.

"Not new," he said, realizing who had returned, finally, after leaving in such haste weeks before. "Just old friends coming home."

The doctor's eyes grew large. "Did that old woman just give me the finger?"

"Were you staring?"

"Yes."

"Then probably."

John stood frozen, his feet nailed to the travertine, as Beverly Spencer and her grandmother approached the center fountain. Beverly looked defeated, much as she had the day she first arrived, and grandmother Louise had that same look of agitation and confusion.

Granddaughter led grandmother to the fountain, dipped a small cup into the water, and aided her as she swallowed. Louise then sat down on the edge of the fountain as if a great burden had been lifted from her shoulders, as if she had finally returned home after being whisked away against her will. But who could blame the granddaughter for taking her away? Regardless of the reasons, here they were, returned, and John still stood there like a brainless statue as Beverly looked his way.

Vitto nudged John. "Go to her. John, go. Remember, barrel of sunshine."

John took one slow step, then another, and muttered, "Barrel of sunshine, Gandy." Slowly he moved toward the fountain, where Beverly stood wiping her eyes and smiling.

"Well?" she said.

"Well what?"

"Are you going to stand there like a lamppost, or are you going to ask me? Again."

"Last time I asked you, you smacked me."

Vitto hissed, "Ask her."

He looked over his shoulder, hissed back, "All right, Gandy." And then he did it. He got down on one knee, paused for a moment, and then lowered the other knee, which got a blushed chuckle from Beverly and a headshake from Vitto, then spurred a few of the watching guests to get out their journals and write that scene down.

"Beverly, will you be my wife?"

"Of course I will."

John got to his feet and hugged her so tight and high that *her* feet lifted from the stones. When he finally put her back down, he said, "We should set a date."

"Sooner rather than later," said Louise, sipping more water at the fountain. "Her grandmother isn't getting any younger."

Thirty-One

*B*everly and John's wedding took place the following week, with chairs set out in rows across the piazza and the vows spoken just as the setting sun painted the sky with broad strokes of red and orange and turned the stone walls to gold.

"Now don't cry up there, John," Vitto had told him while he helped fasten the bow tie around John's thick neck before the ceremony.

"I'll try not to, Gandy, but you know I'm an emotional person. And I thought this day would never come."

"With Beverly?"

"With anyone."

"Barrel of sunshine, John."

"Barrel of sunshine, Gandy."

Vitto patted John's arm and sent him on his way, and at the beginning of the wedding ceremony he thought his friend might make it through without crying. Then John saw his bride for the first time and started gushing like his own internal faucet had been turned on. Cowboy Cane had to walk up to the makeshift altar where Father Embry presided and give John his handkerchief. John blew his nose into it like a foghorn and handed it back. Cowboy Cane told him to keep it and returned to his seat in the middle of a cluster of widows.

John made it through the ceremony, although he had to pull out the handkerchief two more times during the vows. Valerie had slinked her arm through Vitto's and squeezed his hand by that point, and with her lips an inch from his ear, she whispered, "Women appreciate a man who's not afraid to show his emotions."

He whispered back, "She must appreciate him something terrible then."

She rested her head on his shoulder. "I'm just saying, tears aren't always a sign of weakness."

"You saying I should cry more?"

"I'm saying that you should just allow yourself to feel what you feel."

He looked down at the top of her head. "Meet me in the loft of the olive mill later?"

He could feel her smile against his arm. "I'll consider."

They celebrated well after sundown with music and stories on the piazza. Those who could dance did so, while others watched from tables and chairs as their minds began to grow fuzzy. John won last call with a story of bravery from the war—how he'd run across a bullet-riddled field to rescue a fallen comrade. The seriousness with which he told it made everyone believe it. Or maybe they figured he was making it up—that it was probably something he *wished* he'd done—and let him win because it was his wedding day. Either way, after last call, Beverly took him by the arm and led him back to their room, saying to him in a voice everyone else could hear that not all heroes are heroic.

Valerie smiled as she watched the newlyweds go. She yawned and then called William to come get ready for bed. Together she and Vitto walked their son inside, and while Vitto monitored William's tooth brushing, Valerie fell asleep facedown atop the covers of their bed. Vitto slipped her shoes off and covered her up with an extra blanket.

By the time he turned to William, the boy was already under his bedcovers, waiting for the story of the gods to continue. So Vitto pulled up a chair and picked up where he left off last time—with Zeus tricking his father, Cronus, into drinking that concoction that made him vomit up the rest of his brothers and sisters.

"This began the Titanomachy," he explained. "The war between the Titans and the Olympians, who were led by Zeus. The old generation of Greek gods on Mount Othrys against the new Olympian gods, led by Zeus and based on Mount Olympus. Remember the Hecatonchires and the Cyclopes that Uranus had sent to Tartarus?"

William nodded and yawned, too tired to ask many questions.

"Well, Zeus released them all and asked for their help against their brother, Cronus. The Hecatonchires hurled massive rocks against the Titans. The Cyclopes created the famous thunderbolts that Zeus used as weapons. The war lasted ten years, and in the end the Titans were defeated by the Olympians. All the Titans except Epimetheus and Prometheus, the only two who fought alongside Zeus, were jailed in Tartarus, and the Hecatonchires guarded them."

Vitto stopped because William's eyes were closed, but when he started to get up, William said, "Then what happened?"

"Zeus and his brothers, Poseidon and Hades, drew lots, like straws, to see how to divide the new universe. Zeus won and became god of the sky and the ruler of mortals and gods. Poseidon became the ruler of the seas. You hear the waves out there?" Vitto gestured toward the western side of the hotel, where the sound of waves beating against rocks could barely be heard.

William yawned again. "I hear those all the time."

"Well, Poseidon was put in charge of them. And Hades drew the shortest straw and had to go down and rule the underworld. The dawn of a new era in Greek mythology was born."

William snored, so he left it at that.

Vitto kissed his forehead, turned out all the lights, and watched the piazza from the window. The guests had all retreated to their rooms for the night, but the bar area was still lit while Juba cleaned the counters. Vitto quietly left his room and sat at the bar. Juba offered him a glass of wine, and Vitto didn't decline. They spoke casually of the wedding and shared a few laughs on John's behalf. Juba cleaned glasses as they chinned about times both present and past, and as the evening grew to night they finished a bottle of the hotel's red wine together.

"Why did you never tell me my father couldn't see color?"

"Because he asked me not to." Juba glanced into the shadows of the loggia.

Is he looking toward Robert's room? "You're so loyal to him that you allowed me to be kept in the dark all these years?"

Juba glanced at the wall clock behind the bar, the clock around which the shelves holding all the glasses had seemingly been built. "I don't think you were the one kept in the dark, Vittorio. You see color more vividly than—"

"Because I somehow stole it from him."

"You didn't steal it from him, Vitto."

"Then how would you put it?"

"Could it be *he* was only borrowing it?" asked Juba. Vitto grunted, opened another bottle. Juba added, "Or was the ability always meant for you anyway, and he was only holding it for you until you arrived?"

"Is that a question? Or are you telling me some kind of answer?"

Juba shrugged, kept busy wiping the inside of the glasses with a white towel. How many times had he cleaned those glasses over the years? His hair had grown white, but he didn't seem to have aged much over the years. Then again, according to Robert, Magdalena hadn't aged that much until she started drinking the water.

"How old are you, Juba?"

"Old enough."

"Where'd you go?" Juba raised his eyebrows. Vitto said, "You know what I'm talking about. You left when Dad closed down the hotel. You came back. Where'd you go in between?"

"Traveled." He smiled and shrugged. "Saw the world."

"But not for the first time, right?"

This drew a pause from Juba, as if he was wondering why Vitto had put it that way. But Vitto himself didn't really know why he asked it, other than because Juba, more than anyone he'd ever met, looked like someone who'd been places.

"I've been around," Juba finally said.

"So how old are you, Juba?"

This time Juba laughed. "Would it surprise you to hear that I don't really know?"

"No. It would surprise me less, though, if you knew but said you couldn't tell me. But you're all about the same age, right—you and Dad and Mamma?"

"Perhaps." Juba winked, glanced at the wall clock. "Roughly, I'd guess."

"Did Mamma set fire to her house in Pienza? With that man Lippi still in it?"

Juba turned, showed his back, pretended to clean a glass he'd already cleaned twice. "I don't know."

"You do. But that's okay. I assume you and Dad are still trying to protect me from something. Protect her memory even? Her legacy?"

"More wine?"

Vitto nodded, sipped as soon as it was poured. "She did it, didn't she? That reporter is on to something. He wants to smear her legacy, like his father was trying to—all because he thinks his father was pushed off that cliff." He took another sip, set the glass down. "She burned that house down with him in it, didn't she?"

"Enough, Vitto."

"You're protecting her too."

"Of course I am," Juba said quickly, almost in a hiss. "I've been . . ."

"You've been what?"

"Your mother . . . the horrors she lived through—it wasn't that much different from what you . . . what your army doctor called battle fatigue? Combat exhaustion? Hell doesn't always require a war, Vittorio."

"My entire life she battled with memory. An ability to remember that I somehow stole, just as I stole from my father. But at least she lived. She smiled. She was warm when many of my nights were cold. But near the end, those final months—Juba, she was depressed. She turned inward, spoke very little. It pained her even to smile. And she obviously jumped off that cliff to end it all. But why? What happened to her, Juba?"

Juba looked around the piazza toward the wall clock, toward Robert's room, then back to Vitto. "Some roots grow deep."

"What does that mean? I'm not a little boy anymore."

"I told her not to drink the water."

"And you're okay with people drinking it now?" Juba didn't answer. Vitto said, "Explain, or I'll go drag my father out of bed right now and demand that he tell me."

"Your mother was born without the ability to remember."

"I know that," said Vitto. "But after she and Dad met, things changed. They somehow completed each other; she got her memory back, and he could see color. And they lived a life of bliss until I was born, but then they slowly reverted back."

"Your mother was able to remember a lot, yes. But not every-thing."

"Why not?"

"The same reason you shoved your wartime memories down so deep that it took multiple glasses of fountain water that night to bring it all back up. You remember?"

"Of course I remember."

"Well your mother had memories she buried deep, too, so deep they remained buried even during those years before you were born. But she knew they were in there. Not what they were exactly, but that they were in there, like the deepest of splinters, unseen but somehow still poking away at her daily. Feelings of guilt and dread and fear followed her without her knowing why. So she drank the water from that fountain so she could remember. I told her not to, but she did it anyway."

"You knew what the water would do? This isn't recent?"

"No, Vittorio. That water has always restored memory, and it's always accelerated the aging process."

"But the earthquake?"

"Was just an earthquake."

"The creek reversed?"

"It's not the first time that's happened. Ask Father Embry. He'll tell you stories about it happening even before he arrived. That creek, Robert's famous River Lethe, has changed course over the centuries like sand in an hourglass."

"So did the water work for her?"

"Almost immediately," said Juba. "It used to be stronger, the water. It's weakened over the decades."

"Which is why you're okay with handing it out to the guests? Because it's weaker."

Juba nodded. "Back then it was strong enough to bring back those memories your mother feared most but felt she needed to face. The ones her mind had buried so deep she could never bring them back up on her own. But once she brought those memories up, she couldn't handle them."

"Lippi?"

Juba nodded. "He took advantage of her inability to remember, Vitto." The whites of his eyes expanded. "In *every* way."

Vitto's blood seemed to freeze upon hearing the words. His own mother, defenseless against the cravings of an animal. A devil. A devil in the form of a man.

"He beat her. Used her. He said she was his muse, and I suppose that was true—his paintings of her were famous in the day. But he treated her more like his possession. His toy. He kept her hidden away, wouldn't allow her to go out. It wasn't supposed . . ."

"It wasn't supposed to be what, Juba? You speak as if this is some story within a story. Some Greek tragedy script to be followed line by line."

"You pour enough water in, and eventually it will flood out the bad stuff, Vitto. The memories of Lippi surfaced, and Magdalena couldn't handle them. She couldn't handle her battle fatigue. The guilt."

"She killed Lippi?"

"She snapped." Juba looked away, for the first time since Vitto had known him showing anger and some hidden guilt of his own. "I was watching over her. Had been for years."

"Why?"

Juba ignored the question, answered another. "I saw her flee the house that night. I went in, found Lippi's body . . . what she'd done to it. A woman pushed to the brink of madness."

For the first time, Vitto hoped Juba would spare him the details, which he did. Then realization dawned. "*You* set fire to the house."

"Yes."

"So the police would never know what she'd done."

Juba nodded again, fighting memories of his own. He'd begun wiping out the glasses again, his way of dealing with nerves, with stress.

"So did she steal Lippi's money? Or did you do that?"

Juba's lips tightened. "The man was dead. He didn't need it. Besides, she was his adopted daughter." He said that with a bit of a sneer. "His muse. It was hers by right, so I took it for her."

Vitto lowered his head, pondering that new piece of information. Then, "Did Mamma push Landry Tuffant's father off that cliff?"

Juba sighed in defeat. "I don't know, Vitto. What I do know is that your mother was the kindest and gentlest person I've ever known. What happened in that house before I burned it—it wasn't her. It was desperation. And she was never that desperate again—at least not until she drank the water."

Juba placed the last clean glass on the shelf. "As much as his son wants some truth, Melvin Tuffant's death may forever remain a mystery, but I know in my heart she didn't push him. It was raining that night. He was out on the cliffs. Magdalena was out there with him. The next thing I know she's running inside the hotel screaming that he'd gone over. That he'd slipped. That she'd tried to warn him about the wind. I believed her, Vitto. Your father believed her, too, of course."

"But some didn't?"

"Some didn't. They knew why Tuffant was there, investigating Magdalena's past, and in that some saw motive."

"What was the year?"

"1921."

"The year I was born," said Vitto. "Her memory at that point was fine. She was not yet back to writing notes in her journal."

"No."

"But it doesn't mean she didn't write something down." Vitto jumped from the stool. "Juba, are her journals still around?"

"Your father boxed them all up and put them in the basement, Vitto. But leave them be. What good could come from reading them? We know she was not capable of pushing a man to his death."

"For the same reason you've always done what you've done, Juba. To protect her."

"In my heart, I already know the truth."

"But Landry Tuffant does not."

Thirty-Two

*V*itto awoke in the basement to the sound of anxious footsteps above. And voices—not the typical morning pleasantries, but more of a nervous chatter.

"Where's Vittorio?"

"He can't do this. That reporter! Why is Robert allowing this?"

Allowing what?

Vitto leaned up on his elbows, and a stack of little leather books tumbled to the cold floor of the wine cellar, where he'd found all of his mother's journals in boxes stacked in a narrow gap between rows of wine bottles, situated in such a way that he could only pull out one box at a time. He hadn't anticipated so many boxes—the kind they'd once used for wine, each one holding at least a dozen journals apiece. He'd counted at least fifteen of them, and there were possibly more back in the shadows; he'd only estimated the number by how high and deep the visible boxes were stacked. And there were no labels, no way to know what was in each box. The journals seemed to have been thrown in haphazardly and out of order.

He'd come here last night immediately after his talk with Juba, intending to find the journal, if it even existed, that could possibly shed light on Melvin Tuffant, something more tangible than what had been reported in the newspaper in the days after his death—Magdalena had been quoted as saying she saw him slip, but the writer's words had made hers sound desperate and untrustworthy. But the wine he'd drunk had kicked in, and he'd fallen asleep paging through the final journal of the first box, whose contents chronicled the end of his third year and the first month of his fourth. At that point Magdalena had already begun to write down nearly everything she did during the day: conversations she'd had, interactions she'd witnessed, guests she'd talked to, the daily doings of being everyone's muse.

Reading her words had saddened him, slowing his pace despite the urgency to find truth. He'd been too young to understand back then, specifically during the months he'd read about—it almost felt like spying. As he grew older he'd been aware of her memory troubles, had even felt sympathy for her, but had never known the extent of what she'd had to go through, writing down everything just to be able to function. And to think how it worsened by the month, by the year, until she'd felt the desperate need to drink from that fountain and bring back even the worst of it.

Pinpricks of sunlight found their ways through cracks in the ceiling of the cellar. Dust motes hovered. He made it to his feet, straightened the crick in his back, and decided the commotion upstairs was more relevant now than what had happened in the past. Had something happened to the water? Had someone finally died? He took the curved stone steps leading to the piazza two at a time and found the guests, judging from their voices, as out of sorts as he'd imagined.

He hurried to find Valerie, who was walking quickly toward the Roman arches at the hotel entrance. She spotted him, waited, smoothed down a portion of his hair that must have been sticking up from the awkward way he'd slept. "Where were you last night?"

"I fell asleep in the wine cellar. I'll explain later."

She appeared distracted by the goings-on outside the hotel anyway. "What is going on?" he asked. She was reluctant to tell him; she stood there searching for the words. "Is it Dad?"

She shook her head. "No. Vittorio . . . they're digging up your mother's grave."

He didn't wait for an explanation. He ran out the entrance, where more of the guests stood watching the poppy field. Just beyond it stood the graveyard where Magdalena and a handful of staff from over the years had been buried. Vitto hurried across the field, his feet cutting through the tall grass like machetes, with Valerie following closely behind, telling him things like, *Stop . . . There's nothing we can do . . . We've already tried . . . Paperwork . . .*

The small graveyard had been partitioned off by rope and was surrounded by four police officers, two other men with shovels, and the reporter Landry Tuffant, who was smoking a cigarette and exhaling plumes into the morning air as Vitto approached, so out of his mind that he could barely even hear the insults and threats coming from his own mouth. Tuffant hadn't been around in days. Vitto had wondered if he was up to something.

It took three of the police officers to hold him back. One of them took a club to Vitto's knee, knocking him to the grass, hovering above. "I should arrest you now, Mr. Gandy."

"You heard him," shouted Landry Tuffant. "He threatened to kill me."

Did I?

Valerie had him by the arm, begging him to come with her, begging the police to ignore what he'd just said. "He's upset. His mother's grave is being desecrated. How would you react?" she screamed at the officers, then screamed it again at Tuffant, who turned from her, took another drag on his cigarette, and nodded for the two men with shovels to get to it.

The first crunch of blade into soil magnified in Vitto's head. Words warped in and out of focus, loud, then muted, distorted—words from Valerie, words from the officers, words from Tuffant, words from the guests watching outside the hotel. Vitto allowed himself to be led away, toward the pools, then back toward the building.

"Where is he? Where's Dad? How is he standing for this?"

Valerie gripped his elbow, halted him before the entrance to the northern wing. "This is your father's doing."

"He wanted this?"

"No. But he put the idea in Tuffant's head." They both breathed heavily as the ocean rolled in the distance. "A week ago, apparently, your father made a comment when Tuffant was snooping, asking questions of Magdalena's past. He said that all of his answers were buried with her. Tuffant pushed him on it, asked him if he meant evidence of some sort. And your father said yes, there's evidence buried with her."

"What evidence? Why did he say that?"

"I don't know. I asked him if he'd been sound of mind at the time. He said yes, it was in the middle of the day, and he knew exactly what he was doing." She tried to rub the tension from her face, her neck. "He even said the words 'Be my guest.' Like he wanted Tuffant to do this, Vitto."

"Where is Dad?"

She pointed through the entrance, toward the piazza. "In there. At one of the tables, drinking coffee like it's a regular morning."

Vitto took off through the entrance and ran into Juba. "Juba, do something."

"Nothing can be done, Vittorio." Although Juba's eyes showed worry, his voice was stern. "They've gotten permission from the courts. And your father—this seems to be how he wants it."

"And you, Juba? Do you know what they're going to find once they open that casket?"

Juba gave a slight nod.

"Tell me. Tell me, Juba."

"I never should have told you what I did last night. Some things should remain hidden."

Valerie glanced sharply up at Vitto; he mumbled that he'd tell her later. Juba stepped out onto the grounds, his large feet firmly planted in the middle of the bocce court, and watched from afar as shovels overturned earth and cigarette smoke sifted upward like from a smoldering campfire. Juba said, "It'll take them all day. Her coffin was buried deep, and the ground is like iron out there."

Vitto found his father on the piazza just as Valerie had said, sitting by himself at a table and drinking coffee, in view of both the bar and the untouched marble that was to become his final masterpiece. "What is going on?"

Robert looked up from the newspaper on his lap. His legs were crossed lazily at the knees, revealing long, bony legs. "Let them do what they feel necessary, Vittorio."

"How can you be so . . ."

"So what?"

"What are they going to find in there?"

Robert waved it away. "Oh, nothing."

"So this is a wild goose chase? You're allowing them to dig up my mother, and there's no evidence of anything?"

"I'm not allowing them to do anything, son. They have a court order. The original investigation was dismissed for lack of evidence. But now they believe they'll find the evidence."

"And you're telling me they won't?"

"Not the evidence they're looking for."

"Then what?"

"Relax, Vitto. I know what I'm doing."

"Do you? It was only a few months ago that you tried brushing your teeth with a razor. You couldn't find the bathroom, so you soiled your pants."

Valerie said, "Vitto, please."

Robert looked over his shoulder toward the empty bar, and it took Vitto only a few seconds to realize what he'd glanced at. "Why do you and Juba keep looking at that clock?"

Robert said, "To see what time it is, Vitto."

"Tell me about that clock."

"It's a Dutch clock, if I remember correctly. Perfectly handcrafted."

"And Mamma brought it with her from Florence. The orphanage let her take it when she was . . ." He couldn't bring himself to say "adopted," now that he knew so much about the monster Francesco Lippi.

"It seems you already know about the clock then. What more is there to tell?"

Vitto clenched his fists, felt like striking something, anything. He probably would have had Valerie not touched his arm. He pointed in the direction of where the exhumation was taking place on the other side of the hotel wall. "I will not let that man destroy my mother's memory. She was nothing but good. For us. For others."

"The best," said Robert, suddenly melancholy. "A goddess. My muse." And then his face hardened. "That man out there, Vitto, isn't so different from you."

Vitto turned on him. "He and I are not the same."

"Sons desperate for the truth about parents who are no longer around to tell it."

Vitto seethed, but any anger he still harbored toward his father melted as he gazed upon the frailty of him. He stepped away, placed a forgiving hand on his father's thin shoulder, and faced the bar. Beside it was the stone stairwell leading below to the wine cellar. *The journals.* He slid his hand from his father's shoulder and moved toward the bar.

"Vitto, where are you going?"

He didn't answer, but Valerie followed as he suspected she would—had hoped she would. Robert raised the newspaper with a palpable snap and continued reading as Vitto and Valerie descended below the hotel. His mission last night had been derailed by tiredness, by a melancholy lack of urgency, by too much wine. But the shovels digging into the earth outside had now made him desperate. He couldn't legally stop what they were doing out on the grounds, but perhaps he could find some proof, some written words of Magdalena's that were believable enough for Tuffant to put an end to this madness.

Something to bring the man peace so he wouldn't ruin more lives while trying to fill in the gaps of his own.

As he and Valerie pulled out box after box, Vitto explained what Juba had told him last night, about Magdalena killing Lippi and Juba setting fire to the house to protect her, to keep the police from finding what he'd found.

"What did she do to Lippi? How did she kill him?"

"I don't know, Val, and I don't want to. He was a monster. What he did to her, for years, I can't even . . ."

He told her about the water in the fountain, how Juba had said it had always had the power to bring back memory, but that it was growing weaker.

"How did it get there in the first place?"

"I don't know." He handed her another box. "Why don't you take this one and I'll go through the other."

They buried themselves in boxes, in decades' worth of discarded journals, daily notes and reminders, stories and memories. Some were written the way anyone would write in a journal—to document things in need of remembrance. But most were written out of the desperation of living one day to the next.

At noon William brought them a lunch they could hardly take breaks to eat, so determined were they to find something before Tuffant struck wood outside. They were flipping through pages so quickly, they'd reduced their focus to skimming, searching for words about the tragedy at the Tuscany Hotel, the reporter Melvin Tuffant, or the year 1921. But with nothing labeled or organized, it was like finding a needle in a haystack.

Frustration soon led to guilt, as periodically they'd stop to share things they'd skimmed, various thoughts and memories, random musings and an occasional note about something Magdalena couldn't possibly have remembered—vivid descriptions of the Italian

Renaissance, anecdotes about famous art and artists, musicians and scientists and builders. Memories from the fourteenth century, the fifteenth, the sixteenth and seventeenth. And all were jotted down as if Magdalena was not retelling stories she once heard but had actually lived them, as if she had been there herself with Botticelli and Leonardo and so many others in Milan and Florence and Rome centuries before her arrival at the Hospital of Innocents. The more they skimmed, the more they felt as if they were prying into an unstable mind, afflicted not only with memory loss but also with delusions of grandeur, until Vitto finally closed one journal with a loud pop and hurled it across the room.

John and Beverly joined them a little while later and reported that the shovels had hit the top of the coffin. Vitto didn't want to be out there. Didn't want to destroy the perfect picture in his head of a beautiful mother, loved by all, now reduced to bones. According to Beverly, both Juba and Father Embry were pacing the piazza, nervous, as if they knew what would be found. Robert had gotten up a few times to shuffle out the entrance and observe for a moment before slowly moving back inside, where he'd been playing a game of chess with William when she and John came down.

It was John, with fresh eyes and a heart not as burdened by personal memories, who found something an hour later in a box they'd yet to open. Inside one journal were folded newspaper articles from around the time of the tragedy in 1921, when Melvin Tuffant's broken body was found on the rocks below.

One of the articles showed a picture of Melvin from a story he'd done three months before his death about the discovery of a speakeasy in Los Angeles. The grainy photo showed crates of illegal liquor waiting to be loaded into a truck disguised as an ambulance, which had made regular runs up and down the coast. The reporter had posed with one arm atop a whiskey barrel, the contents puddled around his boots and sluicing toward a drain along the street curb, wearing a smile that made him much more human than not.

It had clearly been a proud moment, a big break for the determined reporter who, according to the other articles, had gone on to become well-known for uncovering speakeasies and illegal distilleries up and down the coast. Then he had latched on to the Tuscany Hotel, on the alcohol it served and the gangsters who frequented it, and on Magdalena's past, for his next big story.

That investigation had ended in tragedy. And now Melvin's son, who looked a lot like him, was outside digging up a coffin, searching for his own bit of fame. His own big break.

Vitto shoved the articles aside and dug deeper into the box John had discovered. The four of them worked feverishly for the next fifteen minutes—eyes darting across pages, across lines and words and thoughts. Finally Valerie found the journal they needed, and when she handed it over her hands were shaking. Vitto read, hands trembling as well. Magdalena hadn't pushed Melvin Tuffant. She'd tried to help him up, not force him down—after the gangsters pushed him over.

Vitto closed the book and ran. Maybe if he showed Landry Tuffant what Magdalena had written in her journal, he'd put a halt to the digging, to the opening of that coffin.

But by the time he hit the fresh air of the piazza, it was too late.

Everyone was standing there—the guests, Juba, Father Embry, the police, Tuffant, even Robert, having just ingested a bit of news Vitto was about to hear for himself. All eyes turned to Vitto and Valerie and then Beverly and John, who'd just emerged from the wine cellar.

Vitto held up the journal for Landry Tuffant to see. But before he could explain, the reporter, whose pale face looked like the life had been siphoned from him, said, "It was empty."

Vitto looked to Robert. "What's he talking about?"

Tuffant said, "The coffin. It was empty."

"What? No evidence?"

"No," Tuffant confirmed, still in shock, if not humiliated. *Was that Dad's plan all along?* "Nothing. There was nothing in there. At all."

Again Vitto looked at his father for an answer.

Robert said, "We never found her body, Vittorio."

Thirty-Three

*Y*ou buried an empty coffin?"

Robert didn't deny it. Apparently Juba and Father Embry had known as well. When Vitto asked his father why, he said they'd done it so her friends and only son would have something to visit, some*one* to visit, somewhere to leave flowers.

"For flowers? You did this for flowers?"

"For you, Vitto. For you."

It made sense now—Father Embry's hesitation and nervousness during the eulogy. So many years she'd walked down to the monastery church for confession. Had they planned it all together?

"And I was tired of answering the questions, Vitto. Questions about your mother. The mysteries. Her mysteries. I needed resolution."

Snippets of the past became clearer. Those daily swims in the ocean. The fact that Robert, who'd loved Magdalena more than any man could ever love a woman, had rarely visited her grave. The many hours he'd spent standing atop the cliff overlooking the vastness of the ocean, her true resting place, a casket of endless water.

"I was nearly a man grown when she died."

"But still a boy with little understanding of death, Vitto. Of pain and sorrow."

"I would have—"

"What? Searched the ocean day and night until it consumed you completely?"

"And you? Did you not search for her?"

"Of course I did—for days. But I knew she was gone. I knew she'd gone back home."

"What? To the ocean? To the depths of the sea like some . . . ?"

Like some god or goddess from her bedtime stories.

Vitto hadn't been able to bring himself to finish the question. And Robert, who understood it well enough, had no answer, at least none he was able to give in front of everyone listening on the piazza. He slumped in his chair, his aged body a bag of bones.

Vitto looked to Landry Tuffant and tossed him the journal. "It's near the end. About your father." Then he descended the stairs again to the wine cellar. There, surrounded by aging wine bottles and dust-covered journals—little bits of fragmented truths—he could almost imagine he heard his mother's voice. Valerie joined him, and they silently flipped through pages for thirty minutes before she kissed him on the head and left him alone. Twenty minutes later, footsteps whisked on the stone steps leading down—the tread too heavy for Valerie or William, not heavy enough for Juba, and Vitto doubted his father now had the strength to make it down.

"Do you mind?"

Vitto looked up to see Landry Tuffant standing with Magdalena's journal resting against his chest, his hands holding it like one might an infant. Vitto nodded toward an open spot on the floor. Landry grunted as he sat, cross-legged and surrounded by stacks of journals, stacks of stories, stacks of memories.

Landry's voice was low and soft. "I'm sorry."

"So am I."

And then they both sat silent for a while, sharing the knowledge of what had happened the night Melvin Tuffant died. It was all there in the journal, the story captured in Magdalena's familiar scrawl.

❈

After uncovering that first speakeasy in Los Angeles, Melvin Tuffant was a man with a mission, determined to make his mark and to come down on the proper side of Prohibition. He quickly became as well-known as the agents who tore down doors and spilled the spirits out windows and into the streets. His crusades left him little time for his young son, Landry, but the boy idolized him. And why not? Landry Tuffant's daddy was in the newspapers, always out catching bad guys. A father a boy could be proud of.

And a father who was intent on bringing down the Tuscany Hotel.

The presence of alcohol at the hotel was common knowledge, generally overlooked because of Robert Gandy's position in society and the fame of many of its guests. Less well-known was the fact that gangsters and bootleggers had begun visiting the hotel, unwanted and uninvited. But Melvin Tuffant knew, and he wanted to break the story.

The gangsters knew Melvin Tuffant as well, his reputation for covering the wins for the Prohibitionists, and they didn't like that he was sniffing around the hotel, which was becoming one of their favorite spots to meet and discuss business. They were counting on Robert's popularity and his stature in the community to provide cover. And to make sure he went along with their plans, they weren't above a touch of blackmail.

A couple of these gangsters, Italian brothers named Vitto and Vincent Cornolli, had known some street toughs from Pienza, where Robert Gandy's wife, a woman with blazing orange hair and an inspiring personality, had supposedly come from. Rumor had it that she'd cut up some guy there and then burned him alive. This possibility gave them the leverage they needed to convince Robert Gandy to let them do as they pleased at the hotel.

The reporter, Melvin Tuffant, overheard them talking and set about to write a story about it—the illegal liquor and wine still flowing through the Tuscany Hotel, the presence of the gangsters, and the tantalizing possibility that Robert Gandy's wife was a murderer. The state might have turned a blind eye to everything going on at the

Tuscany Hotel, but Melvin Tuffant wasn't about to ignore it. To him this was the story of all stories.

For weeks he hung around, watching and jotting down notes, until one night when rain poured down and the ocean waves roared and voices were muted by the force of all that water. That was the night when Vitto and Vincent Cornolli decided to teach the reporter a lesson. First they'd get him good and drunk. Then they'd give him a good beating, just for fun. Then they'd drag him out to the cliffs and get down to business.

Getting Melvin Tuffant floppy wasn't hard because he was a drunk, and they knew it. Melvin had made himself famous for helping the Prohibition agents lure so-called criminals out of their hidey-holes like some sneak-thief rat, but he liked to imbibe here and there from what was captured and drink himself goofy every night while no one was watching. So when they handed him a bottle, he guzzled it down good and fast, probably because he knew what was coming.

The two brothers didn't disappoint his expectations. At the cliffs they toyed with him like cats with a mouse. They held him out over the edge, at one time leaning him out and holding on to nothing but Melvin's red silk tie while he pleaded for his life and the breakers foamed against the sharp rocks below. They were about to drop him when they heard Magdalena's voice cut through the downpour—not asking but demanding that they put him down safely.

She'd somehow found one of their machine guns and held it poised, pointed right at them, and from what they'd heard of her past, they knew she might have the sand to use it. So they took their hands off Melvin Tuffant and left him wobbling, drunk, right next to the cliff's edge.

Magdalena told the two thugs to go on, that if they did, nobody would ever hear of it. Melvin was sobbing and soaked to the bone, his glasses broken and lost in the mud as blood from his beating meandered down his jaw and onto his neck, his collar stained red and smeared.

"They threatened to kill my family," he blubbered to Magdalena. "Threatened to find my boy and turn him into soup."

"They'll do no such thing," Magdalena said while Vitto and Vincent laughed under their rain-soaked fedoras—eyes black, faces hard and chiseled.

"I promise I won't write the story," Melvin pleaded. "I promise."

Vitto laughed and then, quick as a snakebite, kicked Melvin's feet out from beneath him. The reporter went down, slipped, and found himself clinging to the cliff side, gripping for mud and grass and roots and rock while his feet dangled and his screams went muted by the rainfall and wind and ocean waves. Magdalena dropped the gun to save him, sliding onto the ground and gripping both of his wrists with every bit of strength she could muster. But she couldn't get any traction, and she felt him slipping through her wet grip. She pleaded for the two gangsters to help.

Vincent shielded his mouth from the wind as he lit a cigarette, and the tip glowed like a beacon in the fog. Vitto squatted down, and at first, Magdalena thought he was going to help, but then he brought his mouth toward her ear and spoke like the devil he was. Too much like a voice from her past. Too much like the degrading, abusive voice of Francesco Lippi.

"You ever mention what happened here, even one word, and I'll come back and ruin you. I don't know what that man you cut up in Pienza did to you, but I'll make it ten times worse. You understand?" She'd nodded profusely, too frightened to cry, but also losing her grip on Melvin Tuffant's wet wrists.

The gangster wasn't finished. "You gonna need reminding? Huh?"

She shook her head no, but he said, "You know how you're gonna get reminded? That little baby you got growing in you—yeah, word travels—you're gonna name him after me. You hear me? You're gonna name him Vittorio. And you're gonna call him Vitto just like I'm called. That way every time you look at him, you'll remember. I'll know you know, and everything will be jake."

Magdalena hissed defiantly, "What if it's a girl?"

He smacked the top of her head, forcing her face into the grass, and laughed. "Got us a funny broad here, Vincent." He hunkered down toward her ear again. "You'll name it Vittorio no matter. We clear?"

She nodded, crying now. They walked away, disappeared into the shadows of the hotel while Melvin Tuffant screamed. A few seconds later she lost her hold, and he slipped to the rocks below, where he was found the next morning.

The newspaper article that day and the ones that followed in the days and weeks thereafter, all written by friends and colleagues of Melvin Tuffant, referred to the death as mysterious, citing Tuffant's fear of heights and stating that there was no way he would have been on the cliffs on his own. An anonymous source claimed to have seen the woman with the orange hair out there with him in the rain, arguing with him over a story he was investigating about her past. But with insufficient evidence and some muscling from Robert and Juba, the accusations soon went away, until the son, Landry Tuffant, dug them all back up again.

❖

Landry placed the journal on the ground, the truth hovering around them like a suffocating hood. He looked like he wanted to say something but wasn't sure if he should. And then he did. "Good thing you weren't a girl."

Vitto laughed, nodded, guessed it was a good thing. They shared a quick smile and then averted their eyes—to the walls, to the wine bottles, to the stacks of journals.

Landry said, "Did she really kill that man in Pienza?"

Vitto shrugged and stared at the reporter for a moment, no longer sensing trouble from him. Any threat had passed with what they'd learned from that journal. "Off the record?" he asked.

"Of course."

Vitto perused the stacks around him and then settled on one he'd set aside earlier in the day—older, weathered books from Magdalena's stay with Lippi, most of which had been too painful for him to read. He pushed them across the floor, close enough for Landry to reach. "Look for yourself. If she did do it, you'll see why."

"I won't write about it. You have my word."

"Good."

"Now I just want to know more about the woman who risked her life to save Dad."

Vitto nodded, folded his arms as if cold. The history of his name had cut sharper than any wind could. He stood from the floor. "I'm heading on up."

"You mind if I stay down here?"

"Go ahead."

"Vitto . . . the water in that fountain. Off the record. Does it really do what your father says?"

"Is it slowly killing them?"

"Yes."

"Maybe it is," he said. "Maybe it isn't. Or maybe it starts when we're born? Are we living or dying?"

"A bit of both, I guess."

"Either way, ticktock goes the clock."

"But if it's allowing them to live, how could it possibly be killing them?"

Vitto paused at the doorway and turned back toward Landry. "You ever heard of the Moirai? The Fates in Greek mythology?"

Landry shook his head no.

"There's a room here on the east wing, second floor, third from the southern tower. When I was fourteen, I did a painting of them on the wall opposite the door—a replica of a sixteenth-century oil painting by Salviati. They were three goddesses who determined how long a person's life would last. Clotho spun the thread of life. Lachesis measured it. Atropos cut it at life's end, and her decision was one that even the gods couldn't change."

"You believe it works like that?"

"I'd believe just about anything right now. But if it is like that, then the thread of just about everybody up there in the hotel is being measured and about to get snipped. Might as well let them enjoy it until that happens."

He started up the steps, but Landry stopped him on the second one. "You do know how those two brothers died, right? The Cornolli brothers, Vitto and Vincent? They were both found in an alley in San Francisco—side by side, neatly placed, facing the sky. Strangled by a rope."

"When?"

"About a year after the night my father died."

"Who did it?"

"Unsolved. I ran across the pictures years ago, doing a story on that new type of organized crime that Prohibition seemed to have started. There was something interesting about how they were found. They had coins over their eyes."

Vitto grinned. "For the boatman."

Thirty-Four

*A*fter leaving Landry in the wine cellar with Magdalena's journals, Vitto went straight to his father's room and gently knocked on the door.

Hearing nothing, he turned the knob and let himself in to find Robert in bed, his frail frame like rocky indentations beneath the white sheets. His mouth was open, his closed eyes lost in shadowed sockets. Vitto hurried bedside, fearing the worst, but then noticed the gentle rise and fall of Robert's chest and sighed in relief. Just sleeping. Thread yet to be cut. Every so often he'd flinch as if a dream or nightmare had clutched him, but otherwise, he was calm, peaceful almost. Under the care of Hypnos, the god of sleep, the twin to Thanatos—death. By the look of it, near the end of one's thread, there was not much to differentiate the two.

For thirty minutes Vitto sat bedside, watching his father and wondering if he'd ever found out about the threat to Magdalena, if he and Juba had had a hand in the death of the Cornolli brothers.

His father had told him once about the boatman, the mythical ferryman called Charon, who carried the deceased souls of the underworld across the River Styx. Coins were placed over the mouth or the eyes of the dead to pay for the journey. A smile bubbled up at the thought of it, and then a full-out laugh when he imagined his mother holding a machine gun and talking the Cornolli brothers down.

Robert slept on, mouth open, drooling slightly, so Vitto wiped his chin with the corner of the sheet and made his way to the door. He turned again toward the bed before leaving and noticed how it now swallowed him.

And also how, after all these years alone, Robert still slept on the far left side of it, leaving the right side open for Magdalena.

✦

"Vitto, have we not been over this before?" asked Father Embry as dusk cast prisms of color through the stained-glass windows of his church and onto the front pew, where they both now sat. "I can't speak about the confessions of others."

"But Mamma visited you daily near the end. And I know she'd begun drinking the water."

Father Embry rubbed his hands together, didn't deny it. "Her heart was heavy, Vittorio."

"Did she tell you she was going to jump?"

"No."

"If we never found her body . . . how do we know she went over the cliff? How do we know she even went into the water?"

"Some things we just know. Your father took to the ocean immediately, convinced that's where she'd gone. He searched for days . . . I shouldn't be telling you this. You should ask him."

"He's asleep. And I want to know now."

"He and Juba searched the ocean for days and nights without returning to shore. We thought we'd lost them as well, but on the fourth morning they returned. Your father climbed out of that boat, his skin beaten by the sun, but otherwise glowing. His smile showed peace. Contentment. I asked if they'd found her, and he said yes, but I looked to their boat and saw nothing. He explained that they hadn't found her body, but in the sunrise that morning, in the shimmer coming off the ripples, he'd both seen and felt her."

"How could he see the sunrise? He can't see color."

"But he did on that morning, Vittorio. And that's how he knew. She'd gone back home . . . somehow."

"I don't understand."

"Did your parents not tell you where they were found as infants?"

"No. They? Only that Mamma was abandoned."

Father Embry stiffened in the pew, crossed himself. "Perhaps I've overstepped my bounds."

"Perhaps you should step the rest of the way, then," said Vitto. "I can see in your eyes that you want to. That you, too, have been burdened by all of this."

Father Embry cleared his throat. "Very well. Your mother was found by a woman on the banks of the Arno River in Florence. Swaddled right next to the water, a few feet from the Ponte Vecchio. The woman—we don't know who she was—carried her to the Hospital of Innocents, the orphanage where she was raised."

"How do you know that?"

"Juba told me. I don't know how he found it out."

"But you said 'they' were found?"

He hesitated. "Your father was adopted as well—also abandoned and found next to water, a river in Alabama. The man who would adopt him heard his cries while hunting. The water was lapping at his feet when they spotted him. And as far as we could backtrack, he and Magdalena seemed to have been found on the same day. Both of them deposited right there by the water. There was a great storm the night before. The heavens rumbled, and lightning split the sky." He glanced toward the altar, then looked back. He had more to tell. "Juba, he was an orphan as well. Found next to a river in the Sudan, in Africa."

"The same time?"

"That's a little harder to ascertain, but we think so. Juba traveled back to the village where he was born—he was actually named after that village. And the elders there spoke of a great storm that happened around the time that Juba was found—a storm so violent they said lightning split the heavens."

Vitto didn't know what to say, so he said nothing while Father

Embry kissed his cross and whispered a silent prayer. Then he asked, "Do you believe in miracles?"

Father Embry grinned at Vitto. "Yes."

"Do you think that's what could be happening here? With the water?"

"I think it would be foolish to try and quantify exactly what is happening here, Vitto, and what has happened in the past. The question you asked me so often as a kid . . ."

"Where do we go when we die? Do you finally have my answer?"

Father Embry paused, smiled. "To heaven, of course."

"That's what you always say."

"Well, what if I said I didn't know for sure?"

"You don't?"

"What, am I supposed to know that with certainty because I wear these robes?"

"I thought they put you closer to God than the rest of us."

"Vitto, at my age, the only thing I'm closer to is death, and I won't know the answer to your question for sure until then. But don't be so consumed with the cutting of the thread, Vitto. Focus on the thread itself."

"So you're saying you have doubt about what you've always told me?"

"No, Vitto, I have faith. And I believe that faith implies a bit of doubt." He smiled again. "Otherwise instead of *belief* we'd call it *fact*. I think it's the bit of doubt that makes it most interesting, don't you think?" The priest leaned back in the pew and peered at Vitto over his spectacles. "Oh dear. You seem even more confused now. Perhaps I haven't done my job very well."

"You believe in God, right?"

"I do."

"My mother was raised Catholic, in Italy. After she moved here, she attended church regularly—daily, even, near the end. Dad rarely went to church. But they both spoke often about the ancients—the Greek and Roman gods. They told me stories about them and spoke as if they truly believed in them too."

Father Embry clenched his jaw like he was holding something in. Vitto said, "I guess I've never been sure what I should believe in. What is wrong and what is right. God or the gods."

"It's the belief in *something*, Vitto, that keeps us going." He gestured in the direction of the hotel. "Even if that something is just hope. Or a cause. A mission."

The sun dropped lower outside the church, moving the colorful prism of reflected light through the stained glass, shifting it from the altar to the steps leading up to it. Vitto stood and approached the colorful light slanting from the northern window. He put his hand through the floating dust motes, watched his wrist and fingers turn red and green and purple and gold. Then he turned toward the pew where Father Embry still sat. "I know my mother came to confession every day. But did my father ever come? Did Juba?"

Father Embry watched him curiously. "Yes."

"How often?"

"Just the once."

"When?"

"I think you know, Vitto." Again, the smile. "They'd do anything to protect your mother." Father Embry nodded, offered nothing more.

"Will they be forgiven? I hear Hades isn't pretty for those who've committed a crime. Tartarus is a constant torture. And then, of course, there's hell . . ."

"Focus on the thread, Vittorio. The thread."

Vitto turned to go, his footfalls echoing off the arched ceiling. But Father Embry's words carried behind him. "Your father has served his penance for whatever he may or may not have done, as you have served yours. Go on now. If you want to make it more official I can add ten Hail Marys and ten Our Fathers. You're forgiven as well, Vitto. Is that not part of the reason you came down here?"

He couldn't deny it. Even now the memories flashed: the woman he'd accidentally shot during the war, the concentration camp survivor eating his chocolate bar, dunking Landry Tuffant's head repeatedly into the fountain water, his hands around the neck of the only woman he'd ever loved . . .

"Thank you."

❊

"You never told me you were an orphan."

Juba filled two glasses of wine and slid one across the bar top to Vitto. "Does that change your opinion of me?"

"No."

"Then consider it unnecessary information." Juba gulped half of his wine, when typically he barely sipped the red and white he poured nightly. "I assume you've been to see the good father."

"Did you see it too? When you and Dad went out in search of her body, did the sunrise my father saw convince you too?"

"It did. It was a feeling similar to the calm we'd all felt when we sat together in the boat."

"Which boat?"

"The one we left Italy in."

"When Father first saw the color orange? Mamma's hair."

"That's right."

"What brought you to California, though? To this land. These cliffs?"

"It's just where the waters eventually brought us, Vittorio. Not everything has a clear-cut answer."

"I don't believe you. I know where you went in the years the hotel was closed. Why did you go there?"

Juba sighed heavily, resigned. "Why? Perhaps the same reason you just visited the church. For answers?"

"But why there?"

Juba finished his wine, glanced at the wall clock. "Why did I go to Greece? To Athens? To the temples of Poseidon and Zeus? To Olympia? And to the village where I was born?"

Vitto chuckled. Juba poured himself more wine. "What?"

"I really didn't know where you went—until now. It's the first time I've ever been able to trick you, Juba."

"The first time I've ever allowed it, Vittorio. Glad that you're amused. I knew you didn't know because I never told anyone, even your father."

"How did you know to return?"

"The same reason birds know when it's time to fly south for the winter."

"You felt it getting colder?"

Juba folded his powerful arms across his even more powerful chest. "You should have been a comedian, Vitto."

"Why did you go to those places?"

Juba's eyes burrowed into his. "If I tell you, will you promise to not ask more?"

"If you insist."

"Every journey needs a road map."

"You always talk in riddles, Juba. What does that even mean?"

"That sounded like a question."

"Because it was. Look, I understand why you went to Africa, but why to those temples of the gods? And what road map?"

"Have you ever been to Athens, to the temple of Poseidon, and overlooked the sea on three sides?"

"You know that I haven't."

"Let's just say it's not too different from the view here."

"So you're saying this hotel is a temple? The final piece on some map . . . to where?"

Juba shrugged again. "To home?"

Vitto laughed, finished his wine, and slid off the stool. "Infuriating as always, Juba." He pointed to the wall behind the bar. "Now tell me about the clock. Why was it so important to my mother that she took it with her from the orphanage, to Pienza, and then across the ocean to the coastal town of Gandy, California?"

Juba stared at him, incredulous, his jaws like a vault, then suddenly they softened. And even more suddenly, Vitto almost didn't want to know. It was as if Juba—and not only him but also Father Embry and even Robert—all sensed the end of something was at hand, and that was why they were willing to talk about things they'd previously kept secret.

"That clock hung on the wall of the Hospital of Innocents for more than a century," said Juba. "I was told that there was a great clash of thunder and a bright stroke of lightning one evening at midnight, rendering the clock suddenly useless. The hands no longer moved, no matter what was tried. But they left it up anyway, for show, its hands stuck perpetually at midnight."

He chuckled. "It became a tradition for the nurses, whenever a new foundling was left, to refer to it jokingly as 'another midnight baby.'"

Vitto watched the clock tick behind the bar, as he'd seen it tick his entire life, although he couldn't help but wonder if those hands were now ticking more slowly than normal, like an aging heart. "I could venture a guess, but when did it start working again?"

"During the storm the night your mother was left in that wheel."

"The same night my father was found during a similar storm here in the States," said Vitto. "And you in Africa. Storms don't reach that far, Juba."

"Apparently this one did, and all those who witnessed it thought the heavens were about to open up and collapse onto the earth."

"And that clock has been ticking ever since?"

"Yes."

Vitto opened his wallet and tossed a couple of bills atop the counter.

"Your money is no good here, Vitto."

"For your travels then. But tell me one more thing. If the clock started about the time Mother was born, did you expect it to stop again upon her death?"

"I did."

"But it didn't."

"No. It didn't."

Thirty-Five

*V*itto restlessly stared at the ceiling of their room for an hour before giving up on sleep. In the middle of the night, he found himself out on the piazza painting while everyone slept.

The image of Melvin Tuffant leaning against a recently emptied barrel of whiskey stuck in his mind, so he painted that. He'd leave it on the easel for Landry to find in the morning—an olive branch in the form of a memory, a moment in time encased in oil and brush-strokes.

He managed to fall asleep soon after finishing the piece and dreamed of wind and sound, the rhythmic chinking of chisel into stone carrying through the open window and hugging him like only the best of memory senses could. The hammering didn't last long, but long enough, and in the morning, he was as surprised as the rest of the guests on the piazza to find Robert's slab of marble covered by a large brown cloth, the same one he'd often use to catch the shavings and chunks and dust.

The sounds last night hadn't been a dream after all. As whispers would have it, Robert had emerged from his room before sunup and carved something into that stone—something he'd immediately covered with the brown cloth. And just as Vitto was about to pull the cloth away to reveal what had been done to the marble, Robert's voice stopped him.

"Not yet." He was hunkered into a wheelchair, and John stood behind it.

"Morning, Gandy."

Vitto nodded toward John and said to his dad, "Then when?"

"When I'm gone." Robert grinned, coughed into a hand of bones. "My final masterpiece."

"Could you get any more morbid? You speak as if this is your last day on earth."

"I've always wondered if my pieces would go up in value after I'm gone."

"Have you had your medicine this morning?"

"I've had my water." He beckoned to Vitto—and Valerie and William, who had stepped up behind him. "Come."

"Where are we going?"

"For a ride."

"Where?"

"Down memory lane," said Robert. "*La passeggiata.* Do you remember the Sunday evening strolls?" Vitto nodded, and Robert explained to John how, once a week, everyone in the hotel used to dress up and stroll leisurely around the grounds, socializing and drinking as the sun dipped under the horizon.

John looked eager to move along; he pushed the wheelchair across the piazza's travertine toward the arches of the front entrance. The rest of them walked behind as Robert regaled them with detailed descriptions of the hotel's construction—where in Tuscany the stones had come from, the size and weight of each block, the time it had taken to build each wall and the piazza, and even the planning of each window and flower box. The four corner turrets had been the final touches to a lifelong dream, a vision, a love letter to Magdalena and the Italian Renaissance.

A temple, Vitto thought, holding hands with both Valerie and William as they followed Robert's wheelchair along the outskirts of the hotel and listened to more stories about everything they passed— picnics and Tuscany-themed festivals in the poppy field, poolside parties and evening tennis matches, strolls atop the cliffs, olive and grape harvests, the making of oils and wines and food.

"Oh Vitto, the foods we ate." Robert glanced over his shoulder. "Your food is just as good, John."

"Thanks, Mr. Gandy."

"But the parties, the courses—so many courses, eating this and that throughout the day. And the desserts . . ." He trailed off as if he'd lost his train of thought, which he did two more times before they stopped outside the entrance to the southern wing, where the olive mill loomed in front of the terraced grove of trees.

They all watched Robert—several of the guests had joined them along the way, a few of whom had written everything he'd said into their daily journals—and he appeared ready to say more but didn't. Instead, he stared out toward the ocean.

"Take me down there."

Vitto told Robert it wasn't a good idea in his condition to go down to the cliffs.

Robert told him his opinion was noted but asked John to take him down anyway, which he did, as far as they could go along the walkway to and around the monastery church and then over the rougher patch toward the shoreline. John lifted Robert out of the chair and carried him toward the water's edge while Vitto wheeled the chair behind them. Then, with Valerie holding one arm and Vitto the other, Robert made his way out into the water—the calm waves lazily lapping around his ankles as he wavered in their hands.

He closed his eyes and inhaled the ocean air, the smell of wet sand and rock and seaweed. Wind blew his thinning white hair against his shoulders and face, and he welcomed it all with a sun-drenched smile, all while Juba watched from the cliff top above. Ten minutes he stood in the low-rolling waves as the tide recycled itself around his ankles and feet. In and out the frothy waves flowed, in and out he breathed in the mist, no doubt remembering the countless times he'd taken to the water for his morning swims. The times he and Magdalena had gone into the water together for private swims under the moonlight or on lazy days in their fishing boat.

"What is the sense most associated with memory, Vitto?" he quizzed.

Seeing that Robert's eyes were still closed, Vitto guessed, "Smell."

"Yes. The smell. Nothing can bring the moment back faster."

Vitto looked back and saw that Landry Tuffant had joined them, and from the tear-filled look he gave Vitto, along with the slight head nod, Vitto assumed he'd found the painting of his father. Another painting of the real, another nudge toward Vitto finding his calling, his faith in the cause. His quest for knowledge somehow complete.

When Robert's depleted legs began to tremble, John carried him back to the wheelchair, and they processed up the monks' hillside toward the hotel. By the time they reached the piazza, the sky had begun to darken. The ocean waves behind them pounded higher. Robert eyed the encroaching purple clouds, almost low enough to touch. "A storm is coming."

But the tempest proved slow moving, the air around them eerily silent. On Robert's advice they moved dinner early, last call even earlier. But instead of the typical social game and trading of stories, Robert gathered everyone around and said he would tell only one story—a short one, for he was tired and could hear his bed calling.

William said, "I don't hear anything, Grandpa Robert. And beds can't talk."

"I promise at my age that they do. Everything talks, William. The walls, the floors . . . the weather. Your bones. They all have stories to tell."

"Then tell us a story."

Robert leaned forward in his wheelchair, bony fingers intertwined, and paused, searching his memory for what he wanted to say. His morning dose of water was well on its way to wearing off. But earlier, when Vitto had offered him a little more to get him through the day, he'd shaken his head in quiet, solemn refusal.

Finally he held up a finger. "Ah, here's a brief story, a quick reminder to sustain you. It's about the goddesses known as the Charites, also known as the Graces. They are usually depicted in art as three beautiful naked women holding hands in a circle and dancing."

William said, "He said naked."

"Yes, William, naked! These Graces are friends to the nine beautiful Muses. And they are goddesses of grace and beauty and joy. Festivity and dance and song, my friends. Happiness and rest and relaxation." He grinned and opened his hands, palms to the sky. "You've all earned it. Before the thread is cut, my friends, I offer this. Ignore the pains and aches and groans of mortality and instead hold hands and dance."

William turned to Vitto, confused. "That wasn't much of a story."

Vitto squeezed his hand. Then the first raindrop fell, and soon fat drops were splattering all over the piazza, plopping into the fountain water and filling the air with the pleasant aroma of earth and stone.

Vitto stood there for a moment, mindlessly watching the guests hunker against the rainfall and slowly move toward their respective rooms. Then he came to and realized his father meant for him to wheel him out of the rain, but not before he'd given both William and Valerie a kiss good night—a kiss to both cheeks with whispers of *buona notte*.

"I'll see you in the morning," said William, Vitto wondering if he'd almost inflected it as a question.

"Not if I see you first, William."

The rain fell harder, the drops covering more stone, as Vitto pushed Robert's chair over the travertine toward his room. Robert, eyes closed, tilted his head up and sniffed. "Petrichor, the smell of rain. Do you know where the word comes from, Vittorio?"

"No, but I assume you'll tell me."

"From the Greek words *petra*, which means stone, and *ichor*. And do you know what ichor is, Vittorio? It's the fluid that runs through the veins of Greek gods."

"Of course it is."

Robert laughed. "Always so arch, my Vitto."

Vitto held the door open with his foot and rolled the wheelchair inside. He helped Robert shuffle from the chair to the bed and got him under the covers as the rain pounded harder against the roof tiles and sluiced down in curtains to the piazza. A comforting sound, a soporific sound from his childhood, the sound of spring rains that produced plump olives and fat grapes and never failed to yield eventual sunshine again.

Robert scooted to his normal position against the wall, leaving Magdalena's side open. His head lolled on the pillow, facing Vitto and the chair he'd just pulled up bedside. His eyes were still so powerfully blue, yet behind them Vitto sensed the onset of confusion, and even more so in the crinkled brow above them.

Vitto leaned closer. "Dad, it's me. Vittorio."

"Vittorio, yes." Robert grinned. His brittle hair whisked against the pillow. "When I first held you, I felt as if you were a part of me, a part of me freely given. The color I'd been granted since reuniting with your mother flickered briefly then, like an old lightbulb might before it eventually goes out. And I somehow knew. I'd always known."

"Known what?"

He smiled. "That you'd somehow be the death of me."

Vitto leaned back in his chair.

"I'm only kidding . . ." His eyes searched, suddenly confused again.

"I'm here. Vittorio."

"Yes . . . Vittorio." He'd begun fidgeting with the sheets. "Where am I?"

"The Tuscany Hotel, Dad. *Your* hotel."

"My temple," he whispered, and then, "Where *was* I?"

"I was apparently the death of you."

Robert grinned, closed his eyes. "The life, Vitto. The life of me."

"You were afraid of the son just like the gods were afraid of the son."

"I was . . . until I wasn't. Until I realized the meaning of my penance here on earth. I wasn't the sun about which all the planets orbited, Vitto. I was merely one of the planets, one of the moons in need of that sun. In need of a son. To give of myself to." His pale lips seemed touched by sadness. "Just another god fallen. Or perhaps never a god at all."

"But look what you created."

"And what *you* will continue." He went quiet again, his eyes now on the ceiling, a fresco of the nine Muses. And then his head rolled toward his son again. "Vitto."

"Yes."

"Do you know what's more boring than watching paint dry?"

"What?"

"Watching an old man sleep." He grinned, shivered. "Go to your wife. And see that both sides of the bed remain occupied, always."

Thirty-Six

*T*icktock goes the clock.

    Waves crash, burying rocks in foam and mist: shoreline erased.

    Thunder booms, heavy drums. Hotel walls tremble, unseen hands grip from above. Wind whistles a rhythmic song, as delicate as a flute, as powerful as the heavens. Lightning streaks the sky, ripping with knives of gold.

    William crawls into bed with them, scared. Vitto and Valerie tell him not to be. It's just a storm, and storms pass. And yet ticktock goes the clock, the hands clicking softly, but somehow still audible through the noise.

    More thunder. More lightning. Vitto holds close to his family, and at some point he dreams of footsteps. Heavy shoes. Juba's shoes. They click-clack across the travertine as he walks, a suitcase gripped in each massive brown hand. He pauses at the fountain, rests the suitcases next to the tiles, and fills a cup with the rain. He drinks, sets the cup down, and turns back toward his bar, which is lit but curtained with rainfall. Rain drips from his fedora, the bill of which he touches and tilts toward the bar, the bar behind which his voice has carried for decades. Last call, *says the ghost of his voice, now a voice inside the walls, inside every stone. He lifts his suitcases and walks across the piazza. He disappears into the shadows, into the middle of the three Roman arches at the entrance, and ticktock goes the clock.*

    Waves soar as they hit the rocks at the shoreline, and Juba stands before it all, looking up, looking in, a suitcase in each hand. He looks up to the cliffs and then again at the sea, the raging waters, and walks right

into the roil, singing, his voice deeper than the ocean floor, more pow-
erful than its cresting waves. And as soon as he enters, the water calms.
The thunder grows silent, the sky dark, and the clouds float quietly like
his hat atop the water. The fedora disappears into the shadows, giving
way to a sun that rises yellow and bold, and ticktock goes the clock.
   But slower the hands go.
   And Vitto hears his father's voice as a child.
   "I am the Renaissance."
   And the hands on the clock grow slower.
   Ticktock.
   And then they stop.

❉

Vitto's eyes shot open.

He sat up quickly in bed, stirring both William and Valerie with
his sudden movement.

"Vitto, what is it?" Valerie hugged her pillow, groggy.

"Just a dream." Sunlight shone through the window, bright white
and yellow. He put his shoes on and tucked in his shirt. The storm
had passed, leaving in its wake a morning to be painted, a cloudless
blue sky and air fresh with spring and birdsong.

"What time is it?"

Vitto didn't know, didn't care, was suddenly afraid to look down
at his watch as he stepped out onto the piazza, where a handful of
guests stood around chatting and noticeably staring toward Robert's
closed door.

"Hey, Gandy?" Vitto turned toward John, who added, "I can't
find Juba anywhere."

Valerie and William emerged from the room, catching what was
just said. "Where do you think he's gone?"

Vitto ran to the bar and noticed the clock on the wall, the hands no longer moving. The clock had finally stopped. "Not with Magdalena's death, but . . ." He hurried to Robert's room, found his father on the bed, unmoving, peaceful, hands folded, fingers interlocked on his chest as if praying.

Valerie had stopped William at the door and then knelt next to him when he asked why Grandpa Robert wasn't moving. Tears, both silent and loud, from all three of them. On Magdalena's side of the bed lay a leather journal. On Robert's side, close to his body, his hammer and tools had been left. Next to them lay a note. Vitto unfolded it.

> Vittorio,
>
>   Your father asked that I give you this journal upon his passing. In it is the last story written by your mother, the one she told at her last call. I translated it from the Italian so that you would understand her words. In a style only befitting your father, he wishes to be buried at sea. Behind the bar, in a freshly cleaned glass, you will find two coins to pay the boatman.
>
>   Ta leme (Greek for till we speak again)
>   Juba

Vitto folded the note. Below his name Juba had drawn a symbol, a small picture of what looked to be an instrument—on second glance, a lyre.

"Vitto, what is it?" Valerie stepped into the room, eyeing what had been left on the bed.

He handed her the note, then whispered, "Apollo."

Weeping sounded across the piazza. Word of Robert's passing had spread quickly, and soon all the guests had gathered—milling aimlessly around the fountain, around the scattered tables, around the slab of marble still covered in the large brown cloth.

The note was now in William's hands. Vitto knew the boy could read the words but would not understand any of the meaning. But he'd heard what Vitto had whispered aloud. "Who is Apollo?" he asked.

Vitto walked his son out into the brightly lit piazza, any sadness now suddenly replaced with a warmth and sense of pride he wasn't yet ready to explain.

"Dad, why are you smiling?"

Vitto stopped, knelt down eye to eye with William. "Juba drew a picture of a lyre. It's the instrument known to symbolize Apollo. He's a very important god, William, the son of Zeus and the god of many things. Of sunlight and knowledge. Of music and art. Of medicine. He's always depicted in art with a face forever youthful." He patted William's tiny shoulders. "And he's the leader of the Muses."

William stared. "Why did Juba draw it?"

"I don't know." But perhaps he did and didn't know how to explain it. He took William by the hand and led him toward the marble slab Robert had covered with the brown cloth, concealing what he'd carved the other night, what he'd called his final master-piece. Together, he and Valerie and William pulled it off. The guests stepped closer, pinched in to get a better view.

The marble appeared as it had for the past several months, seemingly untouched. Vitto walked around it, looking for signs of the chiseling he knew he'd heard.

"Here it is, Gandy."

Vitto moved to where John stood but still saw nothing that could have resembled a sculpture, or even the beginnings of one. Then he looked lower and saw it—not a chisel mark or indentation, but words carefully clinked into the stone, the letters no more than an inch tall but easily readable now that they'd spotted them:

ROBERT AND MAGDALENA
THE RENAISSANCE MAN AND HIS MUSE

"Who does this?" Valerie whispered to Vitto that afternoon as they climbed aboard a gleaming yacht in the small private marina south of Gandy. "Who *chooses* to be buried at sea?"

"Someone who wants to be with his wife."

"If she's out there at all. Vitto, I don't think this is even legal."

"If we're lucky, no one will know."

His eyes took in the rustic wooden casket behind them on the deck. His father's body stretched out inside—the coins to pay the boatman on his eyes, his body and carving tools rolled inside the brown cloth he'd used to cover his final masterpiece, along with chunks of heavy stone meant to keep him below the waves.

Following Robert's instructions had taken some doing. Apparently it was one thing to bury a body at sea when you were far from land, but taking one out for that purpose had proved more of a challenge. But Robert had made arrangements that made it easier. He'd had the casket made months before and stored in the basement of Father Embry's church. And he'd called in a favor from an old friend—a famous writer who lived nearby and remembered the hotel's glory days—to arrange for the yacht. Clearly intrigued and sworn to secrecy, the man now prepared to cast off while Vitto, Valerie, William, and Father Embry donned life jackets and found their seats.

Valerie hugged her husband's arm as the yacht's big motor rumbled to life beneath them. "It just pains me to think of him out there. And what if he washes up somewhere?"

"It's what he wanted, Val." Vitto gripped Valerie's hand. "And something tells me there soon won't be a body to be found."

"What, you think it'll disappear like your mother's? As if swallowed by some great fish?"

"That would make for a story, would it not?"

"Juba will help us understand it all when he gets back." Her voice was infinitely sad, and he knew that Juba's absence was a greater loss for her. No one knew where he had gone. A search of the hotel grounds had revealed no trace of him.

Vitto considered telling her about the dream he'd had of Juba, still dressed in his clothes and fedora, walking right into these very waters and disappearing into the ocean. Perhaps one day he would tell her, once he figured out the meaning himself.

Had it been some kind of vision? Had Juba really walked into the ocean? Or had he simply gotten into a car and driven off in the night after the clock on the wall behind the bar had finally stopped ticking and after he'd left Robert's tools and Magdalena's last journal.

Her final story told.

But reading what his mother had written would have to wait for later tonight. Because once their current task was through, there was celebrating to do. Even now, back at the hotel, Johnny Two-Times and his staff was preparing a feast in his father's honor. They would dine on the piazza and bring up vintage wine from the cellar. They'd congregate and tell stories. Those who could play musical instruments would play. Those who could sing would sing. Those who could dance would dance.

It would be a feast and celebration fit for the gods. A festival to honor the Graces. A fitting good-bye to a man who'd once thought himself a god but had managed to grow into an unforgettable human.

Landry Tuffant had offered to write an article on the celebration. He'd already asked permission to write another article on the heroism of Magdalena of the Wheel, to which Vitto had hugged the man and said he'd be honored. Robert would not want the guests to be solemn, would not want the mood of the night to be full of sadness—but of life.

❁

That evening, while the guests and workers prepared, Vitto stood staring at the slab of marble on the piazza, at his mother and father's name chiseled low and small and the rest of the stone surface smooth and untouched. All that blank space seemed out of place.

William had sidled up beside him, his eyes red and his cheeks puffy from recent tears. He stood in a way that defied his years, the same upright posture he used when he made his pretend rounds on the piazza, checking heartbeats and asking questions. He held up a hammer and chisel. "I found 'em behind the bar. I don't think we were supposed to send these ones out to sea."

Vitto knelt to eye level. "You don't, huh?"

William shook his head. "I think Juba left them there so we could carve more names." He pointed toward the marble. "Too much white space."

Vitto eyed the statue that wasn't really a statue and then ruffled William's hair as an idea struck him. "Can I have those?"

William handed over the hammer and chisel. Both felt heavy and awkward in Vitto's hands, vastly different from his collection of paintbrushes. His first bite into the marble felt completely unworthy of the medium. But after his fourth and fifth blow, when he'd allowed some strength into his strike and stopped worrying about the attention his carving was now bringing across the piazza, he settled into a comfortable rhythm that didn't stop until the last letter, followed by an exclamation point. He wiped the dust clean and stepped back to view what he'd done.

The lettering was clear and substantial, if not quite as polished as Robert's inscription: "Juba was here!"

Satisfied with how it looked and in a hurry to get to his mother's journal, to her final story and the entry made in the hours before she'd jumped off the cliff, which he was to read at last call that night, Vitto placed the hammer and chisel on the travertine. They would remain until Mrs. Eaves passed away three weeks later, her name, along with a few piano keys, chiseled into the marble by the increasingly unsteady hand of Cowboy Cane.

"Miss Elenore Eaves," he chiseled, "was here too!"

Thirty-Seven

*M*agdalena's hands shook as she found the place in her journal, knowing her story would lend a finality to the night's last call that no one would know about until later. They'd heard her stories before and would not think much of this one during the telling of it.

But later, she wondered, *will they understand?*

She noticed that Vitto and Valerie were not in attendance this evening. She'd written down in her journal that the two of them had fought only hours ago and that she'd been the reason for it. Valerie had been right. "Dear Valerie, how astute you are. I am dying. The water is slowly doing this to me, I know, but it is the only way." She found her hands calming as she looked over the guests standing across the piazza, her heart slowing to a comfortable pace as she reviewed the first words of her story, written previously in Italian.

The crowd hushed in anticipation.

"Mnemosyne," she began, "the goddess of memory and time, was also the inventor of languages and words, and so she came to represent the memorization needed to pass stories from generation to generation—history and myth, family sagas and oral history—because writing had not yet been invented."

She paced as she spoke, as was her custom. "After the Titanomachy, when Zeus became the newly established ruler of all the gods, he set out with a plan to seduce the lovely Mnemosyne, disguising himself as a shepherd."

She winked at the crowd. "Now cover your ears because this story is about to get a little naughty." She waited for laughter to die down. "They slept together for nine consecutive days before returning to Mount Olympus, and from that union the nine Muses were born."

Magdalena sneaked a glance at her husband, who stood to the side, listening intently. She found it difficult to look at him, knowing what she planned to do later. Afraid that if she met his eyes she would not be able to go on with the story—or the plans.

"Overjoyed with his new daughters, Zeus first kept them close by his throne to entertain his guests with stories and song. He soon made his son Apollo, the god of music and prophecy, their leader and guardian and sent them to earth, where they inspired golden ages of history—great works of art and music and story."

Here she paused and briefly locked eyes with Juba, who was standing next to the fountain of the piazza. *Dear Juba, thank you,* she said with her eyes, and he nodded in return. "Apollo took his role seriously and never let the Muses out of his sight, promising to always protect them and their mother, Mnemosyne.

"Then came a time when life on earth grew dark. The evils that had emerged from Pandora's box were slowly taking over—pride and envy, pain and greed and suffering." She paused again, closed her eyes briefly to gather herself. "So much suffering. War and poverty, ignorance and abuse, hunger and pestilence wreaked havoc on the human race while the gods watched from their perch on Mount Olympus. Barbarians invaded centers of learning and ransacked great works of art. Learned men and women hid themselves and their books away. A plague known as Black Death devastated town after town. And Apollo, fearing for the safety of his charges, hustled the Muses back to Olympus, to their place beside the throne of Zeus."

Magdalena's energy surged as the story took hold of her, and she played to the crowd, acting out her next words, the next actions. "For a long time, the gods on Olympus watched the swirling darkness below, the ravages of Pandora's evils. But one day Mnemosyne, sitting lazily upon her throne of stone and surrounded by her fountain of water, which triggered memory, reminded Zeus that Pandora had closed her box before all its inhabitants escaped. But that one day it had whispered."

Mr. Carney shouted from the crowd. "What did it whisper, Magdalena?"

She waited for the chuckles to die down and said with a grin, "That there was hope inside that box, and it badly wanted out. So Pandora had opened the box." Again, she gestured, pantomiming a winged thing emerging from captivity. "And out came hope for all mankind."

She mimicked a conversation with the goddess: "What is your point, Mnemosyne? That humans need to be reminded of that? Of hope? Well, perhaps you're right. So what do you propose, now that plague has nearly finished off the lot of them?"

Mr. Carney, drunk and happy, shouted, "What did she propose, Magdalena?"

She pointed at him as if she'd pointed at Zeus himself. "A rebirth, Mr. Carney. Mnemosyne told Zeus that life on earth needn't be so gloomy and harsh, so full of hard work and ignorance and wars and disease. What humans needed was a new way of thinking—or rather an *old* way of thinking. A return to the classical vision of the Greeks and Romans. Of beauty and light and reason and hope."

She gestured to the hotel around them before continuing. "Mnemosyne nodded toward the nine Muses, who danced listlessly around their father's throne. Through the years since their return to Olympus, they had grown increasingly bored. 'We should put them back to work, Zeus, doing what they were born to do.'"

Magdalena turned in a circle, taking in the gazes from all her listeners. "'Life for people below can be enjoyable again, Zeus. They need beauty and comfort and education. Art and science and music and poetry can change the way they think and make their lives more beautiful.'

"'So what do you propose?' asked Zeus."

Mr. Carney again: "What does Zeus propose, Magdalena?"

"'As I said, a rebirth. We'll call it a Renaissance. We'll send the girls down there to inspire and bring beauty and light to a world gone dreary. It's time. Past time.'

"'And where should we send them?'"

Mr. Carney was about to shout it out, but Magdalena's suddenly serious look stopped him. "'To Italy,' said Mnemosyne, 'because the humans there once knew us well. And specifically to Tuscany, because it's the most beautiful place on earth.'"

Magdalena smiled, knowing her listeners were aware of her birthplace and would get her little joke. She went on, "And that's what they did. One by one, over a course of years, the nine Muses were delegated to Tuscany, to the city known as Florence. And soon their influence spread to surrounding cities such as Rome and Milan and Venice. It wasn't long before the Muses spread their influence to all of Europe, inspiring great art and music, architecture and songs, writings and buildings, the like of which no one had ever seen before."

Magdalena paused to take a drink from the cup she'd rested on the fountain's edge before she'd begun—none of them knowing the drink within had come from the very fountain around which they'd congregated. "The Muses didn't stay on earth all the time, of course. They returned often to their home on Olympus, each one somehow transformed by her time on earth, more glorious and beautiful, with tales of great artists and scientists and musicians. And each, upon her return, begged to be sent back down to do more. Every artist needed a muse, and there were too many artists and creators now to count.

"Even Mnemosyne, who watched daily and monthly and yearly from above, itched to go down and see for herself this Renaissance that was her brainchild. She longed especially to see a man her nine daughters had spoken of, a mortal man of strength and honor who had been born with a hammer in his hand, a man with flowing hair that gave him strength, a man who carved beautiful statues from marble that made even Michelangelo rage with envy."

Magdalena surveyed the crowd and noticed that Robert had conveniently walked away, somehow knowing where her story would lead. "A man who claimed to be more than a man. A beautiful but prideful man who claimed to *be* the Renaissance. A culmination of all those who had painted and sculpted and thought and created through the years. This man saw color like no other because he claimed to *be* color. He was stone and canvas and tile and cloth and everything in between. He was a thinker and a scientist, and he walked the Italian streets like a god fallen from the sky, the envy of every man and the focus of every woman, including the nine Muses and now of Mnemosyne herself."

Magdalena drank more water and scanned the crowd again for Robert, for Vitto, for Valerie. But finding them still absent, she continued her story, perhaps now with more vigor and confidence *because* they were not there to hear it. *Because* they were not ready to hear it.

"Then one day"—she held up an index finger to the sky—"Zeus grew jealous of all this attention the Renaissance man was drawing. He sent a lightning bolt down from the heavens that hit the man in the heart and turned him into a statue, frozen in midwalk right there on the streets of Florence." Here she briefly froze like a statue. "And for months he was the curiosity of many, looking even more godlike than before, but unable to live and create.

"Mnemosyne cried to Zeus, pleading for him to undo what he'd done, but Zeus was stubborn. He said the only thing that would free the Renaissance man would be her tears, which would never reach him, because Zeus would never allow her to go to Florence. She hatched a plan to sneak down while Zeus slept, but he learned of her plan and vowed never to sleep.

"'The Muses have outdone themselves,' he told her. 'They've helped create much that is good, only to have let the heads of mortals grow large with pride. They need closer watching—as do you, my love.'

"Mnemosyne fretted, unable to change Zeus's mind but determined to help the Renaissance man. So one day when Zeus was in one of his moods, stomping about the heavens and creating rumbles of thunder with each step, she whispered to the underworld, her voice echoing to the cave of Hypnos, begging for him to somehow force Zeus to sleep."

Mr. Carney's gaze was now fully on her, as was everyone else's.

"Hypnos echoed back that he would grant her request, but under one condition. 'Anything,' she said, for the longer she looked upon that statue frozen on the streets of Florence, the more she fell in love with the man created from her own heart. "'I will give you a beautiful chalice filled with water from the River Lethe, disguised as the sweetest wine,' said Hypnos. 'Zeus will drink of it and fall asleep, as requested. But you must drink from the chalice, too, and forget that this conversation ever took place.'

"Mnemosyne agreed to these terms and followed them to the letter. Zeus did fall asleep that night, and she did sip from the chalice, just enough to forget that her conversation with Hypnos had ever taken place. Then she prepared to go to earth while her consort slumbered. The heavens were still rumbling from Zeus's day of stomping about, and when a lightning bolt split the clouds she traveled with it, landing on the streets of Florence in the middle of the night. She approached the stony Renaissance man and stared at it for what seemed like years before kneeling next to it and wrapping her arms around the front leg. There she wept and eventually fell asleep."

Magdalena wiped her own eyes and went on. "When Mnemosyne awoke it was day, and the streets teemed with people, many talking about the statue and wondering aloud where it had gone. But there was a strong hand gripping her own, telling her they must hide, pulling her through the crowds, this way and that, until they stopped in the shadows of a tall stone building. Mnemosyne looked up and recognized her Renaissance man. His muscles were taut, his eyes blue like the sky. Her tears had undone the stony curse that Zeus had cast for him.

"The two of them spent days and nights on the streets while thunder rumbled above. They agreed to marry, and with a push from the oceans and seas they returned to the heavens, hand in hand.

"Zeus, of course, was filled with jealousy and rage. He pointed toward this mortal man who had claimed to be a god and threatened to lop off his head with a sickle. The man opened his arms and said, 'But I am the Renaissance, created from the heart and mind of the woman I was born to love.' And Zeus couldn't argue with that.

"The Muses, meanwhile, grew jealous as well, because they, too, loved the man they believed they'd helped create. Soon they began arguing with one another, and even Apollo couldn't calm them. Annoyed with their bickering, Zeus bundled them together with rope and threatened to eat them all, as his father Cronus had done with his children. But his love for them overcame his anger and he released them—for the moment.

"The Renaissance man, now garbed in the rich, colorful robes Mnemosyne had given him, asked Zeus to make him immortal so that he and the mother of the Muses could live as one. But Zeus took offense.

"'You!' he shouted, pointing to the Renaissance man." Magdalena's voice grew angry, sterner, as the story called for, although, unbeknownst to her listeners, her anger was real. "'Walking and talking and acting like a god does not make you one. Your pride and your greed will certainly be your downfall.'

"'And you!' Now he pointed to Mnemosyne. 'Your deception must not be rewarded.'

"Meanwhile, behind him, the Muses still bickered. And Zeus, tired of hearing it, rolled them all into a ball, Mnemosyne with them, until they all became one—one woman, one muse, one goddess, fallen—all while Apollo and the rest of the court watched on in shock."

Magdalena scanned the crowd again. Juba now watched her intently from the bar. "Zeus then took the chalice from the arm of his throne, the one still mostly full from what he'd sipped before. He made the new woman drink it all gone and told her she'd return to earth with the waters from the River Lethe flowing through her. And from the Renaissance man, who stood before him in his robes of the richest red and blue and gold, Zeus took his ability to see the color that surrounded him.

"Zeus took away their gifts, you see. He pronounced it as a sentence: 'You must both return to earth and live among mortals, but far away from one another. You'—he pointed toward the new woman—'will no longer remember that you ever knew him. And you who are called Renaissance man'—he pointed toward the man—'will no longer see the color that you claimed to embody.' But then, thinking of Pandora's box, he offered them a tiny bit of hope: 'If you somehow manage to find one another again, all will be returned.'

"'And then I'll be made immortal?' asked the Renaissance man.

"'No,' said Zeus, 'not until lessons are learned.'" Magdalena pointed to the crowd. "'Not until pride is returned to Pandora's box and hope is again set free. Not until giving of yourself becomes more important than yearning for what you have lost. Only then will you be made immortal.'

"Zeus had made his pronouncement, but his anger remained. Anger at Apollo for not keeping a close enough eye on the Muses. Anger at his consort Mnemosyne for tricking him and defying him. Anger at his daughters for doing too good a job on earth. Anger at this man whose pride had tempted fate. And anger, perhaps, at himself, for acting in haste and destroying those he loved."

Magdalena playacted what she said next. "The angry Zeus stomped, and the heavens rumbled. He stomped again, and lightning cut through darkness all over the world. He picked up the empty chalice, still wet with the waters of forgetfulness, and hurled it at Mnemosyne's memory fountain.

"A few drops of the water splashed, escaping through the clouds and mixing with the waters of a little creek that flowed over a small outcropping of coastal land. Mixed with forgetfulness, the creek waters didn't know which way to flow, so it tried one way and then another, eternally confused.

"Zeus then upturned the stones of Mnemosyne's fountain and hurled them, piece by memory-soaked piece, down to the earth, where the stones and water they once held landed a few hundred yards away from the creek. Next, he threw a bolt of lightning through the clouds, opening them vast and wide, and torrents of rainwater mixed with the remnants of forgetfulness fell upon the earth, where it touched the elderly like a plague.

"Zeus stomped again, and the heavens opened wider." Magdalena held her arms skyward, hands to the clouds. "First the Renaissance man tumbled down. The woman who used to be Mnemosyne and her Muses soon followed. Before the clouds closed up, Apollo opened his lungs in song and, as the protector of the Muses, went after them. All of them tumbled toward the raging seas.

"Zeus looked down as they fell and felt a pang of remorse. He called upon his brother Poseidon to not let them drown in his waters, but to spit them back up to the shore instead, where they would start their lives anew." Magdalena closed her eyes, felt her heart thumping now against her rib cage. "'And he sent down to the woman a bit of his own rage to protect her should she ever need it and to parcel it out as she must.'"

Flashes of blood, flashes of that horrible man, Lippi, urged Magdalena's words faster. "The waves then calmed enough for another voice to be heard in the wind. The voice of Zeus's other brother Hades, echoing up like a rumbling belch from the underworld, claiming that one of the stones from Mnemosyne's fountain had been hurled with such force that it had crashed through to the underworld and into the River Styx, leaving a gaping hole through which the light streamed and Mnemosyne's memory water dripped.

"This intrusion enraged the gods of death—Thanatos and his blood-craving sisters, the Keres, all of them agents of the Fates. The Keres looked up through the hole and dripping water and promised violent death to anyone who drank from it. But Thanatos, like his twin brother, Hypnos, had a touch that was gentle. He plugged the hole with the stone that had caused it, assuring Zeus that any death from the water that remained would be nonviolent and brought about during sleep."

She lowered her head, closed her eyes again. "And with that, Zeus was satisfied."

After

*T*he nurse parked Vittorio Gandy's wheelchair in the same place every morning—within arm's reach of the piazza's central fountain, where Cronus wrestled with memory and forgetfulness, close enough for him to reach over the tiled edge and run his fingers through the water. Close enough to hear the trickle coming from the mouths of the chimeras.

From there he could see over the southern crenellations to the terraced olive grove, where plump green ovals weighted down limbs. Around him, scattered throughout the piazza—some standing, some in wheelchairs like his own—were dozens of men and women his age, battling as he was to remember the simplest of things: how old they were, what their names were, what they'd just eaten for breakfast—or whether they had eaten at all. The name of the man who'd tied his shoes for him this morning, the one with the bald spot forming on the top of his head. The name of the lovely nurse who had parked him seconds ago.

"What is your name, dear?" At nearly ninety-eight years old, his voice now rattled like the rest of him. "I know your eyes."

The brunette nurse sat on the edge of the fountain and gripped his hand, a hand now covered in liver spots and curled wretchedly with arthritis. "I'm Amy, Grandpa. Amy Gandy. Your granddaughter."

"Ah, yes. Amy." He pretended to recollect but only had a vague impression, although her eyes reminded him deeply of someone.

She must have sensed his confusion, a daily thing, and pulled a notebook from the side pocket of his wheelchair. She opened the first page for him and pointed to the words. He could still read on most days and assumed she wanted him to do so. "Vittorio Gandy."

"That's you."

He looked back down. "Married to Valerie Gandy, now deceased."

Now he remembered. "You have her eyes, Amy. My Valerie's eyes. What's funny?"

"Nothing, Grandpa. It's just that you tell me so every morning, and it never gets old."

He looked to the notebook—his journal, as it was called. Everyone in the hotel had one, carried at all times to remind them who they were. "It says she was a violinist."

Amy nodded, *yes, go on*, encouraging him. Vitto read, "She started the hotel's music therapy program, which she, at the time, called musical medicine."

"Yes," said Amy. "From the stories I was told, she would play the violin for the guests here on the piazza or in their rooms sometimes at night to help some fall asleep or calm down. She was convinced that music could help restore memory. That it could calm and remind and heal."

"Yes," said Vitto, wheezing out a laugh. "She loved her violin. Where is she now?"

"She passed away ten years ago, Grandpa. She's buried here, though. In the cemetery. We could go now if you'd like, although we normally wait until after lunch."

"Yes." He nodded, tried hard to remember. "After lunch. Do you work here?"

"I'm a nurse, yes."

"And I'm a patient?"

"Of sorts." She lowered her voice and playfully said, "But we don't call them patients here. You're all guests."

"Guests?"

"Of the hotel."

"Ah, yes. The hotel."

"Your father's hotel."

"Yes. Father's hotel." He paused. "You're pretty. You've got eyes I've seen before."

That laugh again. She leaned forward and turned a page in the notebook, where a few pictures had been glued. The same pictures were on the iPad in the wheelchair's side pocket, but they'd learned that the real photos brought back memories more readily.

Amy pointed toward the first photo. "That's you and Valerie at my father's wedding."

"Who's your father?"

"William. William Gandy. Your son. And his wife is my mother. Claire."

"Yes, William and Claire. What do they do?"

"They run the hotel. My father, William. Your son. He's the doctor here." She pointed across the hotel to a white-haired man walking stooped and holding a clipboard, stopping to chat with an even older woman. "There he is. Your son, William. He's been the doctor here for decades now. Since the seventies, I believe. Guests come from far and wide to stay here."

"Why?"

"Well, because of our success with the elderly," she said. "With those with Alzheimer's and other forms of dementia."

"Which do I have?"

"We're pretty sure you have Alzheimer's, Grandpa."

"Sounds like nasty business."

"It is, but we somehow make things work here. As well as they can be worked, I suppose."

Vitto looked around, felt around, his fingers prodding in the side pocket, reaching for the iPad. She asked him if he wanted to take a picture, and he said yes.

"Of what?"

"Of you," he said. "Right there next to the fountain. Like a painting."

She helped him hold the electronic device, reminded him of what button to press, and then sat back down on the fountain to be photographed. When finished, she showed him the picture he'd taken, and then with the pad of her index finger swiped left and right to show him similar pictures he'd taken in the past days.

"You started all of this," she said.

"All of what?"

"The pictures. Every guest here has one of those. Some use their phones. Some still use old-fashioned cameras. They take pictures to capture memories, Grandpa. Do you remember the paintings you used to do? Of the guests here? To help them remember?"

He nodded slowly but didn't really. Vaguely, perhaps.

"You called it painting the real," she said. "At least that's how Dad tells it. So that's what we do with our cameras."

Vitto nodded, grinned, stared into the fountain, at the water as it rippled. "We used to drink from this fountain."

She chuckled, patted his hand. "No one used to drink from the fountain, Grandpa."

"It was like medicine."

"As the story goes," she agreed. "But those were only stories."

Vitto watched the water, the shimmer blurring and distorting the blue and yellow tiles below it. "It worked for a time . . . the water. But then it didn't. Over time it didn't. It became just . . . water."

"That's why so many come here still," she said. "They say there's something in the water. Something about the ocean. The Alzheimer's, it can't be fixed, but there's something about this place that makes it, well, manageable. The senses are somehow stimulated by all of this art and music and . . . the Renaissance."

"Rebirth."

"Yes. That's what you always said this hotel would be for the guests. A rebirth."

"They used to come here to live."

"And they do still."

"There was something in the water. There were miracles in the water."

"No miracles," she said, patting his hand again. "Just us. Humans doing for others."

"Yes, doing for others."

"And it was all started by you. And Grandma. And the stories of Great-Grandpa Robert and Magdalena."

Magdalena. That name. He knew it . . . but couldn't quite grasp it.

He didn't say anything more for several minutes. Then, "Valerie, can you take me for a ride?"

"It's Amy."

"What's funny? Why are you always laughing at me?"

"Because we have to. We have to laugh."

"And why is that?"

"We'd go crazy if we didn't."

"Humor is the universal language," he said. The elevated words seemed to shock her. "Just something someone once said to me. Can you take me for a ride?"

She unlocked the brakes on the wheelchair and pushed him around the fountain, and as they circled, he named all the colors of the doors, the slight variances in shade as one wing angled into another until all the colors of the color wheel were represented. "You never cease to amaze me, Grandpa."

"How so?"

"Every day you tell me the names of each and every color, of each and every door."

"Yes, color. Always color."

They were both silent for a bit as she pushed and the wind

whispered words that could have been song. The wheels went thump-thump over the travertine. "Stop there, please." He pointed toward the large piece of marble on the northwestern side of the piazza, not far from the bar. "Tell me about this."

"It was your father's last masterpiece."

Vitto ran his hands over the surface, the engraving of so many names—hundreds and hundreds of names—all etched under his fingertips.

"The guests," she told him. "After they leave here, their names are carved into the stone."

"You mean die," he said. "Pass away. Not leave."

She didn't argue with him, although it had become legend by now that Magdalena's body had never been found, and days after Sir Robert Gandy's body had been buried at sea, they'd found his coffin floating empty. And no one ever heard from Juba again.

She pointed to his father's name, carved by Robert half a century ago, and then the name of Juba. Vitto's fingers found Cowboy Cane next. Johnny Two-Times and his wife, Beverly. A woman named Elenore Eaves. Landry Tuffant's name was there too. The reporter, who had come on as an employee of the hotel soon after Robert's passing, had continued to write a daily column in the *Gandy Gazette* and started a hotel newspaper, the *Tuscany Tribune,* in the early 1950s.

Vitto pointed next to the bar, so she rolled him there. A man he recognized vaguely was cleaning glasses behind the bar and nodded to him with respect. "Mr. Gandy. How are you this fine morning?"

Vitto sat confused. "I'd be better with some wine in one of those glasses."

The bartender smiled. "How about orange juice?"

"How about orange juice that bubbles?"

The man laughed. "So the usual."

"The usual, Juba." He knew it wasn't Juba, but the way the bartender laughed and then shared a glance with Amy made him think that this, too, was a daily occurrence. He pointed to the wall behind the bar, the place between the shelves where the old clock hung. "The clock on the wall is broken."

"Since the spring of '46, Mr. Gandy." The man handed Vitto his spiked orange juice and the nurse rolled him onward, around the outskirts of the piazza, following the blue mosaic tiles. They passed a cluster of men and women painting, a young woman playing piano, and a gathering of people fumbling through some kind of craft with bright yarn. Vitto could still see the colors so vividly it hurt his eyes.

She rolled him through the front arches to see the statue of Cupid, to the poppy field spotted in brilliant orange and red, past vineyards and olives trees that now thrived again.

Vitto sipped his orange juice. The wind tousled his thin hair. "Beautiful, Valerie."

The woman pushing his wheelchair laughed and patted his shoulder. "Isn't it, though, Grandpa?" So that's who she was. He had a granddaughter. "They say Gandy gets more rain than any other place in California."

He stared down the valley, at the robust vineyards. "Must be something in the water." He had her stop outside a stone building that looked familiar to him. She said it was the building where the olives were made into oil. He smiled, raised his arm. "There's a loft up there."

"Yes, that's where they store the blankets and willow baskets for the olive harvest."

Vitto smiled. "That's not all that happened up there." He didn't elaborate, but she laughed again. He didn't want to tell the stranger pushing him about such things, so he said simply, "I met my wife up there. When we were kids."

"Did you know your wife was my grandmother?"

"She is?"

"Yes."

"Where is she? I think the two of you should meet then."

"She's gone, Grandpa. She died."

The wave of sadness began to dissipate almost as soon as it struck. "When did she die?"

"Years ago."

"Oh, yes, yes. That's right. We should visit her today. I'd like to invite her to lunch. She plays the violin, you know. I'll have her play for you."

The wind picked up as they approached the cliffs, and the woman behind him had to exert herself to get him up the paved incline. He braced his hands on the armrests and leaned back. "Have you ever been on a roller coaster?"

"I have," said the woman. "I hear that you and Grandma once got stuck at the top of a Ferris wheel."

"Yes, yes, we did." He didn't remember completely, but something brought about a smile. He pointed toward the cliff, where it narrowed out to a triangular outcropping that resembled the one in Athens, the crumbled temple of Poseidon. A chinking sound echoed, the sound of hammer and chisel and stone. There was a woman out there, with long gray hair that flowed like a ripped flag might. "Who is that?"

"Your daughter, Grandpa. My aunt."

"You sure?"

"Quite sure," said the woman behind him, now leaning and speaking directly into his ear as she pushed. "You and Grandma had her in 1947."

"Why do you know so much about me?"

"Her name is Violeta."

"Violeta," he said. "Yes. Violeta. William was six or seven when she was born."

"And all that hair," said the woman. "Do you remember? She was born with all that orange hair. With eyes green as olives."

Vitto smiled. "Like Magdalena."

"That's what everyone said. Her hair is gray now, but it was once the color of fresh paint."

The hammering grew louder. "What is she doing?"

"Working on another statue."

"She's an artist, huh?"

"Not just an artist, Grandpa, but *the* artist. She has sculptures and paintings all over the world. In museums and castles. In private homes and estates. The great Violeta Gandy."

"What's she doing?" Whatever the statue was, it appeared to be nearly finished and included several figures, three of them nude women.

The series of sculpted figures were all mounted on a grand marble slab, facing out over the cliff to the vastness of the ocean beyond. "She's calling this her masterpiece." She pointed. "The three who are holding hands and dancing—those are the three Graces. Or some call them the three Charites."

"Daughters of Zeus," he said, his mind becoming clearer the closer he got to the cliff, to the sound and mist of the crashing water. "Goddesses of beauty and charm and creativity. Good cheer and joyfulness."

"And friends to the nine Muses."

"Yes, the Muses." She pointed to the right, down along the cliff's edge, where the land eventually dipped lower toward the tennis courts. Ten more statues overlooked the ocean. "She finished those last year. The Muses . . . and Apollo."

She parked his wheelchair next to the statue the woman with the long gray hair was chiseling. The dancing figures of the Graces cast shadows across his face and torso, leaving his legs warmed by the sun. Next to them was another grouping, the one now in progress, of a man and woman intertwined lovingly, their figures holding hands and spiraling up from waves that reached for them. Vitto somehow knew them to be his parents, Robert and Magdalena.

The creators.

The woman with the long gray hair poked her head out from behind Robert Gandy's marble arm. "Daddy."

He looked over his shoulder for affirmation. *Who is this woman? Who are you?*

She carefully placed her hammer and chisel on the ground. "I'm Violeta. Your daughter."

"Yes. Violeta. Of course." Her gray hair held a hint of gold, and he could see it as fire even still, just as he had when she was born. The wind blew ocean mist, and along with it came memories. "You paint too. Some say better than I?"

"Some say," she laughed. "But I disagree."

More memories struck him. "Father Embry—after Father died, Father Embry told me about that creek out there. The Lethe. That wasn't the first time it changed direction. It did it three times before that."

"And four times since," she added. "There is always a quake before the river changes direction, yet it doesn't always change when there's a quake. We know that now. It's like sand in an hourglass. When one end runs out, it flips back."

"So it didn't only happen when the guests arrived." What the hotel now commonly referred to as the hotel's rebirth. "The water in that fountain. It once restored memory."

Violeta nodded. "So the story goes."

"Then the clock stopped. The water . . . It slowly . . ." He lost his train of thought.

Violeta helped him. "It slowly became just that . . . water." She opened her arms to the hotel behind him. "But look what sprang forth, Daddy."

"Yes," he said, craning his neck to look over his shoulder at the hotel. After a moment he focused again toward the cliff, toward the ocean. He smiled, broad and wide. "Barrel of sunshine or a barrel of stones, Gandy."

Neither woman responded; he'd spoken the words aloud, but somehow for himself. "What's it called now, that creek? William changed it. Not the River of Forgetfulness."

Violeta said, "We call it the River of Life now. People cross the bridge, Daddy, and that's just what they do. They live—right down to their last day."

He stared at her, into her green eyes. "You play the violin. And piano." He remembered now, her voice every evening at last call, so different than Juba's but no less lovely and demanding. "And you sing."

"Yes, Daddy. All of those things."

The woman who had pushed his wheelchair to the cliff leaned toward his ear again. "And she's in charge of our music and art therapy programs here, while William runs the more clinical aspects of the hotel. They're both doctors, just different kinds."

Violeta stepped closer, and the closer she got the more familiar she looked, although Vitto wasn't quite clear why. "Enough about me," she said. "Tell me how your day has gone so far."

Vitto didn't know, so he held up his orange juice and sipped from it, which made his daughter chuckle. Without knowing why— possibly he did the same every day—he blurted out, "Violeta, tell me a story."

And, without hesitation, she did.

A Note from the Author

Tell me a story . . .

This simple line is mentioned more than once in the novel, as the telling of stories plays such a crucial role. *Midnight at the Tuscany Hotel* is an example of that rapidly growing genre of post-WWII, historical, Renaissance art, Greek god, and magical realism mashup! Okay, so maybe that's not a thing. Until now. Perhaps it will catch on? Who knows? The bottom line is, I don't always adhere to a specific genre, and, even though all of my novels are rooted in history, I tend to oftentimes fall under the spell of that childhood bedtime precept: *tell me a story!* Regardless of what genre walls it crosses. And so I've told you a story, and if you've made it this far, hopefully you enjoyed it, as I've done my very best to tell it.

The story, for me, began percolating decades ago, in my childhood, without me even being aware the seeds had been planted: the seeds of my artistic upbringing, raised in a loving house where creativity and art and music and books thrived. My dad was for decades, and still is, a creator of stained glass, with thousands of beautiful windows all over the country. Also a sculptor and painter and poet, his creative influence trickled down to his children. When his turn-table wasn't spinning album after album, my sister's piano music echoed perfectly off the walls and down hallways—walls adorned with framed paintings and hallways where sculptures easily lurked. It was a house where my brothers were allowed to draw on their bedroom walls, not mere scribbles but sketches and world-building that, even at young ages, had the quality of storybooks. On every end table and floor-to-ceiling bookshelf there seemed to be books on art and art history, on Renaissance sculptors and painters and the ancients, and by high school I'd flipped through them all, developing not only an appreciation for the arts, humanities, and history but for books and the written word in general.

All of this helped conjure the fictional Tuscany Hotel, make it real, and inspire the writing of the novel. Although Gandy, California, is a fictional place, the foundling hospital in Florence, where Magdalena was left abandoned, was real and is now a popular museum. I tried to make Magdalena's stay in Pienza as realistic as possible, and likewise with all my mentioning of the Greek gods, which was a daunting task. Any mistakes are certainly mine. Many of the war memories and post-war trauma experienced by both Vitto and Johnny Two-Times were directly inspired by my grandfather's time in Europe during the war, which is why this novel was dedicated to him. As stated at the beginning, to me he was a god of bravery and courage. And his son, my father, is still, in my eyes, a god of creativity and art. Aspects of both men inspired the fictional father and son combo of Robert and Vittorio Gandy. I'd always assumed, and I'm sure my father wouldn't deny, that in fifty-plus years of marriage, my mother was and still is his muse, just as my artistic upbringing and my wife will forever be mine.

Thanks for reading!

James

Acknowledgments

Without the help of others, most novels wouldn't get off the runway, and *Midnight at the Tuscany Hotel* was no different. In a sense, I'd been conceptualizing this story for years but couldn't figure out the best way to build it, until I decided to do what Robert Gandy did with his construction of the Tuscany Hotel and start with the piazza fountain. And after Dr. John Markert gave me some inspiring ideas, I was off and running. But then, after plowing through the first half of the novel quite quickly, things suddenly screeched to a halt, and I was hammered with the dilemma—*I know where I want to go with this, but how to get there?* I needed a bridge, something to connect all this talk of Greek gods and art and memory together, and so I then leaned heavily on my editor, Kimberly Carlton, who read the first half and saved me from bagging it altogether. Instead, after a few brainstorming phone calls, I renewed writing, with gusto, and ended up with possibly my favorite novel to date. So, thank you! To Anne Buchanan for another outstanding line edit. I know this one, especially with the convoluted timelines, wasn't easy. To Laura Wheeler for taking the novel to the editorial finish line. At the risk of leaving someone out, which is why I both enjoy and hate writing acknowledgments, thank you to EVERYONE at Thomas Nelson who worked on this novel, before and after publication, from marketing and editorial to proofreading and publicity and cover design! Thank you to my friends and family for the continued support, and for showing up at every book release party at 3rd Turn Brewing to drink beer. To my parents for instilling in me the drive to be creative. To Dan Lazar at Writers House for giving me the start I so readily needed. Onward, upward, and thank you! To Kim Lionetti, thanks so much for championing my work; the future looks bright! To my children, Ryan and Molly, you continue to impress and inspire. To Tracy, my wife of nearly twenty years—I always save the best for last—thank you for paying my bills when needed and for putting up with my #writerslife.

Discussion Questions

1. There are plenty of flawed characters in *Midnight at the Tuscany Hotel*. Pick a couple of your favorites and discuss how redemption plays a role for them by the end of the story.

2. As a glass half-full kind of guy, I've always looked toward the positive side of life. How do the themes of optimism and hope play out in the novel?

3. At the end of the story, Juba, one of my favorite characters, leaves the hotel under mysterious circumstances. Where might he have gone? And why did he leave at that point?

4. As with the water inside the piazza fountain at the Tuscany Hotel, things in life aren't always as perfect as they seem. If given the difficult choice thrust upon the guests at the hotel, what would you do? Drink or no? Stay or go?

5. The Tuscany Hotel was a place of dreams and beauty and lore. Imagine yourself there in its heyday. I certainly did. Who would you most like to meet, whether it be an imagined character from the book or a person of history from the time period? What would you spend your day doing at the Tuscany Hotel?

6. If you had one story to tell at Last Call, what would it be? Truth or lies?

7. Young William Gandy might not be considered a major character, but how is his role in the novel no less significant than the other, older characters?

8. The parent/child theme in *Midnight at the Tuscany Hotel* is

an important one. Discuss the various relationships, namely Vitto and Robert, Vitto and William, Juba and Valerie, and Magdalena and Vitto. How are they similar? How are they different?

9. When writing a novel, I also like to visualize it as a movie. Who would you have playing the parts of Robert, Vitto, Valerie, Magdalena, Juba, and Johnny Two-Times?

10. During troubling times, especially when dealing with the difficulties of a disease like Alzheimer's, humor, as stated in the book, can be the universal language. I made sure to add plenty of humor to the goings on at the Tuscany Hotel. What were some of the more humorous scenes? Many for me involved Johnny Two-Times, a true barrel of sunshine.

11. In the novel, the Tuscany Hotel is almost a character in itself. Discuss examples of how it not only comes to life but seems to conjure it.

12. Memories can be a double-edged sword. While some memories can heal, others hurt. Discuss examples of both.

Enjoy this excerpt from the book described as "historical fiction at its finest" (Booklist STARRED review).

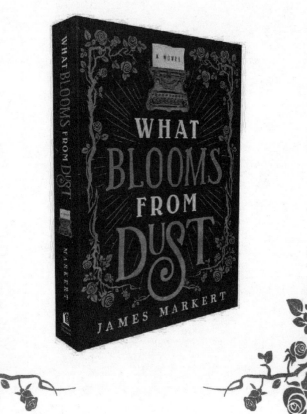

Before

1908
SOUTHERN PLAINS

*T*he train ride out west was free.

Paid in full by the brand-new state of Oklahoma in hopes of encouraging settlement in the land once occupied by bison and Indians. Wilmington Goodbye knew the truth of it. They'd been killed off—the bison, for sure, and too many of the Indians to count. Those that survived the cowboys and Rangers got squeezed together into reservations. The state had earmarked the rest of the land for homesteading. And no place looked more promising than Majestic, Oklahoma.

Wilmington studied the pamphlet for the tenth time in the last hour—glorious pictures of elegant buildings, paved roads edged by flowers, show houses where finely dressed couples wandered about. And that fountain in the town center looked majestic in itself.

With each *choof* of the train, Wilmington and his pregnant wife, Amanda, inched closer to becoming landowners, with fresh soil to plow up and a fortune to be made in a state just one year old.

He folded the pamphlet and slid it back into his suit pocket. He teased the corners of his mustache and straightened the fresh rose he'd pinned to his lapel that morning.

"Health, wealth, and opportunity, love."

Amanda was bathed in sunlight nearly the color of her hair. She smiled. They'd repeated the slogan often enough, as had the rest of the men and women on the train. He'd met half of them already and was proud to call them future neighbors.

Citizens of Majestic.

He had a notion to look at the pamphlet again but resisted. Instead he watched his wife as miles of grassland flashed in the background. The doctor back east said the air would be better for her out here, away from the city pollution. Her breathing had already become less labored. The swell of her belly pressed tight against her blue dress. *She has to have an entire brood in there.* She'd laughed the idea off at first, but had recently admitted she felt more than one baby kicking around.

Tall prairie grass swayed alongside the speeding train. Miles of velvety blades, moving like something Wilmington couldn't quite put a finger on. *Ocean waves, maybe.* They had to be getting close. But where were the buildings? Where were the roads? And that town center? Shouldn't they see it over the horizon?

Two minutes later the train slowed and then screeched to a halt.

"Why are we stopping?" asked a man Wilmington now knew as Orion Bentley, a fancy gentleman in a suit as sharp as his wit and a bowler hat straight from the newest catalogues. They'd befriended each other minutes after boarding the train and had engaged in meaningful, optimistic dialogue for much of the trip.

"Must be something on the tracks," said Wilmington.

Everyone crowded near the windows. A man in a brown suit and matching hat stood in the shin-high grass holding a clipboard and pen. The doors opened. People hesitated, but then, beckoned by the man's hand gesture, they exited the train.

There were twenty-two of them in all, dressed to the nines in their Sunday best—long, colorful dresses, pressed suits, and polished shoes for the special occasion.

Wilmington stepped in front of the group and faced the suited man. "What's the meaning of this? We're supposed to be escorted to Majestic, Oklahoma." He removed the pamphlet from his coat, as most of the others had already done. "See? Right here." Only then did he noticed the rippling white flags spaced out across the prairie land, staked like the homesteading of virgin land instead of one already expertly developed.

The suited man said, "I'm sorry, sir. But there is no Majestic, Oklahoma."

Wilmington showed him the pamphlet, pointed hard enough to crinkle the paper. "There sure is. It has paved roads and buildings and plots of land to grow wheat on."

"Well." The man chuckled. "The land we got." He reached his hand out for a shake, but Wilmington didn't bother. "My name is Donald Dupree. I work for the state government. I'm sorry to say, folks, but you've been swindled, same as the folks just west of here, in what was supposed to be Boise City. Except it looks much like this."

Wilmington pointed to the pamphlet again, this time with a little defeat. "The buildings? The town fountain . . . with all that marble."

"All made up, sir. A horrible fiction, I'm afraid. But I'm happy to say the developers who conned you have been arrested and will be held in Leavenworth until their trial."

The newcomers eyed one another. Tears mingled with the wind. Husbands held their wives as prairie grass whipped to a frenzy around ankles and knees. All those white flags. Miles upon miles of desolation cut by a blazing sun. The orange sky looked to be bleeding in places, swirling just along the horizon.

Grass as far as the eye could see.

"We want to help right this wrong," said Donald. "We've staked the land, and we're prepared to sell it for next to nothing." He forced a smile, the tips of his mustache fluttering. "Health, wealth, and opportunity. Right at your fingertips."

Wilmington studied the land, inhaled the air, and turned to

where Amanda and his new friend Orion stood. "We're out in the middle of nowhere."

The two men locked eyes. Amanda looked from one to the other and knew.

"We're not going back, are we?"

Discover the secrets of the Bellhaven Woods . . .

Where evil can come in the most beautiful of forms.

AVAILABLE IN PRINT, E-BOOK, AND AUDIO

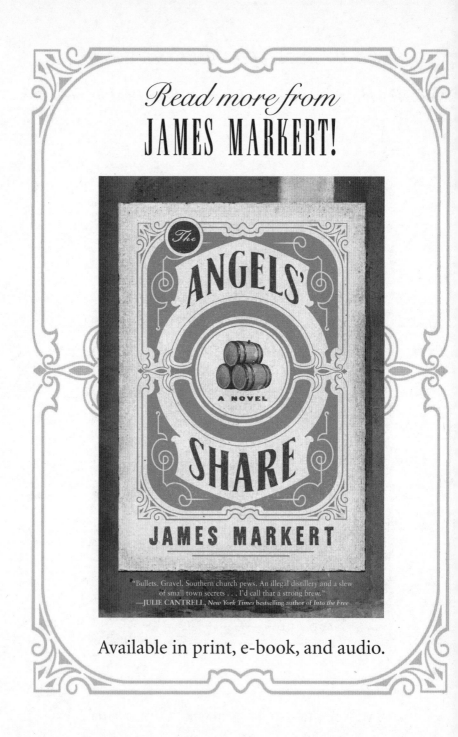

About the Author

Photo by John Markert

*J*ames Markert lives with his wife and two children in Louisville, Kentucky. He has a history degree from the University of Louisville and won an IPPY Award for *The Requiem Rose*, which was later published as *A White Wind Blew*, a story of redemption in a 1929 tuberculosis sanatorium, where a faith-tested doctor uses music therapy to heal the patients. James is also a USPTA tennis pro and has coached dozens of kids who've gone on to play college tennis in top conferences like the Big 10, the Big East, and the ACC.

❉

Learn more at JamesMarkert.com
Facebook: James Markert
Twitter: @JamesMarkert